I0771063

PATCHED TOGETHER
The Together Series, Book 3

Kim Garee

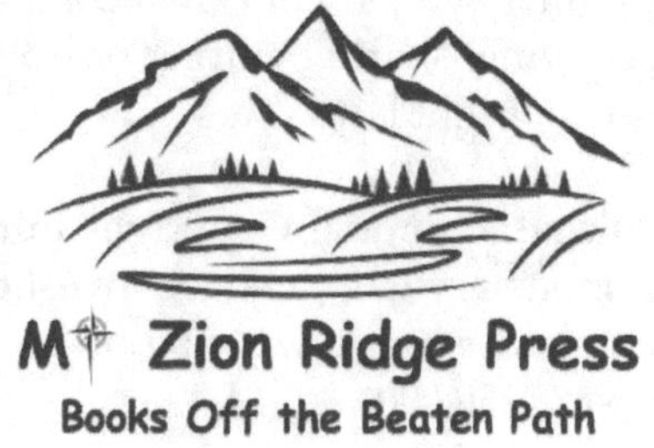

Mt Zion Ridge Press
Books Off the Beaten Path

www.MtZionRidgePress.com

Mt Zion Ridge Press LLC
295 Gum Springs Rd, NW
Georgetown, TN 37366

https://www.mtzionridgepress.com

ISBN 13: 978-1-962862-81-3
Published in the United States of America
Publication Date: September 1, 2025

Copyright: © 2025 Kim Garee

Editor-In-Chief: Michelle Levigne
Executive Editor: Tamera Lynn Kraft
Cover art by Addison Stewart © 2025
Cover art design by Tamera Lynn Kraft
Cover Art Copyright by Mt Zion Ridge Press LLC © 2025

All rights reserved. No portion of this book may be reproduced or transmitted in any form or by any electronic or mechanical means, including photocopying, recording or by any information retrieval and storage system without permission of the publisher.

Ebooks, audiobooks, and print books are *not* transferrable, either in whole or in part. As the purchaser or otherwise *lawful* recipient of this book, you have the right to enjoy the novel on your own computer or other device. Further distribution, copying, sharing, gifting or uploading is illegal and violates United States Copyright laws.

Pirating of books is illegal. Criminal Copyright Infringement, *including* infringement without monetary gain, may be investigated by the Federal Bureau of Investigation and is punishable by up to five years in federal prison and a fine of up to $250,000.

Names, characters and incidents depicted in this book are products of the author's imagination, or are used in a fictitious situation. Any resemblances to actual events, locations, organizations, incidents or persons – living or dead – are coincidental and beyond the intent of the author.

DEDICATION

This one's for Graham, Emma, and Kora — my favorite three-part series of all.

Prologue

Summer 1935
Four miles southwest of Buckeye Lake

Every kid watching out on Old Canal Road froze in fear at the scream of the Model T's braking system.

That piercing noise was the reason drag racing did *not* happen in town.

Tonight's final race had been a near disaster on the curve, but Reggie Black Jr.'s souped-up old car finally fishtailed to rest less than a foot from an oak tree along the abandoned canal. The night seemed to hold its breath. A hiss of smoke sighed from the engine.

Reggie was not driving his own car. Instead, he was the first of the young people to run toward what had very nearly been a spectacular crash.

Young Dottie Berkeley vaulted out of the driver's seat, dark curls flying out of the scarf she'd used to try to contain them. She was breathing hard and pointing at the car rolling to a stop behind her. At the wheel of that car, its driver, Archie Hill, scrubbed both shaking hands over his face.

"I won!" Dottie crowed, tripping over a piece of gravel in the glow of Archie's headlights.

At fifteen, the only car she'd ever driven was this old Model T that belonged to Reggie's family and, these days, featured a flathead V8 engine. The combination of that engine and her reaction time was a weekly money maker for Reggie. As of that summer night in '35, Dottie Berkeley had yet to be beaten.

"C'mon, Reg." Archie blew out a huff and a low curse, easing from his own car and ignoring Dottie entirely. "You can't hop up the T so much the brakes won't even stop it. You could've killed the kid!"

"I'm not a kid." But at least he hadn't called her a "little girl."

"She managed," Reggie said defensively. He glanced at Dottie but quickly moved on to his pride-and-joy: the car.

Dottie went over to shake Archie's hand and edge a little nearer to his humiliation. The guys, all older, hated "losing to a little girl" every Saturday night. Dottie knew she was never what they expected, knew that they hated that, and she loved getting to *see* them hate it up close.

Archie punctuated his "Glad you didn't die, kid" with the eye roll she'd expected.

Something was steaming even more now under the Model T's hood as Dottie went on to seek out the only fan she'd ever longed to impress.

It was not her father. No, even at fifteen, she could only impress him by managing as much as possible of the business of Buckeye Lake's amusement park over the summer. He'd be at the park tonight, and tomorrow it would be Dottie's job to clean up whatever he was currently destroying.

It wasn't her friends she wanted to impress, either. She only had a couple, and they'd never have been allowed out this late at night.

No, it was Levi Black she wanted watching her triumph behind the wheel of his older brother's car. Senior swim team captain and state champion. He was affectionately known as "Smokey" now, ever since his dark hair had turned mysteriously gray two years before.

It had somehow made him even more desirable to Dottie … and to every other girl at school.

A glance confirmed that Smokey was not huddled with his brother, Reggie, as he opened the hood of the car and conducted an investigation into the whistling steam.

Dottie looked for Smokey over by the tree line, where still other folks from school were passing around a jug.

She had not come for those kids or their jug. She had come to preserve her drag race title and, in doing so, to make Levi Smokey Black fall madly in love with her before he graduated.

Smokey didn't always come out for the racing, Dottie knew. He preferred to spend his nights dancing on the pier to Les Elgart's band, tossing summer girls in their silky dresses into the air until *they* fell in love with *him*.

Yet, she knew he was somewhere out here tonight on the Old Canal Road. She'd seen him arrive with his brother at twilight, and the whole time she'd slammed the pedal to the floor, the whole time she'd generated a blinding cloud of dry dirt to cover Archie's car, she'd pictured Smokey's clear, light-gray eyes watching her with admiration.

She imagined him deciding to take *her* to the Crystal Ballroom next Saturday night to toss *her* around to fast jazz.

"Lovely … *hair*."

Dottie turned to find Madge Laugherty standing beside another canal-fed oak and, also, standing in the greatest triumph of all: within the circle of Smokey Black's arms.

He leaned back against the tree, mostly hidden in shadow, but Dottie would know the appealing shape of him anywhere.

She had a moment to wonder just what in the world Smokey was doing with the likes of Madge behind that tree when one of the most thrilling drag races of the summer had just gone down a few yards away.

He must have *missed* it! Then, registering Madge's hair comment and cruel tone, Dottie self-consciously touched her curls. In her mind, she could suddenly imagine what a mess she was.

Didn't Smokey know she'd won again?

"I think my kerchief blew off," she heard herself say. She even sounded stupid to herself.

Madge and Smokey both chuckled, but Dottie noticed it was *Madge* Smokey was looking at in the moonlight. Madge with her perfect style and her careful cosmetics. Her lovely, blue-plaid dress and her grown-woman body.

"But I won." Dottie tried to stand taller.

The others had left the Model T and were drifting back toward them now. The shared-jug crowd was gradually joining them, too.

"Well, well," Madge said, pausing to let the gaze from her black-fringed eyes travel up and down Dottie. She had allowed more time, it seemed, for the others to hear when she said: "Aren't you just every man's … *ideal*?"

It wasn't the words.

It was the way she said them.

Dottie looked down at herself, too, at her high-belted slacks and plain white shirt that now featured smudges of dirt. She looked up into the eyes of the grinning boys who all saw her as some kind of pet, some anomaly who defied death each Saturday night. Some were laughing at Madge's description.

Then she heard Smokey Black laugh.

She heard him, the rich sound of it from the shadows, and she saw him turn to look at her, the word "ideal" flickering around her like the light of fireflies.

Dottie, at fifteen, knew with the knowledge of a grown woman that she was not Smokey's ideal.

Her face burned, her eyes stung, and winning another race was suddenly astoundingly lonely.

So, she simply told herself she would do the worst thing she could think of to Smokey Black. She would *leave* him to Madge. Punishment enough for any man. Leave him with yet another silly girl who didn't care about him at all but who dreamed of being the next Mrs. Black of the famous and expansive Black-Pool Farms.

Just as Dottie's family owned most of the north shore amusement park, Smokey and Reggie Black's family owned nearly all the surrounding farmland.

Swiping an angry tear away and returning to the fast jalopy that wasn't hers but that understood her, Dottie realized how unfair life could really be.

Smokey Black should not be loved for his family's money and property … though maybe it was fair to adore him for the way he looked in his swim captain's suit, waving at the crowd.

And she, Dottie Berkeley, should be loved *at least* for winning the road race another week running.

That had to be *some*one's ideal.

Chapter One

March 26, 1947
Twelve Years Later

Late spring ice storms made it hard to get a roller coaster repaired in time for summer.

Dottie stomped down the midway, gloved hands shoved in the pockets of her father's work coat, but beneath the coat she was decidedly under-dressed for the sudden return of winter.

"Look, we can just talk about it tomorrow, Dottie." Behind her, her brother-in-law Walter had a clipboard held over his forehead like a visor or, more aptly, a hard hat. The slicing bits of sleet hammering from the sky did hurt, but she wouldn't give him the satisfaction of admitting it when they only had two months — and counting — until the summer opening.

The pair stopped on the shoreline of Buckeye Lake's "little lake," where The Dips coaster stretched over the dark water. Hissing sounds echoed loud around them as the ice-rain speared the lake water.

Just yesterday, the spring sun had been shining on that same water. Daffodils had sprung up weeks before, only to be beaten mercilessly this afternoon by wind and ice.

"I despise Ohio." Each of Walter's grumbles was testier than the last.

"Right there." Dottie pulled her hand from her pocket to point at The Dips. "See where those two boards look compromised? At the second hill?"

Walter squinted, his large ears bright red. "Yeah. I see."

Dottie glanced over to make sure he did. She didn't take safety lightly. "I walked it last week. That whole section there needs to be reworked before May." She had to speak up to be heard over the wind, which tried hard to send Walter's clipboard cover sailing away. She watched him fight to make note of the location, the stub of his pencil swallowed by his thick glove.

Walter was her ride manager, a "pity job" Shelby Berkeley, her father, had given him when Walter had married her younger sister, Carla. The kid had been armed with few ambitions and no source of income. This, in fact, had become a pattern in the Berkeley family. Shelby's four children had all been girls, and those girls tended to fall for the kind of man who needed a little guidance.

Except for Dottie. She was the one *offering* guidance, generally. If her sisters tended toward a certain type of man, all she "tended" was the amusement park … and her three brothers-in law. Of them, Walter was her favorite. He did exactly what she told him to do, and in recent years had even offered an idea or two of his own.

"Got it. By May," he growled. "Now, *let's go in.*"

He and Carla had spent the winter in southern Georgia with friends and returned to Buckeye Lake, it seemed, one week too soon.

"Have Watson's crew work on it." Dottie led the way back to the office. "Tomorrow," she added, just to irritate him.

"Tomorrow? This is ice, for Pete's sake."

"The paper said sun tomorrow."

"I hate Ohio." He mumbled other descriptors, and Dottie burrowed her chin deeper into the coat, trying not to smile over Walter's mood. The Buckeye State really could offer its worst in March. Still, she wished she could think of some other repair that would keep them out longer, if only to get Walter's goat. After all, after the Christmas blizzard she'd endured, her brother-in-law's suntan offended Dottie deep in her soul.

Walter drew alongside her. "Your pop's in the billiard hall, you know."

Dottie shot him a look. Walter didn't need to tell her Shelby Berkeley would be drunk there. If he was in the billiard hall—or the drug store or the diner or the bus station or even the post office—he was sure to be drunk by this time of day.

Shelby's drinking was one of only two things Dottie could not control.

The other was the weather.

When Walter peeled off to head home, he called out, "Roads look to be getting bad!"

"Careful, then," Dottie called back. She did like Walter. "See you tomorrow."

"Yeah. Sunshine and all."

She was grateful for the warmth of the amusement park office, where she shucked the heavy brown coat that smelled of pipe smoke and wondered idly if her father had his other coat with him on a day that had turned so suddenly dreadful.

Would he even feel the cold, though, if he'd forgotten it?

"Walter head out?" Sylvia Pool looked up from the desk she claimed every Wednesday.

"Yes." Dottie struggled with the galoshes she'd slid over her heels. "He's going to get with Watson and the fellows tomorrow about that weak area in The Dips."

"It'll get done in time," the older woman assured her. "Mama Pool," as everyone called her, was an accounting genius who was also gifted in telling Dottie whatever she needed to hear. She helped with the books weekly in winter and twice weekly in summer—not because she needed the work, but simply because she thrived on numbers.

These days, her boys had mostly taken over managing the agricultural empire Mama Pool had built.

Sylvia was the "Pool" half of Black-Pool Farms, a massive farming operation west of Buckeye Lake that the woman had created first through the inheritance of her own family's farm and then upon her marriage to Reginald Black, Sr., owner of the adjacent spread of farmland.

Mama Pool had helped make Black-Pool Farms an agricultural leader in the Midwest, raised her two sons to think big, and then found herself bored enough to lend Dottie a hand with some of the park's record keeping. In the years since Reginald Senior had passed, she seemed to avoid idle hours at all costs.

Today, as sleet slapped at the front windows, a second middle-aged woman also bent over a desk in Dottie's office. This one *did* very much need a job.

"Hey, Lil." Dottie patted Lillian's shoulder on her way to hang up the coat.

"Hello."

"Ready for our first night of class?"

"You bet!" Lillian Turnbull Graham was dressed in a conservative business ensemble she'd been gifted from a woman at their church. She was currently stuffing boardwalk rental agreements for the summer of 1947 into envelopes as fast as she could.

Lil, a former dancer, did everything as fast as she could.

"About that class," Mama Pool said from her own perch, and Dottie dreaded what she'd say next as the wind shook the office door in its frame. "Do you think you ought to cancel, Hon?"

"Cancel?" Dottie pretended (even to herself) that she hadn't considered it. "I mean, I'd really hate to do that on the first night of the class."

Dot's Dash to Business was a six-week program she'd developed to expose war widows and single ladies in the Buckeye Lake community to office management. This way, she hoped they could find rewarding work with which to sustain themselves and their families. Dottie was to teach the seven ladies who had signed up the basics of taking dictation, simple accounting (with Mama Pool's help), telephone etiquette in the workplace, payroll, type format, and other skills employers might value.

Dottie didn't like women of a certain age to have to shave ice for snow cones all summer to get by.

"Sounds like the sleet is sticking to the roads in spots, that's all," Mama Pool went on. "I do not think the ladies will come out on a night like this for class. Not the ones who have to drive into town, anyway."

"After the blizzard, this is nothing." Dottie heard how stubborn she sounded.

"After the blizzard, ice is still ice, and it still makes roads slick."

Dottie sighed, noting with the backs of her fingers that her own cheeks were nearly ice, themselves. "What do you think, Lil?"

Lillian blinked, not used to being asked her opinion on anything. She'd arrived in Buckeye Lake two weeks before, accidentally crashing her eldest daughter's wedding after disappearing from her two girls' lives when they were only toddlers.

She'd been easy to convince to sign up for Dot's Dash to Business course, having meekly declared her wish to learn something more practical than dancing so she could earn her own way in the world ... possibly even at her late husband's family's marina.

"Um." Lillian hesitated, shooting a cautious glance at Mama Pool. "Is there harm in starting it a week later?"

Dottie narrowed her eyes, but she knew when she was beaten. "I wouldn't want anyone getting hurt." She propped her elbows on the counter and her chin on her palms. "Would you mind calling the others to let them know, Lil?"

"Of course." She abandoned the envelope stuffing with the same enthusiasm that had fueled it in the first place. "You have their registration forms on your desk?"

The outside door opened as Dottie passed the forms over, and the local newspaper publisher slid in beneath the shadow of a woolen cape. Emily Graham Mathison's newsroom was a couple doors down on the boardwalk.

"Changed to snow," she exclaimed, pushing the hood back and beaming at them. She blinked at Lil. "Oh, hey ... Mom."

Emily was one of Lillian's estranged daughters; namely, the one who'd tried to bring the woman back home after more than two decades. She'd insisted Lil live with her upon the older woman's sudden return, but Emily and her sister, Rosie, were both newly married.

Loathe to push in at such a time, Lillian had jumped at the offer to board with Mama Pool at the big farmhouse. Meanwhile, Dottie had jumped at the chance to offer the woman a little respectable work.

"Hello, Em," Lil replied earnestly to her daughter, telephone in hand.

"Came to tell you all the roads are a mess now." Emily sidled up to the counter, mirroring Dottie's position on the opposite side. "Do you have any more of those Dutch chocolates you keep around?"

"That's really why you came over." Dottie produced the classy little bowl of treats she'd taken to hiding from her life-long friend's pregnancy cravings. "We appreciate the breaking weather news, though. At least you're earning your candy."

"Drew phoned from the Watercraft office," Emily said around an entire piece of candy. "Said it's bad. Ice is turning to snow, too, before it all blows past."

All the women's eyes slanted toward the front window. The patter of ice had, indeed, softened to something more white and more substantial.

"Worst winter I ever saw," Mama Pool declared with disgust. Behind her, Lil was busy breaking the news about the cancelled class over the phone.

Emily nodded. "Good decision. Cancelling. Lottie and Carolyn would do best not to try coming in from Hebron." She popped a second chocolate and worked to form words around it. "What will you do tonight instead, Dottie?"

"Hadn't gotten that far." She was scribbling another note for Walter before she forgot. Then she looked up. "Go ahead and take another piece for the road. Don't be shy."

"If you insist."

"I saw you eyeing them. Your baby's going to come out with a caramel center, though, if you're not careful."

"Ewww."

"Aren't you supposed to be eating broccoli?"

"Broccoli?" Emily gave her a skeptical look, nibbled off the edge of the next chocolate, verifying this one was also, indeed, caramel filled. She showed it off to Dottie before popping it into her mouth. "I'd rather have a baby whose blood runs caramel instead of broccoli. Why broccoli, anyway?"

"I don't know," Dottie admitted. "My mother, the consummate housewife, said she ate broccoli while she was expecting to make sure we grew right in there."

"I ate potatoes when I was growing Reg and Smokey," Mama Pool put in. "My boys turned out *huge*."

"Did you also smoke when you were expecting Smokey?" Emily flashed her a grin. "Is that why his hair turned gray?"

"*No*, smarty pants. That was purely my own daddy's fault. He went gray at twenty."

"Still, older than our Smokey," Emily noted affectionately. They'd all grown up together: Emily and Rosie, Dottie, Smokey, and plenty more lake kids.

"Speaking of which," Mama Pool said, "soon as Lil's done with those calls, I'd like to call my boys and see if one can come get us. Hear that, Lil? Let's let one of the boys drive us on these roads. The farm trucks handle the ice."

"That would be kind of them," Lil said.

"I know it's rotten weather." Emily pulled her hood back up now that her future son or daughter had a dose of chocolate. "But I'm planning a big supper tonight if any of you feel like attempting Towpath Island in the ice."

There was a beat of silence.

Lil was in no position to accept or refuse, since her transportation depended upon Mama Pool. For Dottie's and Mama Pool's parts … well, Emily was not the kind of cook whose food a person braved an ice storm to eat.

"Dinner's to welcome Rosie and Gabe home from their honeymoon trip," Emily went on. "I'm cooking up ham and noodles. Rosie's favorite."

"I don't think so, Honey, though I do thank ya kindly." Mama Pool declined with real warmth. "I had a chicken thawed, myself. But I'm sure one of the boys won't mind dropping you for supper at the island, Lil, if you'd like."

"Then someone would have to be on the roads especially for me, so no thank you." Lil offered her daughter a tentative smile. "Perhaps I could come see the newlyweds over the weekend, though?"

"I'm sure Rosie would like that," Emily said encouragingly, even though they all knew those feelings could still go either way. "Well, I'm off to make my noodles. You all be careful on the roads!"

Dottie lived in rooms over the office, so being careful wasn't what was on her mind as she finished her notes for the next day. Mama Pool's adding machine made its clicking sound, the envelopes were nearly completely stuffed at the back table, and Dottie thought about her father.

Now she wouldn't have instructing her new class to distract from the reality of him, so the night stretched cold ahead. She'd have to track him down at the billiard hall and then babysit him. Again.

It would be embarrassing, as it always was. Fletch, the bartender, would frown over whatever power Shelby Berkeley had thrown around after his sixth or seventh whiskey.

Once Mama Pool had finished her call, Dottie was next to pick up the phone.

"Mom?"

"Hello? Yes?" Winnie Berkeley sounded mousy even over a bad connection.

"It's me. I wanted to let you know Dad's at the billiard hall."

A weary beat of silence. "Bring him home, then."

"I doubt he'll be ready just yet," she responded with a glance at her wrist. There had to be something else to do. She'd go to the towpath. How could Emily mess up ham and noodles, anyway? Dottie made a decision, trying not to wish her own family was different. "Look, I'm headed out for dinner with the Grahams, and if Dad's still at the hall when I get back

… I'll try to get him home. I'll try."

Dottie hung up and opted again for her father's work coat. "Sure you don't want to ride over with me, Lil?"

"Thank you, but then you'd have to take me further out to the farm on these roads."

"I don't mind."

"Chicken dinner with Sylvia sounds just wonderful." Lil gave her a sad smile. All her smiles were sad. Dottie figured things were still a little unnatural with her abandoned family, so she hugged the woman before she left.

"Be careful out there, Honey."

Chapter Two

Smokey Black answered the phone when his mother called to ask to be picked up from work when the surprise ice storm hit.

He, after all, was what the family called their "good time" farmer. Because his livelihood was in pumpkins and Christmas trees, rather than livestock, he was a bit easier to reach by phone during lousy weather than his brother, Reggie.

He had the road to himself as he left the main farmhouse at Black-Pool Farms. That lack of traffic proved a good thing when the truck fishtailed a little on the ice, even with a covered load of fresh feed in the bed. The cab itself was chilly, but Mama Pool was too tough to complain about the cold. Smokey couldn't say yet whether the same was true about Lillian Graham. He was reserving judgment.

He stopped once to un-freeze his wipers. It really had been a miserable winter.

The holiday blizzard that had struck the week before Christmas had been bad news, indeed, for a Christmas tree farm. Now, he told everyone he'd have nearly double the available trees this coming year, adding the positive spin the lake area expected from him. He figured it was a good thing he believed most of what he said.

Even now, as the road curved alongside his own Festival Farms, he was proud and optimistic about those rows of perfect spruces and the way they cradled the falling snow.

This coming November, the sight of snow-covered boughs would warm hearts with holiday cheer.

In late March, though, it was discouraging, to say the least.

Since he was planning for 1947 to be the biggest, most joyous year yet at the farm, Smokey had a long list of things to get done. Now, if spring would be a bit more cooperative …

He tested the brakes on the Lake Road turn, a poorly maintained lane running behind the little waterfront cottages. The road was difficult to maneuver in the best weather. As he slowed, he slid again, farther than he'd anticipated.

Mama Pool had been right to call. It wasn't merely slick. It was also getting difficult to see well in the early darkness and the powdery clouds of snow.

In fact, Smokey barely managed to see Pastor Skip on the curve ahead, bundled and already scooping away at the end of his driveway with a shovel. He was probably hosting a Bible study or some other get-together at his home. Snow did tend to pile there at the base of his drive because of the open shoreline at the church property. A chiseled drift of ice and snow was already forming.

The old guy must've wanted to stay ahead of it, as the white stuff still fell.

Smokey considered pulling over, asking if Pastor Skip needed a hand, but his mother and Lillian were waiting for him. He didn't want them setting off on their own in Mama Pool's car. It wouldn't handle well on ice, and then, there was also the fact he didn't want the old preacher to feel less than capable. The man prided himself on being active.

It was the jerking movement of Skip's fleecy cap in the beam of another headlight that startled Smokey. He sucked in a breath he would never remember letting out.

~~~~~

Dottie was making good time in her '39 Ford five-window coupe since no one else seemed to be out in the storm.

Always kept in top condition, the car purred happily through the ugly weather. Though of course Dottie no longer raced the country roads, she did spend her adult life in a famously spotless car, privately wishing to go faster at all times, wishing spring would just arrive and stay so she could give the thing a good wax.

Soon, she would enjoy being blinded by the sun glinting off the chrome of the coupe.

Being blinded by snow, however, was less fun.

Dark was falling early, but she looked forward to a good gab session with Emily and Rosie. Like any self-respecting woman, Dottie had a list of things she wanted to ask her friends as soon as the three of them could be alone together. *How had the family been coping with Lillian's sudden return? Their grandfather had raised them after their mother had left … how was Hickory Graham handling his long-lost daughter-in-law's presence? How was Rosie enjoying her first two weeks of married life with Gabe Adams? How had her little boy, Charlie, done with his new-found grandparents while she'd been away on her honeymoon?*

Dottie wondered if she could be considered a gossip. She didn't think so. She just liked to know what was going on with her friends. Was that gossip?

She'd been a little uneasy about that after a recent sermon at church. In the end, though, she'd rationalized she just liked the *news*. It was necessary, given her role at the amusement park. And Emily, who had gone to church all her life, was an actual newspaper woman. Her whole *job* was the news, and what really was the difference between news and
~~~~~

gossip, anyway?

As she maneuvered the curves of Lake Road, Dottie thought again about how much she had not wanted to cancel the first night of her business classes. That small group of ladies needed reliable work, and to have reliable work, they needed skills. Excellent record keeping, beautiful shorthand, fast typing, efficient accounting skills.

Dottie enjoyed those basic backbones of her work. She knew her new students would, as well, and she was hopeful she'd even be able to help place them at companies when they'd finished. It would be counted for her as a good deed, as good fruit in her life.

Surely bearing that kind of fruit would cancel out her less-than-desirable habits. Like maybe, kind of, sort of ... gossiping over ham and noodles. Gossip, she thought with satisfaction, was simply another form of accounting.

Humming, Dottie slowed on the curve just before the church. When she came around the corner, though, headlights pierced the slanted snow, blinding her. Pressing a little harder on the brakes out of caution, she felt the layer of ice under the snow take control of her coupe.

Dottie sucked in a breath as she found herself facing a head-on collision with what appeared to be a pickup truck.

Her tires gave her just enough leverage to aim for the ditch as she slid sideways in that direction, trying not to over-correct, but the downward slope on the curve caused the car to go faster, then faster, the brakes useless.

"No, no, no," Dottie mumbled, jaw clenched. She was a good driver.

That was when her own headlights suddenly revealed the form of a man.

The man was standing with a shovel in the very ditch she could not now avoid.

It was ... *Pastor Skip*?

His face was clearly frozen in the crossbeams of both headlights, and Dottie could not look away as her foot shoved uselessly on the brakes, again and again, as she desperately spun the wheel.

Her scream echoed across the half-thawed lake.

Her coupe hit the man, and then it hit a tree.

That scream even drowned out the crunch of metal.

Chapter Three

Doc Larson had a three-bedroom clinic north of the park. Folks referred to it as the "hospital," though only Doc could ever be found there.

Dottie recognized the clinic immediately when she opened her eyes. Her family owned this building, too, and Dottie had collected rent every month from Doc since she was a kid. She knew the plaster work on the ceiling was new because she'd just overseen that project last spring.

Thinking about plaster made her head hurt, though.

No, the light from the other side of the room made her head hurt.

No, *every*thing made her head hurt. Something heavy seemed to be pressing it into a pillow so that she couldn't move it.

She blinked and brought Doc into focus. He was sitting near her. Rent must be due.

No, not Doc. This was … Mama Pool?

She'd just been talking with Mama Pool and … and Lil, hadn't she? They wanted her to cancel the first night of the business course. A storm had hit.

Dottie's heartbeat was an uncomfortable flop in her chest for a moment. It scared her. There was a storm.

Three male figures were suddenly moving into the room. She squinted, still not able to move her head. Ah, *there* was Doc. Then … Smokey Black? He must be here for his mother. Was Mama Pool's head hurting, too? But Dottie noticed he had a bright white sling over his shoulder and arm. The white of it hurt her head when she looked at it.

"Broke his wrist, is all," Doc said as they entered, but he sounded sad. "Lucky, I guess."

Was Mama Pool *crying*? Dottie tried to focus. Was she crying about the white sling on Smokey's arm? A broken wrist, Doc had said.

Smokey sagged onto another of the beds across the room, and that was when Dottie noticed Chief Gunn, the town's police chief, still standing in the doorway.

She considered saying hello to them all. Gunn had always made a pet of her. She was sure she had questions for him or maybe for Doc, but her head hurt, and her throat didn't feel quite right. Somehow, even imagining the sound of her own voice made her head hurt worse. What was it she felt she was supposed to ask them?

Mama Pool crossed the room and placed her hand on her son's

shoulder. The shoulder without the sling. "You know your brother will help out at your place while you heal."

What had happened to Smokey's wrist? Oh, yes. Broken. Dottie's chest felt funny again, but not in the same way her heart sometimes felt floppy when Smokey Black was around. More like she needed … help.

"Not much to show for this," she thought she heard Smokey saying. His throat must hurt, too. He did not sound right.

"You did everything you could." That was Mama Pool.

Sylvia Pool Black always told the truth. Her son must surely have done everything he could about whatever it was. *He'd been there*, was all she could think. A stutter of her heartbeat.

In the corner of Dottie's vision, Doc opened a metal cabinet. The hinges shrieked … like metal when it bent. Like the metal of a car when it hit a tree.

Then Dottie was shrieking too, a breathless and raw kind of shriek that didn't manage to be loud at all. A shriek like metal. Because she'd … she'd seen Pastor Skip's face in a bright light.

"Skip!" she croaked like a warning, and it turned out her head was not pinned down because she lifted it, half-sat, and the room spun.

She could barely find Smokey across the room again. *He'd been there.*

"Smokey … I … Skip …"

Then he muttered, "Skip's dead."

Dottie didn't remember her head crashing back down onto the pillow. The room was still spinning. Mama Pool said, "Shush!" a moment too late, and then Dottie focused sufficiently to see her smack her injured son firmly on the back of the head.

Pastor Skip. Bright light. It had been her own headlights. The coupe's headlights.

The chief's eyes were red-rimmed as they peered down at her, and that was the last thing Dottie saw before she slipped back into the dark.

~~~~~

"You knocked your head but good," Doc Larson explained. He shone a flashlight into her eyes, and something painful pulsed inside her skull. "Try not to sleep, though."

Then he left her in the now dark room, not really bothering to fight the sleep he kept warning her about. What would happen to her if she slept a bit more, she wondered? Would she die?

Dottie could reach up and touch the bandage wrapped around her head, and she could feel that her left eyelid was sore and seemed to be swelling a little more each time she tried to open it.

Her parents had stood near the bed, but they were not there now. It might have been a few minutes before, perhaps. Hours, even? Had a whole day passed? They'd looked at her in the bed there in Doc's
~~~~~

"hospital," but she hadn't known what to say to them.

They, in turn, seemed puzzled by her.

"Doc says you'll be all right," her father had said, the sweetness of rum still on his breath. Dottie had been supposed to pick him up, hadn't she? From the billiard hall. Had her mother retrieved him this time? Winnie stood silent, a step behind him, as she usually was.

Finally, her mother nodded and patted Dottie's leg beneath the light blanket. Then, her parents had talked on the other side of the door in words she couldn't make out.

Dottie slept, regardless of Doc's warnings. Maybe, she thought without alarm, she really would die.

But she dreamed of Pastor Skip.

Silly dreams in which she spotted him operating the Skee-ball game at the park, his hair fuzzy over his ears, and it seemed so realistic that she'd said to him, "I knew you couldn't really be dead."

Another time, another dream, she'd seen him swimming as he did each morning in the summer, the pale bunch of his stringy shoulder muscles freckled, but then the waters of Buckeye Lake had turned to ice all around him, and he could not hear her shout of warning.

"Try to stay awake, Kid," she heard Doc Larson say again after she'd yelled.

Awake, her head felt over-stuffed with something painful, like briars packed tight inside her skull. Awake, Pastor Skip was no longer to be found at the park or in the lake or anywhere ever again on earth. Except, she feared, in every dream she might ever have.

Could he really be gone? She tried to sort it out each time Doc admonished her from the doorway.

Dottie tried to remember when she'd last seen Pastor Skip ... that is, *before*. Before she saw him in her headlights.

Wait. They'd both been at the market on Tuesday. He'd been at the meat counter talking with Burt Strout, and Dottie had waved at them both. Skip had made a little motion at the side of his nose, a private joke between them that dated back to Dottie being maybe five years old. The preacher had managed to convince her as a little girl, repeatedly, that she had something stuck on the side of her nose. She'd fallen for it enough times that he laughed harder with each repetition. Nowadays, she pantomimed her own part to humor the older man, winking to him at the market as she scrubbed at the invisible nose smudge.

When they'd been snowed in at the Island Inn during the holiday blizzard, Pastor Skip had defeated Dottie at chess no less than four times. As he talked about his son during the third game, he had said Gil was finally "right" with the Lord.

"Is that what he said? That's wonderful." She'd also grown up with

Gil, after all, and it had been hard to see him floundering as a young man.

"He said it, but I also know it's true because of the fruit he's producing now."

Dottie had nodded at that and moved her knight on the board, but she'd chewed on those words throughout the Christmas season. Something bothered her—not about Gil, but about herself. Something about fruit.

She'd never thought of fruit as evidence. What was the "fruit" in her own life? Was she a little behind in some heavenly board game and didn't even know it? With little else to do to pass the time, Dottie had snuggled beneath the inn's fine blankets and poured over the Gospels, reading beyond the Christmas story as the blizzard winds had blown.

Suddenly, the concept of "fruit" seemed to be everywhere. True followers were to be known by their fruit.

Dottie had returned to the amusement park's main office to still quieter days following the storm, during which the world dug itself out, and she determined to dig in. *She would bear better fruit.* In fact, she'd *burst* with it.

She had been eager to report to Pastor Skip about her first night with the women in the business class because she just knew it was going to be a success.

She knew how to make things work well.

Instead, she'd cancelled the class that night.

And, anyway, Pastor Skip died last night.

Because of her.

In terms of fruit and scorekeeping, Dottie knew she was profoundly and irrevocably in the hole.

In the "hospital," she learned if she cried hard enough, both her eyes would all but swell shut, probably because of the injury. Through them, she saw that light was beginning to come through the window. Actual *sunlight.*

A new day. But in this day, Dottie Berkeley was a killer.

Chapter Four

Warm, sunshine-squinty days always made Smokey want to put a fresh coat of white paint on just about everything.

On a late afternoon in April, weeks after the accident, he sloshed his brush across the roadside fence in front of his farm. The sun baked his shoulders, the grass smelled freshly mown, and a killdeer bird made persistent, threatening chirps from the gravel berm a few feet away.

"Lays its eggs among the rocks like a fool and then spends the rest of the time hollering at us to stay away." Smokey shook his head, dipping his brush back in the pail.

His companion, Hugh McMullen, did not reply. Hugh rarely replied to anyone, since the war. In fact, though he showed up most days to work, Smokey knew precious little about the man except that he still lived half a mile away, with his folks. Then, there was what he'd heard about him from Al and Beau at the filling station.

Hugh "got spooked" over there, they said, "that's all."

Anyway, Smokey knew a farm was a place a man could feel safe, and he also knew Hugh arrived early, stayed late, and quietly did whatever needed to be done in the in-between. That was enough for Smokey.

A glance told him Hugh was watching the two killdeers out the corner of his eye.

"Grandpa always called them noisy plovers," Smokey continued, swiping the brush awkwardly with his left hand while a burning itch set fire to his right wrist inside its bulky cast. Frustrated, he propped the brush against the can and growled. "I'm cutting this thing off come the weekend. I really am."

He strolled a few feet down the fence line, where a tree had obligingly dropped some twigs from its branches. He jabbed one inside the cast, down past his fingers to the pad of his palm, pushing toward the spot that had needed scratching for most of the week.

Smokey heard the hum of his mother's Fleetline before he saw it crest the little hill on the other side of the farm's drive. Mama Pool's own house, the original family farmstead, was just shy of a mile up the road, but it wasn't uncommon for her to swing in for a chat with her extremely large "baby boy." She pulled alongside, put the car in park, and cranked the window the rest of the way down.

"Fence looks real good," she observed. "Hey there, Hugh."

Hugh nodded, waved, and turned back to his work.

Smokey pushed his hat back on his forehead with his left hand, leaving the twig sticking ominously out of the plaster cast. "Think it needs another coat?"

"Why do you always ask me that? When you never like my answer?"

"Sounds like it's gonna need a second coat, Hugh," he called over his shoulder. He stepped closer to the car and noticed Mama Pool's lavender formal jacket and skirt. "You coming from the courthouse?"

She nodded in response and kept staring at the fence. "Figured I'd swing back by the house, pick up Lil, see if she wants to put in a couple hours at the park office." She didn't have to remind him the two women had been trying to keep up with things there as best they could for Dottie's sake. Mama Pool cut him a glance now, narrowing that glance at his cast. "And just *what* are you doing? Don't go shoving that stick in there, Levi Black. Do you have any sense at all?"

"Itches."

"It'll break off, and then where will you be?"

"I'm breaking the whole cast off anyway in a day or two. It's hot, it's itchy, and my left hand's not worth a plugged nickel. Weather's fit, and I've got farm work to do."

"It hasn't been on there anywhere near two months yet," she scolded, leaning out her window a little to inspect it. "Though it looks dirty enough to have been there two years."

Smokey took a few steps back to his dripping paint brush and proceeded to swipe white paint across the cast with a flourish. "There." He winked. "Freshened right up."

Mama Pool made the face she always made when she was trying not to laugh at one or both of her sons. "Ridiculous."

"So," he said, moving back to her. "What'd the judge end up doing with her?"

Smokey had refused to go back to the court after he'd appeared to give his statement.

Had the roads been slick?

Could you tell how fast Miss Berkeley was driving?

"Involuntary manslaughter."

Smokey looked down to kick a piece of gravel. Hugh moved further down the fence row with his own bucket, and the killdeer even gave up and hopped away.

"You should have come back to the courthouse," his mother said.

He absolutely should *not* have. What good would it have served? Dottie Berkeley had always represented something to him, even if he couldn't quite put into words just what that might be. Seeing her looking so small in that room, the gash still healing on her forehead, the sleeves of her soft pink sweater wrapped tight around her torso as though to hold herself together … *No.* He hadn't spent a minute longer there than he'd had to.

"I'm just saying … she could have used another ally. God knows."

Smokey grunted. She had other friends, didn't she?

"You should've heard the things the Russells said about her." Mama Pool shook her head.

"What? What'd the Russells have to do with anything?"

"Brought up all these stories about Dottie racing cars out on Old Canal Road. I mean … well, I forgot about that, truth be told."

"You *knew* about that?"

Mama Pool smirked. "I knew about everything, son of mine."

He shrugged and worked the stick around again against his hand. It … almost … reached. "That was Reggie's business, anyway. The drag racing. Not mine."

"No. You were all tucked into your bed by nine, of course."

"Anyway, what did the Russells mean, bringing that up? What'd it have to do with the accident? Dottie doesn't race cars anymore. I mean, for crying out loud." At least, he didn't *think* she did. He tried to imagine it, her in those fitted skirts and heels, her dark hair in that low bun, gunning an engine. It almost made him smile.

A lot of things changed in a decade, except maybe not for Glen and Marge Russell stirring up trouble for their neighbors.

Still, Smokey did indulge in a warm memory of Dottie Berkeley vaulting into his brother's jalopy when she was little more than a kid … but little more than a kid who had started looking rather fine in those skirts.

"The judge *asked* her if she races."

Now he did chuckle. "And?"

"She said she does not."

"Of course not. Were they suggesting she was … what, *drag racing* on the lake road in the middle of an ice storm?"

"Zeke Bishop claimed she might as well have been racing coming up on that curve the day of the accident. He watched the whole thing from his living room, he said."

"I don't have any idea how fast Dottie was driving," Smokey said, shaking his head. His mother had heard him admit as much to the court, under oath.

He had no way of knowing what was happening as she'd rounded that curve, except that her fine car slid all over the place in slow motion. It was all blurred now by the memory of trying to get to Skip. Running back to pull Dottie out, his wrist screaming as loud as she had been.

As a Navy frogman, Smokey had seen a good deal in the war, but the war had been over for a spell now. There was no reason he'd just now start dreaming of it, except that maybe Dottie's screams had set it off. Like something had been waiting quietly in his head, and now it was jarred loose.

A late spring ice storm at Buckeye Lake had somehow whirled in his mind to become water explosions and grisly covert ops, mingling with Pastor Skip's blood on the snow, Dottie's head bleeding down over her eyes as she'd cried. He'd woken up sweating more than not lately, and this invisible injury bothered him more than the itch beneath the cast.

Smokey, after all, was not a *nightmare* kind of man. He was *happy*. He'd *always* been happy.

"She won't be driving any time soon, at any rate," Mama Pool was saying. "They took her license for a whole year. I don't know if her daddy pulled some strings to keep it at just the loss of her license, but maybe that's just what people were saying. That he pulled strings. I don't really know."

"People say a lot of things."

Smokey kissed his mother on the cheek before she drove off, and he turned back to the milky paint as he considered how long it might take for the whole business with the accident to blow over. It had to blow over. After all, he'd heard Dottie Berkeley could hardly go into work at the amusement park anymore.

Folks were cruel.

"Her bossy, managing ways won't save her now." That was the milkman who'd shared that. But Smokey couldn't help wondering, as he worked silently beside Hugh in the spring sunshine, what bossiness had to do with losing control of a vehicle on the ice.

Would people have said the same kinds of things if it had been one of Dottie's brothers-in-law driving the car that day?

Anyway, it was no business of Smokey's. He dropped the brush again, jammed the stick deeper into his cast, and heard it snap.

Chapter Five

A box of posters and promotional materials had arrived at the village post office. They advertised the season's opening band, Gene Krupa's orchestra.

Dottie had worked hard for over a year to cinch the deal with Krupa. Still, arranging the contract had been easier than today's task: picking up that box of posters.

Dottie's palms were sweating in her gloves before she reached the door. The post office was attached to the market, with a machine in front, from which cigarettes could be purchased. Dottie didn't smoke much, but she contemplated it now. A sand-colored awning shaded the entrance, which allowed her to see her reflection clearly in the glass door.

She'd taken the bandage off her head for good the other day. The wound looked like a claw had swiped viciously along her hairline and stopped above the temple. It would serve as a reminder to everyone, Dottie knew, that there was no pretending anything away.

The local church was mourning its pastor, and she was the reason why.

She sucked in a shaking breath and gripped her purse strap on her shoulder with both hands to keep them from shaking. *She could do this.*

Dottie took her place in line behind Lynn Boyce, an attractive woman in her sixties Dottie had volunteered with in the USO. When a hush fell over the busy little post office lobby, Lynn turned casually to determine the cause. Her pale eyes met Dottie's, and Dottie smiled at her in greeting. She wasn't surprised when Lynn faced forward again, but she still felt it like another claw swipe.

Others were at their post office boxes, retrieving today's mail.

The pretty little star-knobbed and numbered doors had been a source of fascination for Dottie when she was a child, squinting inside of them to see envelopes of untold mysteries. She'd always loved the scent of ink and paper at those boxes, where Cath Perkins and Liza Saunders now stood gaping. Cath worked at the pizza parlor near the park's entrance. Liza, her neighbor in the village, had a dozen kids who terrorized the amusement park midway all summer.

The two women stared at Dottie for a few silent heartbeats before turning to whisper to one another, their stares unwavering.

"What's wrong with your head?" The question came from a little boy

Dottie recognized but whose name she didn't know. He was holding the hand of Constance Burden, who'd been a year behind Dottie in school. Before Dottie could think of an answer to his question, Constance shushed her son and turned him back into line.

Meanwhile, Cath had moved from the boxes and leaned against the counter, pushing an envelope at the postmaster, Lou Badger. He'd been behind this desk since he'd returned from the first war in Europe, and his buzz cut was now bright white, his apron lined with sharp pencils. Lou said something to Cath that Dottie could not hear.

"Well, it don't seem right." Cath shot Dottie a glance. Dottie held tighter to her purse, like the bar of The Dips coaster on a hill.

"The Lord's ways don't always make sense to the likes of us." Lou glanced up, then back down at his work. "Princess here gets the boo-boo on her crown, and Skip's six feet under. Guess it'll all work out someday. Not for us to understand."

"Heard his son couldn't make it back for the funeral."

"Where *is* Gil, anyway?"

"Don't rightly know." Now the whole lobby was involved in conversation.

"Thank the Lord some of the Grahams were already adopting that odd little girl the pastor was raising. At least there's that."

"Such a good man, to take a little orphan in that way. God rest his soul." Lynn pulled out her handkerchief and patted beneath her eye.

The glass door jingled open again behind Dottie, who stood glued to the floor, staring at a framed American flag on the wall. The flag had been the first flag flown at Buckeye Lake's amusement park. Her father had donated it decades ago. A fine layer of dust dimmed the pane, and Dottie focused hard on it.

Liza grew bolder. "I, for one, will be praying for your soul, Dottie Berkeley."

Why did "praying for your soul" sound so much crueler than "praying for you"? Since thanking Liza for the sentiment seemed awkward, Dottie simply swallowed and looked down at her own navy pumps. Maybe if she stared limply at her shoes, they'd realize their inherent victory and leave her alone.

"I cannot imagine living with that on my conscience," Lynn said to Lou, still propped against the counter like she had nothing else in the world to do. Lou's stamp echoed through the lobby. Lynn clucked her tongue. "I just cannot imagine. I mean, how would a body ever sleep again?"

It wouldn't. A body hardly ever slept again, but Dottie knew she didn't need to confirm that for them. She looked up and around for a path out of this line, but through thick tears all she saw were more bodies between her own and the path to freedom.

"Shame about that fancy car of yours." Lynn took a package from the postmaster and turned around. "Heard there's no fixing it."

"Too much car for a woman." Lou Badger's words might simply be an attempt to deflect the venom in here. Dottie told herself that, so she wouldn't be tempted to thump him with her handbag.

Liza laughed. "Aw, Lou, you caveman, you. Not that you're wrong. What's a woman need with a car like that, anyway?"

Silence. Who was supposed to answer her?

Dottie realized they were waiting for *her* to answer.

"What did you need with a car like that, Dottie?" Lynn's voice was syrupy sweet.

"She doesn't have a husband." There was suppressed laughter in Cath's voice.

"I've got to admit, I'd pick a car like that over a husband any day." Smokey Black's easy, wry humor came from the direction of the door. Dottie instinctively moved toward his deep voice, the laughter in the lobby reluctantly shifting from her to their beloved farmer.

He was leaning against the trim of the doorway, arms crossed, and Dottie fought the ridiculous urge to run to him. She felt him watching her, and she drew a careful breath, determined not to let the tears fall until she was *out* of this place.

"Did you get your mail, Dottie B.?" He stepped aside so she could reach the door, his voice gentle now.

Shaking her head, she whispered, "It's okay."

"I'm here to pick up some seeds. You?"

Dottie couldn't remember. Oh, right. The orchestra. "Posters." She put her hand against the sun-heated door, the room silent behind her.

"Lou, are my seeds back there behind the counter? And how about Miss Berkeley's posters?"

Dottie shook her head again and pushed at the door, putting her head down as a tear did, indeed, escape. Too late.

Smokey leaned down as she brushed past. "I'll get them to you, sweetheart. *Go.*"

~~~~~

The only good thing about Dottie's parents' rambling home on the outskirts of town was that it was on the outskirts of town.

People had to intentionally *look* for her there. There could be no accidentally bumping into her, as so often happened with her little apartment on the boardwalk, above her office.

Lately, any time someone bumped into her, it turned out very, very badly. *For her.*

Dottie lay on her side staring at the leafy wallpaper pattern in her
~~~~~

second-floor childhood bedroom, trying to decide only by sound whose car had just pulled into the drive. Not Walter's car. Not her father's.

Her mother had come in to open the windows to the April air yesterday, but Dottie had yet to rise to shut them again. Not even when she'd shivered in the dead of night.

A car door opened and shut, followed quickly by a second one. Dottie heard voices, and she recognized them.

The Graham sisters.

Well, she supposed they weren't the Graham sisters anymore, technically. Married, they'd be Mrs. Mathison and Mrs. Adams. They had built-in allies now. Dottie felt profoundly lonely, even though Emily and Rosie could only have come here to see her.

People didn't come here to see her parents. Most people in the lake region weren't fans of Shelby and Winnie Berkeley—not enough to visit them, anyway. Even Dottie's own sisters had married young to escape this house, after all.

Rosie and Emily would certainly be here to check up on her, but maybe her mother wouldn't let them come up. Maybe Winnie didn't want anyone to see her daughter this way, either. Or maybe Dottie could slip softly into her own closet before they reached the second floor. Still, that would involve moving. Instead, she tracked the sound of their voices below for a few minutes, the crack of two sets of heels on the steep wooden stairs. A soft knock.

Dottie stayed still.

"Dottie?" That would be Rosie, the sweet one. "Are you awake, honey?"

She lay silent. Let them assume she was asleep in the middle of the day, which was far better than whatever truth this had become.

"I'm not buying it." That would be Emily, the relentless one. "We're coming in."

They did come in, then, but it was a surprisingly gentle entry rather than a bursting in. Their perfume preceded them—the usual soft, lemony scent they'd shared since their granny had first allowed them to dab a drop behind their pretty little ears.

They were dressed for church, she saw. Was it Sunday again *already*? Their hair was neatly curled and pinned, and they both wore post-Easter white gloves.

It was Emily who planted herself directly in Dottie's unblinking line of sight. "Well, look at you, my friend." If Dottie could have managed it, she'd have been worried about the concern in Emily's tone when she whispered, "Are you all right?"

The bed sagged as Rosie sat beside Dottie's knees, and she felt her old friend's hand, glove-free now, laid gently across her cheek. Rosie had been a mother for a decade, so this seemed a predictable first move. If only it were a mere fever laying her low. "Why don't you tell us what's going on?"

"You *know*." They were the first words she'd spoken in days, and Dottie marveled that even her voice was forever broken. One more thing to despise about herself. Her friends, however, truly did know what was going on. There was no need to explain.

"Heard you moved back out here to your folks'," Emily said. "I guess we don't need to ask if it was a good move, from the looks of you."

"Em," Rosie admonished, letting her hand move in a caress on Dottie's arm.

"What?" Emily sounded simultaneously defensive and appalled. "She's not dressed, her hair … well … looks like *that*. Have you even slept at all, Dottie?"

"Emily's one to talk." Rosie laughed. "Take a good look at her, will you?"

"I've been vomiting," Emily said defensively. "It messes with the whole glow of expectant motherhood. But I at least managed to *comb my hair*."

Rosie pelted her little sister with her purse, a clear attempt to make Dottie laugh.

Dottie did not laugh. "Please leave."

"Aww, honey. Come home with us. Come out to Towpath Island," Emily said, warmly now. "We don't even mind you looking like that, do we, Rosie?"

"I can't go. I'm ill."

"Ill, how?" Rosie asked, brushing curls off Dottie's forehead to inspect the healing pink slash near her temple.

"I think it's my heart."

"Your heart?"

"It's doing things it shouldn't." In fact, talking was even making her tired.

"What things, dear?"

"Flopping around. Sinking. Beating too fast." Maybe she would die, and everyone would be so happy.

Well, maybe not these two. Dottie knew she owed Emily, in particular, a thank you. Emily's *Buckeye Lake Beacon* had been the only newspaper in the area, after all, that had spared Dottie the usual awful headlines about the "roller coaster princess turned killer." *The Beacon*, instead, had simply published a beautiful tribute to Pastor Skip Reese.

Somewhere, beneath all of it, she was truly grateful. The trouble was, she was too weak, possibly too indifferent, to show it.

"When was the last time you had a meal?"

Dottie didn't answer Rosie because she didn't know.

"Your heart is probably telling you it needs food, so I think Emily's right. You need to hop in the car with us and come have Sunday dinner. Fried chicken. Sit in the shade while Hickory whittles and smokes his pipe and talks about boat motors."

Dottie shook her head on the pillow. "You two shouldn't be seen with me."

Emily made some sound like, "Bah."

"People hate me so much."

"Not *our* people. Not out on the island, they don't."

"What about Delia? Huh?"

Silence. Delia was the little girl Pastor Skip had inherited, an orphan from his late wife's family. Rosie and her new husband had just finished the paperwork to adopt her so Skip could go away on an extended mission trip, but … still. Everyone Delia knew had died, and now Skip had, too.

"Delia doesn't hate you, Dottie."

Dottie squeezed her eyes shut. "I can't face her."

"You don't have to."

"I can't face anyone."

"Is this about your father?" Rosie asked, brow furrowed.

So, they did know all of it. Dottie had supposed they did, but it hurt all over again that the gossip would have boldly stretched even to her best friends.

The great Shelby Berkeley had, in fact, asked his daughter to "disappear" for a time from the amusement park now that the season was about to start. Local people were being cruel, and it was extending beyond Dottie to impact the family. "This whole business is bad for business," her father had said at the end of their "meeting," when he'd hugged her like it would still fix everything.

"Look, Dottie, he's not thinking clearly. No way can he run the opening of the park without you," Emily insisted. "No way."

"He's not wrong, though. People really do *hate* me."

"Nonsense," Rosie put in. "A few loud-mouthed, mean-spirited old ladies? Since when have any of us waved the white flag in their direction?"

"Actual hate messages." Dottie sighed. "A lot of them."

"I've had hate messages." Emily affirmed it as if the fact solidified them even further.

"Yours came because you were doing something you believed in." Dottie deliberately unclenched her jaw. She took a breath because her heart made a strange flop in her chest again. "Mine is for killing a good man."

"Dottie …"

"Ned refused to bag my groceries at the market." That silenced the sisters. Ned was known for being a very kind man. She didn't tell them about the drug store or the post office. Smokey had, in fact, delivered the orchestra posters to the amusement park office, but Dottie had hidden from him in the stairwell leading from the office up to her little apartment.

Just as she wished she'd managed to hide from these other well-meaning friends.

Rosie got up from the edge of the bed and paced. At the same time, Emily sat at Dottie's old girlhood vanity, the spot where Dottie had first learned to tame her curls. When Rosie turned around, she punctuated the move with a huffing sound. "Okay, here's the thing." She picked up the purse she'd flung at her sister and clutched it in front of her. "Sometimes, in life, there's shame that feels like it just goes on and on."

She stood straight, but Emily just groaned. "That's some pep talk."

"It's no pep talk. I know." Rosie moved closer to the bed again. "Dottie, I *know*. I know what it's like to have everyone talking about you, judging you, filling in the gaps of the story with what they want to believe, whether it's true or not." She swallowed. "Every now and then, believe it or not, I still hear some matron of the town refer to me as 'that fallen Graham girl.'"

Dottie blinked and felt her strength rush back for one dizzying moment in defense of her friend. Of course, girls were the ones held accountable when a baby came before marriage.

Dottie had watched Rosie—arguably the best human being she knew—try to live life for a decade under that cloud of shame and censure. Still, somehow, she envied her friend in comparison to her own situation now, and what kind of ridiculous level of self-pity was that?

"Please don't make me get up," she heard herself mumble, a hot tear she hoped they didn't notice sliding onto her pillow.

Another beat of silence.

"All right." It was Emily, rising from the lace-fringed stool at the vanity. "All right. We'll leave you be for today, Dottie, but only on one condition."

Surprised by the reprieve, Dottie looked directly at Emily for the first time.

"You need to teach Dot's Dash to Business course this coming week. Pick it back up again, as scheduled." Dottie started to shake her head, but Emily pressed on, one hand raised like she was trying to stop the motion. "I mean it. Lillian wants a fresh start." She paused to let that hit home. "Our mother is *counting* on you, Dottie."

With that, the sisters took turns kissing the top of her head and making her repeat her part of the deal out loud.

Chapter Six

Though the countryside greened up under daytime sun, spring nights on the farm could still get chilly. For Smokey, that meant firewood still needed to be chopped. One-handed.

Surviving as a combat diver in active war zones, Smokey Black had never been the kind to admit defeat.

Still, the brand-spanking-new cast on his dominant hand meant another section of dried pine bounced off the side of his axe and flew four feet from the chopping block, un-chopped.

Cream Puff the cat stopped grooming her single hind leg to glare at him as the log rolled into her space.

"Sorry, Princess." Smokey growled and dropped onto the grooved surface of the big stump and let the axe fall amidst the woodchips. His left boot laces were untied, and if there were anything more difficult than chopping wood one-handed, it was tying laces.

Cream Puff nudged that boot, already forgiving him for the flying wood that had put her life in jeopardy.

"I know. There's no place for self-pity here." The cat, after all, had managed fine on three limbs for as long as he'd been feeding her. But what did the fluffy cat know about spring on a farm? Some of the soil needed tilling. The wagon needed new tires.

Sure, his brother and the ever-silent Hugh helped where they could, but the rest of the colossal Black-Pool Farms would always take precedence over Smokey's eccentric seasonal wonderland of pumpkins and evergreens.

Looking out across the farm soothed him a bit, even with all the work it entailed. The cabin he'd called home since his discharge sat on a low hill that offered a staggering view of the patchwork fields below. Evergreens, fields half-plowed for pumpkin patches, newly sprouting cornfields, and his cheerful red barn sprawled out before him in the low light of evening.

He hauled Cream Puff up when she started clawing at his work pants, and she snaked around his neck, a fluffy, long-haired scarf he would endure cheerfully even in the hot months ahead. "Anyway, it's half my own fault," he continued, regarding his fresh cast with disgust. As it turned out, cutting the original off early had revealed a wrist still broken. "No one to blame but me, is there?"

The fact was, Smokey could afford to talk to this cat all he wanted, just as he could afford to name her Princess Cream Puff. Once his shoulders had gotten to be a certain width and size, once he had proved capable of lifting a grown man with one arm, he'd discovered he could do about anything he wanted without folks being bold enough to say much about it.

Together, he and Cream Puff regarded a cloud of gravel dust far down the lane as a blue car wove its way toward him through the evergreens. This would be Lucille Armstrong from Millersport on her twice-weekly crusade. Upon arriving and turning off her engine, she observed Smokey standing with the cat nestled in his arm, his boot laces still dragging in the dirt.

He nodded as she swung out of the driver's seat, and it didn't take him any time at all to notice the pie she carried. "Hello there, Lucille."

"Hey, Smokey." She had the whitest teeth when she smiled, which seemed to be any time she was in his presence. Flaxen hair she curled and arranged with pins behind her ears. Thin but very red, shiny lips. "I opened a jar of peaches from last fall and made you a pie, honey."

"I love peach pie."

"Of course you do. Why else d'you think I'd spend the afternoon baking you one?"

He smiled his thanks as she sidled closer, remembering that last time she'd brought a cherry pie. Whatever recipe she used for crust worked just fine. The other day, it had been a loaf of raisin bread. Right after the accident, she'd arrived with some of the best stew he'd ever tasted.

"Thanks a lot, Lucille."

She touched his right arm affectionately, carefully avoiding Cream Puff, who had wood chips in her fur. "Thought the cast was done?"

"Turns out, I jumped the gun. Earned myself a brand new one."

Lucille was still smiling, but she shook her head. "I'll just put this on your counter inside, then."

"Counter" was a generous word for the slab of treated wood he'd built for his kitchen area. Smokey didn't mind her charging into his home if it meant pie for dinner. A glance at the sun told him he'd forgotten about dinner again, anyway.

While Lucille was inside, probably poking around his cabin, another cloud of dust up the lane announced the Fleetline. Mama Pool. It seemed to be his night for visitors.

Left thumb hooked in his pocket, Smokey nodded as Lucille came out and stood devotedly at his side just as his mother pulled up behind her car. The look on Mama Pool's face told him he'd have to explain this cozy, domestic scene later.

Lillian Graham, Emily and Rosie's long-lost mother, gave a timid wave from the passenger seat, where she stayed put as Mama got out.

"Stopped to see what Doc said." She scooted between cars in her mint green dress. "Hello there, Lucille."

"Mama Pool." Lucille beamed and hugged the older woman. For the length of the hug, Smokey endured a probing look from his mother.

He grinned affably at her and waved the fresh cast, which somehow managed to be larger than the first. "Still broken."

"Of course it is!"

He nodded in the direction of the car and offered Lillian a smile. "Where you two ladies off to this evening looking so pretty?"

"Dottie's business course is finally starting," Mama Pool said with enthusiasm. "Lil and I get to learn about accounts management tonight, don't we, Lucille?"

Smokey laughed. "Can't you manage accounts in your sleep?"

"*Lil* is going to learn about accounts management tonight," she amended, and then she slanted a look at the younger woman still finding opportunities to touch her son's arm. Mama Pool cleared her throat. "I guess I'll see you there at class, Lucille?"

"You will not." Lucille's smile was gone.

"I thought you enrolled in the Dash to Business classes."

"A lot of women did that, Mama Pool," Lucille said in her usual sweet voice "... *before*."

"Before?"

"You know."

Mama Pool visibly stiffened, and Smokey bent to scratch Cream Puff under her fluffy little chin as he waited for the inevitable showdown.

"I think it's important to remember Dottie is trying to *help* the ladies of this town."

Lucille shrugged. "Dottie Berkeley has enough on her plate trying to help herself, if you ask me."

"Because she lost control on an icy road?"

"Because she was reckless and killed Pastor Skip."

Smokey watched Lucille smile again, this time in an unpleasant way, and he hoped his mother didn't pop her one. He knew from experience Mama Pool hit with a closed fist, like a man. And, if that happened, Lucille might take his peach pie away.

"I'm not sure what Dottie has to teach respectable women in this community that they should even be learning, is all."

Mama Pool's nostrils flared. She cleared her throat. "I see how it is, then." She did her angry-walk back around the car, but before she got in, she said, "I see your back-up plan to learning a useful skill is to sink your claws into some clueless man. That way you don't have to learn to take care of yourself."

With that, she slammed her car door and left a small groove with her tire in the lane.

Smokey bit back his grin and sighed. "Well, I think there was an insult for *me* in there somewhere."

Lucille rallied with a shaky breath and forced another blinding smile. "She's a dear woman."

Lucille did leave the pie, of course. Smokey knew he'd get another tomorrow or the next day from Grace Fielding. Maxi Baker, on the other hand, tended to bring processed meats artfully arranged on trays, sometimes with homemade biscuits.

He never asked any of the women to feed him. Nor did he ever, ever ask them to help him tie his boots, even when they offered.

Word had gone out, about the same time as the accident, that Smokey Black of Festival Farms and Black-Pool Farms would be breaking ground soon on his own, brand-new home. But word also spread that he was figuring on holding off on the details until he had a wife.

Those words were true.

After all, by his calculation, his wife would want a say in how the newly built house was designed. He did have the foundation staked out up the hill above the cabin, but he'd grown up hearing Mama Pool bemoan the wall that separated the dining room and kitchen at the farmhouse, along with the way the south-facing windows baked a person in the living room most of the day. Smokey knew enough not to proceed with his homestead without consulting first with Mrs. Smokey Black.

He kept meaning to find her.

But he'd always been a blessed man, so he wasn't too surprised when the women of the Buckeye Lake region began trying to find *him*. With renewed energy, it seemed, and no requirement of energy on his own part.

At some point, he would have to figure out which one she was. But, first, pie.

Chapter Seven

An hour later, in the public library's Community Room, Dottie Berkeley listened to the clock on the wall tick its way well past the time Dot's Dash to Business was to start.

Dottie focused on not swaying where she stood. Lil Graham sat straight-backed and expectant behind one of the dozen adding machines Dottie had purchased months ago for the women in her class. Lil, the only person registered who had shown up, simply watched her.

Dottie offered her what she hoped looked like a smile.

Mama Pool had gone out to the main entrance on a mission to point "the ladies" back to the room where the class would take place, taking her nervous chatter with her and leaving the silence behind.

"I do like your dress." Lil smiled and studied her instructor with her usual wounded look. Dottie wondered if her own eyes had started looking haunted, sunken, and shadowed.

"Thank you." Dottie tugged on her light knit jacket. Getting dressed had been its own kind of accomplishment today, but she'd done it because she'd promised her friends last week she would. She'd grown winded and a little dizzy putting the clothes on, which had her more convinced than ever that her heart was about to give out and she would soon, mercifully, keel over dead.

Maybe now, in this silent room at the Buckeye Lake Public Library.

Her hair, which had mysteriously begun falling out in curly clumps, was gathered back into its professional bun. She supposed it was a good thing there'd always been plenty of it to spare. Now, she couldn't help wondering what Lil Graham saw when she looked at the woman who was supposed to be instructing a class to which, it seemed, no one else was coming. Could Lil tell Dottie was barely standing? That when she slept at all, she woke up shaking, and that the shaking came and went all day?

How could it *not* be obvious to anyone who saw her?

She'd even had to pin her skirt to keep it from sliding off her hips.

Mama Pool re-entered the room and cast a meaningful glance at the clock. Ten minutes ago, she had suggested the ladies must not be a very punctual lot, that they'd "have to work on that" as part of the curriculum. Now, marching back in, the older woman wore a stern and stoic look.

"No one else is coming, are they?" Dottie knew the answer.

Mama Pool gave one brief shake of her head.

Dottie lowered herself into a chair beside the front table, where alongside the adding machines, she'd arranged guide materials, charts, steno pads, and the ballpoint pens she'd purchased.

"I'm …" Lil began. Then, in a stronger voice: "I'm still eager to learn."

Dottie wasn't even embarrassed when the tears came, even though she never, ever cried in front of people.

Yet, here she was. Crying in front of her one student: the former chorus girl who'd abandoned her infant daughters after her young husband's death, eventually extorted money from them, and recently returned from a life of unguessed-at intrigue.

And who was now looking at Dottie with *pity*.

"Now, listen." Mama Pool moved closer. This woman had raised two strapping sons, so Dottie expected her to be alarmed by a crying girl. Instead, Mama Pool's long, strong fingers began a gentle massage on her shoulders that didn't betray any alarm at all. "Maybe we just need to do a better job getting word out again, since there was such a delay in the start."

But Dottie knew the word had gone out. There'd been signs all over for the class's new kickoff this week, and everyone who had originally enrolled had received a personal call. Some of the calls had gotten mysteriously disconnected, just as some of the signs had been torn down.

"We can stop pretending there are other explanations," Dottie tried to say without hiccupping.

"Um. Hello?" In the doorway stood Julia Fey, a young, pretty widow who lived near the park. "I'm sorry I'm late, but I had trouble getting little Penny settled with the neighbor. I can … go, though. If this isn't a good time?"

"There we are!" Mama Pool moved forward. "Welcome, Julia. I'm so glad you could be here. Two is plenty for a class, I think." She helped situate Julia next to Lil, clearly giving Dottie time to mop the tears off her face.

Dottie braced her hands on the polished table and pushed herself to a standing position, dread snaking its way along her spine.

Then that same dread increased when Constance Day eased into the room. She was not on the class roster. She was the head librarian, and she looked apologetic and grim. Constance cleared her throat, then squared her shoulders like preparation for a battle she didn't want to fight.

These days, Dottie recognized the body language well.

"What is it, Connie?" Mama Pool asked.

The librarian folded her hands in front of her and regarded Dottie's tears. Dottie had just enough pride left to swipe the last of them away with her handkerchief.

"The library board just contacted me."

Dottie did not need her to continue but knew she would.

"I'm to convey to you that this room is not to be used for classes like this, after all. The library board discussed it, and they only just now told me their decision. I'm very sorry."

"You're *sorry*?" Mama Pool looked like a warrior queen in a lace-trimmed mint dress.

Dottie just shook her head, raising a hand as though she had the ability to calm the whole world down. "I'll … pack up."

Constance backed out of the room, looking regretful and sheepish. Dottie blinked back more tears, but she made a project of getting the crate back out from under the front table and loading the adding machines into it.

"Julia, thank you for trying." Mama Pool said it as chairs scraped. "We'll be in touch, I promise."

Then Mama Pool was right there, in Dottie's path.

"Is this Dottie Berkeley in front of me?"

Dottie didn't look up, just carefully stacked supplies. She tried not to remember buying them, how eager she'd felt.

"Dottie Berkeley who beat the boys every Field Day? Dottie Berkeley, class valedictorian? Dottie Berkeley who nearly doubled the size of an amusement park during a war?"

"Mama Pool. Please."

"You've broken out in hives, dear. Enough is *enough*."

"I don't know what to do," Dottie admitted as she hiccupped her way through new sobs. "My family. They want me. To take. To take a trip somewhere. I told them I couldn't because of the class."

"For heavens …"

"I'm so ashamed. I don't know." Hiccup. "What to do."

She'd already had to ask Emily to drive her and the boxes of adding machines over here to the library tonight. She was stranded now, waiting two hours to be picked up again, like a child. Unless Mama Pool could drive her … somewhere. Somewhere else where no one wanted her around. She'd basically been kicked out of a public library now, a thing that hardly happened to vagrants.

Dottie couldn't dam up a cascade of self-pity, an inability that somehow made her feel even sorrier for herself.

"*I know*." It was the soft, hesitant voice of Lil that made Dottie realize the thin woman had risen and had also placed a hand on her shoulder. "I don't know exactly how you feel, but I … I know how it feels not to know what to do or where to go."

Dottie nodded and scratched her chest. She, in fact, *was* breaking out in hives.

"You need a good ride on a hay wagon." Mama Pool said it thoughtfully, and for some reason that made Dottie laugh a little. She was mildly allergic to hay. It made her sneeze, so it would probably be great for hives.

"No, I mean it. Don't laugh. I'm serious. Let's pack this stuff up. It will still get used, Dottie, just not in this season of your life." Mama Pool said it with determination, and Lil joined her in re-boxing the supplies. "Then we'll clean *you* up."

"Clean me up?"

"Mop your face," the woman said with a wave. "We'll pack you a bag. You're coming home with me, out to the farmhouse."

"Oh, yes!" Lil clapped once, then got back to work. "The farmhouse is the perfect place to go when you're not sure if anyone wants to see you at all."

Dottie couldn't help but shake her head at that, too. "The thing is, I know very well that no one wants to see me at all."

"Well, we do."

"And then what? We're going to have … hayrides?"

Mama Pool picked up the receiver of the black phone on the corner counter of the Community Room. She murmured some directions to the operator. Then: "Hello. Hello, is this Shelby Berkeley?"

Dottie's eyes went wide.

"I understand you instructed your daughter to take a leave of absence. … Yes. Yes, it's Sylvia. Well, don't send out a search party for her. Not that you would, you sorry excuse for a man … That's right … Uh-huh. Well, you just have fun trying to fill her heels at the park, Mister. If you can even stop drinking long enough to try."

Behind Mama Pool, Dottie's mouth had fallen open. Lil Graham picked up a box of adding machines and gave Dottie a wide-eyed look. "This is why I've decided to stay on her good side."

Chapter Eight

Seedlings were planted two feet apart on the southern slope from Smokey's cabin. This way, he could keep an eye on his little army of spindly, tender-needled babies.

On that late April morning, they needed to be mulched.

Reggie was out planting beans through most of the week because the weather had held. Hugh, quiet and adverse to large machinery since the war, was happy out in the fir tree plot, where those newest trees grew.

Later, as three-year-olds, they would be transplanted to grow to Christmas tree size in the larger fields, five feet apart. Hugh had reinforced the knees of his old trousers so he could kneel to arrange the mulched wood around the base of each seedling in a perpetual war against weeds.

Young Silas Peterman had appeared this morning, as well, as the boy would occasionally do. The kid was up at the northeast corner of the seedling beds with his own pile of mulch and shovel. Mostly deaf, Silas periodically skipped public school and showed up at the farm, where he made no attempt to communicate with anyone, but he did watch Smokey's mouth when Smokey talked.

There was no real need for Silas to watch Hugh's mouth, though, since Hugh hardly ever said a word. The pair worked well together.

In fact, they made for an exceptionally quiet little work crew. At the end of the day, they would collect their pay. Silas might return the next day, or he might decide to go back to school. Smokey never knew.

Smokey himself usually did the work of five men, but on this morning, he speared his shovel into the mulch on the wagon and, steadying it with the edge of his plaster cast, flopped it at the base of a little fir. One-handed, he was clumsy and slow. Then he spread the mulch around the weeded, twiggy base of the tree with his left hand.

"I'm starting to worry I've put on a little weight," Smokey called out loud to Hugh, one row over, as he moved to haul another shovel full. Lucille Armstrong had been back this morning, this time with her sister, Peg, and twice as many homemade cinnamon buns as last time. Smokey had left the plate out on the seat of the tractor for Silas and Hugh. He looked down and confirmed his own pants seemed to be fitting tighter at the waist. He'd have to change to a new hole in his leather belt, if he weren't careful.

Being wooed by women came at a price, it seemed.

The sun was high, and a roll was sitting heavy in his belly when Mama Pool's Fleetline once again crunched the gravel at the entrance to Festival Farms. He flexed his left wrist to peer at his wristwatch beneath the leather glove. It was only mid-morning. Usually, Mama Pool had found a project for her day by now.

Smokey squinted as the car rolled to a stop. Then he greeted his mother with a wave of his cast as she proceeded to unload her own flower-patterned shovel and familiar green gardening gloves. This was new. His mother did *not* mulch or fertilize.

Then, to his even greater surprise, he saw none other than Dottie Berkeley emerge from the passenger side and stand there looking uncharacteristically lost beside the car. She wore ill-fitting coveralls cinched around her waist with a little rope. Smokey moved toward her, finding it somehow strange to see her away from town, out of her heels and skirt suits.

"Dottie." Since his mother was there and he'd been raised right, he lifted his hat in greeting, but he made no attempt to disguise the fact he was looking her up and down. "What are you up to today?"

"I know you're a bit behind on work out here." Mama Pool answered for her, passing the shovel to Dottie. Then she dropped a fancy-looking bag near the younger woman's booted feet, which were barely visible beneath the pile of extra coverall fabric mounded at her ankles.

Smokey did not know what to say. The amusement park wouldn't open without Dottie Berkeley. This should have been her busiest time of year, but here she was, standing on his farm with a shovel.

"She's here to help." Mama Pool gave Dottie a side hug. Then she smashed a wide-brimmed hat down over Dottie's tight, dark braid and shocked Smokey even further by blowing kisses, getting back in her car, and promptly pulling away.

Smokey would've shoved both hands in his pockets, but the cast just didn't fit. "Um." A glance over his shoulder told him Hugh and Silas, on opposite side of the wee seedlings, stared.

"Not sure I know what to do with a pretty girl who hasn't brought me food." Smokey mumbled it into the silence that followed. He stepped closer to Dottie, who was not laughing. He sometimes forgot how small she was in real life. She raised her jaw to meet his eyes, and his heart broke a little at the pale vulnerability beneath the hat.

"Just tell me what to do."

He wondered if she'd ever said that sentence in her whole life. She'd always known just what to do.

Regarding her new frailty, Smokey understood what *he* was supposed to do, as well. If there was one thing Mama Pool had passed down to her youngest son, it was the idealism that farm work fixed all things in time. So, he didn't need his mother to tell him why she'd lugged the lost-looking roller coaster princess out here and dropped her at his feet like a spare barn cat.

"We're mulching." He breathed deep and raised his voice. "I'd say we could just about finish this plot today, Crew! The good Lord sent us plenty of hands to make up for my useless one. C'mon, Dottie B. You two, Hugh and Silas, back to work!"

He helped her shovel mulch to dump at the start of a row of seedlings and then knelt beside her to show her how to make sure there were no weeds at the base of the little trunks. "Weeds grow faster than trees," he told her, always happy to talk about growing things. "So, these little babies are a lot of work."

He showed her how to arrange the mulch around the base and how thick to make it. As silent as the rest of his wacky work crew, she listened and nodded.

"We don't mound it around the base like a volcano," Smokey warned. "That keeps the moisture right up against the bark of the seedling, which can make it decay. See? We want to make more of a donut shape around it." He smiled privately because now he was even communicating in terms of baked goods. "Out to about … here. See?"

"I see."

He watched her arrange the mulch carefully, her arms surprisingly thin where they poked out from his mother's gloves. She needed a cinnamon bun or two, herself. "I don't reckon this is too complicated for you to handle."

She'd been a whiz in school, he knew. Good at everything. Smokey had no doubt her little mulch arrangements in his seedling plot would look far better than his own lopsided, left-handed piles.

Chapter Nine

Mama Pool didn't play fair.

The woman had talked of hayrides in wagons. Fresh air, bread baked at dawn, a silent porch where her only visitors would be deer and cardinals. Dottie should have known, however, when the seasoned farm wife had awakened her today with talk about the healing power of physical labor in the fresh air, that she would wind up ... perspiring.

Even with gloves on, Dottie found she did not care for touching manure.

To be fair, it was really a dirt-manure mix, Smokey had explained. After eating a soggy sandwich Mama Pool had packed for her like a child with a lunchpail, Dottie found herself relocated from the seedling patch to a pumpkin patch. Her job, she'd been told, was now to create mounds of this dirt-manure mix in a large, seemingly endless plot of fresh-tilled ground.

"You want them the size of a pitcher's mound." Smokey patted her on the back with his one good hand and a dose of his boyish enthusiasm. "Later, we'll plant the pumpkin seeds inside the mounds, see?"

That directive had been hours ago. Many hours.

Dottie's back had been hurting almost the entire time. This was, after all, more than she'd moved her body in many weeks. Also, when she'd removed the gardening gloves to eat the sandwich, she'd been dismayed to find dirt beneath her fingernails. How had the dirt managed that when she'd obediently kept the gloves on?

Did that mean there was manure under her fingernails now? She was afraid to take the gloves off ever again.

Smokey kept disappearing on his orange tractor, to return with a wagonload of the dirt manure. She had no idea where he went to get it. Once back on site, he'd distribute it with his one-armed shoveling, whistling at times, grumbling at others, apparently about his cast.

He seemed as frustrated as she was hopeless. Dottie figured the two of them made a charming pair.

Then he'd ride off again, leaving her yards from two other silent field hands. She'd figured out over lunch that the one named Hugh *could* speak but simply didn't. Silas, though, could *not* speak or, it seemed, hear. Instead, the lanky kid stared hard at Smokey's mouth when he talked, nodded, and went about his work in perfect understanding.

Dottie remembered a time in her own awkward younger years when she'd stared hard at Smokey Black's mouth, as well, but for a different reason.

"Shouldn't Silas be in school … somewhere?" she'd asked Smokey after he'd eventually made introductions. Not that it had anything to do with her, but Silas was obviously still a long way from manhood.

"If I drive him back to the school, he'll simply hike back out here to the farm." Smokey shrugged. "He doesn't go back until it's his own idea. Usually after a day or two out here. Silas likes to be outside in the fine weather, that's all."

And so, the hours had passed in easy silence.

Dottie let her mind wander as she sculpted tidy hills the size of the prescribed pitcher's mound. She thought about pumpkins, naturally. She noticed how different the sounds were in a silent field in the middle of the countryside, compared with the sounds up at pier boardwalk on the lake. Even the birds were different out here, just a few miles outside of town. She wondered idly if she would be paid for this labor, or if she herself would be paying for the privilege of mounding manure in the name of healing, like some kind of camp for people who couldn't cope.

Then Dottie thought about the bed she'd slept in last night in Mama Pool's farmhouse. It had to have been Smokey's room years before because there were still championship swimming pendants hanging on one wall.

She also thought about the fact that no one really knew where she was today, not even her family. Sure, her father knew she was with Mama Pool somewhere (which, of course, she was not), but Dottie simply could not remember another time she'd been off everyone's radar.

That, of course, had her mind wandering to the park. Had the crew fixed that last spot on The Dips? Had the new contracts with the vendors all been signed by Shelby? Was he training the new workers, or was he just setting them loose with a few coins for the billiard hall as a hiring bonus?

Mama Pool promised she'd go check on things.

Sitting back on her haunches now, Dottie let those thoughts float away. They came in. They went out. She couldn't face any of it anymore, which turned out to be fine since no one *wanted* her to face any of it anymore.

Instead, she built another mound. She'd thought enough for one day, and if there was one thing more exhausting than pumpkin mound sculpting, it was thinking.

Groaning, she pressed her fist into her lower back after she'd helped empty the wagon again. What time was it? The sun was starting to feel like late afternoon or early evening. She was getting light-headed. She'd half expected her heart to finally stop today, if she worked as hard as she could, but it stubbornly beat on.

Then, to her surprise and mortification, her stomach growled. *Audibly.*

Looking up, at a loss for when she'd last felt hunger, she met Smokey Black's eyes over the pile of smelly dirt and knew he'd heard it when he winked at her.

"I'd say you've more than earned some dinner, Miss Berkeley."

"Oh, no. I'm fine." Mama Pool would have to come back for her at some point, wouldn't she? Surely, she hadn't just dropped her off here indefinitely.

Her boss waved in Silas's direction until he had his attention, and then he enunciated with a pointing gesture. "Hop on the wagon, and we'll go get some chow."

Dottie watched as Hugh and Silas tossed their shovels deep into the back of the wagon, still half-filled with the soil mixture, and then she watched as they literally "hopped on." *Onto the manure.*

She felt certain this was not what Mama Pool had advertised as a "hayride" in a wagon. But then, the seasoned lady farmer had probably known "manure-ride" wasn't going to win Dottie over to a day at the pumpkin patch.

She took off her floppy hat and looked over at Smokey, who was watching her.

"I'll walk."

"It'll be dark before you get there." He climbed cheerfully onto the seat of the tractor in one smooth motion. He was beautiful to watch move, in water or on land. From up top of the Allis Chalmers, he regarded her with his easy smile and turned the key to start the engine. "Come on. Climb up here. There's some leftover bean soup that's gonna taste like heaven after the day you've put in."

She looked up at his enormous body on the seat. "Is there ... room?"

"We'll make it work, darling. For the sake of your tummy. C'mon." Smokey's eyes, she noticed as she climbed up, made perfect half-moons whenever he grinned, and he grinned often. Dottie situated one hip on the sun-warm metal above an enormous tire, which still put her very, very close to him. Her one foot was braced between his legs. She remembered again how damp with perspiration she was, but it was hard to care when her blouse also now boasted animal dung.

"Feel free to do the steering," he said as they lurched forward, his cast wrapped around her waist to keep her in place.

"No, thank you."

"Left hand isn't great. I only sort of end up where I'm aiming to get to these days."

"I'm not driving anymore." She said it softly, but she knew he'd heard her over the engine when he spoke next, the playfulness gone.

"Oh. Oh, right. Sorry, sweetheart." The arm holding her onto her seat gave her a half-squeeze. "That was thick-headed of me."

Dottie shrugged. "I never thanked you."

"For making you work like a dog all day?"

"No, I mean for not … you know, not making me look as bad as you might have. To the judge, in court."

Smokey didn't respond to that for a moment as he steered them through the lane that wove between two sprawling fields of different sorts of pine that managed to overpower the smells from the wagon. There were so many shades of green out here. Dottie had stopped expecting a response when he finally said, "Hopefully you're headed for a season now, Dottie B., where you don't have to thank people for telling the truth under oath, eh?"

She nodded, ready to change the subject. She could not think about that night, not now when the fresh air might be making her tired in a better way than she had been.

Smokey understood what she needed. "Ever hear the story of the Three Sisters?"

"Hmm?"

"The Iroquois legend about three sisters: Maize, Red Bean, and Pumpkin?"

She enjoyed the timbre of his voice over the hum of the tractor as they bounced along toward … she knew not where. Toward bean soup.

"As the legend went, they're the daughters of Sky Woman, all of them very different. The maize, or corn, grows tall and protects her sisters. Red Bean nourishes Maize's roots, while Pumpkin, or Squash, protects the soil with her leaves. They do best together, all three, whether growing or in a meal."

Dottie nodded, thinking not of her own sisters but of her best friends. Emily, Rosie, and her. They also did best together. "They're stronger because they're different," she said, not really trying to raise her voice enough to be heard. "That makes sense."

He turned left this time, and Dottie caught sight of a large pond off to the north and, up a hill ahead, his cabin.

"From an agriculture standpoint, those crops protect from pests and disease. At any rate, I dream of someday having three daughters of my own, named the same."

Dottie slanted him a look, imagining those daughters: tall, lanky, and saddled with the names Maize, Red Bean, and Pumpkin. Unexpectedly, she chuckled. "Your middle daughter will be named Red Bean Black? Hmm. It does have a ring to it."

"Doesn't it?"

"I'd have thought you'd want sons, though, Smoke. You know, for the farm."

"Sons? What in the world for?" He made a comical expression. "Did you *see* how hard you worked today, little lady?"

The tractor chugged its way up the incline to Smokey's rough-hewn home, where a shiny car was parked, looking out of place. Against it, Nettie James leaned in a pale pink evening dress, a basket tucked against her curving hip. Dottie sat straighter, glancing up at Smokey, but he had not reacted in any way to the sight of Nettie.

Were Smokey and Nettie going steady?

Dottie's empty stomach clenched at the thought, making her irritated that she'd still *never* stopped caring who Smokey Black was going with. Weary of herself and him and all the females in the greater Buckeye Lake area, she hopped down as soon as the tractor rolled to a stop.

Nettie was staring pointedly at her, and Dottie's face felt hot. Smokey, of course, seemed comfortable as he dropped to the ground behind Dottie.

"Nettie, hello!" he said in his usual pleasant, Smokey way.

"Hi there, handsome." Her lashes seemed too heavy to stay up all the way above her feline smile. "Guess what I have in a roasting pan in the trunk?"

"Enough for all of us, I hope?" he said, loping over to her car. She tip-toed a kiss, which he leaned down to permit.

Nettie ignored his question. "How does a roast sound? With all the trimmings?"

With that pronouncement and her opening of the hatch, Dottie watched Hugh and Silas appear as if by magic, grinning ear to ear. Which seemed to make Smokey smile.

"What d'ya say, Crew? Can we make do with Miss James's roast instead of leftover bean soup just this one night?"

Nettie, to her credit, did not seem to resent the intrusion of the other two silent men on her romantic plans.

Dottie, however, appeared to be a different kind of intrusion altogether. The other woman, a childless war widow of about thirty, had originally been signed up for Dot's Dash to Business course. Not only had Nettie not shown up, of course, but she seemed not to be able to decide now whether she hated the sight of Dottie here at Smokey's farm or *loved* the sight of Dottie in shapeless coveralls, smeared with dirt and waste.

"Nettie, I know you know Dottie." Smokey muscled the roasting pan out of the trunk, half-balanced with ease on his cast. Could he be pretending away Nettie's scorn?

Nettie gave a slight nod but did not even look over at Dottie.

"Come along, then, friends," Smokey said, leading the way into the cabin with a spring in his step that belied the work he'd done all day.

Dottie hung back, only to notice a long-haired tabby cat walking with an unusual gait around the corner of the house. The cat was missing a hind leg. Head held high, it made its way to a wicker-woven chair beside the door, where it curled up in a contented ball. Upon closer inspection, Dottie decided this was a girl cat because she boasted a dainty yellow bow around her neck. With polka-dots.

Smokey put a bow on his three-legged barn cat. She could hear his laugh now, inside.

When Mama Pool's car pulled up at the same time the laughter rang out, Dottie straightened from rubbing the cat's satiny ear. She waved in acknowledgement of her ride, very hungry but still very relieved to leave, and then walked to the door to bid her—Employer? Host? Parole Officer?—farewell.

Inside, Hugh and Silas regarded the contents of the steaming pan on the small, round table. As Smokey carved the roast, Nettie pressed adoringly against him. Dottie, who hadn't cowered to another female since she was fifteen, slunk off without a word.

Chapter Ten

The windows of Mama Pool's farmhouse kitchen opened to mid-morning, and clean plaid curtains moved like breath, in and out, with the breeze.

At the kitchen table, Dottie waited for her coffee to cool. By contrast, beside her, Lil Graham was content to scald her tongue. It reminded Dottie of Emily.

"You two are quiet this morning," Mama Pool said, moving back into the room while tying her apron.

"It's May Day," Dottie said, her eyes on the wall calendar. An ink illustration of the local sawmill adorned the top, like the one she kept in the park office.

"So, it is."

Lil hissed another sip and aimed questions at Dottie with her eyes. "I thought the rides don't operate until the end of the month?"

"Right." Dottie tried to take a sip, only to find the brew still needed more time in the breeze. "They have a pageant at the park today and the traditional May pole celebration. Dancing on the pier later."

"Oh."

"And you're sitting there on this glorious spring day wondering if someone remembered to book the band," Mama Pool said, glancing over her shoulder.

"And the five hundred other things that happen for May Day to work. But I did book the band months ago. I know that's done."

"Well, May Day's workin' just fine here."

"It's a lovely morning," Lil added.

Dottie had woven a green scarf through her braid before tying it back into a bun. She couldn't deny it really was a lovely morning.

Apron secured, Mama Pool positioned herself before the other two women like a teacher, hands on her sturdy hips. "And on this lovely morning, you'll learn how to bake bread."

Dottie looked at Lil, who returned the look, and then they both looked at Mama Pool.

"Me?"

"Both of you. Unless you already know how." Silence. "Ladies, everyone needs to know how to bake bread."

"Not showgirls," Lil countered with a fresh little grin Dottie had never seen before. At least, not on Lil's weathered face. She'd seen the same grin on Emily's face, though, when the reporter knew she was getting under someone's skin. Funny the small things a person passed on to a child.

Dottie, however, couldn't muster a smile. *Everyone baked bread?* "Not amusement park managers, either."

"I used to smack my boys with a rolling pin. Do not think you two are exempt from that. Grab that flour sack, will you, Dottie? From the pantry?"

Mama Pool kept her supplies on pantry shelves with checkered fabric curtains drawn over the contents. The fabric matched the seat covers at the table, where Lil was wiping everything down.

Dottie found herself still weak. Her dresses didn't fit right anymore, and everything felt heavier these days. Cradling the full flour sack, she wished Reggie, the oldest of Mama Pool's sons, had hauled it out when he'd stopped by on his way to church.

Dottie wondered if Smokey ever popped in for coffee at his mother's house.

"Wait. A. Minute." Dottie grunted the sack onto the counter. Mama Pool emerged from the lower cupboard with a bowl the size of a garden fishpond. "You're not teaching me to bake bread so I can join in this race to win your son's heart with baked goods, are you?"

Dottie could see it now. Mama Pool driving her over to Smokey's cabin and coaching her to present hot-buttered rolls to Smokey with a sassy swing of her diminishing hips.

The older woman cackled with delight. "Never crossed my mind, darling." She made an efficient ruckus then, banging the bowl and measuring cups and spoons onto the little table. "Though watching you get so overshadowed by that nasty Nettie the other night was rather painful."

"I ...." Dottie's mouth opened, but what could she say to any of that? She could see herself at fifteen again, in her overalls while Smokey snuggled with a blonde girl. "I was there to make mounds of dung, I might remind you, which was *your* idea."

"I honestly didn't know about the dung, dear. I'm very disappointed with my son about that."

"You told me it was *fresh air* I needed. You never said anything about catching a husband."

Dottie couldn't exactly make out what Mama Pool said when she bent over again, but it sounded like "meet me halfway." When she rose, she said, "Manure is one thing, fresh-baked bread another."

"I wish I understood that." Lil grinned. Dottie didn't even want to.

Mama Pool had harped on her "healing powers of fresh air" mantra all week, but Dottie noticed she herself was being consistently dropped at Smokey's farm rather than at Reggie's expansive livestock barns.

"Reggie doesn't have a broken wrist, now, does he?" Mama Pool huffed when questioned. Now, she said, "Anyway, Smokey doesn't need my help finding a wife any more than you need my help finding a husband."

"I think we all know I'm not much of a candidate right now, anyway." Dottie had screamed twice in the night, after all, and awoken with both an aching head and stomachache.

"You said it, not me," Mama Pool said, but she added a laugh brighter than the May sunshine and a playful hip bump that nearly knocked Dottie over. "Your sermon this morning is about *yeast*. Gather 'round, ladies."

Dottie and Lil obeyed because neither of them had been ready to attend First Community Church on Sunday mornings. They might have different reasons, but Dottie figured both came back to shame. Mama Pool had applied no pressure, but they'd been mildly surprised when their hostess stayed back at the house with them this morning.

"Now, look here." They watched her measure out the meal-like yeast into the bowl. "There's nothing to bread baking once you figure out how to keep your yeast alive and growing, and that's all to do with water temperature. Mark my words."

"Should I be writing this down?" That question earned Dottie a light tap from Mama Pool's rolling pin.

"Just pay attention."

But neither the career dancer nor the businesswoman proved an easy student. When Mama Pool said to test the water temperature on the inside of their wrists, both struggled with her next instructions: "Just a smidge hotter than you'd give a baby in its bottle. You know, when you mix the milk and corn syrup with the water."

Once again, Dottie and Lil shared a baffled look.

"Do I need to point out I was a terrible mother, and it was a very long time ago, at that?" Lil asked, and Dottie didn't feel the need to point out she'd obviously never mixed a bottle in her life.

Still, Mama Pool proved herself capable of adapting. She was clearly determined.

"How much bread are we making? That's a small bit of yeast, it seems," Lil observed.

"Exactly so." Mama Pool rolled up her sleeves. "The parable of the yeast in the Bible was all about a small beginning, a little bit of faith that grows. It's alive, like the Spirit in us that fills every corner of our lives." She gestured broadly and made Dottie smile a little. "You just watch it fill this bowl in the sunshine and see."

The scent of mingling ingredients began to fill the kitchen. Dottie watched the dough stick to the older woman's freckled forearms, mesmerized in the same way she was easily mesmerized by ordinary things these days.

She wasn't even sure how much time had passed before Mama Pool flicked a clean towel over the bowl and placed it in a warm beam of sun.

"And, just like us, the yeast needs to rest from time to time." Dottie blinked back tears when she felt Mama Pool's soft kiss on her temple where the slash would soon be a scar. "It will be more effective later from that rest."

"And from the fresh air," Lil put in with a wink at Dottie.

Chapter Eleven

When the light spring rain began to fall, Smokey gave up on fixing his tractor one-handed. He knew Dottie Berkeley would be stranded at his farm in this rain unless he tracked her down and gave her a ride back to his mother's place. She had no other way to move about in the world.

Things like that, things that smacked of helplessness ... well, they had to sit very badly with the woman he'd watched run the lake's amusement park since she was a schoolgirl.

About the time the rain had started, Smokey figured Dottie had been weeding around the bundle house — his name for the little structure where they bundled and loaded holiday trees. He loped across the field through the raindrops to find her.

He knew his mother had gone to Columbus with Reggie and Pam on a supply run, having dropped his prettiest little laborer off at the front gate at dawn. Mama Pool wouldn't be home until supper, rain or no rain, which meant that laborer without driving privileges was stuck in the wet.

At any rate, it was never hard to find Dottie.

Almost from the first, she'd been drawn to the menagerie that was Smokey's little petting zoo: a ragtag collection of docile goats, donkeys, rabbits, and other barnyard characters. The zoo inhabitants had free run of half the inside of his barn and access to the little fenced yard beyond.

Dottie, whom he also allowed free run of the entire farm, could often be found there with the animals. Sometimes he discovered the barnyard raked, fresh beds of straw arranged with comical precision. Food troughs would appear freshly scrubbed. Nel, one of the oldest goats, had lately been sporting a paisley kerchief on her neck that Smokey could swear he'd once seen all mixed up in Dottie's braid.

Now, as the steady rain fell, Smokey stopped just inside the barn door to take in the sight of Dottie Berkeley doing ...

... absolutely nothing.

When all that motion of her stopped, it was, somehow, riveting.

She'd shucked her coveralls and sat on an overturned bucket in a pair of fitted cotton pants, her knees drawn up to her chin. He stared at her bare feet in disbelief. People were not supposed to go barefoot in a barn, but of course she wouldn't know that. Smokey spotted work boots beside the discarded coveralls.

She'd also taken her hair down. When had he *ever* seen Dottie

Berkeley's miles of curls unbound?

Smokey considered turning back into the rain, somehow feeling he shouldn't be seeing her like this. He'd only just begun to adjust to the woman's uncharacteristic vulnerability and silence, and now here she sat, wild-haired, barefooted, and *still*.

Instead of leaving, he pulled his own handkerchief out of his pocket and mopped the rain from his head and face, considering her from behind while his big, lop-eared rabbit, Carlton, stared at her from the front, sitting at the base of the fence. Dottie stared back, still motionless.

Smokey contemplated what it had been like, growing up adjacent to Dottie Berkeley. She was a bit younger. Smokey had once hidden Dottie's entire collection of marbles at school. He'd wanted to see if he could make her cry because none of the other boys ever managed it. But she hadn't cried. Instead, she'd created a grid on a piece of school paper and carefully mapped out all the places her bag of marbles could be. Of course, she had systematically and calmly investigated all the possibilities. In short, she'd ruined all his fun.

Back then, she had looked like a dark-haired Shirley Temple, except he'd never thought of her as "cute." Dottie had been too capable and focused to be cute.

And here she was, bare-toed, still focused fully, but this time focused on an overgrown rabbit while the rain tapped on the barn's metal roof.

Smokey realized he did not know Dottie anymore. Not really. He simply could not mesh that determined little girl with the bossy manager of an amusement park with the woman who had taken to hiding here on his farm.

"I'm afraid Carlton is thinking about chewing the nose right off your face." He stayed where he was by the door, his voice mild.

Dottie glanced back over her shoulder but otherwise remained still. "Carlton would never do that."

"How do you know I haven't trained him to attack?"

She considered the rabbit. "He'd have done it by now, I think."

Smokey approached her, still unsettled. By the time he reached the pen posts with their chicken wire, he was greeted by a welcoming party of animals, the scent of them mingling with the hay and with Dottie.

Dottie made no effort to rise as he looked down at her. Below her linked hands, her toes were pale and perfect.

"I didn't finish with the north side of the bundle house, Boss."

He shrugged. "I didn't finish the tractor, either." Then he reached down and scooped Carlton up with his good hand. Carlton was larger than any rabbit had a right to be, dark gray in color. Smokey identified with him on several levels, so the rabbit got a mid-day head scratch.

"I know what you've done here, you know." Dottie looked up at him with her mass of hair framing her face, shadows like bruises beneath her eyes.

"That's a loaded sentence." He grinned at her, but she didn't smile back. It occurred to Smokey that he missed Dottie's smile. He'd been so used to it since boyhood, he'd certainly taken for granted the way her dimples flashed with it. "And just what have I done here?"

"You've built some kind of refuge for broken things, haven't you?" She rose from her perch, and Smokey watched in horror as those soft, pink-soled feet came in contact with the mix of dirt, gravel, and straw.

"Why in the world are you barefoot, darlin'?"

"It took me awhile to see it," she went on, joining him at the fence to pet Pee-Pee the goat, whom Smokey was always quick to point out was named by Reggie's little girl. "This goat here seems to be blind. I'm right, aren't I? Then, there's Cream Puff the cat, missing a leg."

"Cream Puff stays at the house with me. She thinks she's too good for the barn." He'd have said the same thing about Dottie Berkeley a month ago, though.

"And how *old* is that turkey, Smoke?"

"Sir Lawrence? Hmm … I think he turned ten a few weeks ago. Happy birthday, fella!" he called jovially.

"He's missing feathers in places."

"Aren't we all? Sir Lawrence has been around Black-Pool farms since I planted the first spruce trees out here, I think. Only fitting he retires here."

"Ten years of not being eaten."

"Well, he's good with kids. Why would someone eat a turkey like that?"

"Mm-hmm. Also, I'm not even going to ask what happened to that donkey's ear."

"Very polite of you. She can still hear out of it, and she's pretty sensitive."

"Then there's Hugh."

"Who is a person and whose ears are fine, I might point out."

"He doesn't talk."

"He needed some fresh air after the war, that's all."

Dottie huffed a laugh, somehow managing it without really smiling. He knew because he glanced over to check. "You and your mother," she said with a shake of her head. "I won't go into all the other 'fresh air' patients you've collected here … the least of which I know very well is me."

"The least? *You?* Least in what way?"

"Least useful on a farm, maybe?"

"Nonsense." He gestured with the woefully obese rabbit he still held.

It occurred to him, for no obvious reason, that this was the first time he'd been alone with her since the accident. "Actually, I was coming to find you to see if you'd like a ride back to the farmhouse. Or anywhere. Also, to pay you for work very well done."

She waved that away. "You'd better not try to pay me."

"I do pay my workers. All of them."

When he glanced down, she was studying him. The top of Dottie's head came up to his chest, where Carlton was.

"You're the only one here who's whole, aren't you?"

He sighed. He ought to let her keep thinking that. But this was a different Dottie, somehow. One who, if he hid her marble collection now, might actually cry.

"I'm almost whole. When I'm here, anyway."

Smokey placed Carlton carefully back into the fenced area, where the rabbit continued to stare out at Dottie, besotted. Walking back toward the barn door, Smokey knocked a few spiderwebs off a milking stool and pulled a braided chair out from behind a barrel. "For the sake of your feet, at least slide those boots back on."

He was pleased she understood the invitation in his suggestion, but it still surprised him when she shuffled over in the untied boots to join him just inches out of reach of the rain.

Shallow puddles were beginning in the lane that connected the barn to the bundle house. The barn marked the starting point of the pumpkin patches on the west side of the farm but looking to the east were rows and rows of evergreen trees in shades of sage and shadow.

Next to where he'd folded himself onto the stool, he noticed Dottie's thin pants had diamond patterns in blue. If she were at the park, she would be in heels and stockings and armed with her clipboard.

"It must seem strange to you out here," he observed. "Compared with the midway."

"Yes."

He wanted to ask if she liked it here, but he knew that shouldn't be important. Somehow, he didn't want to know. She would have to go back to her life, regardless. No way Buckeye Lake's amusement park would survive a season without Dottie Berkeley.

"Ten years ago?"

He looked over at her.

"You just said you planted the trees here ten years ago. Smokey, you'd have still been in *school* ten years ago."

"I did the planting after school and in the summers." He floated her a smile, but he didn't get one back.

"But what kid that age plants acres of Christmas trees?"

"What kid that age manages an amusement park?"

She made a sound. "*Touche*. Is it fair to say it kept us out of trouble?"

"Speak for yourself."

"You were swimming the length of the lake whenever it wasn't frozen," she pressed. "Helping your parents and Reggie with the farm, and, of course, dating all the girls."

Smokey laughed, delighted.

"And planting Christmas trees?!"

"I didn't realize you were watching me so carefully, Dottie Berkeley."

She waved that away. "You're hard to miss."

"Yeah, well. I had a vision, I guess." He looked over to see if she'd settle for that or if she'd demand more. Her eyes, still so sharp no matter what else had changed for her, told him she'd always expect more.

~~~~~

Dottie had never been in a barn in the rain, but she found she liked the way the scent of the fresh hay seemed to wrap around her in ways it didn't when dry air moved through. She didn't even sneeze. And she'd always liked the way Smokey Black's eyes had an unexpected, dreamy quality in them.

Especially when he talked about his trees.

"There's that forested area," he was explaining. "At the north of the Black-Pool property, you know?"

Dottie nodded. She didn't exactly know where the sprawling family farm ended, but she did know the popular hunting woods to the far north.

"I think my very earliest memories are of heading back there with our wagon and chopping down a tree for Christmas," he said. "We'd take the dogs. Mom and Pop sang carols."

Dottie nodded, swamped in envy.

"There was really nowhere folks around the lake could just go and chop a tree."

"True."

"So, we'd always invite friends and their families out to find a tree, too. The thing is, there were only so many the right size, and even as a kid, I started worrying we'd run out."

"We used to buy our tree from the ones someone trucked in. Remember? In front of the market."

"Right. From someplace out of town," Smokey said with a nod. "So, I went to the library and read up on evergreens. As it happened, President Roosevelt had just started a Christmas tree farm on his estate in New York."

"Really?"

"Really. It was the first time I'd thought about farming in quite that way, you know? I mean, I used to love going out with the other families to the forest and pointing out the best trees to them. Somehow, I think it
~~~~~

made me even happier than it made them."

"So, you planted your own between swim meets and school." Dottie could imagine it, now that she let herself. There'd always been so much magic in him.

"I asked my dad if I could use this area around the lake, and then I used my own money from livestock sales and everything. Every year I cleared and planted a new section of the field."

"Did you mean for it to get this big?"

"By the time I joined up with the Navy, I did. Reggie and the guys kept it going for me while I was gone." Looking out over the fields, his lips tilted on the corners with a smile. "While other men were writing love letters home, I was writing pages and pages of instructions about the trees."

Dottie also considered those fields, how organized they were. The subtly different heights in different sections. She didn't know much about evergreen types, but for the first time she noticed the slightly different shades of green in the misty rain.

"Combat diving requires a lot of waiting," he went on. "Staying very still, very wet, waiting. To keep myself from losing my mind, I made plans for this place. I knew the first field of trees would be ready for cutting, so I started picturing it as a ... a destination, you know? For families."

Dottie nodded. She knew all about destinations. It was her business, too, after all. She knew Smokey had come home from war and gradually drew more and more people out here to appreciate the planning he'd done.

"That's when I thought about pumpkins, during the war. I wondered what would happen if I took all those bits of holiday magic and concentrated them right here, where folks could pull a car up with their whole family and get to do the things you don't get to do in town or the city. Hayrides. Picking your own pumpkin out of a field, picking your own tree out of a field. Apples, eventually. Bonfires."

"Petting mildly deformed barnyard animals."

"Definitely. A place where that magic of the holidays was always just waiting for you."

Dottie understood. "I get that."

"I knew you would."

For some reason, the words and the warmth in his eyes filled a little aching spot in her heart. She hadn't had a single kind word from anyone lately, so something as simple as "I knew you would" was enough to keep her going for another day.

"The lake keeps folks entertained for the summer," Smokey went on. "Your park, of course. The water itself. But the fall ... the fall is for the farm. It's for the harvest and for the holidays. For magic, you know?"

"Hope," Dottie said a little sadly, biting at a fingernail she'd already bitten to the quick. "Not magic. Hope. Hope that the harvest will be good, that the jack-o-lanterns will be glowing again. That a tree can take up residence in your house once more and that you'll find a surprise under it."

Smokey nodded, but she found him staring at her chewed fingertips. She tucked her hands under her thighs.

"That's where the broken things tie in." Dottie told herself to stop talking, but it all made perfect sense. "Broken things might need more hope than the rest."

On cue, Pee-Pee bleated loudly behind them, and they shared a smile.

"Also, I'm a sucker."

"A softy."

He blew out a breath and winked again. "Okay, a softy. Don't tell."

Because she had a crazy desire to crawl into his lap and cry, a kind of panic made Dottie stand up and realize she'd forgotten to pull her wet hair back into its bun. Feeling warm and suddenly itchy all over, she felt Smokey's eyes on her as she pushed the curls back and wrapped them into a rope. The rope became a bun. Or, she thought wryly, a loaf.

He cleared his throat but didn't comment on her hair, thankfully.

"I like the hope thing," he said, instead. "Hope mingling with magic."

Dottie made an affirming sound as she focused on tying the scarf sloppily around the bun.

Smokey glanced over. "The amusement park is like that, too. Families surrounded by the lights, the wonder, the sounds, the food. You don't know what might happen next."

"I do."

"Because you make the magic happen, don't you? Face it. We're simply the same person at the core, Dottie B."

That made her huff out a laugh even as he did. Nothing could be farther from the truth.

"Anyway, I can hardly believe they had the nerve to banish you from your park."

"They didn't *banish* me. I'm just not great for business right now, that's all."

"Most of the visitors to the park don't even know what happened," he countered, sounding irritated but, at least, not with her. "They're coming from out of town."

"It was in all the newspapers, Smoke."

He waved that away. "C'mon. As though they'd decide not to come ride rides because the owner's daughter had a traffic accident."

"Manslaughter, you mean." Hair in place now, Dottie carefully tied her boots. "I guess you can take me back to your mom's for now. Since the rain isn't letting up." She wondered what she'd do there, was half afraid of being alone with herself now. "If it isn't too much trouble."

Smokey wordlessly rose from the stool and put it and her chair back in their place. Then he joined her again at the barn door, where they both considered the soaking they were about to get.

"I'll run up to the house and get the truck."

"You shouldn't get that cast wet." What was the alternative? She couldn't help. No way was she driving his truck, not even down the gravel lane back to the barn.

"Hey, Dottie," he said, and she looked up to find him looking down. "Have you considered your father might be trying to protect you?"

"You mean from the comments and hate?"

"Right. I know *I'd* rather you hang out with Cream Puff and Carlton than get verbally pummeled by all our well-meaning neighbors. And you're not even mine."

The word "mine" hung there like another place she might crawl and hide. She wondered if Shelby Berkeley had ever thought of her as "his." *Had she ever belonged to anyone?* "You're giving my father a lot of credit."

Dottie could say it to Smokey. Folks who'd lived at the lake all these years tolerated Shelby as a powerful presence, but they also gave him a wide berth when he was drinking. Which was understood to be most of the time. Dottie still struggled not to be embarrassed by it, so she changed the subject.

"Smokey, there's a war widow working there. At the park. I just arranged for her to have a job at the restaurant. The Park Terrace. She signed up for my ..." No, she thought. All they needed right now was to talk about the little business courses she'd planned, which was sure to make her cry. "Anyway, she needs to make money." She looked up to make sure she had his attention. "Her name is Julia, and she has a little girl to support."

"All right."

"Well, it's just that the restaurant is only going to work out for her for the summer. I wondered if you might, you know, need someone to run the cash box or something come harvest time?"

"Ahh." She knew he'd caught up. "You're hoping I can create a position for a grieving woman in need."

"Right."

He grinned and winked again. Dottie had not often been on the receiving end of that wink. "I think you're getting the idea of this place, Miss Berkeley."

"Good." She thought of the homemade rolls she'd deliberately left behind in Mama Pool's kitchen. She couldn't bring herself to offer them to him and become another one of his adoring tribe, no matter how kind he'd been to her. "You can drive me home now." Dottie retrieved her discarded coveralls and thrust them at him. "Use those to cover your cast, maybe."

Chapter Twelve

"This is insulting." Surrounded by a field of white spruce, Dottie held large shears and watched Smokey point again at a specific branch.

"Here."

Growling, she obeyed, lopping off several inches of a stray branch that had the nerve to disrupt the cone shape of the four-foot tree. It was the first sunbaked day of the summer, and Dottie was covered in a layer of sweat.

"Here." He shifted to point to another little cluster of branches that needed trimming. With his cast still on, Smokey couldn't operate the shears one-handed. He'd begun the morning of shaping trees being sulky about it, which Dottie had secretly found endearing. Then, as the sun had risen higher and the air heated, he'd started to take a bit *too* much pleasure in directing her with the shears.

Endearing had quickly turned to *irritating*.

"Here."

She obediently sheared off a few inches of lighter growth.

"Look, we've been at this long enough. I think I can tell what needs to be trimmed," she grumbled, following his pointing finger to another branch. She fantasized about lopping that finger off. "You don't need to keep pointing to every branch."

"Here," he said, the right side of his lips raising a little. "I do the shearing of the four-year-olds myself. *Always.*"

"Basically, you don't trust me."

"How many Christmas trees have you shaped? Here." He pointed. She followed and sliced.

"Why don't you let me tackle one tree, and then you can inspect it and tell me what I missed?"

"Here."

Blowing a stray piece of hair out of her eyes, Dottie used both arms to pull the shears apart and bring the blades back together. Smokey reached over with that annoying pointer finger and tucked the damp curl back behind her ear.

"I want them to look the way I want them to look." The note of apology in his voice disarmed her enough that she didn't glare when he turned back to the tree, pointed, and said, "Here."

This section of white spruce trees was nearly Dottie's height already.

The field sloped gently down toward the pond just ten yards away, where dragonflies jetted over the still water. There wasn't a spot of shade to be found in a field of four-foot trees, though, so she'd worn a long sleeve cotton blouse and Mama Pool's floppy hat again.

Now, she regretted the blouse. She debated rolling her sleeves up, but her skin was too fair for that. Her body was battling enough problems, after all, without adding a blistering sunburn to it. Her stomach was often upset, too upset to eat. Sometimes her hands shook so hard she had to sit on them. Her heart and breathing were almost never right.

A drop of perspiration ran slowly down her lower back and into her waistband.

"Here."

Staying busy was better than sitting, she'd found. Out here, no matter the heat or the inane task, Dottie couldn't hear her heartbeat skipping in her ears. When her hands were busy, they didn't shake as badly.

Instead, she listened to the birds and was learning to identify them by their call.

"Get down low here," Smokey said, his voice relaxed amidst the birdsong.

She stooped and lopped, stooped and lopped. Heard a female cardinal. Imagined jumping in the pond to cool off.

Dottie did miss Buckeye Lake. Sure, she missed the amusement park, of course, but she was surprised by all the ways the lake itself had woven itself into the fabric of her workdays. She had never in her life experienced a warm summer day that wasn't also punctuated by boat motors and laughter from the water. There was the chatter of fishermen on the bridge over to Picnic Point. Ducks and geese bobbing along on the surface, herons tall and watchful amidst the green growth along the dam.

Mama Pool said she was keeping up with the books in the office, but Dottie had done far more than tracking debits and credits. She needed to personally review the expenses and income. Were they having a good year? Just as Smokey didn't trust her ability to shape something into a cone, she was reluctant to believe everything was operating just fine at her park.

"I know the shape Christmas trees are supposed to be, you know," she pointed out, following him to the next tree in the tidy rows. Smokey did keep his farm and his trees immaculate.

He ignored her, assessing this next tree with his warm, perceptive gaze. He reached out with his good hand to touch a few branches, leaning in to inspect the needles. "It's not just about the shape," he finally said. "Here. Start with this little section at the top."

Dottie obeyed. He was paying her to obey, after all, and there was also the fact he hadn't yet referred to her as a killer. She owed him this much.

"It's just like pruning any growing thing." He pointed silently this time. "When we shear, not only are we shaping the tree, but we're allowing the rest of the branches to fill in and grow even healthier. See? This part has a little pest damage. You're removing something that's keeping the tree from being its best."

"Sounds pretty profound," she said, slicing. Then she sliced him a look. "Want me to cut your hand off at the forearm since it's keeping you from being your best?"

"Tempting, with as hot as this cast is."

Smokey was easy to be with. He could hardly be riled, which was sometimes an irresistible challenge.

"There's a reason Jesus talked about trees when He talked about walking in the light," Smokey went on after another minute had passed. "Here, right here."

Dottie lopped.

"Healthy branches bearing fruit stay. But pruning allows a tree to grow healthier, to produce more fruit." He glanced over at her. "Being pruned, as a person, is never fun, though."

She cut again, thought about that as the tree before them became tidier. Was that what was happening to her? Was she being pruned?

The problem was, she'd been deliberately *trying* to bear more fruit before the accident. The classes she'd put together were going to help women who needed money to support their families. She'd been poised to use her gifts, eager to use them to help meet the needs of others. It made *no sense* to prune her right when she was getting ready to blossom, when she'd been working to impress her Maker.

She couldn't say out loud that God must have made a mistake with the shears. She shouldn't even think it.

"Well, if a tree gets pruned at the wrong time, it might end up dying," was all she did say, hearing her own stubbornness. She hated to think she was dying inside, but …

"Hmm." Smokey pointed to another branch, and she followed him around the tree counterclockwise. "Maybe the roots need to drink up the water a bit. To focus less on fruit and more on the nutrients coming from what it's grounded in."

Dottie frowned, trimmed more. She thought of yeast and rest; she was getting better at baking. Resting dough wasn't the same as drinking up water and nutrients, but it wasn't exactly different, either.

Was Smokey suggesting she'd put the cart before the horse? That she hadn't started at the right place? A little spark of resentment kindled. He didn't know her or her heart.

"Look …" she began, but then Smokey made a strange sound that stopped her in her tracks and made her lower the shears.

Horrified, Dottie watched a yellow jacket dive down past Smokey's throat and into his plaid shirt.

They stood completely still. Met one another's eyes for a split second.

Then Smokey made a sound that could only be described as a yip and began fumbling with the buttons of his shirt with his cast. Dottie thought she should offer to help, but help with what? *Undressing* him? While he was *writhing*?

Instead, she stood there, mouth agape, as he did an urgent dance. He ripped his shirt open, buttons flying one direction, the yellow jacket another.

Dottie was caught off guard, though, when he reached for her wrist with his good hand, his shirt trailing now off his cast like a flag and began to drag her toward the pond. She dropped the shears and tried to plant her feet.

"There will be more," he called out. "When they sting. It calls the others. Move!"

They did move.

Dottie succeeded in tugging her sweaty forearm out of his sweaty grip just before he took a mad leap into the pond, his cast raised up in the air above the splash, still half-wrapped in his shredded shirt.

Once the water settled around him, the late morning grew calm and quiet once more. Standing on the bank beside a cluster of cattails, Dottie crossed her arms and regarded Smokey standing in the water.

He'd always been sun-browned and strong. Now, the water slid off his powerful shoulders, beaded on his chest, and zigzagged down the ridges of his stomach. Two angry welts were forming amidst all that perfection.

Squinting against the sun, he grinned up at her, and then his grin turned into his booming laugh. It had always been a contagious laugh, and Dottie gave into her own.

She had the sudden urge to bake Smokey some fresh rolls. She might even try giggling when she handed them to him, brushing her hand accidentally over one of those biceps.

She'd watched the others do it enough, and Dottie knew herself to be a fast learner.

Chapter Thirteen

It was time to get back to business.

Dottie crept through her own family's amusement park at midnight on a Tuesday, bending low to the ground. Behind her, she just *knew* Emily was rolling her eyes. Her friend had already used the word "ridiculous" a few times.

"You don't have to stay," Dottie whispered.

Emily did not whisper, though, when she replied, "You have every right to be here. Why are you acting like you're doing espionage? And how do you expect to get out of here *without* me?"

She meant her car, of course. Dottie had asked Emily to pick her up at the farmhouse and bring her into town in the middle of the night. It had cost her a good deal of pride.

"You can go home and go to bed, Em. I'll call someone to get me in the morning."

"I'm not leaving you."

"As you just pointed out, I have a right to be here. I'll be fine."

Emily didn't respond but walked beside her as they rounded the empty boardwalk. The strands of bulbs that made up the festive atmosphere of the park were still lit in most places, while others had been unplugged after the final run of The Dips. Dew was already heavy in the air, and Dottie drank in the familiar scent of her home. The park always seemed haunted to her at night, like the specter of laughing crowds somehow hung there like the ghostly smoke of a spent firework against the night sky.

She used her key on the door to the park office and flipped the light switch. She assessed the room for changes.

No one had watered her spider plant. The tips of the leaves had curled and browned.

She assumed it was Mama Pool who had kept papers stacked neatly on the desks behind the main counter. All the little hand-written signs for season passes and band tickets were the same, in Dottie's own tidy writing.

"Seriously," she said in a normal voice now, turning to Emily. "I'll be fine here alone. I just want to go through the files, make sure everything's in order."

"What if you fall asleep, Goldilocks? And someone from your awful family finds you in the morning?"

Dottie tried to smile. Her family could be awful, sometimes, and Emily was loyal all the time. "Expectant women need their rest," she argued, trying a different approach.

"This baby knows we keep a strange schedule. Don't you?" She bent her head toward the mound of her belly and patted there with her hand. "Besides, I can crash upstairs, in your apartment. Just come get me when you want to go back to the farmhouse, okay?"

"And Drew is fine with this?"

"Drew?" Emily blinked. "Why would he weigh in on it one way or another?" With that, she ran an affectionate hand down the length of Dottie's arm and went through the door at the back of the office that led upstairs, as she'd been comfortable doing most of her life.

Alone, Dottie tried to make sense of her own feelings as she reached out to touch the polished wood of the counter. What did accounting have to do with feelings, though?

The squeak of her desk chair was like a lullaby. She arranged ledgers, explored folders. Had all the rent been collected? Where were the maintenance records since March? She couldn't find any information on the special gimmicks, the acts free to the public that drove attendance up. She'd pumped her friend for information on the drive over, but Emily had changed the subject.

Dottie hated being handled with care.

She had originally arranged for an ice sculptor named Sam to deliver an extravagant piece each Saturday morning, and guests could place bets on what time of day the creation would be completely melted. It was exactly the kind of thing folks loved. But Emily said she hadn't seen a sculpture last Saturday. Dottie took a deep breath as she pulled another drawer out. She could phone Sam from the farmhouse tomorrow and make sure it would happen this coming weekend.

In the back of her mind, she thought of the similarities in this work and the work Smokey did on the farm. Both jobs were a strange mix of idealism and hands-on, tedious labor.

Lately, she'd only been doing the hands-on work part.

Here in the office in the dead of night, though, she could hear her heartbeat in her ears again. Now and then, her heart made a flop in her chest, and her breathing would get tight. A cool damp gathered on her brow.

Dottie slammed the drawer and stood, wringing her hands.

This wasn't her. *What was wrong with her?*

Just as the amusement park outside seemed haunted by the ghosts of happy guests, this space was haunted by another version of herself. A version that she missed very much.

She rose, looking out the wide windows at the park. Everyone despised her, evidently even her own family. It was a profoundly lonely feeling. For the first time, she had a sense they'd all been waiting for this, waiting for her to fall. Found pleasure in watching her fail to rise again. Amidst the strange sounds of her own heartbeat, Dottie could hear them all in her head, probably at Sunday dinner, talking about someone who hadn't quite gotten what she deserved.

Those voices were slithering their way right into her soul.

Too weak to go tell Emily she was ready to leave, Dottie dropped onto the floor behind the counter and hugged her knees to her chest. She wrapped her fingers around her calves so she could keep the shaking contained.

Chapter Fourteen

On a mid-June afternoon, when the pumpkin plants were beginning to blossom under an encouraging bright sun, Smokey hauled a small wagon of old tractor tires into the woods adjacent to the pumpkin patch.

Dottie was waiting for him there like a tidy little sprite, fists on her hips as she poked around his Enchanted Forest.

It was a space amidst the trees that he wanted ready for the pumpkin harvest season in the fall, something he'd begun to build last year. A deliberately rustic wooden sign announced the shaded, green clearing as the Enchanted Forest, and it already boasted a treehouse with ropes to swing down on, a tree stump obstacle course, giant rocking horses with unicorn horns, and a bridge over the tiny creek with a carved troll beneath it.

Smokey had shown the forest project to Dottie two days before. She'd grown even quieter this past week, but instinct told him she would not be able to resist the potential of this little forest clearing. He'd been right. She'd lit up about it. She hadn't said as much in words, but Dottie clearly saw the Enchanted Forest as its own kind of amusement park, and a bit of her spirit revived.

She'd instructed him to bring her tires. Happy to see her eyes sparkling, he'd obeyed her without question.

Until now. He did have a question now.

Hopping off the tractor, he considered the tires he'd spent hours sawing into half-moons. With his cast finally off, he'd loved every minute of actually controlling the saw with two good hands. Now he called out to her. "When do I get to know what we're doing with these?"

Spinning, Dottie rushed over in her canvas work pants with their woven rope belt, and she also peered into the wagon bed. Baggy as those pants were, her curls were still slicked back in tight, dark rivers to a no-nonsense bun. Two soft curls were left around her face. "Oh, good!" She clapped once. "They're different sizes."

"I can follow orders." He couldn't be certain whether he found it amusing or confounding that she'd started giving him orders regarding his own property.

Now, she surprised him by reaching in to grab one of the biggest tractor tire halves. "It's going to be ..." she grunted, re-balanced against the awkward weight of it. "... a Loch Ness Monster!"

Smokey didn't move her aside, but he did reach in with one hand to help her steady the giant half-circle of thick rubber.

"This can be the monster's head," she declared, bouncing it on the ground before her.

"You'll have to show me your vision," he said. Not that he didn't trust Dottie's vision. After all, she'd single-handedly redesigned half of the lake's north shore by the time she'd turned twenty.

"It's the Enchanted Forest. Full of mythical things." Smokey followed her deeper into the trees with more tires under his arms. "You're not suggesting the Lock Ness Monster isn't *real*, are you?"

Nessie was in all the papers since they'd been kids. At Buckeye Lake's little community beaches, they'd played many games based on the water beast.

Smokey dropped the two tires where Dottie pointed. "I want her to be real."

"That's allowed." She nodded before she marched back to the wagon. "I want that unicorn over there to be real, too, I suppose."

They made another trip, and then she started arranging the various sizes like a sea serpent's back arching in and out of imaginary water … or, in this case, a loch of mulched pine chips.

"Listen. I got green paint from the hardware. I stored it up in the shade of the treehouse," Dottie told him, rejecting a half-tire and reselecting. "We can paint before dark still, don't you think?"

Smokey watched her adjust her rubber creature by mere inches here or there, chattering about paint and brushes as she worked. Standing back, he was surprised to find the thing beginning to look like a sea serpent. It took shape in a bare spot right alongside the treehouse and only feet from the troll's bridge.

"I suppose I'll need a shovel to bury the ends of each tire," he noted when she stood back beside him to inspect the layout. She nodded, and he caught the fresh scent of her perfume mingling with the scent of last fall's leaves below them. It was like a pleasant punch in the gut.

"That root sticking up there needs to be dug up, as well, Smoke. Or axed or something. It's not safe if the kids are going to climb on Nessie."

"Yes, ma'am."

"And when we bury the big one there, we'll do it a little differently," she explained, reaching for his hand and tugging him over to it, where she explained only one cut end would be underground. On the other, she'd attach a long, red tongue so the thing would look plenty lizard-like.

"Paint first or plant the rubber first, Boss?"

They secured it first. As it turned out, the shadows began to grow long by the time Nessie was rooted enough for children to be able to safely hop from hump to hump on her back. Smokey felt his stomach rumbling with hunger, which was a new sensation lately. Though he wouldn't be broken-hearted if Lillian or one of the other ladies came tooling up with a basket of fried chicken, he couldn't bring himself to stop Dottie from muscling open a can of bright green paint.

For once, she'd been full of chatter.

"You need bird houses decorated so fairies could be living in them, you know?"

"A giant, rope spider web anchored to the trees would be fun for climbing."

"You could line the path back here with scenes from fairytales, even."

They also laughed over shared memories. The way Mr. Bender wrote half-inch chalk letters on the board in History, and they had to clump up a foot away to take notes. The time Russell Boyd had kissed Caroline Lee, and Freddy Garvin had thrown him right through the cafeteria window. Had Smokey heard Caroline had married a traveling salesman? Had Dottie heard their old principal, Mr. Boone, had gotten remarried just two weeks after his wife had died last year?

Together, they linked squares in the blanket of gossip in their old schoolmates' lives. Dottie knew things from the park, and Smokey learned things from his holiday visitors who crowded the farm beginning in October.

For a glorious moment, they were two people whose distant past was strong enough to overshadow the recent past.

Smokey stabbed his brush into spaces he was supposed to paint green. "Boy, it's kind of a pain getting in between the tread here."

"Bet it's easier with your right hand, though."

"You know it."

"This tire barely has any tread to work around," she said from the arch beside him. "But don't think for a second we're swapping."

Smokey slanted her a look, wondered if she ever thought about food.

"When the green dries, I'll come back out with yellow to make the top parts look even more like scales." She was lying on her side now to get up under the edge of the tire. He continued trying to force his brush between the tread, and Dottie seemed to hear it because she rotated her head to investigate, virtually upside down.

"Whoa, careful not to fray the bristles."

Smokey didn't think. He simply swiped his slightly frayed brush right down her bare arm.

Dottie sat up slowly and considered the bright green swath along her skin. No gasp or any sign of outrage, but then, Smokey wouldn't have expected any from her.

"Well, that was not very mature," she said, calmly.

Instinct and memory combined to tell him he was doomed, so

Smokey rose to his feet.

"Where are you going, sweetheart?" she cooed, dipping her brush into the can between them.

"Nowhere." He coughed to cover the laugh that escaped. "I think I can paint standing up just fine."

"Chicken," she muttered.

She returned to painting as though her arm wasn't dripping.

"Look, I know what a tempting palette the top of my head must be, that's all." He rubbed his right hand over the soft stubble of his buzz cut, noticing how sensitive his skin was where the cast had been.

"Afraid green might be worse than gray?"

He squatted to reach the curve of the tire with his brush, but he was determined to stay on his feet. "Who says I don't love my gray hair?"

He'd never minded, really. Hardly thought of it after he'd made peace with it at seventeen.

"It would just confuse everyone if you had to change your name from Smokey to Mossy or something." She snorted a little laugh, shocking him and evidently delighting herself. He peered over to check for the dimple, but there was still no sign of it.

Dottie finished her tire and rose to her feet, stretching her back and arms, green brush still in hand. Smokey watched her movements warily. Then she set the brush down.

"I'm thirsty. I brought a Thermos out with water if you'd like a cup."

"Sure," he said, preparing for her to fling the water at him. He could handle a mild soaking, if that was to be her revenge. Instead, though, she simply poured some water out into the tin cap and handed it to him.

Smokey recognized the faded Thermos as the one his father had carried around in any kind of weather. Instead of drinking straight from the container, Dottie waited for him to drain the little cup. Then she refilled it and sipped it herself.

Smokey found himself transfixed by her damp lips. Idly, with zero expectation of finding out, he wondered what it would be like to kiss Dottie. It wasn't the first time he'd wondered.

"I want to see what Nessie looks like from above," she announced, handing both Thermos and lid over. Moving a few feet to the ladder of the treehouse, she said, "Help yourself to the rest of the water, okay?"

But there wasn't much water left, Smokey realized, pulling his attention away from her movements on the ladder. He re-capped the Thermos and regarded the early twilight of the forest. They'd have to finish before much longer to keep from starving or dying from thirst.

Smokey bent back to his task, determined to finish this tire and then call it a day. He worked the brush between the tread, careful this time not to fray those precious bristles. He figured he'd beg dinner off Mama Pool when he drove Dottie back down the road.

His mother usually had ...

Smokey had no warning before the jelly of paint splattered over the top of his head from above. Unlike Dottie, he *did* gasp in shock, tipping his head back instinctively to keep rivers of green from running into his eyes. Instead, the paint ran over his ears and down his back collar, as if moving to the soundtrack of music that was Dottie Berkeley's laughter.

Clearly, she'd brought *two* cans of green paint for this job.

And she had the high ground.

Smokey chucked his brush at the can on the ground and reached the tree ladder in two strides. Vaulting himself up like the special forces soldier he'd been, Smokey exulted in Dottie's uncharacteristic squeal from the platform above. Yet, he wasn't half as surprised by that girlish squeal as he was when he saw her grab the rope on the opposite side and, with a wild glance behind her, launch herself out the opposite doorway.

His heart stuttered at her wild cry, but when he reached that gap in the treehouse, the woman was already on the ground and running. Fast.

Releasing a belly laugh, Smokey called out what he figured was his line in their drama: "You can run, but you can't hide!"

He prayed the rope would hold him, though his descent was really more a leap than a swing, anyway. When he loudly hit the ground behind her, Dottie hysterically half-screamed, half-laughed again. He imagined her amusement was partly the sight of him, dripping swamp monster green all over himself as he ran.

Smokey didn't realize he was still laughing, too, until he closed the distance between them. He could grab her now, as she darted between trees back toward his tractor and wagon, but her hair was starting to untuck from its bun and fly about her, she had a dead leaf stuck to her green arm, and she seemed to be having ... fun.

So, he let her scamper around the wagon and regard him with wild-eyed delight. Her cheeks were bright pink. He dodged right. She started left. He reversed. She went right. She tried to say something, but she started laughing so hard again that she ended up bent over to catch her breath.

Smokey pounced on that moment of weakness, rounding the tractor in quick strides, and though she did take off again, she seemed to know she was caught. Turning, she moved backward in a stumbling sort of run, hands out as though warding off a charging bull as she howled with laughter.

Playing the part of a bull, Smokey decided, would be a lovely form of revenge. Reaching her, he charged, painted head first, gently into her stomach. His arms circled her waist to hold her in place while he transferred the green from his head to her cotton button-up shirt, like cleaning a brush against a rag at the end of a job.

Now, he laughed harder because he could *feel* her breathless laughter against his head, could sense it drenching him. Her hands clawed at the back of his shirt, probably to keep her balance, but he was careful not to let her fall backward …

… until … right … now, when he meant for her to, when he could spin to take their fall entirely on his own back.

~~~~~

Dottie found herself on the grass, half-green in color and trying to catch her breath. Every time air hit her lungs, though, she laughed all over again.

Above her, propped on an elbow on his side, Smokey looked ridiculous, like he was wearing a green swim cap, and some of the paint had worked its way into those laugh grooves bracketing each side of his mouth.

Dottie had to wipe tears from her eyes, her paint-splattered tummy delightfully sore from laughing. Those were other muscles she hadn't used in too long.

"You've still got your dimple," she heard Smokey say with something like relief as he dropped onto his own back beside her. She hoped he hadn't re-injured his wrist when she'd crashed down on him.

"My dimple? Of course I do." She was finally breathing again. "A dimple isn't a thing a person outgrows."

Smokey made some skeptical noise in response to that, and she rolled her head to the right to find him studying her, his eyes still squinted with a grin.

"Do I look as much of a mess as you do?"

"You look perfect," he replied, and there was such gentle sincerity in it that Dottie's remaining amusement got all caught up in her throat.

"Are you as hungry as I am?" he blurted.

For one heart-flopping second Dottie wondered what he meant by that, because she really had seen something like hunger in Smokey's eyes at non-mealtimes.

But then she heard *his* stomach growl this time, and it somehow managed to set off her laughter all over again.

He helped her up, and they trotted back to the Enchanted Forest and made quick work of the paint can lids and brushes.

"Why don't you ever leave your hair down, Dottie?"

Her brow furrowed. The truth of *that* was the last thing this lovely moment needed. "Maybe I'll tell you another day. Okay?"

He nodded, and she was grateful. They took the tractor along the lane that ran back past the pumpkin patches and through the trees to where he'd last left his truck.
~~~~~

Dottie had chosen her perch next to him again rather than bouncing along in the wagon like cargo, but this time the arm he looped around her had no cast blunting the end. Now, she felt the strong grip of his hand on her hip.

"It's been a while since I've simply played." Smokey seemed happy.

Dottie started to put in an automatic "Me, too," but she stopped herself. Thought about it. "Hmm." Thought about it again. "Now that I consider it, I'm not sure I've ever really played much."

She'd spent her childhood at her dad's amusement park. *Shouldn't she have been an expert at play?* But her memories there were of following Shelby around, watching, listening. She loved stepping in to help, loved it when he recognized her as capable. Even when she'd been very small, she'd run food out to the freak show folks without him telling her to.

She remembered sitting with those unusual people, watching and listening to them.

No one could have considered it play, though.

"I suppose riding the coaster was my version of playing," she decided as Smokey turned the tractor toward his cabin.

"You rode it every day, I bet."

"Sometimes several times a day. I loved the speed of it."

"Not me."

She looked over, his face just above hers. A small, green smile still played around his mouth. "Not you?"

"Have you ever seen me on The Dips coaster, Dottie B.?"

She tried to remember. Saw flashes like mental snapshots of Smokey Black winning a Cupie doll for a pretty blonde girl, of Smokey in his blue-striped swim uniform with whatever trophy he'd just won, of Smokey at the ballroom …

"*No.* I guess I don't remember seeing you on the coaster. You didn't like it?"

"Never tried it."

Dottie gaped.

"I was too scared." He said it with a little shrug of his shoulder she felt against her back.

"Everyone's scared. That's the point. But they still ride it!"

"Not me."

He didn't even sound ashamed as he shut the tractor off. He was down and reaching up for her before she could shimmy down herself, and Dottie paid extra notice to those huge hands and muscles and the way he could have carried her one-armed all the way back to his mother's house if he had to.

"*You* were scared?"

"Still am, if you want the truth." He winked when he opened the passenger door to the truck for her. "We'll see what Mama Pool has in the fridge for dinner, eh?"

Dottie situated herself on the seat and waited for him to walk around and climb in.

"So, if we were to go to the park right now …"

"No way," he declared. "I need food."

"You would *still* refuse to ride The Dips?"

He grinned over at her, backing onto the lane and switching gears. "Have you lost all respect for me?"

"Smokey." Dottie checked to make sure they weren't getting paint on his seats, even if it was a work truck. "Word is you were part of the invasion at Normandy."

"So?"

"Correct me if I'm wrong, but did you swim out in the middle of the night to disarm bombs or something before troops landed? In the water? In total darkness?"

"Utah Beach, yeah. The western-most sector of the invasion. You must have read that braggy article Emily wrote."

Dottie shook her head. "Smokey, *that* sounds scary."

"It was."

"But you did it."

He grinned. "Well, I've always been told I'm a decent swimmer."

"Yet, you still won't ride the roller coaster at the park."

"I don't think I want to, no. I don't see what one has to do with the other. What's it matter?"

"I …" Dottie wasn't sure it did matter, though she was sure it was somehow funny. She couldn't seem to laugh about it, that was all. Somehow, strong as he'd always been, and as much as he really could swim like some sea creature designed for it, she suddenly and deeply resented anyone sending this man out in the middle of the night, surrounded by explosives and enemy troops.

How had he even made it back to his Christmas trees?

"Don't you worry about me and your roller coaster, sweetheart," he said, reaching across the seat to squeeze her hand as though he'd read her mind. "I'll always find plenty of ways to play. I promise."

Chapter Fifteen

By Independence Day, Dottie had practiced "resting" a handful of times under the careful supervision of the Black family.

Mama Pool had made her spend a full hour on a blanket under her weeping willow tree, for no reason Dottie could see. She was not even permitted to read a book while she lay there. It was just her and an umbrella of swaying branches all around.

And, of course, that fresh air they all boasted about.

Smokey had invited her to walk two nights before. Where had they been walking to? Nowhere. He revealed his young apple orchard to her, beyond the pond and the furthest ridge of fir trees. The orchard wouldn't be ready for picking for some years, he'd explained just before he made her sit between two of the trees to watch the sunset.

"Shhh," he'd said whenever she'd tried to question what they were doing. So, it had been just the two of them sitting there while a pastel mess smeared the sky.

It had been the two of them and a good deal of that fresh air.

So, when Independence Day came and rest was decreed across the expansive Black-Pool Farms, Dottie felt slightly more qualified to indulge in sitting on a rectangular float in Smokey's pond, a glass of iced tea balanced in one hand and her floppy hat firmly in place.

Bright heat played over the ripples in the water. The pond was too small for ripples caused by anything but Smokey's little niece and nephew, Felix and Betty, who took turns jumping off the platform at the edge of the water.

In the trimmed grass near that platform, Mama Pool had laid out a simple picnic, and she lounged in a chair there chatting with Pam. Lil Graham was spending the Fourth on Towpath Island with her own family. She'd been nervous, but last night's tutorial with Mama Pool had been about baking apple pies, so Lil had gone to the family festivities armed with her first homemade dessert.

Dottie watched Reggie and Smokey play with the kids through her sunglasses, deciding there was more to enjoy than just fresh air here on the farm. She'd been witness as Smokey swam his way from boyhood to adulthood, of course, but now he bore an eagle tattoo with inked waves over his shoulder and, like the day of the yellow jacket attack, she noticed scars here and there on his bronzed skin.

He'd gone from swimming for medals to swimming for her freedom.

Instead of making her feel in awe of him, the reality of it continued to wash over Dottie in the form of some emotion she barely understood. It was almost as if she wished she could have *protected* him somehow, which made no sense.

She tried to think through it now, letting her feet move lazily just below the surface of the cool water. Perhaps it came down to the fact a man who thought in terms of childhood magic simply should *not* be dodging bullets. No matter how well he could swim.

He tossed little Betty into the air like a slick, squealing bomb and cheered when the splash landing soaked Reggie. The elder brother, their father's namesake, had always been one of Dottie's favorite people because they'd shared that love of fast cars all those years ago. Reggie was more introspective and reserved than Smokey, though the two brothers were about the same height. When Smokey had been swimming as a young man, Reggie had been tinkering. When Smokey's hair had made its sudden and dramatic switch to gray, Reggie's had stayed black.

Reggie was a good father, and Pam seemed to genuinely like being around him, which Dottie figured must say a lot about any man. A wife would always know the truth, she supposed.

Her reverie was disrupted when she noticed Reggie's irresistible younger brother lazily working his arms through the water in the direction of her raft.

"Smokey." She waited until he was within hearing distance. "Do not even think about it."

He drew back, blinked those long lashes beaded with droplets, and treaded water in some way that made it look like he wasn't even moving.

"Think about what?"

"Don't pretend you didn't swim out here to dump me off this raft."

He grinned. "But I thought we decided play was good for us, sweetheart."

"Don't," she snapped. "I have this lovely glass of your mother's that she wouldn't want at the bottom of the pond. Besides, I'm *resting*."

"And how's that going?"

"I was doing well at it, actually, until you swam out here and made me … tense."

He laughed at that and kicked onto his back to float and grin at the blue sky.

"Reggie wants us to take the boat out tonight. For the fireworks," he said after a full minute of floating. Then he flipped over, aiming back at the edge of her raft, water sliding off his forearms when he stacked them against it. "Relax. I'm not sending you into the water. Anyway, I think I'll go. Out on the boat, I mean. Wouldn't mind watching the fireworks with the kids, and last year I was … otherwise occupied."

Dottie knew he'd been helping their friends, Emily and Drew, outsmart the mob this time last year, though she'd forgotten that whole business until just now. *Had that really been just a year ago?*

"Will you come out on the boat with us?"

She sipped her tea, which wasn't cold anymore. She knew the Fourth at the lake so well, knew how many people she would know there. How many she would have to face.

Would they still be as cruel to her on their nation's birthday? Did scorn take holidays? Was there any chance they'd started to forget at all?

"I'm not certain I … should."

She felt like a coward as he looked up at her, so she reminded herself he feared The Dips. Being frightened of being called a killer was less cowardly than that, surely.

Still, she couldn't stay hidden here on a farm forever. She knew that, too.

Or could she? She regarded the settled pattern of the pines around her. *Why not?*

As it turned out, God answered a question she hadn't even been addressing to Him when she saw an unfamiliar car pull up on the nearby gravel lane.

At first, Dottie assumed this was some other guest the Blacks had invited to their lazy picnic. But she sat up a little straighter, feeling like she was sinking right through the raft, when she spotted Gus, one of the bartenders her father referred to as a friend, getting out of the driver's side of the car.

Like a disaster that couldn't be avoided but that she supposed she might always be anticipating, her father wobbled from the passenger side, stumbled a little, and immediately began looking for her.

~~~~~

Shelby Berkeley was not a very tall man, but his personality had always made his wiry frame appear far larger than it really was. Today he was dressed in rumpled clothes Dottie recognized, and his usual summer boater hat with the patriotic band was probably more an accident than intention for the holiday.

The hat was dented.

Dottie, wrapped now in one of Mama Pool's wide towels, tried to make sense of her father standing here in the grass. Mama Pool had offered him food, but he'd declined politely and instructed Gus to wait for him at the car.

Smokey stood sentry at Dottie's shoulder, and she wondered if she should send him away, too, before he learned more than most people wanted to know about the Berkeley family.
~~~~~

She would let him stay, though. On some level, she needed it.

"I need your key," Shelby said to his oldest daughter. He didn't look or sound well. Certainly not happy. One side of his face was oddly puffy and turning unpleasant colors. "The one to your apartment. I can't find a spare key anywhere."

"What do you need with my apartment?" She told herself it was useless to wish he'd asked how *she* was. That he'd sought her out because he thought she might need the support of her family after such a painful season. That he worried she might have been homesick or something, on a national holiday.

"Looks like I'll be spending a night or so there in your place." He looked miserable, maybe even a little embarrassed.

"Why?"

"Your mother," was all he said, but he pulled the hat off where it rested low on his brow, and Dottie saw his left eyeball was morbidly red, the lids swollen badly around it. That puffiness on the same side of his face must be a bruise that would extend from the eye down over the cheekbone by tomorrow.

"I don't believe for a second that Mom socked you, Dad, though I can't say I'd blame her if she had."

"Now, now. Show some respect."

"What happened?

"Fell off the stage at the billiard hall last night."

"And Gus brought you *here*? To Smokey's place? Why?"

"The key. I told you. Your mother insists."

Acutely aware of Smokey close to her arm, Dottie worked through her surprise at her father's words. "Mom won't let you come home?"

"She locked the house to me." He tried to laugh a little, like he was just telling "the fellas," but it was a pathetic laugh. He still smelled strongly of alcohol, as he typically did.

"I can't believe she finally put her foot down." Dottie mumbled it mostly to herself. She tried to imagine her meek little mother, turning those door locks against Shelby, the fall-down drunk and love of her life. "You must have really done it this time."

"I just need to crash at your place."

"Dad," Dottie sighed, studying him.

"Don't worry. I'm not drinking anymore."

Right. "How'd you fall off a stage, then?"

"I mean today. Starting today, I'm not drinking anymore."

She raised her brows. Smokey would have no way of knowing that Shelby had never gone so far as to make a vow like that before. This was a first. His face, and his pride, must hurt very badly, indeed.

"Who's running the park today?"

"It runs itself. You know that."

Dottie huffed a short laugh. "It absolutely does not."

"Look, I'm not …" His words slid off, as though he didn't know what to say.

"It's July Fourth, Dad. The biggest day of the year."

That snapped his head up. He shook it. "I can't, Dottie. I can't today."

Something about the sadness and humiliation in the words slid right into Dottie's heart and found good company there. If there was something she did relate to, it was sadness and humiliation. And an inability to face the day.

"I mean it, I'm stopping. No more drinking," he said miserably. "But I need a place, and your mother … I need the key to your place, okay? I need somewhere to just … go."

"You can stay here," Smokey said simply.

Dottie turned to look up at him. "What?!"

"Here?" Her father looked around at the rolling fields of green trees.

Smokey shrugged. "Just think it'd be easier to stay away from the stuff if you were, you know, actually away from it for a bit."

Dottie closed her eyes. Smokey did love to wrap his arms around the broken, didn't he? But this was *her* hiding place. And *her* broken father. "Smokey …"

"He can stay in the cabin. There's a cot. Spend a few days here, Shelby, since you can't go home, anyway. The fresh air might do you good."

Chapter Sixteen

The Buckeye Lake Amusement Park did *not* just run itself. Smokey had that on good authority an hour after Shelby Berkeley had arrived at his farm.

Dottie had grumbled about it as he drove her back to town. She'd applied fresh makeup and dressed in a summer knit sweater and skirt with a wide, blue belt. From the corner of his eye, he'd noticed her picking at the beads on her bracelet.

"You okay?" He maneuvered through the thousands and thousands of cars lining the roadway near the amusement park. It was the busiest day of the year, and getting Dottie anywhere near the entrance had proven tricky.

"Yes."

"It's just you've got a lot to … deal with just now."

"You mean the park?"

"And your father." To say nothing of the fact she hadn't exactly been thriving herself, lately.

"I can only deal with the most pressing of those just now."

"Just don't go feeling embarrassed or anything. Around me. Promise? You know I don't judge your father."

"I can't believe you invited him to stay." She shook her head. "And I can't believe he's *doing* it."

The night before must have been dreadful, Smokey figured. Shelby Berkeley wasn't the type to hide away from everyone, any more than his daughter had been before.

The July heat was thicker here at the amusement park, where the sun made a stone oven of the parking areas and walkways. Any breeze that might have come off the lake was blocked by restaurants, dance halls, a skating rink, a host of rides and attractions, and, most oppressively, tens of thousands of people.

Smokey walked with Dottie to the front of the park office, which had always been her domain, pleased their arrival had been socially uneventful for her. He hadn't relished flattening anyone with his fists for being cruel to her.

"How can I help today?" He shoved those fists into his pockets.

Dottie shook her head. "You don't have to stay, Smoke. Thanks for bringing me here. I don't know *what* all I'm walking into, so you don't have to stay."

"I'll stay."

She waved her hand, distracted in a way he hadn't seen her in days. "You've got the boat. The fireworks. Go."

"I'm not leaving you."

Her gaze darted around at the crowds. She finally sighed. "Let me treat you to dinner somewhere later, then, okay?"

He couldn't read her emotions now. Was she worried about what needed to be done? Worried about her reception here after weeks away?

He wouldn't be leaving until she looked far more settled than she did just now.

"I'll check back after a bit." He gave her shoulder a squeeze, and then he gave her the space she needed to be Dottie Berkeley.

As Smokey made his way down the boardwalk to Rosie's studio space, he determined things seemed to be running all right, despite the owner and his daughter having been MIA. There were plenty of balloons, sticky faces, bells ringing at game stations, and shouts of happiness and delight.

He saw it differently now than he had before, now that he knew Dottie better. He saw the work in it, the *job* behind the fun.

Rosie's studio wasn't empty but was still less crowded than the boardwalk when he entered. He walked past displays of blown glass items to walls lined with framed prints of the park and the lake. Some would go home with guests later as souvenirs. Rosie Graham — Adams, now, he reminded himself — was talking with an older couple, her vibrant red hair waving around her face.

She smiled at him and raised a finger to let him know she'd be over. He waved that off, so she'd take her time, then arranged himself on a stool next to her counter. Beside him, on the cool glass of the display case, a cat had draped itself in meditation. He ran his hand over its brindled back, igniting a purr.

Rosie was beside him within minutes. "What are you doing here?"

"Hey, now."

"It's a crowded holiday. You despise this kind of thing."

"Brought Dottie in."

Rosie's brows shot up in question. "And how *is* Dottie?"

"Better than her father."

"I heard."

"What'd you hear?"

"I guess there was quite a scene in more than one place last night. Is he alive, still?"

"He's out at the farm. My mother is feeding him and lecturing him."

"Huh." Rosie seemed to let that digest. "So, Dottie came in to run the park today."

"You got it."

"How's she holding up, though?"

Smokey didn't know how to answer that. He was friends with both women, but it still felt like some kind of betrayal to say Dottie was still a long way from being Dottie. So, he shrugged. "You think she'll run into trouble with folks here at all?"

Rosie sighed. "It's a busy day. Hopefully that'll be a distraction for people, you know?"

So, yes. Dottie would run into trouble.

Smokey thought he'd better stick around.

~~~~~

The sun was going down when Dottie finally hooked her arm in Smokey's elbow and led him to dinner. She'd apologized for making him miss the holiday with his family and scolded him for waiting.

Just the same, he'd seen the relief in her eyes when she'd found him still there.

She took him to the Park Terrace, where they settled at a table and Dottie had immediately ordered from a menu she apparently had memorized. Now, she daintily sawed off a bite of breaded perch.

"Did you know this fish gets shipped down from Lake Erie?" She raised her eyebrows at him to punctuate the question. Smokey watched her balance her knife gracefully back on the rim of her plate, even as she raised the fork with her left hand. The lamps over the tables put out an orange glow from their bulbs, which drew a host of small bugs. Smokey watched the light flash off Dottie's fork when it left her lips.

"I didn't know that. About Lake Erie."

No one else in the restaurant would realize Dottie was uncomfortable. She was eating, after all. Smiling and talking.

But he knew her body language, and she was holding her shoulders unnaturally high.

As he chewed and swallowed and listened to Dottie tell him a story about the restaurant's owner, Smokey also knew *why* tension had drawn those shoulders up. She'd spent the day feeling the nearby conversations of others spotlighting her, not unlike the orange bulb above them now.

A local couple behind her—people whose names he didn't remember—were discussing her with ugly judgment all over their greasy, pursed lips.

Smokey cleared his throat and looked away, but across the room were two servers—one male, one female—staring hard and having plenty to say. They had to be gossiping about them. Or, probably, just gossiping about Dottie.

He brought his gaze back to her and noticed that the end of her
~~~~~

perfect nose had burned a little while she'd floated on the raft earlier. The sun's rays had found their way around her floppy hat. He conjured the image of her, soft and relaxed in his pond, while around them, the ugly whispers continued.

Smokey drew a slow, careful breath to keep from standing and smashing someone's face. Anyone's would do.

"What's wrong?" She sipped her tea.

What could he say to that? *Excuse me while I go overturn a table full of people who don't understand you or care about the truth of who you are.*

"How were you … treated today?" he asked instead.

Awareness moved into her liquid eyes, and the truth was there right behind it. She'd spent the day making sure *they* all had a magical day, and now they smirked at her. Smokey decided he would take her back to the farm. Specifically, he would take her to the barn. She needed Pee-Pee and Carlton.

She shrugged one of those tense shoulders. "This hasn't been easy from the start, Smokey. You know that."

"That's not an answer."

"You worried about me?"

"Yes." That seemed to surprise her, so he ran with it. "You don't have to stay here, you know. At your place."

Dottie smiled at that, and her dimple flashed. "Ah, but I do. The park can only have one of us broken at a time. I mean, between my father and me. It's usually him, actually, so I'm used to this."

"You hardly need to point that out, honey."

"Anyway, we can't *both* be licking our wounds at the same time. Talk about bad for business."

He smashed a white square of perch into his plate like a sulky child. "I want you at the farm, not him."

"So sweet."

"Has he always been like this?"

Dottie sat back, seeming to consider him. Smokey watched as she glanced over to where the waitstaff was still discussing her in apparent detail. She sighed. She'd probably still insist on tipping them.

"Never mind," he said. "It doesn't matter."

"Like a lot of bad parents, my father was also a good parent." She looked like she was visibly drawing the past around her shoulders to shield herself from the talk. "When I was a kid, my dad was larger than life to me. Do you know what I mean?"

"Yes." Smokey did. His own father had been the same.

"He could imagine things and then make them happen, even if it meant he stayed up two nights straight in the maintenance shop or worked under a spotlight on the midway. He fascinated me because his ideas were … fun, you know?"

"I guess they'd have to have been. This place wouldn't be so popular if his ideas were dull. Still, when I look around, I see a lot of your influence here."

"Now, sure. But when I was a kid, of course this place was his vision. His own father had traveled with the circus. Did you know that?"

"I did not."

"I think Dad's worst habits might have started during that nomadic childhood. I don't know for sure. Dad was super smart and good at making money, from the time he was young."

"You're the child most like him. In the good ways, I mean."

She nodded. "That's a whole other story, but it would have to be me. And, to his credit, he let me."

"Let you?"

"Let me be who I wanted. He never said anything about me staying behind to learn to cook with my mother. When I showed him I could do something, he entrusted it to me like I was … I don't know. An equal or something. Capable. So, I grew up thinking I was."

All that gelled with the girl he'd always known. "A gift."

"Do you want the rest of my potatoes, Smoke?"

"You're done?"

"I can't eat any more." She nudged her plate over, and Smokey speared a potato with his fork. The couple behind Dottie watched the whole thing, but then Dottie pulled his attention back. "That freedom was nice, but … but maybe a little careless, too. On his part."

"Careless in what way?"

"That's the thing about my hair." She cleared her throat, picked up her glass. "You asked why I keep my hair pulled back."

A pit formed in his stomach. "It has to do with your dad?"

"Yes and no." She sipped, ran one of her fingers along the vine pattern on the tablecloth. "It was always one of my jobs to collect the rent from the shops. For the businesses here at the park who rent from us."

"I can't remember you *not* working up here."

"I liked visiting with everyone. Listening to their triumphs and their complaints. Sometimes I could solve their problems, make things better. Most of them were really very kind to me, treated me as sort of a pet when I was growing up." She swallowed, kept focusing on the embroidered pattern before her. "It meant a lot that Dad trusted me with all that."

Smokey ground his teeth. Somehow, this had to do with her hair.

"One day … I think I was maybe … fourteen? Thirteen or fourteen. There was a man who ran the candy store. The one with the big jars of taffy on the table. Remember that place?"

"I remember him, yeah. He always had us call him Uncle Sugar,"

Smokey said with distaste. He already didn't like where this story was going, wishing now he hadn't asked Dottie about her hair and its tidy bun.

She was clearly thinking about the man, too, based on her own expression. "I wore my hair down back then. People always complimented me on how shiny my curls were, and the one thing my mom did teach me that I paid attention to was how to take care of my curls." She drew a breath. "One day, I went in to get his rent." She didn't say his name. "It was the first of the month in August. He'd been touching my hair a lot that summer. All summer. You know?"

Smokey frowned, involuntarily shaking his head. "Touching your hair."

"Yes. He'd reach out and pluck at the curls to make them bounce, and sometimes he'd just run his hand along them."

"No."

"I didn't like it, of course, but I didn't think much about it until that day. That one day. I was the only one in the shop. And he ... said some things."

Smokey held himself still.

"Things about how I'd grown into an attractive woman, only the truth was, I didn't feel like a woman yet. You know? He said he liked how I didn't cover my assets like some women did." Dottie's cheeks turned a splotchy pink with the words.

"Your assets?"

"I thought he meant my hair. I didn't really know. But I felt ... I don't know. Dirty. The way he talked about me seemed so dirty."

"I'm going to murder him."

"He's gone." She cleared her throat. "He started touching my hair again, and I tried to step away, and I definitely told him not to touch me, then. But he backed me into a table. I still remember one of the taffy jars falling over and rolling off, crashing to the ground. They were pink pieces, in their little waxy paper, all over the tile floor."

Smokey kept his voice low, careful. "He hurt you?"

"He kept touching me. I don't really want to talk about it. The way he looked at me, the things he said. I didn't understand, really, except that I felt so ... wrong. Wrong about who I was, somehow."

"But you got away."

"I did. I got away. I ran and found my father. I hardly knew what to tell him. I mean, nothing had happened, but it felt like something awful had happened."

"But you told him what happened?"

"I did. I was crying."

"Oh, honey." Smokey reached across the table and put his hand over the fingers she was using to pluck at the table cover. He hooked his pinky with hers. *Where had he been that day, himself?* When Uncle Sugar, the worm, had touched her and scared her and made her cry? "What did your father do?"

Smokey imagined Shelby Berkeley beating the man with a ball bat, but somehow, he knew the answer before Dottie said it.

"Nothing." She shrugged. Laughed a little, ruefully. "He said I needed to be more careful with men, was all, and at least nothing bad happened."

"*Nothing bad happened?*"

Dottie shrugged. "In the end, he just touched me."

"Against your will." Smokey would now return to his farm, find her alcoholic father, and use a ball bat on *him*.

"Anyway, I understood that day that it must be my hair, you know? I had a job to do, and I took the job seriously, but my hair must be making men think I wasn't serious, somehow. That I was showing off my 'assets,' whatever that meant. I'm still not sure I know." She gave Smokey a wry smile.

He said, softly, "That's when you started with the bun."

She nodded.

Another voice cut in. "Smokey Black."

Startled, he realized there were people standing alongside their table. A couple, to be exact: Lucas and Regina, married, friends of Reggie's and Pam's. How long had they been there, while he'd been fantasizing about violence involving a Louisville slugger? With his pinky hooked in Dottie's.

Shaking off the thick disgust, Smokey reoriented himself to the restaurant, the crowd, the gathering darkness that would soon bring fireworks.

"Hey, there, you two," he said, standing up to shake hands with Lucas and nod at Regina. Smokey cleared his throat. A combination of Lucas's reluctance to return his handshake and Regina's cold eyes had alarms going off too late in Smokey's sluggish mind.

"We're so surprised to see you here," Regina said, carefully giving Dottie her back. "I didn't think it was true, but now I don't know what to think."

"Folks are saying you're … carrying on …" Lucas gestured with his whole head toward Dottie but did not meet her eyes. "I guess it's true."

"I can hardly believe it," his wife whispered on a hiss before Smokey could say a thing, and then she yanked Lucas away.

Smokey turned to go after them.

"No."

He felt Dottie's hand firm around his arm.

"Smokey, no. Let them go."

He hated that the other people in the restaurant could see his shoulders heave with frustrated breath. He unclenched his fists, calmed himself by looking into Dottie's enormous, tea-colored eyes.

He would start carrying the ball bat *with* him, whether it was good for either of their businesses or not.

~~~~~

"*Carrying on …!*" Dottie breathlessly repeated the phrase, her face so, so warm. She couldn't bring herself to meet Smokey's gaze again as he lowered himself back into his chair at the restaurant table.

Carrying on? What did *that* mean? Dottie would have to check with Emily to be sure about the connotation of that phrase, but her own impression was that it implied a good deal more than mounding manure for pumpkin seeds or mulching evergreen seedlings.

"Well." That was all Smokey said, his jaw tight. Every muscle in his body looked tight.

The window of the Park Terrace didn't allow them to see a firework explode out in the sky, but Dottie did catch bits of red sparks reflected on the lake water. Also red were the tips of Smokey's ears.

He must be humiliated. She'd made *him* a topic of gossip, when all he'd done was treat her with kindness.

"I'm so very sorry."

He looked surprised. "*You're* sorry? Sorry for what?"

"For. You know. Everyone thinks we're … carrying on. Whatever that means."

Smokey let out a breath and managed to smile at that, while she remained mortified.

"Nothing to apologize for, sweetheart. It's just gossip, and in this case, the gossip makes me look pretty good, all things considered."

Dottie gaped in response. "Smokey. People despise me. It absolutely does *not* make you look good."

"People think you're with me? That we're a couple? It's outrageous that a woman like you would even look twice at me, so I'd say it's rather a point of pride that they've paired us together in their talk. If anything, I'm proud."

Sure. He gave her one of those winks.

Dottie folded her napkin carefully on the table and sat back, shaking her head. Of course, she was grateful to him. "Sometimes I can't tell if you're delusional or enlightened. But it doesn't matter. I just need to thank you for letting me come out to work on the farm, Smokey, and for saying the kind of things you just said. Thank you so much."

"'Thank you' is a step up from 'so very sorry.' Anyway, no need to thank me, either. You're a good farmhand. I've been glad for the help."

"Just the same, I think I'd better be done with that work." People
~~~~~

were talking about *him* now. Being mean to Smokey Black in public. She couldn't have that.

"Ah, so you're staying here for keeps." He said it with a sigh, his eyes intense on her. "I wondered all day about that."

"You've got a new project now, anyway. My father." She tried not to roll her eyes.

"I just hope people don't say I'm carrying on with *him*."

Dottie tried not to laugh. Failed.

"Dimple sighting."

"Stop it."

"Your father will be a step down for me in the gossip mill, I suppose. Plus, there's the fact I'll miss you."

"Maybe I could still come out and see Nel and Carlton and Sir Lawrence? Now and then? For a visit, I mean."

Another body appeared alongside their table, and Dottie glanced up with wary dread. She was relieved to be met with a friendly smile.

"Julia!"

"Dottie, I thought that was you!" The pretty young woman bent to hug Dottie's shoulders just as if there was no such thing as social contagion. "It's so good to see you here."

Dottie rose to return Julia's hug, determined to hold tight to anyone who still tolerated her. Younger than herself by a couple of years, Julia was relatively new to town. She had honey-colored hair that waved around a lovely, open face.

"Smokey," Dottie said, turning, "this is Julia Fey. The lovely mother with the sweet little girl I told you about. The one you said could come out and help run the register during harvest and tree season?"

"Oh, sure." Smokey, ever the gentleman, had also risen again, and now he extended his hand to Julia. He flashed his white grin, and Dottie knew all too well how disorienting it felt to be on the other end of it.

She supposed it might be especially jarring to be faced with that smile for the very first time, but she couldn't recall. She figured she'd probably been in pigtails the first time Smokey Black had smiled at her, and he'd probably smiled because he was trying to cut one of her pigtails *off*.

Julia, sure enough, blushed.

"It's nice to meet you, ma'am."

"Julia, this is Levi Black. Everyone calls him Smokey, and you should, too."

"Hello, Smokey."

"Will you pull up a chair and join us?" Smokey was the one to ask.

"Thank you, but I can't. I'm waiting tables on the other side until whenever we close here for the night. It might be hours more."

Dottie thought about Julia's daughter, wondering who was keeping an eye on the little tyke on this festive night. The poor thing. A couple of years ago, she'd have had both her mommy and daddy on either side of her for the fireworks show. Now, they had a framed flag in their little living room for his memory, and Julia was wearing herself out working two jobs.

A lightbulb, rather than a firework, lit for Dottie.

"I was just telling Smokey how I can't help him at the farm now. I'm going to have to be here at the park more again." The words made Dottie's heart stutter uncomfortably. Out on the farm, her heart had stopped doing those kinds of things. In truth, she did not want to be here, and she did not want to go back to feeling so alone. Back to not playing, to not resting.

Nor would she let the place fall apart, though, just because *she* had fallen apart. Not after all the hard work.

Smokey nodded. "I don't know what I'll do without her," he said, and Dottie tested his words, trying to detect sarcasm. There was none.

Keeping her voice low, Dottie told Julia, "To be clear, the two of us, we're certainly not … you know. *Carrying on.*"

Smokey barked a laugh across the table, which drew more unwanted attention. He winked at Dottie, understanding instinctively what she was angling for. As he usually did.

"I may need help out on the farm well before the harvest season," he said, folding his own napkin on his plate. "The pumpkins will need a good deal of water as we get into this dry heat of July and August. Your little girl is welcome to come and help, too, if you think she'd like it."

Now Dottie surprised herself by winking back at him in gratitude.

There was a lot to be said for friendships, she decided all over again, that went back decades.

Chapter Seventeen

In the end, Smokey refused to leave her at the park that night.

He insisted on taking her back to Mama Pool's, so they'd slipped away even as the sky lit with the lake's Independence Day fireworks display. On the water, boats bobbed so thick they touched one another under the colorful lights. On the road leading away from the crowds, however, all was comparatively silent.

"I suppose I should gather my things from your mother's place, anyway." Dottie told herself one more night at Mama Pool's was logical.

"Whatever keeps me from having to be the one to pull away and leave you here. No way I'm doing that."

Her heart squeezed. "Don't be silly. This is my place, just as the farm is yours."

"And remember my farm can be your place any time you need it to be, Dottie B."

There was something sad in his voice, something sad in her soul, that left them silent as they crossed the country roads. She told herself she was glad to have the farm as an option. It was always good to have a spot reserved for nervous breakdowns.

The truck windows were open, and the air smelled intermittently of barbecue, smoke, and corn fields.

Dottie had never realized cornfields had a smell, but now she knew they did.

When their feet crunched across the gravel of Mama Pool's drive at the old farmhouse where Smokey had grown up, both their steps slowed. The house was completely dark, which was no surprise. Mama Pool, who would be up well before dawn, was usually sound asleep by sundown.

Dottie found she didn't know what to say to Smokey. She'd already thanked him. She'd already apologized for involving him in gossip. What else was left?

He was the one who spoke, his hands in his pockets. "Are you tired?"

"I don't know." Glumly, she considered it. "I guess I always am."

"Come here."

Dottie followed him around the corner of the house to the giant maple tree with its swing, a broad piece of wood with thick rope knotted to each end. "Hop on."

She looked up at him, just a shadow on a silver moon night, but she could make out his smile.

"I'll push you. Get on."

"Why?"

"*Play*. Remember how you're newly committed to playing? Come on."

Dottie allowed herself a private grin as she considered. *Why not?* She placed her handbag at the base of the tree and obediently climbed onto the swing, pushing herself off with her foot. Smokey strolled behind her, waited for her to glide back to him, and gave her a gentle shove. The swing arched forward a little further. On the backswing, both of his hands were there again, pushing with more firmness.

Dottie didn't pump her legs. She just let them dangle, let Smokey do all the work.

He was the one who finally spoke. "Is your dad going to be a grump these next few days?"

"Without whiskey and rum, you mean?"

"Right."

"I don't know. I've honestly never seen him deny himself." The swing went back, then forward, rope groaning against the bark. "You're in uncharted territory, Smoke."

"I'm impressed he's willing to try."

"I still can't believe my mom kicked him out." Dottie knew she needed to pay her mother a visit, check on her. This was more uncharted territory. "She's built an entire life on looking the other way. Preparing his meals, mending his clothes, and looking the other way."

"He won't find living with me these next few days to be as easy, I don't think." Smokey's hands met her lower back. Each push forward seemed to first involve a split-second embrace. "Especially not knowing what I know now. About how he didn't fight for you when he should have."

"Which time?"

"Exactly."

"Do you want him out?"

"No. I'll try to help him if I can."

"You're a better person than most."

"I don't know about that. Mostly, I'll try for your sake."

"He's not good at being told what to do," she warned. She could see this going so badly. She fully expected her father to return to the park no later than tomorrow afternoon. He wouldn't be able to stay away. For the first time, she wondered if it was only alcohol that had the man addicted.

Perhaps she even understood that other addiction.

Didn't she, herself, know the satisfaction of engaging in the next problem-solving adventure at the amusement park? It was easy to thrive on it. There was always something to be done, and when a person was doing all of that, it hardly left room for convicting silence or stillness. She and her father both had lived for so long according to the pulse of calliope music, squeals and splashes, the ding of bells.

The stillness of summer at Smokey's farm was another world. Shelby would not be able to cope with it.

Dottie, conversely, was surprised to realize she'd miss it.

"Tell me what you'll be doing this month," she ordered, enjoying the coolness of the air rushing against her face when she swung forward. "On the farm, I mean."

"Well, I wasn't kidding about those pumpkins needing plenty of water. Hopefully your friend Julia takes me up on the work."

"I'm certain she will. Thank you for that."

"You'll have to find out what she's making at the restaurant and whatever else she's doing at the park to get by. In the office or whatever. Let me know. I'll make sure she earns more here."

"It will be nice for her not to be spread so thin. Her little girl, Penny, is precious. You'll love her. I'm grateful to you."

"Stop thanking me, darling. I lost friends over in Europe. Men with wives and babies. I'm counting on folks giving those families a helping hand in the same way."

She already knew that, and she meant it when she said he was a good man. So different from the cocky state champion she'd had a crush on a decade before. But the stillness of the summer night already felt a little too intimate, and she figured Smokey must know, didn't he, that he was everyone's hero? Maybe even her own? Surely, he woke up each day, considered himself in the shaving mirror, and felt deeply satisfied with the man he saw there.

It stung, the contrast to the way she felt looking in the mirror each morning.

With no warning, gliding forward and back through the warm night air, she had to swallow back tears she couldn't have explained. *Don't think about yourself, Dottie. Think about him. Focus.*

"You know." She paused to clear her throat because it was coated in those tears. "I've been thinking you should change the name of your farm to Holiday Farms."

"*Holiday* Farms?" He tried it out a few times as the rope made its soft sighing noise. "Why not Festival Farms? You don't like the name?"

"Your farm celebrates the holidays, though. Festivals are different from holidays. Your farm is about Halloween and Christmas. Holidays, right?"

"What about when the orchard is ready for apple picking? Peach picking? What about the acres of sunflowers I've planted?"

"Labor Day, right? September? Holiday."

Smokey chuckled. "I just figured the alliteration worked. Festival Farms. The double F. But you don't think so?"

Dottie had given it no thought at all, but now she had to pretend she had. "I just like Holiday Farms. It sounds more ... I don't know ... regular. A predictable rhythm for the year and for the memories people can create there."

"I'll consider it." He pushed, and she soared. "You know, I wondered how long it would take for you to start making business suggestions to me. And now you have. You must be feeling more like your old self, I suppose."

Dottie considered those words, felt them echo like a lie inside of her. *Her old self?* She wished he hadn't said it like that. It seemed to conjure that ghost of who she'd once been. She wondered, if she were to meet her *old self* now, whether she'd even be able to have a conversation with that woman.

That Dottie had been immensely capable, confident. There'd been a kind of fire inside of her, but when she looked for the same flames now .... She missed them. She wasn't sure she'd been a better person, that "old self," but she had been an *easier* person to be. She'd felt better looking in the mirror, at least.

"I'm not," she heard herself say, but the words were strangled in her throat again. They burned up from there to her nose and to the backs of her eyes.

"What?"

Ridiculously, it suddenly felt like no time had passed at all. She was right back there on an icy road in March. Right back in that courtroom. *Vehicular homicide.* Right back to the library classroom where no one had shown up. Right back to her father's frustration. *Maybe it's better if you go away for a little while.*

Her chest tightened, and she squeezed her eyes shut. Time had passed. This was a different moment. This was none of those moments. She was on a tree swing on a warm summer holiday.

Take a breath. But that breath didn't make it all the way past her throat, which was still burning.

"Dottie?" His voice seemed to come from a great distance.

"I'm not," she said louder. Her breath came with a gasp, but at least it came. Smokey's hands weren't there when she swung back this time, shaking her head as the leaves blurred above her. "I'm not ... feeling like my old self at all."

This time, when she swung back, Smokey's arms grabbed her around her middle and tugged her right off the wooden board. She squealed in surprise, and he shushed her, mumbling something about waking Mama

Pool.

Then he mumbled an apology against her temple. "I'm sorry. I'm sorry if I said something ..."

As the empty swing bounced forward, Dottie found herself cradled like a child against Smokey's chest. His arms wrapped under her lower back and the back of her knees, and none of it was a struggle for him. Slowly, saying nothing, he strolled over to the maple and leaned casually back against its thick trunk, keeping hold of her. She let her forehead fall against the stubble of his jaw.

Maybe it was because she'd been thrust back to the turning point, the moment that separated her old self from this new creature of uncertainty, or maybe it was the scent of the man's aftershave when her nose pressed against that warm neck and she felt her own tears there, but, whatever it was, a memory surfaced.

One her mind must have rid itself of. Until now.

"You held me." She was reeling with the sensory details of that night, of the side of that road. Icy sleet on her face, the hiss of her smashed car's radiator, the silence of death. "That night. At the accident scene. You held me."

He had. He'd held her in his arms that night in this same way. He'd held her just like this while her head was bleeding, while she'd stared in horror at the scene before her.

Now, she started to tremble with the memory of that scene. She shook with the things she'd needed to forget. Smokey felt her shaking, surely, because she felt his lips press to her forehead in comfort as he whispered, "Shhh. You're okay."

The shaking was hard, though, as it sometimes was. The kind she hadn't wanted anyone else to know about. She hated that he not just knew about it now but that he even felt it. Somehow, she couldn't have him *worry* about her. She couldn't have *anyone* worrying about her.

She needed to go inside. She couldn't breathe.

"Dottie. Hey. Dottie?" His lips stayed near the pale streak of a scar at her hairline. "Take a deep breath for me, will you?"

"Can't."

"Yes, you can. You're safe. Breathe."

"I didn't remember."

"Do you want me to put you down? Is that what you need?"

It was too late. Now he knew she sometimes shook this way. "No." The breath made it past her throat this time. She wheezed.

"Another."

She hiccupped a sob. Worked to breathe. Minutes passed.

"Maybe you need to talk about that night. Maybe not right now, but maybe you'll want to talk to me about it sometime." More minutes passed.

"When you're ready, you know where to find me. Any time. Take another breath."

She obeyed. "I wonder why I forgot. That part." Another tremor shook her, and his arms tightened.

"Sometimes your brain doesn't bring things back until it knows you're ready to handle them. Not before."

"Well, I … I'm clearly still not ready."

She felt his deep chuckle against her cheek, and the next breath came easy. This was different from curling up in a ball on the cool floorboards of the upstairs bedroom. Different from the panic that sometimes destroyed her there in the night.

"Smokey, I'm afraid it's never going to … to be all right," she choked. She had never said that out loud, had barely said it in her own mind, but it was the absolute truth. "It's always *there* now. Under everything, ruining absolutely everything." She shuddered with another breath. "It's never going to go away. It's always …"

She couldn't go on. She was crying.

He let her.

When she finally quieted, she was too weary to feel embarrassed. He waited until she'd drawn several long, full breaths before he said, "Don't even think about apologizing."

"Why do you bother with me?" With her, with her father, with all of it. "I'm a load of trouble now."

"I figure you're less trouble than you used to be. Besides, I've got my reasons."

Dottie lifted her head, her face wet like his jaw and neck.

He sighed, somber. "In case I ever get the nerve up to ride The Dips."

"What?"

"The coaster. If I ever want to ride it, I figure you'll be able to get me in for free. So, I put up with you."

They were close enough their laughing breaths mingled a little.

Too close, really. Dottie wriggled and slid back to the ground, wondering how he was so good at making things seem okay when they were not even close to being okay. "You're a good friend, Smokey. I hope you'll at least let me thank you for that."

"Will you be able to sleep?"

"Maybe. After I finish tonight's breakdown in peace." But she knew this one had nearly passed. She stooped to pick up her purse, turning toward the paving stones that led to the kitchen door.

"Dottie."

She turned around. She wished he didn't look so good there, under the tree.

He said, "I have nightmares sometimes."

"About the accident?"

"About the accident. And the war. They get mixed up together."

Dottie tilted her head. She had trouble imagining this man of strength also knew the feel of cool floorboards in the middle of the night when they might be the only thing left to cling to. What did she have to offer, though? "Well, we'd better talk about that sometime, too, I suppose."

Chapter Eighteen

Lillian Turnbull Graham was in her forties, and today, in the office of the Buckeye Lake Amusement Park, she would use a typewriter for the first time.

Dottie had blocked off time on hot July afternoons to teach Lil the basic office tasks she would have learned in Dot's Dash to Business course, had the course happened as planned. She would do the same for Julia one day, but Julia and her little Penny had been spending their days together in that proverbial fresh air at the farm. There'd be plenty of time for typing later.

"You don't have to force the paper in like that." Dottie corrected Lil, patting her shoulder and turning the dial to roll the slightly crumpled paper back out of the machine. "You can just set it in there. Like this, see? It will catch."

"Ah." Lil nodded. She was an eager student. Not close to competent, but eager. She followed Dottie's directions and only mangled the paper a little the next time she loaded it. It occurred to Dottie she would love to see this woman in her element, dancing.

"Emily said I could start typing up items for the community calendar for the newspaper. Once I figure this out."

Dottie made a pleased sound, enjoying the vision of mother and daughter partnering on something for *The Beacon* that came out each week. Could Emily have taught Lil to use the typewriter herself? *Yes.* Would their relationship have survived? *Most likely not.*

Dottie wasn't the most patient woman at the lake, but her friend was even further from it.

She showed Lil how to place her fingers on the keys. "The trick is to start slowly but to use the correct fingers on the correct keys. Even though it's going to be slow at first, okay? It will pay off later."

The hour between noon and one on weekdays was quiet in the park office. The morning was usually filled with the unexpected, during the season: a wiring issue that had popped up the night before, someone whose shift would need to be covered that day, a delivery delay, a broken-down car blocking the entrance, prize theft from one of the games, a minor kitchen fire.

Then there were the usual routines of the day to squeeze in there: bank deposits, supply orders, correspondence, timecards and payroll.

With the basics done and the literal and figurative fires put out, Dottie typically tried to spend the rest of the stifling summer afternoons planning. She booked bands, booked shows, booked company picnics.

In summers before, she would stroll along the midway and out to the pier during those afternoons, walk down to the pool or the beach. She'd slide her sunglasses down and let her imagination run wild. *"What if?"* she'd ask herself.

What if they trucked in a giant tub of seals? How many people would rush out to Buckeye Lake for that? What about a truck of sand for a sandcastle competition? A synchronized swimming act that might run for a week? Was it time for another skating marathon?

This summer, she was better off doing her imagining inside the office.

Hard stares and murmured conversations could be distracting.

"Type the word 'write' with the correct fingers," Dottie said after Lil had spent ten minutes doing rows of top-line letters. "Like 'write' as in writing a note. Type it over and over."

The gunshot clicking of the typewriter keys was loud in the office.

Then it stopped.

"Dottie." Lil was looking over at her, an eyebrow arched. "Was that your stomach?"

"What?"

"Did your stomach just growl?"

Dottie blinked. Had it? "I … don't know." She thought of that first day on the farm, when Smokey had grinned at her stomach growling and held her one-armed on the tractor.

"Did you even eat lunch?" A pause, and then Lil sighed. "Dottie, Dottie, Dottie. I think you might be an even sorrier case than me."

Dottie thought the statement might have infuriated her once upon a time. Especially coming from a derelict mother and dancer of previously questionable reputation. But who *was* Dottie, and what *was* her own story? The answer came quickly: far worse. Far worse than any of that. Not that it was a competition, but she nodded.

"The sorriest of us, sorry to say."

"Let's go get you a fish sandwich." Lil, who mostly let everyone tell her what to do since she'd returned to the lake in March, rose before a surprised Dottie could respond, grabbed her purse, and handed Dottie her own bag off her desk. "Come on, now."

Dottie followed her. She hesitated at the door, but the older woman turned impatiently.

"You've got to eat."

Into the sunlight they went. Dottie scanned the boardwalk the way she always did now, trying to anticipate the next attack.

Last week, she'd been un-invited to a wedding. Pastor Skip had been scheduled to perform the ceremony, since he'd baptized both the bride and groom. The bride's mother explained it would be uncomfortable to have Dottie there, casting a shadow of loss on their special day. Dottie had quickly agreed not to attend.

Otherwise, July was going so, so slowly, though attendance was good here at the park. The fire last year had garnered its own publicity, so some came out to watch the final touches on the rebuilding of the pier. Even on a Thursday afternoon, there were plenty of groups on the midway playing games.

Because it wasn't exactly midday and wasn't suppertime yet, there was no line at The Feedbox. Soon Dottie held two fried fish fillets in grease-darkened slabs of white bread, a thin square of paper between the bread and her fingers.

She walked beside Lil toward the swimming area at the little lake.

Dottie looked away quickly when she spotted Doris from the ladies' auxiliary headed right toward them with two mean-eyed friends. Dottie pretended total fascination with her fish as they passed.

"Princess" was the only word she heard, but it was not said kindly, which confirmed they were referring to her.

What would they have done if she'd smiled openly at them?

But she knew. She'd already tried that. It had only made things worse.

"Here," Lil said, claiming an empty bench where tufts of summer-dry grass began to meet with sand.

Dottie sat, passing a sandwich to Lil. Lil stared at her until she obediently took a bite of her own.

In front of them, families made the most of the afternoon. The nearby coaster was one kind of soundtrack, a radio at the towel cabana another. Young mothers were chatting waist-deep, some of them balancing pudgy babies in the water, the little ones squealing and kicking. Near them, older children splashed and chased.

Dottie wondered what would happen if one of those kids started to drown and she ran in and rescued it. Would she be forgiven in the community's eyes?

At any rate, Dottie thought, these would be the summer families from the cabins around the lake. Husbands would drive into Columbus for work each morning and back out to the lake each evening for supper. In fact, the ladies would be leaving the water soon to make meals of summer squash casserole and perhaps berry cobbler.

Dottie blinked back a familiar sting in her eyes, desperately wishing for the first time to be one of them. They laughed so easily, talked earnestly, knew they *belonged*. They belonged here among the women and children. They would belong later with their husbands and families, and they would go on belonging tomorrow.

"Being different is lonely," Lil said, startling Dottie out of her reverie. Had she shared her own thoughts out loud?

Dottie made a sound of agreement as she chewed. Because *yes*. Being different was starting to feel unbelievably lonely.

"There's nothing quite as isolating as shame, either."

Dottie glanced over, but Lil didn't seem to require a response to that. She thought this was the closest Lil had come to openly speaking of her own past. She was an undeniably attractive woman, even in middle age. It wasn't anything she did, simply how she was made. Not, Dottie thought, unlike Emily and Rosie. People called it "good bones." Lil's good bones were covered with weary skin, though, and a tension around her eyes. Added to that was an unhealthy thinness that Dottie worried would soon mark her own frame.

She hastily took another bite of perch and greasy bread.

"I brought the shame on myself," Lil continued. "I made clear choices that resulted in shame. I put my love of a lifestyle over whatever love I felt for my babies. Look at those women out there. They would never do such a thing."

Dottie didn't point out that none of them looked like they could so much as square dance well, let alone be Lindy Hoppers. And could anyone really predict those women's true hearts, anyway?

"You came back," she said into the guilty silence, because what else could she say?

"After it mattered," Lil said. "Everyone knows who I've been, what I've done. There's no escaping that. Especially not in this little lake community I spent most of my life hating and avoiding. Still, our circumstances, our shame ... yours and mine ... they're not really alike, are they?"

"Beyond the fact I can't escape either?"

"I made a choice, Dottie."

For the first time, she thought Lil sounded like she could be someone's mother. Maybe Dottie was just the only woman she felt she could advise. What was the fallen, guilt-ridden Lil Graham to offer her two daughters? Emily and Rosie had turned out fine, more or less.

Anyway, Lil seemed to have plenty to offer Dottie.

"I made a choice, but you didn't."

"Didn't I?"

"What were you guilty of, missy? Driving out to see your friends for dinner?"

"In an ice storm."

"Oh, stop. It's not the same thing. Though I suppose that doesn't matter when it comes to public opinion."

"There you go. People decide what matters, I guess."

"What you think of yourself is what matters. What God thinks of you. But it's still lonely."

Imagining this woman beside her, younger, Dottie couldn't help but wonder what her late husband, her friends' father, had been like. She thought his name had been Jesse. How had the two of them fallen in love, Jesse and Lil? How had Lil felt when she'd still been so young, her baby girls so young, and had to process all the grief of his sudden death? How had it felt moving in with her in-laws? To go from the thrill of those dance shows, touring the nation, to Towpath Island?

Not for the first time, Dottie considered that she'd been far too self-absorbed lately. She hadn't stopped to wonder if it felt difficult for Lil, when she'd walked away.

Regardless, that wasn't something Dottie had any right to know.

"How's it going for you, Lil?" she asked, instead. "I mean, with your family?"

The corners of Lil's lips were framed in shallow lines when she smiled.

"What can I say?" She took her time. "I suppose I knew it would be a bit before anyone would trust me. I mean, I barely trust myself."

"Not to pack up and leave again?"

"That. Or whatever the easy way out seems to be this time. I've been very good, my whole life, at walking away from the hard things and chasing whatever seems easier."

"What would that be now? What feels easier than being here, getting to know your family?"

She smiled again, bowing her head in a way that made her look younger and a little vulnerable. "Between us, just about anything would be easier than this."

Dottie hid her surprise. She knew Rosie and Emily better than most people did. "It's hard to imagine them being unkind to you."

Lil's surprise, by contrast, was not hidden. "No! No, they're not unkind. I didn't mean that." A degree of relief washed over Dottie. All she needed now was to be wrong about her favorite people in the world. "No, it's not them. I only mean that it's not easy for me to see them. To talk with them, watch them living their lives. Thinking about what we could have meant to one another. To think of the memories we *don't* have together. To learn to know Hickory for real this time, but now without Louisa by his side. To face again what it meant when I bought that one-way ticket to a life that seemed easier back then."

"To be fair, I always figured life as a professional dancer would be anything but easy."

"Dance was what I knew. All I knew before I met Jesse. Crying babies, fevers, skin rashes, cooking, laundry … that all made twelve-hour rehearsals seem plenty easy, I'll tell you."

They both laughed at that, watching the toddlers play in the water. Dottie thought Lil's words made a little too much sense, were a little too relatable, and there was no comfort in that.

"No one claps for you when you do those things. When you wash those diapers," Lil went on. "But when you rehearse the steps and you follow a careful diet and you give everything out on the stage … there's applause at the end of it, you know? The same is simply not true for taking care of little girls."

"You don't have to explain your past decisions to me. I hope you know that."

"I know. I know I don't."

"It must have taken a great deal of courage to come back here."

Lil reached over and put a warm hand on Dottie's forearm. "I could say the same of you. You came back here, too."

Dottie leaned into the other woman's shoulder affectionately and straightened again.

Shame.

Dottie, whose brain naturally sorted things onto line graphs, considered her own shame alongside Lil Graham's. Whose was greater, then? Dottie had ended a man's life, and not just any man's life. A man of God. Certainly, it hadn't been on purpose, but it was still her actions that had resulted in his death. Lil, by contrast, had left on purpose, but she had not killed anyone. She'd deprived two amazing girls, now amazing women, of a mother just as they'd lost a father.

Whose shame was greater? Again, she wondered if it mattered.

Before, she might have gone to Pastor Skip and asked him. Which grieved God more? How did they move on from here?

But Pastor Skip was gone. Because of her.

For no reason she could explain, Dottie longed for Smokey. The shame let up a little when he was nearby, though he never spoke of it as Lil just had. There was warm acceptance in his eyes, that was all, and Dottie was having trouble finding it in the eyes of other people.

If Lil's "easy escape" had once been dance, Dottie was afraid her own now was a farm full of pumpkin vines and pines.

"I'm enjoying little Charlie and Delia," Lil said after she'd watched the children playing in the water again for a time.

Any mention of Delia made Dottie's stomach hurt. Pastor Skip was one more person taken from the little girl. Dottie placed the uneaten half of her sandwich beside her on the bench.

"Kids have always confused me," the older woman went on. "But being around Rosie's, well, I realize in many ways they're … easier than adults."

"Shorter memories."

"Yes."

"Emily's baby will know you from its first day, Lil. To that child, you will always have *been there*. A loving and devoted granny."

Lillian smiled at that. "I have thought of that. Emily and Drew are moving into the bigger house on the towpath before the baby comes, now that Rosie and the kids are with Gabe at the inn."

"Yes, she mentioned that."

"They want me to move into the old barge house." It was a cottage, really, constructed around a barge from the old Ohio-Erie Canal. Just big enough for one or two.

"That makes sense. Will you do it?"

"Only if Hickory lets me earn my keep working at the marina. And I can help Emily at the paper. I don't want to feel they're taking pity on me or that I'm some kind of charity case. I've always made my own way, for better or for worse. Not well, always, but I don't want to be a burden to anyone now."

"I don't think they'd have ever thought of it like that. They're not like that."

"I know. I would, though."

"What's Mama Pool think?"

"She's the one person I don't mind accepting help from. Isn't that funny?"

"I feel the same way."

"She wants to make sure I can cook meals without setting anything on fire." Lillian laughed softly. "Those are the conditions of her letting me graduate from her farmhouse to the barge house."

Dottie smiled, wishing she'd been required to meet a similar objective before moving back into her apartment over the office. She'd been accustomed, before, to grabbing food from the dozens of restaurants to keep herself alive, but now going to those restaurants tended to destroy her appetite.

There were always people there, and with those people, there was more shame.

"I think it's going to take time," Lillian said now. "Just as you say the kids' memories are shorter. I think time will help us both."

Dottie considered it. Would people still talk cruelly about her as years passed? She wasn't sure. She could picture herself, easily, as a spindly old lady with a cane, and when she walked by, older generations would tell the younger: "See that crone there? She used to race jalopies as a kid, and then she killed the best man in town with her car."

The younger people would try to picture her behind the wheel, would abandon the image, would resort to steering clear of the old lady who had nothing but money in her life.

"I hope you're right." Dottie couldn't hide her skepticism.

"It's all new, fresh. That's why it's hard to imagine."

"It doesn't feel fresh. It feels like forever."

"Rosie tells me I need to stop defining who I am based on how the community defines me," Lil said. "She's pretty wise, though of course she didn't get that from me."

Rosie Graham Adams was allowed to weigh in. After all, she did know about shame, as she'd tried to point out to Dottie months before. She'd brought Charlie into the world at sixteen, with no wedding ring on her finger.

"Rosie's one in a million."

"She keeps reminding me to focus on what God says about me. Not what the others say."

"Sometimes, Lil, that scares me more."

"Well, I'm certainly no expert, but I've been reading the Good Book. And Rosie makes a point."

"She does."

"I like the part where it says God takes *delight* in me. So much that He sings over me, just like I am. I try to remember that when I'm fantasizing about packing up and running back toward something easier, where no one knows what I've done. But it's not what anyone else thinks. And, in the end, it's not even what I think of myself that's true."

Dottie nodded. This would be a kind of consolation. But there were still scales in her mind, line graphs, the measure of good and bad, better and worse. She appreciated, though, this flawed friend who offered even a glimmer of hope. "Thanks for that thought, Lil."

"It's not my thought. Look it up. A little book right before you get to the New Testament. Zephaniah."

"Anyway, you might have better mothering skills than you think. My own mother has been … quiet in the face of all of this."

"There's no manual for these kinds of situations. Just like you, like me, your parents are feeling their way along, too. Making mistakes the way people do."

"Again, don't sell yourself short when it comes to wisdom." Dottie rose. "I appreciate you."

"Don't think I haven't noticed you didn't finish the sandwich."

"I ate. I'm fine."

"No, you're not. I'm not either. But we will be."

Chapter Nineteen

The passenger seat of the Fleetline was as hot as July when Dottie journeyed back to the farm again. She had a question for her father, and there was no telephone in Smokey's cabin. No one would answer if there were, anyway. Dottie could hardly believe Shelby was still out there, but she spotted him—and a fishing pole—at the pond.

There was no sign of the pond's owner.

"I'll meet you up at the barn after a bit," Mama Pool told her before she drove away.

Dottie stood in the heat, wishing she'd thought to grab a hat before leaving the office, watching the dust mark Mama Pool's journey back to the road. The older woman had decided she could get a load of "wash" done before they headed back to the park. The day was young.

Beside her father, cattails grew in a clump. As Dottie approached the greenish water, she thought back to Smokey taking that running leap into the pond when the yellow jacket dove into his shirt. The memory brought a smile. She'd been floating in this very pond, learning to rest, so recently. Now, she was back in her work heels, and it was her father's turn to rest.

Shelby looked up when his daughter's pumps crunched the pale grass behind him. July had been even dryer than usual, which had Dottie hoping her pumpkin plants were truly getting all the water they needed.

The hat her father wore could only belong to Smokey. Lures and hooks left little rust stains on the brim, and it was too large for Shelby's head. It occurred to Dottie she'd never seen Smokey fishing out here.

She wished she'd come to see Smokey Black, but she hadn't been able to invent a reason to do it. She still had too much pride to go baking the man a cobbler. *Way* too much pride to beg someone to drive her out here to hand it over to him.

"That man lets the fish grow plenty big in here." Her father gestured to a bucketful beside him by way of a greeting. "Leaves them alone more than not, from what I can tell."

"He's too busy to fish much, I imagine."

"I am, too, normally." Shelby patted the grass beside him, but Dottie considered her skirt and remained standing. Her father breathed a long, contented sigh. "Can't recall the last time I cast a line. Up to this week, anyway."

"Are you frying them up, as well?"

"I fish in the early morning and in the afternoon, and then, yeah, dinner's all me." Now it seemed even her father was compelled to feed the handsome owner of Festival Farms. In this case, at least, it could be considered payment.

Her father's stillness was striking. No twitching fingers or feet. Dottie wished she could see his eyes, wondering if she would remember what they looked like sober.

"Sometimes Hugh comes out here and fishes a bit. Doesn't say a lot. You know Hugh?"

"Yes. Hugh and I worked together some days."

"Good man. Told him we'd find a spot for him at the park if he ever wants it. Same with Silas. The young man who can't hear?"

Dottie wondered if Hugh or Silas were ready to face the crowds at the park, though. She barely was.

"How are you feeling, Dad?"

"Good. Real good."

"Have you talked to Mom?"

He shook his head in defeat. "You?"

"Yes." Dottie didn't know how much to say about that. Her mother had cried, and she'd said she regretted sending her husband packing. If Shelby went back there, Dottie knew he would be re-admitted to his life as it had been.

She considered the yellow traces of bruising evident under the hat. The trouble was, his life as it had been was consuming the man she'd once admired. So, Dottie thought better about telling him what her mother had said. Let him think he was banished a little longer.

"No drink since you've been out here?"

"Where would I come by it?"

She was surprised to realize she'd missed this strong and steady voice she'd known as a child. How long had his dialect been one of slurred words?

"Tell me how the park is."

"Actually, I came out to ask you about arrangements for next week. I saw the posters for The Cardinals performing, but I can't find the folder with the contract or anything."

"Ask Walter."

"Walter's the rides, you know that. Who booked the Cardinals?"

"Thought you did. Before."

Dottie sighed. These were the kinds of balls that had been dropping all around her since she and her father, the chief jugglers, had lost focus.

"I didn't. I made initial contact back in February, but I didn't handle the booking."

"Then Hank or Richard must have." These would be two others of her sisters' husbands. "Wasn't me. Don't forget, the platform will need to be set up. I can come back and oversee that, though. I know the specs."

"You wrote them down. It's done."

Shelby nodded. "What'd we clear over the holiday weekend?"

Dottie told him, and he nodded again.

"Almost seems like the place is in good hands," he said with a sardonic laugh.

Dottie ground her molars. "It is in good hands."

"My own hands have been a bit shaky of late," he said. "I owe you an apology for that."

Of late? More irritation flared. They'd dealt with one another as business partners longer than they had as father and daughter.

"And you're really done with it? The drinking. Just like that?"

He cranked the reel on his rod, a soft whirring. "I mean to be."

This was simply too new an approach for her to know what to expect. Was it merely a gesture, designed to appease her mother? It was probably easier to make such an overture out here, with not a drop of booze to be found.

But the vacation destination, the get-away oasis where the two of them typically lived every waking minute ... that place was a different story. Temptation was always at hand there.

"There's no rush to come back. The place *is* in good hands, Dad."

Skepticism was clear in the glance he gave her. "Fact is, you're not yourself, Dottie."

"You mean people think of me as a killer."

"If that's what I meant, I'd have said it, wouldn't I? I mean you're not yourself."

And just how would he know that anymore? She ground her heel into the crisp carpet of grass. She thought about the father she'd needed these past few months, tried to imagine him keeping her close, standing up for her, taking care of her the way she didn't like admitting she'd needed to be taken care of.

Then she considered Shelby Berkeley as he reeled the line in, checked his bait, and cast it back out with a practiced flick of his arm.

This was her father. The one she'd been given here on earth. And if she wished things were different in some ways, what about it? *This* was what had made her. *Who* had made her, and hadn't her father's hands-off approach to his oldest daughter been somehow important in its own way?

Not good, but definitely important.

Just as Lil's walking out on her daughters had been important in Emily's and Rosie's stories. There was what she and her friends wished for ... and then there was the truth of the choices human beings made.

There had to be a path forward through that truth, rather than some wishy-washy side trail that got a person nowhere.

"You're right," she said to her father at last. "I haven't really been myself."

Turning away, Dottie reminded herself it wouldn't be his or anyone else's responsibility to do something about it.

~~~~~

When Smokey finally saw Dottie again, she was dressed once more in her usual professional clothing. She sat, though, with her legs stretched before her on the barn floor, Carlton the rabbit snug against her thigh.

Pee-Pee the goat was nudging her cheek, and she was slicing off bite-sized chunks of pears for him with a small paring knife. Pee-Pee scarfed the pieces out of her fingers, drawing a soft laugh from her each time.

Crossing the barn to her, watching her, Smokey knew he would do absolutely anything in the world for this woman.

He didn't go so far as to put a name to that emotion. He only knew that there was no end to what she could ask of him, nor to what he would happily take on.

"You're back." He leaned above her on one of the posts of the animals' pen.

She looked up, as though she was uncertain of him now. Would it be because she'd fallen apart that night he'd dropped her at Mama Pool's? They hadn't seen one another since.

Sensing her discomfort, Smokey set out to put her at ease. "Hugh told me he saw my mother drop you off a little bit ago."

"I can't stay long. I just needed to ask my father a few questions."

"There's plenty to do here if you do decide to stay."

"Don't tempt me with back-breaking labor, Smoke." She sliced off another piece of pear when Pee-Pee started nibbling at her tidy bun. "How is he doing? My father, I mean. Is he behaving?"

"There are no stages for him to fall off of here, if that's what you mean." He opened the gate wide enough to get closer. "Julia and her little girl come out a few days a week, and they're accomplishing a fair amount of work. Thanks for referring her."

"Thanks for employing her. She seems so happy, when I see her."

He rubbed a hand over the goat's head. Pee-Pee stared in his general direction, blinking long-lashed lids over his mostly blind eyes. "And how are you doing, Dottie B.?"

"Fine."

"Eh. Don't just say 'fine.' Not to me." They were past that.

When Pee-Pee got a little aggressive with her bun, Dottie awkwardly rose to standing in her pencil-line skirt. Smokey casually noticed her curves like he always did. More distracting this time, however, was a saliva-covered chunk of pear skin stuck to her backside.
~~~~~

"I saw you," she said, distracting him from the distraction. "At the concert. The other night, over by the pier? I saw you from a distance."

"I was checking up on you." What was the point of pretending he didn't care? They were past that, as well. "It had been nine days."

"Why didn't you come say hello? While you were over?"

"Just wanted to make sure you were ... you know."

"Fine?"

His face split into a smile.

"You used to dance a lot up there, at the ballroom," Dottie said. "Before the war. Why didn't you stay to dance the other night?"

"I guess I like it better out here now. Dottie ..." He was thinking about how to say he had missed her, but Pee-Pee the goat chose that moment to snag the significant remainder of the pear right out of Dottie's fingers.

Dottie screamed. Smokey stood there, wondering why she'd screamed.

Pee-Pee, also alarmed by her scream, darted past Smokey's legs, nearly knocking him over where he was leaning against the pen, and suddenly the blind goat was free in the world.

Indeed, Pee-Pee was off and running, but not with any speed. It was more of a dramatic and directionless meander.

Through the barn he wove, Dottie in comical pursuit, her stride hobbled by her skirt to the point she was not any more effective than Pee-Pee at covering distance. Smokey watched, trying to make sense of it.

"He's going to choke!" she exclaimed, moving to trap the goat at the corner by the door, which was when Smokey noticed she was still armed with the paring knife.

"The goat is fine, sweetheart."

Pee-Pee really was fine, but he was not cooperating. He worked what was left of the pear further into his mouth, which prompted more shouts of alarm from Dottie.

"The book says they can choke!" She was gasping. Lunging, missing, and gasping.

Pee-Pee, for his part, cleared the barn door with a lazy lunge of his own, pausing to look back in their general direction with what Smokey interpreted as a smug expression. Could the goat see well enough to know there were hundreds of acres of freedom before him? Pee-Pee did seem to be calculating his next move even as Dottie lurched her way toward him, hollering breathlessly about his airway.

Smokey was afraid the woman was in greater danger of dying today than was the goat.

Having secured the gate so the rest of his little menagerie couldn't join the game, Smokey reached for the metal feed bucket. At the edge of the barn door, he banged it against the threshold.

Pee-Pee had successfully swallowed the pear during the chase. Now, he turned, barreled right past Dottie and her pursuit, then ran full tilt at Smokey. Or, rather, at the bucket. Amused, Smokey guided the ornery animal back inside the gate, tossed the bucket to the side, and met Dottie back at the barn entrance. He brushed off his hands and shoved them in his pockets.

Dottie's shoulders heaved as she caught her breath. Two stray, dark curls were plastered to her neck.

"The book," she said, sucking in air. "It said to cut up the pear in bite … in bite-sized pieces. Or they would choke. The goats."

"Last week, Pee-Pee ate one of my leather work gloves."

"But …" There was a worry line between her eyes as she looked past him, presumably to verify the goat did, indeed, live on. "What if he'd choked today? What if I'd brought him that pear, and he'd choked today and died?"

Smokey took in her wide pupils, her pale cheeks. He remembered her passing out last Christmas when Rosie had sliced her hand in the kitchen of the Island Inn. "Honey, hand over that knife, will you?" He unraveled its handle from her white knuckles as she let visibly tense shoulders drop back against the doorframe. "There we are. Pee-Pee is fine."

How long would it take for her to stop seeing herself as a killer?

And wasn't that a question haunting so many in the aftermath of war?

Smokey shook off the thought and imagined Dottie, alone at the library reading a book about goats. Imagined her at the market buying a pear for Pee-Pee, carefully tucking it into her stylish handbag alongside a paring knife.

He had not lived adjacent to *this* woman for decades. Not *this one*. No. This one, he was still learning.

And he was enjoying the learning.

Smokey took two steps, pulled the other hand from his pocket, and used his thumb to caress a spot just under her ear. He smiled at her. "You made that goat's day. You did not hurt him one bit. I promise."

Dottie's eyes were still wide, her lips so pink. Her breath was moving fast over those lips. Was she about to cry again? Panic again? Smokey had only begun to wonder which it would be when she did the absolute last thing he was expecting.

She went up on her toes, stretched herself long, and pressed those same lips to the knot of Adam's apple in his throat.

"Dottie?" He blinked at her as she worked to reach him. He was a giant. She was on the small side. What was a man to do but help her? And, after all, he was the kind of man who liked to help others.

So, he slid closer, dipped his head, and let her move her lips right on up to his own.

Her arms also moved to snake around his neck, and he leaned into the kiss. Pear juice. She tasted like summer heat and pear juice. She must have cut a slice for herself before he'd arrived, and Smokey let himself enjoy it, enjoy her as he smiled against her mouth. Until he discovered he'd lifted her a little, and the wood of the broad doorway had her lightly pinned from the opposite side, and …

… and his mother sounded her car horn from almost *right beside them.*

Dottie's eyes flew open, and she was instantly in a kind of wiggling frenzy to drop back onto those heels of hers.

Mama Pool leaned her head out the window as the car rolled to a stop. Smokey waited for a scolding as he watched Dottie scramble in through the passenger door, but Mama Pool simply pushed her sunglasses down her nose until Smokey could see the icicles in her eyes.

Oh, he knew that look well.

There would be consequences, he figured, as the woman who'd brought him into the world stepped on the gas and covered him in a cloud of dust.

Looking down, Smokey spotted Dottie's paring knife sticking up from the packed dirt of the barn floor like it had fallen from the very great height of … well, his own hand.

Had he chucked the thing like a spear when he'd reached for her? It bothered him that he couldn't recall. He decided he'd better be much, much more careful.

Chapter Twenty

What had she been thinking?

In the days that followed that visit to the farm, Dottie hid in her office, agonizing over killing one of her favorite people. On top of that, she now found herself thinking about also killing one of her lifelong friendships.

At least the goat was alive.

"Smokey is so considerate." Julia Fey had stopped by the park office one morning. The woman's rented cottage was just a block away from the park, and she'd brought Penny—all pigtails and perfectly trimmed bangs—to feed the ducks off the boardwalk. The little girl had new shoes, thanks to Smokey Black's generosity as an employer. "Penny loves riding on the tractor with Smokey. Don't you, Honey?"

"'Mokey!" Penny's smile was pure sunlight. "Ride tractor!"

For possibly the first time, Dottie felt herself relating to a small child.

Julia went on to suggest Dottie join them out at the farm some evening, after supper. "It's a good time to water the plants. Cooler, you know?"

Dottie knew that very well. Times like this, she thought of herself as a seasoned farmhand, rather than what she'd really been: a career woman who had hidden among Christmas trees for a few weeks so that angry villagers would stop trying to destroy her.

The angry villagers still lurked in public places, of course. She'd fallen into a pattern these days of doing her shopping ten minutes before the market closed, which was a great way to avoid them.

Dottie had not yet been back to church.

Still, she told herself she was leading a full life. When Emily wasn't out covering a story, she would swing by to have lunch with her. Rosie would sail in now and then with a plate of cookies and an invitation to dinner. Dottie, who found reasons not to accept even those invitations, told herself she had all the friends and socializing she needed. Clearly.

Sometimes she found herself looking for Smokey on a crowded night, though. Construction on the new pier was close to complete, so she would venture out to check on progress. She was pleased with the new ballroom, the restaurants and rides. She didn't see Smokey out there, but why would she want him checking up on her, anyway? Who would want that?

Not her. Of course not.

July passed that way.

Though she'd had no sighting of Smokey at the park, Mama Pool would sometimes bring notes from him on folded sheets of paper when she'd come to help in the office.

I have a surprise for you. Come by the farm, read one note.

But she was very busy. And there was the fact she'd *kissed him*. Unfortunately, Dottie had lately added mortification to her constant state of guilt.

After all, the last two times she'd seen Smokey, she'd nearly hyperventilated, cried hard, and tried to kill his blind goat. And then, as if all that weren't enough, she'd kissed his *throat*. She hardly knew what to expect of her own behavior any longer, but the word mortification was what she kept settling on to describe it.

Mama Pool never spoke of what she'd seen that day in the barn door. As Dottie worked hard not to think about what it must have looked like, she also tried not to be insulted by the fact Mama Pool was apparently ignoring the whole incident.

The older woman's character was more given to open meddling than to quiet contemplation. When Dottie let herself think about it, she found the silence mildly insulting. Instead of butting in like Pee-Pee the goat to arrange love and marriage for her youngest son, instead of plotting a wedding between two people she wanted to see together … well, she wasn't doing any of it.

Even though Mama Pool loved her, she likely thought Dottie was crazy. That had to be it. No woman wanted her baby boy joined for life with a nervous-natured woman who boasted a criminal record.

At any rate, there was nothing romantic about the notes Smokey was sending through his mother. One missive featured a hand-drawn circle in the middle of the page roughly the size of a muskmelon. *Your pumpkins are averaging this size*, the scrawled note read. *Come see*.

But Dottie had plenty to occupy her in the stuffy office. Her father had returned, looking a little healthier, but his return had seemed to increase her workload rather than reduce it. After all, she had to keep a careful eye on him throughout the day in case her threats to his "friends" didn't discourage them from offering him booze.

Then, as the hot, dry month ended, a different message arrived, this time from the new preacher at the church: *I'll be stopping by your office on Thursday morning to introduce myself.*

So, early that Thursday morning, Dottie met Mama Pool at the office door dressed in crisp, new denim work pants, boots, and a floppy hat of her very own.

"I'd like to go out to the tree farm today," she said. "Would you mind driving me?"

There was only one person she wanted to face less than Smokey

Black, and that was the replacement of the man she had killed.

~~~~~

Smokey had helped his brother cut wheat at the main farm.

By the time he'd finished that, Shelby Berkeley had announced he was sober and ready to go back to his life.

Another broken-winged bird fixed and ready to fly. Smokey had cheerfully driven Dottie's father back to his house in Hebron so the man could make amends with his wife.

"Who will you go to when you want a drink?" Smokey had asked him on the way back to town.

In a way, he'd miss the camaraderie he'd developed with the energetic, visionary man … once he'd chewed him out about not protecting his daughter from scoundrels at the park. Beyond that, the pair of them had more in common than Smokey might have supposed.

"Maybe more important is who I *won't* go to when I want a drink." Shelby had punctuated that with his usual rich laugh on his way back to town. "But there's always Rip Carver. He kicked the liquor a few years back, Rip did. I reckon I could go pay him a visit."

"Rip's a good fellow. I can lend you an ear whenever you need one, too, for what it's worth."

"Wouldn't mind coming out to help with the harvest and the holiday tree cutting and such, when the time comes. To return your kindness."

"You're always welcome. But you owe me nothing."

He'd honked the horn of his truck in farewell as he'd pulled away from the Berkeley house. That was days ago now.

Today, as he mowed his way between fir trees on the tractor, a cloud of pollen and dandelion fluff floating around him, Smokey wondered how Shelby was doing balancing his lifestyle at the park with his new commitment to sobriety.

And he wondered, as he always did, how Dottie was doing there.

Was she pleased to have her father back? Was the man one more source of stress and worry for her, or was he now the ally she so desperately needed? Had Dottie considered managing less of the workload so Shelby, sober, would step back up to his responsibilities?

None of it was Smokey's business.

After all, she hadn't responded to any of his notes.

Still, she *had* kissed him.

In the war, Smokey had learned that sometimes, faced with panic, a person simply had to take some sort of action. Any sort of action. That kiss Dottie had pressed to his neck in the barn … a desperate need to act was probably the best way to explain why she'd done it.

She'd been on the verge of another meltdown, that was all. Thinking she might have endangered his goat, she'd simply moved impulsively.
~~~~~

There had been nothing romantic about that kiss, of course. It had simply been a distraction.

Just the same, there was the memory of the soft heat of her lips and that subtle flavor of pears. He thought about it more than he should.

He wished he *didn't* know now the way it felt to kiss Dottie Berkeley, no matter the reason she'd started it. How many times had he casually wondered about those lips of hers, off and on, over the years?

Not having to wonder—knowing—turned out to be far, far worse. Almost as bad as mowing on a day when the thermometer was reading ninety or more.

Smokey kept a handkerchief in his back pocket to wipe his face and neck. He pulled through the last row of firs, removed his hat to mop his brow, and paused mid-swipe to blink in surprise.

She was *here*.

His eyes burned with sweat, but there was no mistaking Dottie for anyone else. It was possible she was some kind of heat-induced mirage. But no … she was no hallucination, if only because he would never have built a fantasy about her in what appeared to be newly purchased denim work pants.

Or, at least, he never would have built a fantasy about her that way before *today*. He might every day after this, of course.

He watched her lead little Penny into the barn, bending to hold her hand.

He debated for exactly half a second. The barn, he decided, was getting complicated, and so was Dottie Berkeley. Nevertheless, he turned the tractor and mower in that direction.

Julia stopped weeding to join him, offering him a perky pumpkin update as they entered the barn. To Smokey's surprise, Hugh also relaxed in the shade of the barn. All of them—Julia, Penny, Dottie, Hugh, most likely himself—were red-cheeked from the heat. The others had just had enough sense to seek some shade.

Smokey's eyes tracked immediately to Dottie, wondering how she'd treat him after that kiss, wondering why she was here, wondering if she could get those dark curls into any tighter a bun at the top of her neck.

When she took off her sunhat and draped it on a post, the softer curls that usually framed her forehead were damp and stuck to her temples.

Penny was giggling over Carlton, who was eating out of her palm. "Bunny teeths tickle," she informed Hugh. She hardly needed to squat to get onto the rabbit's level, and Hugh was standing by with more food for her little hand.

Dottie looked down at the child, as well, smiling an uncharacteristically soft smile.

"Hi, Dottie." Smokey felt like a boy instead of a war hero.

"Hi. I, uh, hope you don't mind an extra pair of hands today." She met his eyes briefly, and he saw his same uncertainty mirrored there. Again. This was an aspect of the new Dottie that continued to unnerve him. Had she ever been uncertain about anything in her life?

Had he?

"I'm always happy for the help, especially since it seems most of my help prefers the shade to that blazing sun. Can't imagine why."

"I've been weeding for an hour," Julia put in, clearly worried her pay was about to be docked. The very idea made Smokey shake his head.

He smiled, too, to put her at ease. "I've been baking out there, myself, on the tractor."

"Tractor!" Penny jumped up from her squat to wave at him.

"Anyway, I was just thinking it's a better day for swimming than working."

"But …"

"Julia, I'll *pay* you all to jump in the pond and cool down."

"I didn't bring anything to swim in." This was Dottie.

"Whatever you jump in with will dry back out in the sun in ten minutes, darling. C'mon. Penny, tell the others it's play time." He tossed Dottie a slow wink at the word *play*, which he knew she would have ignored before. The new Dottie got redder in the cheeks. "Later, we need to cut boards and place them under those lovely pumpkins you ladies have got growing. But the sun won't set 'til near ten, and the pumpkin patch is better work for evening, don't you all think?"

"Swim!" Penny exclaimed now.

Hugh wordlessly rose and unbuttoned his ratty shirt. Beneath the shirt was a white-ish undershirt. They all watched the man stroll wordlessly out of the barn and turn in the direction of the pond. Hugh had decided to swim, indeed.

When Smokey looked over at Dottie and Julia, the three of them all burst into laughter.

It was laughter born of relief. With joy, Smokey mentally logged another sign of healing for his quiet friend who had served his country so well.

"Nothing for us but to follow his lead, then, ladies."

~~~~~

Wet denim most certainly did *not* dry in ten minutes, no matter how hot the sun was or what Smokey Black had decreed.

Dottie was comfortable enough beside the pond, on a blanket next to Julia, but she wished she'd brought her bathing suit out to the farm. Unlike the picnic on the Fourth of July, the little party of swimmers had nothing fancy among them. No fresh-squeezed lemonade. No salads or bread or cheese. Not even a towel.
~~~~~

They had only this blanket and the music of happy laughter coming from the water. Hugh liked to swim, it seemed, though he was sloppy about it compared with Smokey. The two men were in their sleeveless undershirts playing with Penny. They'd take turns holding her while the other did tricks. Then they'd found a turtle on a rock along the bank.

Smokey's skin was significantly darker by this time of summer, Dottie observed, her mouth a little dry as she watched him. Penny had demanded detailed explanations about his Navy tattoo. The child had decided she wanted a "birdie" tattoo just like that herself, which had prompted the former sailor to apologize to Julia.

Julia was watching Smokey more closely than she was watching her daughter.

"He's so good with her," she said, wringing out a clump of her own honey-colored hair.

"Yes. He's always loved kids." Dottie hadn't meant to lay claim to "always," but she accidentally had, just the same.

"I never would have expected a man that … *strong*, to also be so gentle."

There was something whimsical in her tone that had Dottie glancing over. "What was your husband like?"

Julia plucked a piece of thick grass and began to systematically shred it into strips.

"I'm sorry. It's none of my business. I know it must hurt to talk about him."

Julia merely shrugged. "It's been two years since he died. But everyone avoids talking to me about him. I don't mind talking about George, though. He was a navigator. Did I ever tell you that?" She glanced over, and Dottie shook her head. "Anyway, he was a good man. Penny was just a little thing when he left for the war, so it's hard to say …" Her voice trailed off as she watched Penny try to climb up Smokey's shoulders to escape the turtle he'd lifted in one hand.

"That's not a snapper," Dottie assured the child's mother. Running wild at the big lake all her life meant she could identify a turtle from any distance.

"I wasn't worried. Smokey would never let anything happen to her."

It was spoken with the assurance of experience, and Dottie realized most of a month had now passed since she'd arranged for Julia and Penny to spend time out here at Smokey's farm. And a month, Dottie well knew, was more than enough to develop a hankering for Smokey Black.

How much of that time had the three of them spent together, exactly? Uneasy, Dottie wondered if she was outside looking in today, and she'd only just picked up on it.

She pushed up off her elbow and reached for a grass blade of her own. Instead of shredding it, she rolled it into a tight straw.

Her first, most uncharitable thought was to find Julia a more regular position at the park office. *Away* from Smokey Black. Wouldn't Julia be happier out of the sun and heat? She could build her office skills with more and more experience. Another worker would be a relief. The office staff often got busy during the season, after all.

Dottie could use the extra help. Little Penny, too, would be welcome in the park office.

She looked over at the young mother, and she couldn't help seeing how sweet and kind she was. Those qualities shone all around the woman, a sort of golden aura.

Sweet, kind, lovely.

Meanwhile, Dottie was a monster, plotting to remove Julia from this place and this man she and her little girl both seemed to think was absolute perfection.

Smokey had always been romantic, fanciful.

Dottie dealt in facts.

And the fact was, Julia seemed quite smitten with Smokey. Which made her think this churning in her stomach was some kind of … jealousy. *Was* she jealous? Could it be termed something simple like "jealousy" after she'd nurtured it for such an embarrassingly long time?

First, there had been those girls from their school days who had hung all over him. He hadn't seemed to mind them, but Dottie had minded. Though she was younger than him, she'd minded. She'd minded that they wanted to trap him into an ordinary life. She'd very much minded the idea that he would let them. That he would love them.

She'd never been in the running for his heart, anyway. So, was it even jealousy Dottie felt as she considered, for the first time, how perfect Julia and Smokey would be together?

She'd been afraid he'd be trapped into some ordinary life. The fact was, though, the ridiculously romantic and idealistic Smokey Black seemed like he might *want* that ordinary family life.

Maybe she'd been more worried about herself, rather than him. Had she been projecting her own fears? Dottie did not expect an ordinary life. Less now than ever. She could root for other people to enjoy it, but even when she looked around at them, she still couldn't bring herself to anticipate anything normal for herself. Perhaps she'd been ruined early on by horses diving off platforms into flaming pools, by the misfits in the freak show, by dancers like Lil and their stories from the road.

Smokey had been brought up on whimsical expeditions for the perfect Christmas tree, his daddy's banjo on the porch on sleepy Sunday afternoons, his mama's homemade pie.

A life like that—full of lovely, ordinary things—would be a dream for sweet Julia Fey. And a fine way for little Penny to grow up.

Were she to marry Smokey Black, Julia would have leisure time to care for Penny, and mother and daughter would never have to worry about money again. Julia could have even more sweet children. She was clearly a wonderful mother. Julia could help Smokey design his house up on the hill overlooking the Christmas tree farm, and she would make it a welcoming home for him with all her domestic talents.

Julia's black raspberry cobbler had been a highlight at every church gathering, and the woman was a talented and stylish seamstress. She and Penny were always clean, well-dressed in simple fabrics, and kind to everyone they met.

The late George Fey, the navigator who had died for his country, had been blessed in marriage, indeed. Then, there was Smokey, of course, who had a heart for his fallen comrades and the families they'd left behind.

No, Dottie decided with a sense of sorrow that might once have been jealousy. Julia didn't need to learn office accounting or shorthand. *She needed to marry a good man.* One who was good with kids, who had land and endless patience and security.

Accepting what she knew she needed to do, Dottie threw her little rolled ball of grass back to the ground and sighed a little louder than she meant to.

"Are you okay?" Julia's powder blue eyes were pure, innocent concern across the blanket.

"Depends. Whose definition of okay are we using?"

Chapter Twenty-One

When Smokey returned to the blanket, Penny riding on his hip, Dottie disciplined herself to look away from the picture they made. The charming nurturer who lit up all over whenever a little child lit up all over. The angelic little girl looking up into his face with total trust.

This was a man for another kind of woman, as he'd always been. Always. So, Dottie averted her eyes, let Julia go on drinking him in, and contemplated her status as an old maid.

She'd had a good life alone. She'd simply have to work to make it a good life again. Dottie was sure, especially now that she was so broken, that a life like her mother's or lives like her sisters' would simply not work for her.

Unfortunately, she was attracted to Smokey Black. So, what? She'd always been attracted to him. Who hadn't been? That was merely a normal, female reaction to a fine-looking man. And if she felt pulled to him beyond reasonable explanation, well, that didn't mean such a pull was automatically healthy.

She'd also been pulled to fast cars, and everyone at the lake knew where that had gotten her.

Dottie's thoughts were interrupted by a long, high-pitched, "Nooooooo." Penny claimed all their attention when she was plopped down against her will on the edge of the blanket.

Dottie liked Penny better than she liked most very small children, but the little girl did love to test the power of the word "No." It was usually followed by some babel only her mother understood.

"Swim time is over, Baby." Julia reached for her daughter. From the corner of her vision, Dottie noticed Smokey pulling his shirt over his dripping torso.

Meanwhile, at the edge of the pond, Hugh waved farewell and turned to walk away. She wondered where he would go now. He must have reached his limit on interaction for this day.

Penny *definitely* had. Now she was running around in the dry, prickly grass, crying because the blades were hurting her tender, bare feet but also crying because staying on the blanket meant putting clothes on.

"No blanket!"

"No dress! No!"

Another old maid might find Penny's temper tantrum reprehensible, but Dottie was enjoying it. For one thing, she herself resented clothing on such a hot day. Running about in damp underclothes did seem wiser, so why wouldn't the child challenge buttons and collar? She was the smart one, really.

For another thing, Penny was rather adorable in a fit. Her bright pink cheeks, her spiky little lashes below dripping bangs, and that pouty, dramatic lower lip … Dottie felt some absurd instinct to gather her up.

But then what in the world would she do with her?

Penny opted to wrap herself firmly around Smokey's tree trunk of a leg, crying with gusto. Once again, who was Dottie to judge the little tyke's preferences?

"I can take her back into the water if you want," Smokey stage whispered to Julia, looking helpless in the face of the meltdown. Julia, flustered, was gathering her daughter's socks in preparation for her next move in the battle.

"Thank you, but no," she sighed, embracing Penny's favorite vocabulary. "I hoped being late for her nap would work out today since she was having such fun, but clearly, she needs to rest. Come on, sweet girl. Let's get you home."

That plan was the opposite of play time in the water with her favorite friendly giant, so Penny only cried harder. "Nooooo!"

Even as she wrestled Penny into her dress with firm hands, Julia got Dottie's attention. "Would you like a ride back to town with us?"

Dottie was wondering how the pinwheeling little girl would be smashed into a vehicle when Penny simply melted onto her mother's shoulder in surrender. She closed her eyes, and that was that.

What time was it? Dottie tried to find her watch in her purse. She'd taken it off when she got into the water. She must be careful not to return to the office until the new pastor would have come and gone.

But Smokey entered the conversation, his gaze on Dottie. "I could still use some help sliding those pieces of board under the pumpkins, if you don't have anything pressing back at the lake. I can run you home in the truck when we finish."

Dottie knew she shouldn't stay. She needed to keep an eye on her father, not on this man the Good Lord might have tapped to solve all of Julia's troubles.

"I probably should get back for supper." Even she knew that was ridiculous. She rarely felt like eating.

"Believe it or not, I do keep food at my place," he countered with an easy smile, bending at the waist to scoop up the blanket he'd snagged from the barn. "Princess Cream Puff would probably be honored to dine with you."

She rolled her eyes but smiled at the thought of the three-legged cat she had missed. It was the cat, not his charm, that had her nodding in defeat.

The two of them walked Julia and Penny to the car. Dottie watched for signs that she was cutting in, that she was destroying this sweet widow's long-term plans by remaining here to tend pumpkins with the most eligible man at Buckeye Lake, but Julia was reliably perky and pleasant as she bid them a good night.

"See you tomorrow," Smokey called, also pleasantly, a hand raised as Julia guided the car down the gravel path that wound through the farm to the road.

He was so open, so giving, that Dottie had trouble reading the man. After all, didn't he treat Julia, Hugh, his mother, her own father and even Dottie herself with identical kindness and respect?

They strolled in silence toward the cabin.

How did a person like her decide who mattered to a person like Smokey? Certainly, it seemed *every*one mattered to a person like him. Especially the broken and needy ones. Dottie knew herself to be one of his projects. A project who, regretfully, kissed him on the throat and then on the mouth the last time they'd been alone.

She felt certain that neither Hugh nor her father nor that ancient turkey in the barn had ever put Smokey in that kind of position.

Had Julia, though?

On cue, Princess Cream Puff appeared around the corner of Smokey's cabin, hobbling straight for her owner like she knew she mattered to him.

"There she is." His voice rumbled like the pitch of Cream Puff's comically loud purr as he scooped her up. "Looks like her highness needs her belly scratched."

Smokey flipped the cat into the crook of his arm like a baby, and Cream Puff predictably went along with it, stretching her three remaining legs into the air while he gave her tummy a rub.

"Um. I saw the sign out front," Dottie said over the cat's weird purr.

Smokey grinned. "Welcome to Holiday Farms! Formerly Festival Farms. Are you pleased?"

"Smokey." She couldn't help but smile back. "I only suggested it lightly that night, that you change the name of this place. You didn't have to just ... go *do* it!"

"I know I didn't." He rocked the cat a little, and Cream Puff's eyes slit with lazy contentment. "The more I thought about it, the more I liked it. I told you in the note I had a surprise, but you sure took your time coming back out to see it."

"Yes."

"Anyway, I figured you'd be pleased I let you boss me around." Then he gave her one of his usual winks.

"I mean …" Dottie said, thoughtful. It really was a better name. "You know, you can do a whole concept with this holiday angle. I have loads of ideas."

"Of course you do, and I want to hear them." He said it like he *enjoyed* that she had the ideas and like he *did* want to hear them. "Maybe over supper?"

Dottie nodded.

He set Cream Puff gently onto the ground, where the cat rubbed the side of her head against his pant leg. It was a mirror of the same scene minutes before with little Penny. "How about I change into dry clothes and go load the boards into the wagon? The ones we'll slide under the pumpkins."

"Look, I know this should be obvious, but why exactly are we putting boards under the pumpkins?"

"Gets 'em off the dirt as they grow bigger. This way they don't get all ugly in the mud on one side. While I do that, maybe you could whip us up something to eat?"

He said it casually, already heading into the cabin to start executing his plan. A cold unease slid through Dottie, defying the heat. Dottie Berkeley did not "whip things up." At least, not *edible* things. Perhaps he'd consider trading her tasks? She could certainly load wooden boards onto a wagon.

After he'd changed into dry clothes, though, he had, indeed, left her in control of his cabin. Dottie shamelessly took advantage of the opportunity to explore, which was as good a distraction as any from preparing food.

The little space was two rooms with a fireplace in the dividing wall that would warm both rooms in winter — one room had a bed made with military precision, and the other had a scarred oak table and two chairs. A wide rocking chair of dark wood that certainly had stories of its own sat on a braided oval rug of rust and yellows.

Dottie touched a glass evergreen tree on the rustic fireplace mantle. With her thumb, she rubbed a bit of dust from the green glass. Clearly, Rosie had made this. Dottie smiled, thinking of her artist friend trading this lovingly crafted glass tree for a live tree for her little boy.

Then she thought of the spot Smokey had staked out farther up the hill that would boast a bigger, more finished home. He talked about that future home a good deal. The electric cooperative had come this far out now, and the man seemed to have grand plans for indoor plumbing. When that home was finished, which of these trinkets and cast-off family furnishings would make the move up there?

Would he keep this quaint little cabin with its laundry line stretched between trees, or would he tear it down?

The cabin had been rapidly assembled, she knew, by Reggie Black and his farmhands as a "welcome home" surprise for Smokey at the war's end. Dottie had heard updates regularly from Mama Pool at the park—how she'd donated her old cookstove to the project as an excuse to buy a brand new one for her own kitchen.

Moving into the little kitchen nook, Dottie ran her hand over the Andes stove now, imagining her older friend "whipping up" farm-worthy meals for the hungry men in her family. The stove didn't seem fancy enough for projects like that, but Dottie wondered if the secret rested more in the cook than with the stove. Mama Pool could likely feed a football team with a few logs and a match.

Dottie's own stomach fluttered at the thought of feeding herself and one man.

She took a calming breath and considered a basket of potatoes under the open window. Potatoes were so non-threatening. Above those harmless spuds, hooked onto a rough beam of wood, was a slightly more intimidating cast iron skillet.

Potatoes. Pan. Dottie experienced her first moment of hope. The coals would already be kept hot, she knew, so she added wood from a pile beside the stove. It was the last thing she wanted to do in the already stifling cabin, but now she had plenty of heat going.

She figured that was an important first step. Though her own mother's stove was gas, Dottie remembered as a girl hearing that the left side of a coal stovetop burned hotter because of where the fire burned. So, she used the handle to pull up the cover of a burner on the left and placed the empty skillet on it to heat up.

Determined and pleased she'd spent hours peeling potatoes with Freddy the French Fry Man on the pier, she located a peeler next, and soon she was happily slicing white disks a quarter-of-an-inch thick. She even tested her ability to cut spuds and hum a tune at the same time, which also turned out fine.

Now she wished Smokey would wander in and see her happily chopping in such a domestic and capable manner. If only she had an apron to cover her still not-entirely-dry denim slacks. An apron with frills on the edges would be ideal. Perhaps Dottie had been too quick to assume she wasn't cut out for this kind of task. *Ordinary* was turning out to be rather fun.

Next, she knew she'd need to push those slices of potatoes into the pan, and then all she'd have to do was flip them around until they turned golden-colored. Though her mother had early given up teaching Dottie to cook because she was always "up at the lake" with Shelby, Dottie remembered watching her mother fry up potatoes on occasion.

Men liked fried potatoes. She was certain.

What she was less certain of was whether the pan she'd placed on the burner was ready for the potatoes or how to tell if it was. She chewed on her lower lip. Experiences with her mother and watching Freddy make the fries told her a *sizzling* sound was crucial for success. There was nothing to do, she supposed, but dump the discs into the pan and see what happened.

When she did, they sizzled. *A lot.*

And then they stubbornly resisted being flipped.

~~~~~

Smokey sang his usual questionable mix of hymns and sailor ditties as he pulled the Allis-Chalmers alongside the cabin. He felt content in the knowledge that Dottie would climb up onto the seat next to him in a few minutes. He thought about how good she always smelled. He thought about enjoying the prolonged twilight in the pumpkin patch, knowing they would laugh together there.

Dottie had a magnificent laugh, and she was one of his oldest friends. She was a dazzlingly smart businesswoman. She'd always been pretty as a picture. These days—since she'd kissed him in the barn—he wondered if she enjoyed him as much as he enjoyed her.

Or the *way* he enjoyed her.

Smokey didn't make it more complicated than that. He wanted to be alone with her tonight, with Dottie and their pumpkins, and that was all he needed.

Then he smelled something. Something like sweet smoke. No, *acrid* smoke. Nothing like dinner and everything like disaster.

But when he shut down the tractor and dropped to the ground, he was greeted not just by that smell but also by Lucille Armstrong's shining Oldsmobile. She must have followed the tractor and its board-loaded trailer up the drive. He hadn't heard her approach over the tractor's engine.

"Hey there, Smokey Black," Lucille called in her sing-song soprano.

"Hey there, Lucille." Like Dottie, he'd known Lucille for a long time, yet it struck him that he knew her very little. She had platinum hair in perfect, frozen waves. She had grown up around show ponies, and she congratulated herself on throwing tasteful parties that Smokey had a talent for avoiding.

Which reminded him that Lucille Armstrong was also relentless regarding those parties.

"Missed you Saturday," she said, predictably.

"Lots to do 'round here."

"What's that smokey smell, Smokey?" She giggled at her play on words. "You set fire to your quaint little … abode?"
~~~~~

Smokey couldn't answer that yet but was determined to as he moved to the door.

"I cooked you up a pork roast so juicy it'll make you cry."

Smokey didn't cry over food, but he didn't say so. Lucille was right there with him, her and her roasting pan. The mouth-watering smells coming from the pan warred with the increasingly disturbing smoke as he reached for the doorknob.

Then, there was Dottie.

She flung open the door before he could, leading with a pan of chaos. "Watch out!"

Stumbling backward, Smokey's first concern was for Dottie, whose hands were covered in quilted mitts, quickly assessing to make sure she wasn't hurt. Something was sizzling under all the smoke.

It was Lucille who exclaimed, "My heavens!"

Dottie's curls had gone from pond-damp to smoke-frizzed around her red face, and Smokey thought she was either crying or reacting to the smoke, based on her streaming eyes. She rushed past them and all but threw the billowing pan onto his wood chopping stump. In it, a congealed mass of black still burned. Was the pan itself *melting*? Was that even possible?

"Are your hands burned?" he asked, reaching down to pull the mitts off her forearms. "Dottie?"

All she seemed capable of doing was coughing and gasping for breath, but her hands did look just fine. They shook a bit, that was all. As he inspected the soft pink of her palms, Lucille was inspecting the contents of the pan with the expression one might use to determine the cause of death in a grisly murder. She still toted her own shiny roasting pan.

"*What* was that supposed to be?"

Dottie spoke for the first time, her voice a little raw, probably from inhaling all the smoke. "Potatoes. They're potatoes."

"Well!" Lucille's gaze moved to Dottie's person with similar disgust. "Good thing I brought supper, I suppose."

~~~~~

Maybe it was too much smoke and too little oxygen.

Maybe it was the overpowering heat of the kitchen where things had gone so wrong. A pan too hot, like the day.

Maybe it was those stakes up on the hill where Smokey Black was waiting to build his bride the house of her dreams. And maybe Dottie Berkeley had always, always known that ideal woman couldn't be her.

Or, likely, it was the fact Dottie had been looked at *in just that same* condescending way by Smokey Black and other females so many times before. Amused pity. She was suddenly a gangly kid again, dressed for back road racing in Reggie Black's jalopy. She was the girl in the bun with
~~~~~

the clipboard organizing the beauty pageant Lucille won. Dottie herself bore the dubious honor of having mail-ordered the tiara Lucille had worn in that pageant.

Whatever the cause, something new snapped in Dottie's mind as the pan smoked. She was still that same pitiful girl, after all, and added to that, she was now a killer and an outcast. One who couldn't manage to fry up a *potato* in a pan.

For reasons she couldn't entirely explain, Dottie decided she would simply leave.

Smokey had followed Lucille inside the cabin, presumably to make sure Dottie hadn't started any actual fires. She had not. She knew she had not. She had merely melted potatoes onto cast iron.

Before Dottie managed her exit, she heard Lucille through the open window, exclaiming over the mess and the smell. "Really, Smokey." A dainty cough. "Don't you worry about what having *her* out here will do to business come fall?" From there, Dottie couldn't understand what else Lucille said, but her tone was easy enough to discern.

Aren't you just every man's … ideal? The words were always there. Implied, if not directly said, by all the ones who *were* that ideal.

Dottie glanced at Lucille's Olds, at Smokey's truck parked over at the ridge, even at the tractor, and she remembered that she was forbidden to drive.

Also, she was *afraid* to drive, when it came down to it. Very afraid.

So, she began walking. Up the rise behind the cabin, past the orange-tipped stakes for the homestead and into the trees that bordered this side of Festival Farms. Holiday Farms. Whichever. She would cut through the little wooded area until she came back down onto the road, which led to Mama Pool's sprawling farmhouse less than a mile away. An easy walk.

Dottie did not let herself cry. There had been enough of that. Crying was getting her nowhere.

One thing was certain. She would not put herself in a position to watch Smokey Black make happy sounds over Lucille Armstrong's roasting pan, whatever was in there. She would not observe Lucille squeezing his muscles and trying to toss her lacquered hair. Nor was she even in the mood just now to think about Smokey settling into a happy life with Julia Fey, however much Julia and little Penny deserved it. And however much Julia was infinitely preferable to Lucille.

Dottie stormed through the narrow forest.

She realized she'd assumed Lucille was the problem, that Lucille was the reason she needed to find somewhere else to be this evening. But the truth was, it was Smokey. Dottie decided *she despised him.*

She hated the way he made everyone think they mattered to him, until a woman might bring him food for years, clinging to the way he made her feel. Poor Lucille. Poor Nettie. Poor all of them. She hated the way he *knew* how his smile got him whatever he wanted, the way he shamelessly used children and lame animals to seduce, the way he never looked anywhere but into a woman's eyes when she was talking to him.

All of it was by design.

He'd made a study of human hearts, and he used the data to ensnare.

He could even lure women who didn't want the kind of life he wanted.

Dottie was livid, and she felt her own heart pounding as she marched through last autumn's crumbled leaves over the uneven ground, emerging into the tall grass of the roadside ditch. She could see the Black-Pool farmhouse ahead. Jumping the ditch, she felt her left ankle twist, which only made her angrier.

This, too, was Smokey Black's fault. Her ankle throbbed. How would her cream high heels feel on that foot tomorrow morning when she met with the ballroom contractor?

She reached the rocks of the roadway. At the same time, a cloud of dust announced a truck approaching from the east. Of course, it was *his* truck. Chin high, she concentrated on not limping and on maintaining her pace.

No matter what.

~~~~~

Smokey spotted Dottie with relief when she leapt from the high weeds on his side of the road like a clumsy deer. *What was she doing?* She must have hiked through the woods. But *why*?

His truck window was already rolled down when he pulled alongside her, his foot on the brake to keep the vehicle at a crawl. He leaned out the window, just two feet from Dottie's flushed cheeks. She was stomping a little unevenly, swinging her arms. She smelled like smoke.

His confusion didn't prevent him from seeing the absurd picture they made.

"Uh. Dottie?"

She somehow managed to walk faster, stretching her stride in those work pants.

"What are you doing?"

No answer.

"Get in. Let's talk."

There was only the hum of the truck engine and the determined crunch of the country road beneath her boots. Was she limping?

"Are you hurt?"

Still nothing.

Smokey had been in many a battle overseas. He had led his unit,
~~~~~

made decisions under fire, strategized in ways that always got the job done. He even had some medals to prove it.

But he had no idea what to do now, as he paced this clearly livid woman from behind the wheel of his truck. Her forehead glistened, and her lips were set in a grim line. Should he stop the truck and get out? Grab her and make her talk to him? Somehow force her to help him figure out what he'd done to make her pretend his existence away?

"Dottie, please."

Was this about his pan? Had she been worried he'd be cross with her about it? He didn't care about the pan. And he didn't care that much about the potatoes stuck to it. Why would she think he *did* care about those things?

He wanted to work in the pumpkin patch alongside her, that was all. That was all he wanted tonight.

"I'm not upset about the pan, you know."

Smokey stopped the truck, then, when Dottie took off *running*. Like some kind of track star, she pumped her arms and ran—yes, she was, in fact, limping a little—across the road right in front of him, over the culvert and into Mama Pool's front yard. He watched her, amazed, as she zipped across the lawn to escape him.

Of course, his mother appeared on the porch, a dish towel in one hand, shielding her eyes with the other to see what was going on.

He was in very big trouble. Again.

Chapter Twenty-Two

Smokey had slid boards under pumpkins until the sun had set. Alone. Then he'd risen with the sun to finish the job. Alone. Now, he brooded in his mother's kitchen.

Good help was sometimes hard to find.

Good help sometimes even ran down the road to *escape*.

"You only get to drink my coffee after you explain what you've been doing to Dottie." Mama Pool moved across her kitchen to block the coffee pot, arms crossed.

"When you phrase it like that, look at me like that, it almost seems like you expect the worst of me." He was tired, and the coffee smelled good. "My own mother."

"Don't give me that. I kept my mouth shut about whatever you two were up to in the barn that day."

"You kept your mouth shut to *her*. Definitely not to me. Like I told you, we kissed. One quick kiss. You're making everything sound so sordid."

"Says the man who chased a woman down in his truck last night. You caveman."

"Cavemen didn't have trucks."

He needed that coffee, but she remained in his path. Instead, he sighed and reached for the loaf of raisin bread on a sunny yellow plate. He considered ripping off a hunk of it, but experience with his mother told him the proverbial ice he was on was too thin for that.

"Need a knife to cut a slice, Son?" She said it sweetly, too sweetly, so that he was barely surprised when she turned to the counter and back around with a knife pointed at his chest in one smooth, fast move.

"What, now you're going to stab me? Slice my jugular?"

"If you don't start talking."

"You've been watching too many movies, Mama. Besides, this is my business. I'm handling it."

"What do you mean by 'this'? Which 'this' is your business? Huh? Dottie Berkeley? Are you referring to Dottie as your *business*?"

"Well, not when you say it like that. Will you please give me a break? Or, at the very least, some coffee?"

"That woman belongs to God and to herself, Son, and don't you forget it."

She was enjoying herself, he knew, and he ought to just let her. And he *would* just let her if it weren't for the fact he was missing important pieces of the puzzle that made up his own personal life. His life might be his business, but he might have exaggerated handling it.

He swallowed whatever was left of his pride. "What did she do last night, anyway? After she got here?" He had not been permitted entrance, of course. "Did she say anything?"

"And now you think you're in the position to ask me questions. Answer mine, first."

"I'll go to Reggie's for coffee." Sure, Smokey could have made his own, but he hadn't wanted to be alone with his thoughts in that reeking cabin.

"Reggie? What good would he do you? Reggie didn't drive Dottie home last night, now did he?"

"How would I know?" He blew out a breath in frustration. "Look, was she limping? Did she look like she was favoring her right leg when she got here to the house?"

"She mentioned her left ankle was sore."

"You can't think *I'm* responsible for that."

"Of course not. I think you're responsible for making her run down the road away from you. What happened last night?"

"She didn't say?"

How he longed for a clue. His mother just stared him down.

"Everything seemed fine, but then Lucille showed up."

"Lucille Armstrong."

"She brought food, said some things." He didn't tell his mother about whatever Dottie had done to his cast iron skillet. It felt like betrayal. "I told Lucille to leave."

One of Mama Pool's eyebrows went up. "You really told her to leave?"

"Yes! Honestly, she was being cruel."

"She can be."

"Well, it's not something I put up with, even in exchange for pork roast, and I told her that."

"So, you stood up for Dottie."

"Of course, I did." He had no idea what Dottie had been trying to cook. A pile of potato peels told him potatoes had originally been involved, but that was between Dottie and his wrecked pan.

"Are you two a couple? Are you *seeing* Dottie Berkeley?"

"No." Last night had been the first time he'd seen her in too long. He'd spent days building the big, new sign for Holiday Farms, nailing straight branches within a frame to create the charming letters. He'd painted the letters white like the fence beneath it. Dottie would relish giving him directions on embellishing the sign with colored leaves in the fall and evergreen boughs at Christmas.

He could already see it in his mind's eye, the potential magic of that sign. But he wanted Dottie to own that magic, too.

"Smokey, that girl's going through a lot right now." Mama Pool said it as though he'd confessed to using her for some nefarious purpose.

He kept his mood in check. "I know. I was there for the accident, remember?"

She sighed and turned again, slowly this time. She cut him a thick slice of raisin bread, and she paired it with a cup of coffee that she placed beside him. He immediately slurped from the cup. It was so hot. From her look of satisfaction over his wince, he figured he'd effectively washed away the rest of her motherly chagrin.

"I don't want to see her hurt, that's all," Mama Pool said, gentle now and a little sad.

But Smokey knew it was too late for that. Dottie, he was beginning to think, had been hurt over and over again all her life.

~~~~~

It was merely coincidence, Dottie told herself, that a deformed duckling found her on the north shore boardwalk that morning.

These days, she only walked the pier when it was very early or when she had to meet with the contractors about the final touches to the new ballroom. She'd been too restless to stay in bed this morning, so she'd decided to watch the sun rise from the end of the pier.

There was fog, which made an impressionist painting of that sunrise, turning the air around the sleepy park a soft marmalade color. She bent to pick up an occasional piece of trash, already knowing it would be a very humid day. It felt like it might even storm later.

Had Smokey gotten his boards under the pumpkins? She didn't figure Lucille Armstrong would have stayed to help him in her stylish outfit. Lucille would cook for the man, clearly, but something told Dottie she'd draw the line at dirty work.

Just as Dottie drew the line at cooking, it seemed.

After a fitful night of sleep, she had to admit she didn't despise Smokey. Not exactly. She was simply disappointed in him.

She was disappointed in all men, really, but other men were so much easier to forgive. Smokey Black should be better, should know better than to prioritize certain qualities over others. He should know better than to be friendly to Lucille, to dine on the contents of the pan she'd provided, to let her say the things she'd said inside the cabin.

Dottie might not be able to plan and execute a home-cooked meal that a human could digest, but she could plan and execute this new pier with its enhanced attractions and bigger-than-ever ballroom. She could
~~~~~

make a hundred split-second decisions all day to keep thousands of people safe and happy. She could even invest profits wisely.

Why hadn't he stood up for her?

Not that she expected him to eat potatoes that were partially flaming. But … still.

She was so lost in trying to justify her existence, in trying to convince herself she had any value to the males of her own species, that she almost missed the mustard-colored duckling in the morning mist.

It drew her attention, though, because it was alone, stumbling about on the pier.

His fuzzy neck was S-shaped and curled backwards. He lost his balance, beak turned up to the foggy sunrise, and then he couldn't get up again. Dottie watched his dark, webbed feet wiggle in the air, half-spinning his body on the wooden walkway. Instinctively, she knelt and gently righted him. Once on his feet, she watched his neck bend backward so that the dark-striped top of his head rested on his fuzzy back.

"Oh, dear." Dottie considered the little thing, knowing her sore ankle was making her stumble a bit, too. She also knew how hard it was to get back up after falling, especially when a body was all alone. "Poor little guy. I think you're looking for a farm and a fool of a man named Smokey Black," she told it as it lost its balance all over again and sprawled upon the boardwalk.

Dottie chewed on her lower lip and sighed. This little creature was unwell, too unwell to mind being handled, it seemed. She scooped it up, knowing she never would have done so before she'd spent her time with all the misfits in the petting zoo at Festival—no, *Holiday* Farms.

"The trouble seems to be with your neck, little fellow." She checked her wristwatch. The library would open in two hours. Dottie did not like going to the library any more than she liked going anywhere during daylight hours. She'd become like some vampire or other creature of the night. Anyway, there were painful memories at the library now, just like at the post office.

She'd stopped expecting people in general to be kind.

At least at the library she could tell herself that they avoided talking to her because it was a quiet environment. She had to visit there periodically, anyway, because she often needed answers to her questions. It just so happened that she knew the Dewey Decimal System quite well.

"Just let me do some research, and we'll fix you right up," she told the duckling. It stared up at her because its head wouldn't go any other way. She hoped the duck thought she sounded confident. In truth, she desperately wanted to call Smokey. He would know what to do without even going to the library, and he'd make a successful project of the fuzzy little guy. Smokey would have him strutting around his petting zoo and swimming on his farm pond. Goodness, the man would probably get into the water alongside him to demonstrate proper swimming techniques.

The thought made her lips twitch.

Then she remembered how disappointed she was in Smokey Black. He hadn't stuck up for her. He didn't deserve this precious, deformed duckling, and he certainly didn't deserve her own presence on his stupid farm.

Julia could have him, Dottie decided with a sense of what she told herself was peace. Julia could be the one to dust his glass evergreen on the mantle and face those cursed cast iron pans three times a day every day for the rest of her life. She seemed to like such things.

Dottie's life was already ruined. The least she could do was secure Julia's and little Penny's futures.

In fact, if she did, that might just be a mark back in the credit column for her own soul. While it was true that ending Pastor Skip's life was a huge blot in the debit column, perhaps there was still time for her to bank some good deeds. To produce that good fruit Pastor Skip had inspired her with before she'd messed up everything so badly.

Dottie ended her morning walk with two projects before her.

First, she would fix this duck. Then, she'd encourage Smokey and Julia to live happily ever after.

That second part still made her stomach hurt, but at least Lucille Armstrong wouldn't get him.

Chapter Twenty-Three

Smokey swallowed his pride.

He finally asked his mother when the best time was to find Dottie Berkeley in the park office on the boardwalk.

He'd driven in every day to talk with her, and everyday Lil Graham had grimly informed him Miss Berkeley was "out this time of day." Changing his visits to varied times, however, had not changed this message.

"She can see me coming up the boardwalk, can't she?" he'd asked Lil yesterday. In response, the woman had stared hard at a typewriter, but from inside the park office Smokey could see out that wide picture window that overlooked the better part of the midway.

The question was, where had Dottie run to when she'd seen him coming? Upstairs to her apartment? Out the back door and through the alley to Emily's newspaper office or to Rosie's studio?

And he hadn't done anything wrong!

He kept repeating that mantra to himself as, today, at midday, he approached Dottie's office through the back alley that ran in between a bank of trees and the amusement park's sprawling parking lot. It was a crowded day. The lot was already overflowing along Route 79. Smokey had parked at the post office up the road and hiked in through the back.

Instead of flowers, he held a large Bell canning jar in the crook of his arm as he tapped on the locked back door of the Buckeye Lake Amusement Park office.

His mother wouldn't be there today, he knew, but she'd assured him Dottie would be. Lil might or might not be. She sometimes worked at the marina. Julia also came in during the heat of the day, he knew, so she could learn bookkeeping while Penny napped on a cot.

So, he was happy, indeed, when Dottie herself opened the back door and then opened her eyes wide in surprise.

"Smokey!"

"Dottie."

She didn't look particularly pleased, but that didn't change the relief he felt at laying eyes on her again. Her hair was in its office mode rather than its farm mode: neatly braided and bunned, with a dark blue band circling the top of the curls that framed her forehead. She wore a sleeveless white blouse, the kind she would pull one of her pretty linen jackets over, and he desperately wanted to brush his knuckles against either her shoulder or her long neck.

Either would do.

Instead, he handed her the canning jar. "My mother told me to bring you cooked butternut squash as a peace offering."

Dottie's eyes lit a little at that, and she accepted it eagerly. He wished for the thousandth time that this woman made sense to him. "I don't know *why* you need squash so badly, but I'm glad you're pleased."

"Thank you," she said, making no move to let him in, to explain herself, or to explain the squash.

He waited.

So did she.

He raised his eyebrows.

So did she.

"May I come in?"

"Why did you come to the back door?"

"Because I know you can see me coming up the boardwalk, and because you like to run away from me now. Quite literally *run*, for some reason." He crossed his arms and dropped his volume. "Because I wanted to see you."

Dottie stepped back to let him in.

The office had space in the back filled with shelves, stacked files, and a small Bakelite table. Against one of the table legs was a box with a hole in the side. Poking through that hole was what appeared to be a beak. Smokey used a finger to pull open the top of the box.

"Is that a … duck?"

"Yes. Meet Dudley." Dottie leaned close to Smokey and regarded the young duck in the box, as well, with something like maternal satisfaction. "Dudley is a mallard duck."

"What's wrong with him?" Smokey knelt. Dudley's neck appeared to be braced with a rolled bandage, and his body was ensconced in a large, woolen sock. Smokey was baffled by the sight of the creature, but his curiosity and a desire to survive kept laughter at bay.

"He has wry neck," Dottie said. "He was abandoned by the rest of his duck family because of it."

Smokey looked up to see Julia join them in the doorway leading out into the main office. She waved at him and stared at the duck-in-the-box with them. She'd already put in a few hours watering at the farm this morning with Hugh, but she somehow never looked weary.

Julia made Smokey feel old.

"The butternut squash you brought is rich in the vitamins Dudley needs to overcome this little setback," Dottie continued.

She'd been to the library again, Smokey figured, thinking about the pears and the goats. She confirmed his suspicion when she added, "He's named after Dr. Dudley Allen Sargent."

Smokey rose and, using only his eyes, asked the question she was waiting for.

"Dr. Sargent was a Harvard man who developed the first neck strengthening device," she said matter-of-factly. He'd gone to school with this version of Dottie Berkeley, and she'd always made him grin.

"And the sock?"

"It keeps him from moving about for now. When he tries to walk, he falls. I can't have him hurt himself. I'll get him out for his exercise here in a bit, though, after I help him eat the squash. His neck trouble prevents him from feeding himself, but that should be temporary. Thank you so much for bringing it. Truly."

There was a little medicine dropper in the corner of the box. Smokey imagined Dottie on her knees in her business skirt, carefully feeding Dudley several times a day.

He was in love with her.

He *loved* her.

Those were different things, being in love and loving, but Smokey realized he felt both keenly.

His mother had called him a caveman the other day, which felt accurate now, because he had the strangest urge to scoop this woman up and haul her back to his place forever. She could bring the duck. In fact, he'd take her on any terms.

The problem was, she'd literally just run away from him *and* from that farm. He wanted her for a lot of things, but he did not want her for a prisoner.

"Dottie, I wonder if we might talk." He managed to clear his throat twice during that short sentence. What he would say to her, he didn't know, but he mostly needed to hear *her* talk. He needed to know what was going on in her mind, now that he knew what was going on in his own.

~~~~~

It was time to produce good fruit. That was what was on Dottie's mind as she deliberately walked back into the main office with Julia, trusting Smokey to follow them.

She held her back straight, concentrating on not favoring one foot so he wouldn't remember how she'd stumbled and twisted her way through the ditch on his road a few days before.

Smokey was a better man than most, she reminded herself. This would work.

Julia was a truly angelic woman.

Dottie, by contrast, had a lot of good that needed doing if she was going to ever be right with the Good Lord and with herself again. It began
~~~~~

today. In fact, she might already be feeling more like her old self. After all, she'd slept three hours straight the night before.

Smokey said he wanted to talk, but Dottie didn't have anything to say to him that he would want to hear.

How could she tell him that it hurt when he was kind to Lucille Armstrong even when Lucille was cruel to her? Or that it hurt when he was kind to *every*one and absolutely no kinder to her, to Dottie, than he was to any of the others … after she had foolishly let herself want to matter to him. Again.

It was all so mortifying.

How did she tell him, when it was all said and done, that she was still stuck in her fifteen-year-old fantasies? That she wanted to be *looked at* differently than the others. That she did not want to be one of his projects.

There was no good way to say any of that out loud. So, instead, she would simply make *him* her *own* project. That was what she'd do. It started today. She was a good fruit producer.

"Look at sweet little Penny," she prompted Smokey in a whisper when he followed them into the office, gesturing to the pallet on the floor next to the desk Julia had been using. "Isn't she a doll?"

The little girl was sleeping soundly, her right thumb hanging half out of her open mouth, her grungy little cotton blanky pressed up against her chest.

Dottie looked at Smokey to see if he was as affected as she knew he would be by the beautiful innocence of childhood. She was gratified when the creases by his eyes deepened as they did just before he smiled. Children, after all, were what inspired him on that wonderland of a farm he'd conceived.

"Isn't she perfect?"

"She is, indeed."

There. Now, for the little girl's equally perfect mother.

"I know you said you want to talk, but this isn't the best time for me." Dottie kept her voice down. She hoped he couldn't see her heart beating in her throat. "I promised Emily I'd go over to design this week's ad." She glanced significantly at her wristwatch. "I'm afraid I'm late."

She swallowed and looked way up to meet his eyes. Then she wished she hadn't. There was something about the way he looked at her, and she wondered if the rest of his female fan club felt the same way.

"But," she went on with forced cheer, "I know of a certain chef over at the new German place who's been begging me to come try a sausage sandwich. For a taste test, you know?"

Smokey released a breath. "That sounds good."

"How about you and Julia head over there for a nice lunch and tell Friedrich I sent you? What do you think, Julia?"

Now Dottie carefully avoided Smokey's eyes and wrapped an encouraging arm around Julia's belted waist. Julia was looking at her like she'd lost her mind.

Dottie pressed on. "When was the last time you got out for a leisurely restaurant meal, my friend? I know you'll love it. And you'll have to report back. Think of it as an assigned work task."

"But you just took Penny and me out for fish last night."

"Yes, but you need time just for *you*, don't you? You work so hard. I bet you were already out on the farm this morning, weren't you?"

"Well, yes, but ..."

"And then straight over here. Look at that stack of payroll you helped finish. You and Smokey will have a lovely time as Friedrich's honored guests."

"But Penny ..."

"*I'll* take care of Penny."

"I thought you had an appointment with Emily," Smokey said, curse him, but Dottie didn't look in the direction of his deep voice.

She cleared her own throat. "Well, Em can come down here for our planning session until sweet little Penny wakes up. Maybe you could bring her back some potatoes, eh?" Dottie's face heated. Why, *why* did she have to bring up potatoes? "Or sauerkraut! Or whatever Friedrich is especially proud of today," she went on quickly. Dottie put a hand on Julia's lower back and gently pushed her in Smokey's direction. "Like I said, just tell Friedrich you're my guests there. He'll take great care of you, and the meal is on me."

"Dottie." Smokey's voice was grim when he said her name in two long syllables.

"Please," she said firmly. "Please let me do this for you both."

For a moment, none of them moved. Then Dottie gave another little push to her friend, who looked so fetching in her polka dot day dress.

Dottie watched them leave at last, taking her time to draw a deep breath and taking her time to let it out. They looked very good together. She thought she actually felt her soul get lighter.

Chapter Twenty-Four

Smokey figured Hugh was easy to talk to because he typically didn't say much back. Some men had returned from war with purple hearts and commendations, but Hugh, who had been caught up in the worst of it, had come back an award-worthy *listener*.

Smokey sat beside him on the front stoop of the cabin, a bucket of green beans on each side, another bucket for the snapped ones between them.

Mama Pool had transferred the beans from her car to his truck after church. She was spending the day at the ladies' bazaar, but the beans needed to be snapped today. It was easy for Smokey to recruit Hugh for a peaceful hour in the shade of the cabin. In exchange for his help, Hugh would get a pot of those beans cooked up with bits of ham and potatoes.

The centers of the beans made a hollow plunk in the wooden bucket, a steady rhythm against the separating cracks of the hard tips. Later, Smokey would gather those tips from the tarp he'd placed beneath their feet. Mama Pool would want some for making vegetable stock, but he'd also haul some off for the goats. They loved a treat.

Treats for goats made him think of Dottie.

He supposed he could dice and cook some of those discarded ends up for her duckling, as well. Not because he wanted an excuse to see her again, of course, but because wry neck in ducklings did call for vitamins. Dottie's research had been spot on, as usual.

Which somehow annoyed him.

"You know what, Hugh?"

Hugh, predictably, said nothing, which Smokey figured meant he was eager to know *what*.

"There's nothing worse than realizing you're in love with a woman only to find out she's trying to set you up with *another* woman. All on the same day."

The beans dropped systematically into the bucket, and Smokey told himself he was glad he'd finally said it out loud. It felt real now. He was in love with Dottie Berkeley, and now he wasn't the only one who knew it.

Hugh surprised him by making a snorting sound. "*Nothing* worse?"

"Well, I suppose there are one or two worse things."

"I think we've both seen more than one or two."

"That may be the most I've heard you say about the war." Smokey nudged him with his elbow. "I'm talking about love now, man."

"All's fair …"

The audacity of Hugh being … sassy. Then the man had the gall to make it even worse by pushing for details.

"You talkin' about Dot Berkeley, then?"

"Yes."

"That's all right, I guess." Translated, that meant Hugh was happy.

"Well. Thank you."

They snapped another handful of beans. It really was official. Smokey was in love with Dottie.

"You love the regular Dot? Or the hurt, scared Dot?"

Smokey glanced over. Snapped a bean. "I'm not sure what you mean by that." But he did know what he meant.

"You're not mistakin' her for some kind of wounded critter? That's what I mean."

Smokey huffed at that. He wondered what Dottie's reaction might be if she heard herself compared to a *critter*. She'd jokingly identified with the wounded group more than once, though, hadn't she? On his farm of "rejects," as she'd affectionately referred to the place.

It was strange, but he'd never thought of his farm that way until she'd said it. Yet, there was Cream Puff bathing her single hind leg in the shade just beside them, like some kind of advertisement for the place.

"Just something to think about," Hugh mumbled. The silence had stretched too long.

Men of few words, men who listened more than they talked, tended to make points worth considering. Smokey knew that well enough.

Certainly, he had no trouble at all remembering Dottie Berkeley before the accident on that terrible March day. Hadn't he known her for nearly forever? Had he loved her then, too? Before? Sometimes, when you knew someone for such a long time …

In his mind, he considered her cool decisiveness, even as a kid. Her long, purposeful stride, the self-sufficiency and focus that had seen an amusement park through a war. Somehow, she'd always managed to be irresistible while also being completely and utterly unromantic.

"I guess I've always *seen* her." He wasn't certain he could explain it any better than that. It felt like a type of love, but also not like what he'd ever thought of as love. "In truth — and I'll pummel you if you tell anyone this — in truth, I think I've always been a little scared of her."

Hugh grinned at that, and Smokey did too.

"Folks say love and hate are sides of the same coin or whatnot," Hugh said. "Could be, there's a healthy dose of fear in the mix."

Smokey laughed.

"Question is," Hugh went on, chewing on one of the grizzled ends of a green bean. "Question is, if tomorrow she went back to being, you know, *Dot Berkeley*, would you still want her?"

It had never occurred to Smokey that Dottie had ever stopped being Dot Berkeley. Regardless, Smokey knew he'd always wanted her. He didn't tell Hugh that or that the man was a little off base with his question.

The real question, he knew now, was: If Dottie Berkeley no longer needed the kindness and peace denied to her in the empire she'd built, would *she* want anything at all from *him*? And, if so, what in the world would that even be?

She'd arranged a date for him with another woman.

Smokey felt about as discouraged as the discarded bean tips piled up around him.

Chapter Twenty-Five

The Buckeye Lake Beacon would run a big, front-page spread promoting the upcoming Grand Opening of the Pier Ballroom.

That meant Emily Graham Mathison and her trusty reporter's notebook were getting Dottie's first official tour of the place.

"Oooh! Are those lamps being installed all the way around the walls, then?"

"They are." Dottie steered a very pregnant Emily around a ladder with a construction worker balancing at its top.

All around them were the continued sounds of saws, of bangs and thumps, and of deep, masculine shouts from one wall to another. The finishing touches to the actual ballroom area were all that remained, but it was easy to envision the final dazzling effect of the place. A surge of anticipation moved through Dottie.

"It's simply going to take everyone's breath away," Emily said. She hadn't once reached into her satchel for her notebook, which didn't concern Dottie. Emily had been nosey enough throughout construction to have most of the who, what, when, where, and why locked down two weeks before the Grand Opening.

The Who was Dottie and an investment from FH Resorts.

The What was a sprawling, second ballroom on the end of a pier stretching off the amusement park over Buckeye Lake.

The When was nearly upon them, at the end of the summer season. Construction simply couldn't have been completed in time for the 1947 crowds, which they'd known all along, but this soft opening would prompt a list of changes to make for the following spring.

The Why had been a fire set the summer before that Emily knew plenty about. After all, she'd been out among the flames rescuing their mutual childhood friend from the middle of the collapsing pier.

Now, Dottie realized Emily had turned from the tarp-covered expanse of the shining dance floor to glance her way.

"I can't believe you're settling for one week on the front page." Emily arched a brow. "Shouldn't you be pestering me to stretch the news coverage to two weeks leading up to the big night?"

"You *want* me to pester you?"

"I came ready for it." Emily blew a stray blonde curl out of her eye. "I mean, really. Who am I dealing with here?"

"I'm grateful for a full front page next week, Em. You don't owe me more than that."

"But you purchased an enormous double-page ad on the inside that will cover my printing costs for September and October."

Dottie stilled. "Emily." She narrowed her eyes. "No woman of business reveals a thing like that. Who am *I* dealing with here? Pregnancy has rotted your brain."

"Don't deflect. The old Dottie would be harassing me for more exposure."

Dottie smiled because it was true, and then she jumped in surprise when a piece of scaffolding rattled to the ground mere feet from them.

"Come on," she said, steering Emily across the space. "I want you to see the second floor, and it's a little quieter up there." Their shoes clicked amidst the buzz of a saw. "Can you still climb stairs and everything?"

"I'm pregnant, not dying. I'll race you to the top."

But they climbed at a slow pace while Emily scanned the newly printed Grand Opening handbill in maroon and gold.

"What's this?" she asked, pointing to a box on one side of the invitation. "You hadn't mentioned this cheaper ticket option before. Thought you were aiming for black tie, deep pockets, that kind of thing. For the opening, at least."

"Changed my mind."

"You've got Louis Jordan lined up for this, Dottie … at this price, the common folk can attend."

"If you mean Buckeye Lake year-round residents, then yes. That's the idea."

"You trying to work your way back into their affections?"

At the top of the stairway, everything smelled of fresh paint. Dottie shrugged. "It occurs to me sometimes, lately, that I'm not sure I was ever much in their affections. Even before."

Emily narrowed her eyes. "Whose affections do you mean, exactly?"

"Everyone's." Dottie led Emily over to the railing overlooking the ballroom where they'd been standing minutes before. The narrower second story was also lined with tables not yet covered with starched white cloths. "I'm just saying, I'm not sure people liked me that much before I was a killer. I'd never considered it before. And they like me even less now."

Dottie had not said this out loud before, had barely allowed herself to think it. Testing it on Emily, though, she knew it to be true. Emily leaned on the rail, silent, and regarded the workers.

"Don't feel pressured to tell me I'm wrong." Dottie gave her a sardonic smile.

"I guess I don't pay much attention to that kind of thing. I can't really say whether you're being fair to yourself or not."

"You don't have to think about it too hard, Em. *You* haven't even always liked me, and I count you as one of my very best friends."

"Maybe I haven't always liked what you've done, Dottie, but at the end of the day … I've always understood it."

"Well, you're a questionable judge of character, anyway."

"Undoubtedly." Emily fanned herself now with the handbill. "Wouldn't you know I'd choose to grow a baby during the hottest summer on record?"

Dottie slanted her another look. "It is not anywhere close to the hottest summer on record. Where are you getting that?"

"From my gut, that's where. It's the hottest summer in *my* record."

"And you call yourself a journalist."

Emily snorted a laugh, and Dottie was surprised when her friend reached over and squeezed her hand on the railing. "I'll say this, Dottie Berkeley. You've given my sister some of the very best things in her life, and that goes a long way with me. Even when you were trying to carve up Cranberry Bog last year, I couldn't ever forget you gave Rosie a way to make money with her artwork. You offered her that studio right on the boardwalk after Charlie was born. Then, you stepped back and let her have the man of her dreams. Guilt free, even!"

It was Dottie's turn to laugh.

She had been dating Gabe Adams when he abruptly fell in love with Rosie Graham the Christmas before. Ending her own casual romance with the man had been far from the biggest sacrifice of her life. "She got Gabe herself. I was just … the anti-Rosie who helped him see she was his dream woman. Instead of me."

I'm good at that. She considered Smokey and Julia Fey. Was this to be her role in life, then? To help good men recognize their happily-ever-after by contrasting her own disaster of an existence with that of a better woman?

How dreary.

Emily crossed over to the opposite rail, open to a view of the park's midway. It was idyllic from this slight distance, its colors and lights mirrored in the shallow water of the lake. The shapes and motion always danced to the soundtrack of squeals of joy.

"Labor Day is just about here," Emily said.

"Yes."

"Usually, I dread it. You know I prefer the summer pace. But this year, I'm ready. Ready for everything and everyone to just … rest."

"You do have a lot to look forward to this fall." Dottie wrapped an arm around her friend's shoulders, partly from an instinct to try to soak up some of that precious sense of hope.

"The baby is moving." Emily gestured down at her belly under its floral-printed wrap dress. "Here, feel it."

Dottie stepped away. "No, thank you."

Emily grinned. "She won't hurt you, you goon. Just put your hand right here. I can tell that's her feet."

Oh, no. Dottie tried not to cringe and knew she failed, but the idea of a human in there under Emily's cotton dress, moving human *feet* around where Emily's vital organs would normally be … it did not inspire Dottie to "feel it." She supposed this was another way she was not like other women.

"Emily," she said, desperately changing the subject. "Have you learned to cook well?"

Her friend laughed again, rubbing her own hand over the spot she'd indicated on her stomach. "Cook *well*? I don't know if I'd say 'well.' But I can throw together some things when I'm home."

"So domestic life isn't … stifling you?"

"No. But Drew's not like a lot of men. And I'm not sure I can answer that accurately until the baby comes. The stifling might still be coming, but I just don't expect it to be, you know? I'm excited about spending more time working on the kind of family I've always wanted, if that makes any sense."

"It does. But, Em, I think something is wrong with me, and it's nothing to do with the accident. I think it has something to do with the domestic stuff."

"Of course there's something wrong with you."

"I'm serious."

"I know. And look, I think all of us, all us women, think something's wrong with us. It's something done to us and something we do to ourselves. It's one of the crummy things about being a woman, right up there with menstruating and giving birth."

"Of course you've given this some thought."

"I have. It's this impossible … what? Box? A kind of box we feel we must fit neatly into, and the box is built mostly by other people. And the walls, the four walls of the box, are about an ideal appearance, an ideal home, being an ideal wife, being an ideal mother. It hardly leaves room for the other things we may feel we're called to be or do."

Ideal. Dottie nodded. "That feels true."

"Sure, it does. And Dottie, we will all live our lives and die whether we fit perfectly into that box or not, so maybe we can just agree to take a deep breath and let it be what it's going to be. Maybe enjoy it."

"So wise. You're so wise, except a box would technically have six walls to it, not four."

Emily elbowed her, and Dottie huffed a laugh.

"The fact is," Dottie said, "I'm hanging too far out of that box you're talking about to have anything like a normal life. That's what I'm afraid of."

"Do you know anyone living a normal life? Because I don't."

"Emily ..." She tried to take that deep breath her friend had encouraged, and because her chest expanded like the chests of other humans this time, she decided to lay it all out there. "Sometimes, for no reason at all, I feel like I can't get enough air."

"What do you mean?" It was the response of a newspaper reporter trying to get to the bottom of things.

"Sometimes I can't take a full breath. For no reason, I just start to feel like I'm not ... all right. Like I'm in danger or I'm dying, but nothing is actually wrong *around* me. It must be wrong inside of me, and I can't breathe when it happens. I know it makes no sense."

"Like you're dying? Not getting air? Remember, that's why that Frasier boy had to stop running track, right? Trouble breathing when he ran?"

"No, not like that. Not asthma. I don't know how to describe it. It starts with this sense that nothing is all right. And then there's a heavy feeling in my abdomen ... not like the one you're probably feeling." Dottie nodded at Emily's belly, and they shared a quick smile. "After that feeling, there's a prickly sensation in my hands. And then my chest gets tight. And there's no air any longer, and I'm sweating."

"What do you do when that happens?"

"Hide. Mostly, I hide." *Or shake in Smokey's arms.*

"Go see Doc, Sweetie."

"I don't think anything is *wrong*, though. Not in real life."

Emily's brow creased, and she looked mildly annoyed, the way she always did when an answer wasn't apparent. "When did it start? After the accident?"

"Mostly, I guess."

"Then maybe it will just, I don't know, clear up?"

"I hope so. Because the whole normal life thing seems even more out of reach in light of these ... episodes. You know?"

"Like I said, I'm not very convinced anyone's life is normal."

"Sometimes it sure seems like they are."

"I can't believe you're saying that with a straight face after being friends with Rosie and me all these years."

"Yet, look at you two abnormal women. Getting married, having families ..."

"Is that something you want now, Dottie?"

Dottie shook her head. "I don't know. I don't have what it takes, I do know that."

Emily ran a hand over the mound of her stomach. "You mean you don't have what it takes to patiently care for a vision and the details of something magnificent and see it through?"

Dottie didn't answer. She just watched Emily's eyes taking in the warm bulbs of light already tucked into the perfect white trim around them. Those lights were reflected like festive puddles on the oiled wooden floor beneath their feet, just as the amusement park lights reflected in the lake. It was all very beautiful, and Dottie knew it was. "Seems to me," Emily finally went on, her point made, "like you *do* know how to see a vision through with love and be successful."

Dottie had nothing to give Emily but a grateful smile.

She did know how to make things and how to love things. But was the ballroom really the same as a child? Was the amusement park the only family she'd ever get to build? She didn't have the heart to tell Emily how lonely it all felt.

But, for now, it was nice to have someone proud of her for something.

Chapter Twenty-Six

Smokey hadn't been expecting the crew of workers at first light. They'd arrived with a flatbed trailer, and on the trailer were the pieces and parts of an enormous slide for children. A gift, the workers told him, from the Buckeye Lake Amusement Park.

By the time Smokey had directed them where to install the slide back in the Enchanted Forest, Hugh and Silas had wandered up from the fir trees to see what all the fuss was about.

In his hand, Smokey had a neatly folded letter. It was signed Shelby Berkeley, but the script was Dottie's handwriting.

"We hope you'll accept this piece of equipment by way of thanks for the refuge and counsel you provided us this summer." Smokey read the letter out loud to the guys. "The slide is double-width and should make a nice addition to your children's play area. It came down to us from Cedar Point, but we thought it would better suit Holiday Farms than the lake's amusement park. Here's wishing you the start of a successful busy season even as our own wraps up. Please let us know if we can assist you in any way, at any time. Sincerely —"

A second piece of heavy cardstock had slid out of the envelope, as well.

Maroon, it was bordered in golden curlicues and embellishments, and it announced an invitation to the Grand Opening of the Pier Ballroom the following Saturday. It was addressed to "Mr. Levi Smokey Black and Ms. Julia Fey."

Smokey shielded his eyes with his hand. A beam of light through the trees of the forest was glinting off the wavy metal of the new slide's surface. He supposed he'd have Hugh and Silas dump some extra pine mulch at the base of the slide for safety's sake.

"This is awful nice," Hugh said finally.

"She's settling accounts." Smokey swallowed a sense of panic.

The next move would need to be his.

~~~~~

It had been sprinkling off and on all day, which was a little unusual for early September. Dottie had asked Rosie for a ride out to Holiday Farms, since Black-Pool farmland wasn't far out of the way from Towpath Island. Rosie's windshield wipers made a groaning sound against the raindrops on the glass.
~~~~~

Dottie wore a comfortable dress, her journey prompted by a short note inviting her to have supper at Smokey's farm. The note had included a scribbled addition at the bottom: "Bring Dudley."

So, the duck rode in his box on Rosie's back seat, and Dottie craned her neck back to check that he was riding okay.

"His neck is so much stronger," she told Rosie.

"He couldn't ask for a better nurse."

Dottie didn't argue. She'd devised a little exercise routine for Dudley, gradually weaning him off the neck brace for his workouts several times a day. Now, he could walk without falling. Dottie understood better every day why Smokey was so attached to his imperfect barnyard. She wasn't sure why such creatures found him, but she knew why they were treasured.

The duckling's improved health meant she should probably consider re-introducing him to his natural habitat, but she didn't relish the idea of turning him loose at the park. Well-meaning people would feed him bread and French fries there, cutting his little life short.

"I think Smokey asked me out here so he could examine Dudley."

Rosie smiled and made a humming sound.

"Also, he probably wants me to see the giant slide in the Enchanted Forest."

The wipers groaned across the windshield again. Rosie reached down to shut them off, the drizzle over.

"And he probably wants me to see the pumpkins all grown and ready for the season."

"Sounds like a busy night," was Rosie's observation.

Rosie had seemed to hint there was more to this dinner invitation than these practical aspects of Dottie's time at the farm, but then Rosie didn't know about Smokey's and Julia's future the way Dottie did.

She wondered if Julia and sweet little Penny would be at supper. He'd invited Dottie for a meal, so surely there could be no expectation that *she'd* be cooking it. Grimly, Dottie imagined a parade of unmarried women with covered dishes marching up to Smokey's cabin to make this meal possible. Yet, it was far more likely Julia had made herself at home in the man's tiny kitchen and was, even now, "whipping up" something delectable.

Dottie would eat it all, cheerfully.

She told herself she *hoped* Julia was there. After all, she liked Julia.

And it was best, these days, if she were not alone with Smokey. She tended to behave unpredictably when she was.

~~~~~

Smokey was glad to have Dottie all to himself again.

The clouds were low, but the rain had stopped for good while they'd
~~~~~

shared a simple supper in the cabin. The scent of wet grass on cooler air leaked through the open windows, and Smokey reflected this would be one of those Labor Days that seemed to truly hint at autumn.

He dried the soup bowls, sneaking glances at Dottie where she sat in his rocker, her bare feet drawn up under her skirt. On her lap was the leather-bound book in which he kept a record of the farm's finances, and she chewed lightly on the end of a pencil as she slowly flipped another page.

Smokey placed the dry bowl on the shelf beside him with the others, congratulating himself because Dottie had eaten not one but two bowls full of the corn soup and dumplings he'd managed.

At first, she'd been quiet and skeptical about the soup.

He made sure to brag about cooking it all himself.

After he had, she'd tucked into it with real gusto. And here he was, still replaying in his mind her wondrous request for "a bit more."

"Where's the record of the paint, Smoke?" Dottie didn't look up from the book but scanned pages with a furrowed brow.

"You mean the paint for the fence? It's in there. Look at April, I think."

"No, I mean the green paint." Her pretty eyes met his now, and a shared memory lit the space between the rocker and the sink. "The paint we used for Nessie."

"You brought that paint, Sweetheart."

Now Dottie's tentative grin erupted into a laugh. How he'd hated going without that laugh. "I brought it, yes, but I sure as certain charged it to your account at the hardware."

Flinging the damp cloth over his shoulder with a chuckle, he crossed the room as though searching for proof that green paint did not appear in the ledger.

"How's a man supposed to keep the books balanced when his farm hands are out charging things willy-nilly?"

"If I were on your board of directors, I'd insist you fix this shoddy bookkeeping."

"I'll talk to the turkey and the goats about it, see if they're displeased."

"That's your board of directors?"

"As of right now, yes. I suppose that pretty dress you're wearing was somehow also charged to the farm account as compensation for the dresses you ruined meeting with those same board members?"

Dottie surprised him by batting her lashes. "I'm sure you don't mind."

"How could I?"

"Seriously, though." She unfolded her legs and leaned toward him.

"You do need to get word out to the public."

"About green paint?!"

"About the change from Festival Farms to Holiday Farms. Unless you're just playing with the name change."

Smokey lowered himself to the unlit hearth and shrugged. "Folks know where this place is. Does it matter what the sign out front says?"

"Yes, it matters!" Dottie smacked the heel of her hand into her forehead. "You're offering more and more reasons for families to come out each year, and people need to know about those. They need to associate the place with the holidays. It's called advertising, Smoke."

"I'll run an ad."

"With Emily?"

"Yeah. Of course."

"You need to advertise in Newark and Lancaster, too. In the papers there. Pay one of the guys at *The Beacon* to create a logo, a design for Holiday Farms, and … Smokey. Are you listening?"

He sat up straighter. Yes, of course he'd been listening. He'd thought of all those things as the season approached, but if she needed to coach him in the ways of business to get the two of them back on stable footing, then he'd let her do that all night.

"I'm listening. Tell me more."

As she did, he took a chance imagining the two of them this way in years to come. Smokey cooking supper? Dottie doing farm work? Hugh's words haunted him. Was she the old Dottie right now, rattling off marketing strategies like the ones she'd used at the park? Or was she the new Dottie, a little vulnerable in a lovely dress that probably didn't fit her form as snuggly as it had when she bought it?

Was he possibly in love with *both* of those versions of the woman who was pointing at his ledger now?

He thought of how uncertain she'd been when she arrived tonight, looking around as though for spies in his cabin, clutching her duckling box to her chest.

What would she say if a man offered her his love?

Would kissing her again provide an answer to that question?

"Do I have food in my teeth?" Her sudden question, interrupting her own strategizing and his plotting, made him raise his brows.

"Uh. I don't think you do. No."

"You were staring at my teeth." No, he'd been staring at her lips, most likely. "I thought maybe there was a piece of food … you know, stuck."

"Sorry. I guess I was just thinking." Shaking those thoughts off, he pushed up off the hearth. "What are your feelings about leaving little Dudley here with me?"

The two of them crossed the tiny cabin to look once more at the duckling, as they had for a time when she'd arrived. Smokey was impressed that the little guy no longer lived in a sock, and Dottie had even demonstrated how he could feed himself now that his neck didn't flop back.

"You think it's time he left his box?"

In this, he thought in amusement, she recognized him as an expert.

"I do. You've done an amazing job with him, but he probably needs to move about in the world. Do you think he'd like to try the barn, with the menagerie?"

"Well, I suppose." She bit her lip. "I don't think he'd do well at the pier. Do you?"

"No." Smokey bent to swipe his knuckle over the soft back of the duck. "I mixed up some special feed for him, with supplements I give the other animals. The kind we use for Reggie's and Pam's chickens. I thought you could either take the tin back with you, or we could try the feed here, in the barn. Your choice. You're his mama."

Dottie laughed at that. "Normal life, indeed."

"What?"

"Never mind. Let's take him out and introduce him to the others!"

~~~~~

Dottie couldn't think of a time she'd felt so content.

Sitting half-on Smokey's leg on the tractor, her belly full of warm soup he'd made just for her, she felt lingering satisfaction in the way little Dudley had settled right into the barnyard. The other critters had ignored or befriended him, and he'd waddled around with his head mostly straight, looking as proud of himself as she was of him.

She'd cheered like a parent on the sidelines of a ballgame.

After that, Smokey showed her the finished play area in the Enchanted Forest, the large slide in its home there rounding out the attractions. She'd admired their Loch Ness monster, remembered the rush of swinging down from the treehouse. She imagined dozens of children playing there.

It occurred to Dottie that many of the same children who had smiled sticky cotton candy smiles all summer at her amusement park would soon come here to revel in the harvest. They would explore the pumpkin patch, just as she was now from atop the tractor.

The pumpkins were spread before them, acres of warm color.

"Oh, would you *look* at them!" She leaned forward, delighting in the way Smokey's arm tightened around her middle to keep her in place. "They've grown enormous, haven't they?!"

"They're right on track to be the pumpkins the Good Lord intended them to be," was his answer, in that deep voice of his that always seemed
~~~~~

to be verging on a laugh.

The soil, free of weeds, was dark from the day's light rain, which had also left the orange of the pumpkins shining in the soft twilight.

"They're only the most splendid pumpkins I've ever seen."

"As they should be. You put a lot of sweat and love into them."

"So did Julia."

"She did, at that."

Dottie sat back against his side, appreciating the way the pumpkin vines were still somewhat green, like thick yarn anchoring orange pom-poms to an earthy quilt.

"Speaking of Julia," Dottie said. "Did you receive the invitation to the opening of the ballroom?"

She felt his arm stiffen.

"Yes, I received it."

"And you'll come, won't you?"

"I've never received an invitation quite like that. One that involved me replying on behalf of someone I'm not dating."

"Oh, don't worry about that. Julia will come. She's so excited."

"You asked her *for* me, though. Don't you think that's ... odd, Dottie?"

"You're welcome. I heard what a nice time the two of you had at the restaurant."

"Dottie."

She waited, but he eventually just sighed. He was so warm against her, and she felt so grateful to have known him all these years. Grateful to have someone who'd let her just lean.

"This farm of yours really is magic, you know?" Now she breathed in, enjoying that her lungs fully inflated, enjoying this feeling that she was all right, even if it was temporary. If only Smokey could bottle and sell this peace around them. "You're really onto something with your whole 'fresh air' thing, you know. It's *healing*."

"Mmm." He cleared his throat, and she shivered when she felt the vibration against her shoulder. "Fresh air is important. But even fresh air only gets you so far."

The laughter was gone from his voice. Had she said something wrong?

"What do you mean?"

"Just that good, country air will only heal to a point. For it to really work, the good Lord's gotta be involved, too."

Dottie straightened. She started to tell him he had a lot of nerve insinuating that the Lord wasn't fixing her up just fine. After all, what did Smokey know? She hadn't cried in weeks ... in front of him, anyway.

"I've upset you." He said it like he didn't mind, which made her feel no better at all.

"I'm not mad."

"I wouldn't blame you if you were mad. You've been through the worst season most of us can imagine. I figure there must be times when you feel like getting good 'n mad."

Dottie made herself relax again, hating that tears pricked her eyes after she'd just congratulated herself on crying less. It was only that the same relentless memory surfaced again, of him holding her at the accident scene. It occurred to her he'd already seen her worst, up close.

And the worst of her he hadn't seen, it seemed he might have guessed.

"What I'm about to tell you is terrible," she finally admitted, glad he was behind her, glad the cheerful pumpkins were before her. "It's not about being mad. That's not the problem."

"What is it?"

"I … I can't seem to pray."

"I don't know about terrible, but it does sound familiar."

"Familiar?"

"Sure. Honey, a lot of us came back from war not too long ago."

"That's true, that's true. I've nothing to complain about in comparison."

"That's not what I said." She could feel him breathe in and out against her back. "Besides, you weren't complaining. You only said praying is hard. I'm just saying, I get it."

"It's something I would've talked to Pastor Skip about," she went on with grim humor, relieved that Smokey wasn't shocked and dismayed. "But that's not exactly possible anymore."

"No, it's not."

"It's like I don't know what to pray. I think that's the problem. I just end up asking for forgiveness, over and over. I say, 'forgive me,' and then I say it again, but …"

She paused to watch a hawk swoop down along the far side of the field.

"But?"

"I never end up feeling forgiven. It's like I can see that prayer floating out of me, like a balloon, but instead of going up, it … it just sinks down to the ground. Does that make any sense at all?"

"Sure, it does. And maybe that image accounts for a little bit of your trouble." He tucked her closer, and she knew she would listen to whatever he said. "Who says prayers need to go up to some unimaginable height, anyway? Who says God's so far away?"

No one needed to say it. Dottie knew it. Just like Emily Mathison knew in her gut this was the hottest summer on record, Dottie knew her prayers for forgiveness were bobbing along the floorboards, far from God.

"So, you keep praying for forgiveness."

"Over and over."

"What if you switched it up? All you're focused on is who you are. Maybe pray about who God is. That could do the trick."

"Anyway, it's hard to imagine being forgiven when I can't even give myself a free pass on this."

"Forgiveness and a free pass seem like different things. To me, anyway."

"I suppose."

"You think I never killed a man, Sweetheart?"

Dottie twisted around to see him, until she almost fell off her already precarious seat on his leg. "In the war, you mean?"

"Yes, in the war. I was behind enemy lines more often than anyone would want to be. It was kill or be killed."

She eased forward again, blind to the pumpkins now, picturing Smokey fighting for his life. "That's different."

"It sure was. You lost control of your car on ice. I killed on purpose. Do I get a free pass on that?"

She hesitated, then said a decisive, "Yes."

"Shows what you know." He squeezed her again. "I'm forgiven. I absolutely am, but a free pass ... I don't think that's the same thing."

"But you saved more lives than you took, surely."

"There you go again, thinking life is like that leather book of income and expenses again." He gave her a moment with that. "How do you see it all, Dottie B.? You think heaven is about some big ledger?"

She was quiet. In her heart, she suspected the answer was yes. That was how she'd always seen it, just as she'd seen her prayers as balloons that needed to make it up to the sky. Something about his tone, though—and another thing in her own soul—suggested she was off-base about this, too.

"The ledger's never coming out balanced. That's why Jesus died. You *know* that."

"I do. I know. I want it to be as simple as that, but ..." she said, thinking back to the verses that had spurred her into helping the widows, her deep conviction about using the gifts God had given her.

"I'm no Pastor Skip. I do know that." There was humor in his tone again.

"You're doing all right. But ... but here's the thing. Jesus is clear about good fruit mattering."

"For sure."

"Well, that means the good column of the ledger *does* matter, Smoke."

"Only if you're thinking about it in terms of a transaction. Maybe think about it as a relationship, instead." Smokey said it with affection. "And speaking of good fruit, just look at it spread out before us there."

He half-hugged her against him again, bouncing his knee, and Dottie smiled over the pumpkins she'd held as seeds in her hand. She hadn't thought of these pumpkins as literal fruit any more than she'd thought about them as some kind of figurative lesson.

"Sometimes it's easy to put the wagon before the tractor."

Dottie cracked a smile. "Is that like the proverbial cart before the horse?"

"Modern farm version, yeah. You can't put the fruit before the relationship. The work before the trust. It can't start like that and work out."

"The fruit comes naturally. A by-product."

"Bingo."

She hardly noticed when he put the Allis-Chalmers in gear and slowly steered them in the direction of his cabin again.

Dottie realized the same worldview that had made her good at business may have, definitely *had*, skewed her entire concept of faith. She would have plenty of time to ponder that, though, since she chose loneliness most of the time.

<p style="text-align:center">~~~~~</p>

Smokey had never told a woman he loved her before.

Sure, he was good at giving compliments or flattering. After all, he did love women in general. They smelled good and were nice to look at, even talk to.

But this was different. This was *love*.

Sure, Dottie did smell terrific, and he loved looking at her, and he never tired of talking with her. But this was something much more than all of that.

He thought the time was probably right to tell her, though. Dottie was soft and relaxed against his side on the tractor seat. The patch of bright pumpkins in the muted sunset had been truly beautiful.

So, he stopped the tractor when he reached the cabin and hopped down. He would reach back up for her, hands on her waist, and not let her go until she understood what she meant to him. He would somehow find the words.

Unfortunately, though, she had already hopped down on her own, so his hands weren't anywhere near her when he said, "It was sure nice having you back out here again."

"Yes. I missed it. Thank you for having me." She folded her hands in front of her. "Everything looks perfectly ready for the harvest season. Talk about good fruit. You must be so proud."

Pride was not exactly what he'd been feeling, so Smokey took a second too long to make sense of her words.

"Before you drive me back," she was already saying, the phrase washing through him like a wave of chilly water, "I just want to say I hope we can move forward from here. It's been a strange summer, a terrible one in so many ways, and I haven't always behaved … um." Those lower parts of her cheeks darkened crimson with embarrassment, not passion. "I haven't always behaved in ways that made sense."

He wasn't sure he knew what she meant by that. She mostly did make sense to him. Was she referring to crying, to the kiss she'd initiated, or to sprinting down the road because of blackened potatoes? Or did she refer to obviously trying to arrange a romance between him and her friend?

That last part continued to trip him up, to make him hesitate.

Surely, she couldn't have feelings for him and still be scheming to pair him with someone else, could she? It didn't add up. If she didn't share his feelings, what would she say if he told her how he felt? Was he about to ruin everything?

When he didn't respond quickly, she cleared her throat like she was nervous. "Smokey," she said in that husky voice he adored. "I want us to always be friends, okay? *Please.*"

He shoved his hands into his pockets.

His feelings were his own responsibility and, apparently, the last thing she needed just now, at the close of this terrible summer.

"I think we'll always be friends," he said carefully, and he took a muted sort of pleasure in the relief that washed over her face before it blossomed into a sunny smile.

Chapter Twenty-Seven

The Grand Opening celebration of the Pier Ballroom happened after the season ended, yet still managed to be the event of the season.

Even the weather had cooperated, gifting the venue that stretched out over the water with a pleasant breeze under a clear sky. Darkness was beginning to fall as hundreds of guests made their way down the well-lit and splendid pier.

"I feel so under-dressed," Julia told Smokey, her gloved hand tucked in his elbow. She was quite a bit shorter than him, so he walked a little lopsided to accommodate her.

"You look perfect," he said, smiling down at her and her emerald green gown. He'd made sure Julia's paycheck last week had a little extra to put toward a dress. All she was lacking were the jewels that the other women in front of and behind them wore, but somehow Smokey couldn't imagine Julia in jewels.

Instead, she looked fresh-faced and dazzled by the pomp involved in this event.

Orchestra music was already thrumming out the open second floor balcony and the windows of the first floor, spilling warm light along with it. There was a buzz of excited voices from within. Lanterns were lit up and down each side of the pier leading the way to the entrance, which sparkled in twinkling yellow lights like gold.

"Dottie outdid herself," Julia said in awe.

"She usually does." Smokey looked around at the crowds hurrying past one another to get that first look within. He nodded to some of his mother's friends from church, decked out in their pearls and embroidered bags. Just ahead of them were some of the vendors from the park, a couple of firefighters' families, and some former classmates. "It's funny how the local people have decided they hate Dottie, but they don't quite hate her enough to miss out on *this*."

"True," Julia said with contempt. "I want to feel sorry for her about it, but it's hard to manage tonight. Sometimes I hear her called the princess of the park, but that's never struck me as accurate. She's an actual queen. I mean, *look* at her."

Smokey hadn't noticed Dottie yet, until Julia pointed her out. Ahead of all those folks he'd been tallying, just around the edge of the twinkling yellow lights, Dottie stood beside her father in a dress that looked like spun gold. It picked up every one of those lights and threw it back out into the world like a prism. The gown hugged her figure, dipping and gathering and flaring in ways Smokey didn't understand and from which he would likely never recover.

He let out the breath he'd been holding. He thought he should say something in response to Julia, but he couldn't quite make words yet. Dottie was magnificent. She was stunning. She frustrated him to no end. "She may be a queen, but she's a meddler," he finally managed.

Julia looked up at him. "A meddler?"

"Yes, a meddler. Look what she's been doing to us, without our permission."

"That's very true." But Julia only laughed. "Are you sure she's purposely throwing us together, though? I mean, I know that day at the office was strange, when she sent us to lunch without her. But I know she had a lot on her mind that day."

"You. She had *you* on her mind. Dottie likes you, and she likes me, and she's decided I'm the answer to all your problems."

"My problems? I don't have problems Dottie needs to solve."

"Yet, somehow, that never stops her."

"Oh. You mean figuring out how to support Penny and me? But I *am* figuring that out. We're doing just fine!"

"You don't need to tell *me* that. I know you are. You're a strong and admirable woman, Julia Fey, and Dottie wants you to fall in love with me because she thinks I have problems, too."

Julia laughed, enjoying herself. "That explains why we were weirdly paired on our invitations to the opening tonight."

"Yes."

"I'm not in love with you, Smokey," Julia said casually, with that laughter still in her voice. "Has that ever happened to you before? Someone not falling head over heels?"

"Oh, I'm betting the world is full of women who are not in love with me." There was one just across the way, glittering in the doorway like a jewel he couldn't help wanting.

"I do think you look very fine in your suit, though."

Personally, he thought the collar of his white shirt was fitting too tight for comfort. Coming off a full summer of outdoor labor, he was broader than he'd been the last time he'd had reason to wear the black suit. He tried not to fidget as they joined the line to enter.

Across three yards of pier that remained between them, he met Dottie Berkeley's eyes, dancing with golden light from the entrance and from her dress. Her hair was styled into some kind of dramatic updo, with flowers ringing her dark curls and flowing down into a matching choker around her neck.

Julia had spoken of love.

Every man here would enter the place wildly in love with Dottie Berkeley, whether he admitted it or not. Smokey admitted it, at least to himself.

"It's funny to me," Julia was saying, pulling his attention back to her. "It's funny Dottie would try to match the two of us. All along, I've gotten the feeling she was sweet on you herself."

The very idea that a woman like Dottie would be "sweet" on an evergreen grower seemed more preposterous than ever, this evening. "Well, she's not. She just likes to play these games with other peoples' lives."

"That sounds kind of mean."

"I didn't intend it to." He took a breath. "Last winter, when we were all snowed in together during the blizzard—the one that hit during Emily's wedding?"

"I've heard the stories. You were all holed up in the inn out on Lieb's Island, weren't you?"

"That's right. Anyway, she was involved with Gabe Adams when we got there."

"Gabe!? You mean Rosie's husband?"

"Yes, but he wasn't Rosie's husband yet. That's what I'm trying to say. Dottie had dated him a few times, but she was all too happy to step out of the picture and clear the way for Rosie to have Gabe. I watched it all happen. Something tells me she likes to add checkmarks to her good deeds column that way."

"I'm not completely sure what you're …. Good deeds column?"

"Sorry. Ignore me."

"But maybe I do see the pattern," Julia said thoughtfully. They stepped closer to the entrance in line. "Rosie was an unmarried woman with a young son, wasn't she? Did Dottie see that as a problem she needed to fix, as you just suggested she views me?"

"Mmm. Not in quite the same way. Rosie and Gabe had fallen head over heels for one another, in that case. But you're right about the pattern."

"Well, we're not cooperating, then," Julia said with a humorous sigh. "You and me, not falling in love … that has to be irritating to her."

"Only the Good Lord knows what goes on in that mind of hers." That brought them right up to the entrance, where Shelby Berkeley rushed forward in his tuxedo to grasp both of Smokey's hands and make a bow to Julia.

"I'm so glad you could make it!"

Smokey was relieved to see Shelby's eyes were still clear, and the flush on his cheeks appeared to be natural excitement.

"You look good," Smokey said, smiling and meaning it. It took courage to change your life, Smokey knew, and Shelby sure seemed to be experiencing more wins than losses these days. Smokey wondered how the man's marriage was faring. He wondered how his relationship with his eldest daughter was, as well.

But it was hard to tell much amidst the roar of exclamations surrounding them. Through the twinkling archway, he could see more lamps glowing on the walls, floral arrangements on every surface, waiters and waitresses moving about with trays, wearing white uniforms to match the walls and the tables.

"Don't you two look breathtaking together," Dottie exclaimed, and she hugged first Julia and then him. Smokey thought her hug hurt a little. Meanwhile, Julia shot him a look at Dottie's wording, and they shared a smile that must have satisfied their hostess that her plans were working perfectly. "Go in, find a table, enjoy the music. I'll come find you once we get everything underway!"

~~~~~

Sometimes after Dottie had suffered one of her episodes, she felt a little weak and weary the rest of the day. Today, on such a big day, she was relieved to find she was still able to carry out her role in the Grand Opening.

That was despite the fact she hadn't been able to breathe when she'd gone to her apartment to get dressed, wheezing and certain she was dying at the foot of her bed. She tried to find solace in the fact it was happening less often these days.

There was also solace in the fact the party was truly underway, so Dottie was on the move, brushing against the crush of bodies, bending to retrieve a napkin from the floor, nodding to the manager regarding the switch to dinner music.

"Miss Berkeley? Excuse me. Everything looks amazing." A man, who might have been a little younger than her, intercepted her path. "I hope you'll save me a dance later."

He was clearly from out of town. The son of one of their large vendors, if she wasn't mistaken. Otherwise, he'd never want to go out of his way to be seen dancing with her.

"Thank you. Ask me when the dancing starts." What she really meant was *good luck finding me*.

Dottie worked her way toward one of the stairways that would take her to the balcony, checking to make sure food was being served on schedule on both floors. An enormous temporary wait staff was executing flawlessly, twirling covered platters about them as though to the orchestra's music. A breeze fluttered her way on the stairway, and Dottie tested her breathing.

It was fine. Now.
~~~~~

The greeting line at the entrance had been her father's idea. At first, she'd balked. She didn't need to go looking for opportunities to be snubbed; they presented themselves daily. But he'd worn her down, and it had worked out. Those who wanted to avoid touching a madcap jalopy-racer-turned-killer could shake her father's hand and leave Dottie to greet the wealthy out-of-towners.

Upstairs, the effect of the decorations, music, crowds, and lights was even more spectacular. Those at tables overlooking the dance floor had already been served their main course. The acoustics were superb even up here, and the view over the lake was all moonlight glitter and the magic of a waning summer.

Dottie decided to celebrate all that successful splendor with a few moments of hiding. She had earned it.

Nodding and smiling as she passed tables, she inched her way to the rear of the second floor, where a wall with a door on each end led to the upstairs kitchens. Alongside the edge of that wall, like the deck of an ocean liner, was a little walkway. Dottie had already hidden there occasionally during the summer construction updates, so she headed there now.

Everything was fine. She breathed in. The evening was already a success. She breathed out. She loved this kind of thing. Breathe in. She'd been born for it. Breathe out.

Reporters from half a dozen papers had greeted her earlier, and she knew they'd rave about the ballroom and about Louis Jordan's coming performance — his first at Buckeye Lake.

Dottie pulled off her heels as she rounded the far corner, past the kitchen door, which swung open to belch out a tall waiter with a tower of covered plates. She darted around and drew a deep breath, stepping back into the …

She stopped cold.

Someone else had found her hiding place: a fashionable woman in a flawless gown who, when she turned, displayed makeup very much flawed by tears.

"Lucille?!"

Sure enough. Lucille Armstrong, one bane of Dottie's existence, was slouched against the railing. She appeared to be trying to cry her perfect blue eyes out.

What reason did Lucille have to cry? Her family was enormously wealthy.

Then again, Dottie was also quite wealthy in her own right, and she'd done plenty of crying lately.

Still, Lucille Armstrong was a legendary cook. Anyone could ask Smokey Black to attest to it. She was an accomplished pianist, and she had never appeared to be lonely one day in her life.

Until now.

When she looked up through bloodshot eyes, choking on a sob, Dottie stopped trying to remind herself how mean Lucille could be. What she remembered, instead, was that Lucille had stood up for her kid brother valiantly when they were all in school. He'd been … different. Lucille had protected him. She'd also been jilted — not once, but twice — in love.

Did Lucille, apparently perfect in every way that seemed to matter, ever wonder if there was something wrong with her, as Dottie did? As Emily had said they *all* did?

Could she be crying about it, even now?

"Is there anything I can do for you?" Dottie moved closer and slid down a little against the railing, kicking off her heels. Lucille had commandeered the stool Dottie kept hidden here for her own meltdowns.

"You can just leave me alone."

Unfortunately, Lucille's crying voice bordered on comical. She sounded just like an intoxicated puppet master attempting the part of a dragon. Dottie knew because, of course, she'd encountered an actual intoxicated puppet master during her years in the park.

Lucille must despise Dottie seeing and hearing her this way.

"You found my spot." Dottie waited for her to ask for more information. *What spot? What do you come here to cry about, Dottie?*

But all Lucille did was continue to sob. She pressed her face onto her knees as though she'd abandoned all hope of leaving here with a shred of pride.

"Well, now you've done it. You've transferred your mascara onto your dress."

The response was muffled. "I said leave me alone." When Lucille raised her face from her knees, not only was there a smudge of cake mascara on her gown, but a fake eyelash was dangling precariously from the top of her eye.

"I'll get some club soda from the kitchen, and we'll work on those marks. So that they don't stain. If you're not here when I get back," Dottie said practically, "I'll know you were serious about wanting to be alone." She glanced back at Lucille as she slid her heels back on. "I'll also know you're very brave because I *really* don't think you should walk out there looking the way you do just now. I'll be quick."

Dottie spent her brief journey to the kitchen being jostled by trays and working to harden her heart all over again toward Lucille. She told herself the woman was crying because Julia had snagged Smokey as her date, while Lucille had been plotting to get her claws on him since school days. Or maybe she was crying because someone caught her kicking puppies. Or she'd heard there were fewer homeless children in the city this year than last.

"You're still here." On her return, Dottie extended the club soda and the napkin. "Maybe use the napkin on your face first. Then on your dress."

Lucille didn't accept the offer. Instead, her shoulders slumped, and her head plopped in a very unladylike manner into the railing, until it pressed against her cheek in a way that would also certainly leave a mark.

This woman was a mess. It was all a bit refreshing, since Dottie was used to thinking that about herself.

Dottie pulled her own gown up before she dropped to her knees in front of Lucille and got to work blotting the mascara smudges on the dress. It was a pale pink satin. For long minutes, she tipped the bottle to the napkin, blotting. Used a clean bit of napkin to blot some more. She noticed Lucille was struggling with more tears, her sobs quiet and shaky like a child's.

Dottie knew she, herself, cried just about that same way.

"It occurs to me for the first time that the word *stain* and the word *satin* are made of the same letters, just in a different order. Isn't that something?"

She wondered if Lucille was crying because that box Emily had spoken of was so hard for a woman to squeeze herself into.

"Why are you helping me?"

How could she explain that she just felt she was supposed to? "I wouldn't have done so before," was all she had. Last year, if faced with this same situation, Dottie would have come back with the newspaper reporters to ensure Lucille's total humiliation.

Lucille reached across with shaking fingers to grab Dottie's wrist. "If you knew the things I've said about you to people, you wouldn't be helping me."

"Well, I really can't keep up with all the things folks say about me anymore, Lu, so don't you worry about it."

The woman cried for a while longer, and though she refused to tell Dottie what had happened, she assured her she was safe. She stiffly received a side hug from Dottie. She eagerly accepted Dottie sneaking her out through the back stairs down through the kitchens. After all, in the end, the club soda hadn't worked perfectly on the stain or on the satin.

Chapter Twenty-Eight

Smokey hadn't danced much in recent years.

As a young man, he'd treated the ballrooms and dance halls like training facilities for his next swim race. Being blessed with strength, agility, and lightning-fast reflexes, Smokey knew he'd been a commodity on those dance floors, too. He could toss a girl high in the air and catch her without hurting her. He could shoot her right back through his legs and bring her forward again into a dizzying spin and never miss a step.

Then there was the war.

After that, there was a farm he'd longed for while he'd been gone.

Smokey tended to stay on the farm more often than not now, even on weekends. He realized it hadn't occurred to him to miss dancing with pretty girls. He'd been too busy reveling in the silence of the fields and the broad sky. He'd needed that silence.

Tonight, however, he remembered that there was also a time to dance.

And this was *it*. Julia loved to jitterbug.

She was full of stories about growing up with those dances in her uncle's club in Cincinnati. Smokey was as much out of practice as she was now, but they settled quickly back into the rhythm. They ended every song laughing and gasping for breath, at least until they were split up by other partners for the rumba and foxtrot.

He'd shed his suit jacket, and Beverly Williams had broken his suspenders during a hilarious Lambeth Walk. Alice Waggoner had claimed him for Louis Jordan's famous "Choo Choo Ch'Boogie."

Then, he whirled around during the conga line. And there was Dottie Berkeley.

He'd lost sight of her during dinner and for much of the dancing, but he noticed she still looked cool as the September evening when she fell into the conga line beside him. It was no hardship to lean forward and place his hands on her hips, to catch the sweet scent of her bouncing hair as the line drove them forward.

"You seem to be enjoying yourself," she called over her shoulder. He couldn't tell if she was happy.

She scrambled to grab the fella in front of her, and he lost contact for a moment.

"You're not nearly warm enough to have been dancing for long," he shouted back, catching up with her again.

"I've been busy with other things."

That seemed predictable. And sad.

"Can I have the next dance, then? Do you think you can make time?"

Dottie moved with the music, the new floor practically vibrating. He saw her glance around, like she was trying to figure out if the party would survive her joining it for more than a few minutes.

"Please," he called up to her.

She agreed with a nod.

The next song, blessedly, was a slow one.

They regarded one another and smiled, the swirl of energy coming to a rest around them as the crowds headed off the floor for drinks and a breeze. Dottie stepped into his arms, and he didn't even have to think about moving with the music.

The fingers of his left hand closed around hers, and he drew her near with his right arm around her back. They fit here, as they did everywhere. This close, the need to shout over the crowd and trumpets had passed, but they remained silent for a time.

Being quiet with Dottie was easy, somehow.

He thought about apologizing for the fact he'd worked up a sweat on the dance floor, but he told himself even a farmer didn't mention sweat during a romantic song, especially not to a woman who was shimmering gold.

"Where's Julia?" she finally asked, looking up from his throat to his face. Of course, that would be what the woman was thinking about as they moved to the music: orchestrating a love affair that didn't involve her. He worked to curb his irritation.

"She left with Lillian a half hour ago. Her sitter needed to be home."

"Ah."

"Don't look at me like that. I offered to take her home, but she'd arranged for Lillian to take her a week ago."

"Did I say anything?"

Smokey swung her out with some force and pulled her back in, settling his arm back around her. He took a patient breath.

She smelled different tonight than she did when they were on the tractor together. Not better. Just a different kind of good smell. Her fingernails against the calluses of his hand were manicured to perfection, and below them a glittering bracelet hung on her wrist. Gold-sprinkled lace kissed the freckles on her shoulder, and Smokey felt keenly that he had little right to touch this woman.

This was the "old" Dot Berkeley, as Hugh would call her. He moved her in the dance in such a way that she had to look up again and meet his eyes, and in them he searched for the woman who led a duckling in exercises and cried over the mere thought of a choking goat. He squinted and tried to imagine those tame, smooth waves of hair all frizzled in the heat and dirt of a summer afternoon.

"You seem to be back in your element," he told her.

Did it change the way he felt about her? He considered and decided it didn't. She was allowed to be both, to be many, versions of herself, just as he could be a war hero who grew sentimental holiday crops.

"In my element? Yes," she decided, and she looked satisfied. "I guess it's nice being back in the heart of things, juggling all the balls it takes to pull this off. I've had a lovely time, both tonight and the days leading up to tonight."

It sounded like a quote for *The Beacon*.

"Folks are being … kind?"

"Kind enough. Anyway, who cares?"

She seemed to care lately. But the old Dottie might not care as long as the money was pouring in. She smiled and waved to someone he didn't know nearby. "I just love the noise. The music and all the people everywhere I look."

"Hmmm." Was she telling the truth? Did she prefer this to pumpkin patches in the twilight? "Well, you've done a fantastic job. Seems to me the night has gone off without a hitch."

Suddenly, as though on cue, there was an olive-skinned man beside them with a finger raised. "Excuse me. Miss Berkeley?"

Smokey relaxed his arms as they came to a stop.

"What is it?"

"Small plumbing leak, ma'am, in the downstairs kitchen. It's being addressed, and there's no damage. Your father is there. We all thought you should know, is all."

"Thank you," she said with a nod, affirming that was the right thing. "I'll come take a look in a bit. Has someone called the plumber?"

"Your father already did."

Dottie nodded again in satisfaction and launched herself back at Smokey as though "finish dancing" came right before "fix a pipe leak" on her to-do list.

"So much for without a hitch," he said wryly.

"That's nothing. That hardly counts as a hitch."

"You look beautiful tonight. I'm not sure I told you."

She smiled. "Thank you."

"Anyone looking at you tonight would never guess that you don't sleep or eat regularly."

For some reason, she stiffened in his arms. "Now, what's that supposed to mean?"

"Uh." He meant what he'd said. Unless she'd miraculously started sleeping and eating regularly, she'd had a lot to overcome this evening.

"Are you saying the way I usually look is sleep-deprived and emaciated?" Her mouth was tight.

"It was supposed to be a compliment. Why are you making it into an insult?"

"Unless I'm mistaken, you're complimenting me for *faking* looking passable this evening."

"I believe I said 'beautiful.' I told you that you look beautiful tonight."

"And then implied it was a miracle I'd managed it."

Had he said the *miracle* part out loud? He tried to think back. At any rate, Dottie was difficult to fluster, Smokey knew. Seeing her angry was an unusual thing, and he wasn't even sure what had got them there.

"Look, I didn't mean to make you mad."

"I'm not mad."

"You look mad."

"Well, I'm *not*." Her back was very straight as they danced, and she was looking everywhere but at him. Smokey tried to replay what had just happened, but he was feeling confused. Maybe he needed a drink of water.

Dottie sounded sullen when she spoke again. "Somehow, I figured all along you'd be pleased when one of your wounded, disabled creatures recovered and made its way in the world."

"Ah. And I suppose you're the wounded, disabled critter here?"

"Clearly."

"So, this is you … what?" He waited until she turned her gaze back to him. "Released back into the wild?"

"Into my habitat, I suppose, yes. Shouldn't you be happy that I'm *making* it? That I'm swimming with the other fish, flying with the other birds, hunting with the … with the jaguars?"

Smokey laughed at that, squeezing her to him affectionately. "I knew I was missing something in my petting zoo. I'll have to look into finding a jaguar with a limp. He should get along great with Dudley."

But Dottie didn't smile. Smokey registered that he had been an idiot, somehow.

"Look, Dottie …" *What was she looking for from him, again?* Oh, right. Pride in her successful launch back into her old life. "Of course I'm happy for you."

"*Thank* you. Was that so hard?"

"It honestly *has* been a little hard, keeping up with you."

She stomped on his foot, and he covered his grunt with another laugh.

"You're putting on a very good show tonight, darling, and if that makes you happy, then it makes me happy." He looked down, expectantly, and saw her pretty nostrils flare.

"There you go again!" She'd raised her voice. "Putting on a *show*?"

"All right, let's face it …" Smokey faded off. He considered how hard she'd worked. At everything. What was he doing right now? "Never mind."

"No. Say it."

"Dottie."

"Let's *face it*, as you suggested."

"Okay. Let's face the fact that you're the only one here who thinks you're recovered or healed or reacclimated or whatever it is you're priding yourself on." There, he'd said it.

"Because *you* know I haven't slept well in months."

"Because you haven't."

"Because *I* told you that. And I told you I don't always have an appetite."

"I've shared a few meals with you. I'm holding you in my arms. You hardly need to tell me you're not eating enough."

Her jaw was tight, so much that a little muscle visibly worked below her ear.

"I've told you a lot of things, Smokey Black, that I haven't opened up about to other people, and now here you are, throwing those things *back in my face*. Why? To keep me in my place? Some friend you are."

Her *place*? She tore herself from his arms, and the song ended then, anyway.

"Wait. Hold on. That's not what I'm doing! I'm not trying to … to mess with what makes you happy." It was unthinkable. He wouldn't do that, would he?

"You're trying to knock me back down, make me question myself, so I have no choice but to run back out to your little farm of broken things."

"I …" Smokey tried to hear and understand all of that. It was a lot. *Was* he trying to knock her down, in her golden gown? *Did* he want her to be the vulnerable Dottie, so she'd need him and stay with him?

Equally awful was wondering if she found Holiday Farms pathetic, somehow. *Little farm of broken things?*

He watched her storm off toward a leaking pipe, and he let her go.

He had hurt her, and he needed some time to figure out why he had.

She had hurt him, too, though.

But he already knew that maybe she had to.

Chapter Twenty-Nine

The gigantic pumpkin tower had been Dottie's grand idea. *And where was she now?* Smokey mumbled about it as he slid another twenty-five-pounder onto a round shelf.

The two of them had cut the wood for this tower back in June when the afternoon had gotten too hot to trim trees. The contraption consisted of a large, wooden pole with pegs. The pegs supported a series of wooden discs to make a tower, with larger discs at the bottom leading to gradually smaller ones at the top, and these round platforms were designed to hold hundreds of pumpkins.

A pumpkin tower.

"It's time to re-imagine the farm stand," Dottie had told Smokey early in the summer, as she'd painted a picture with words of how it would look. He remembered the caramel lights in her eyes as she'd chattered and gestured. "Put it out front, by the road, the way you usually do the sawhorse tables. Only, this giant tower *itself* will be worth driving out to see!"

That was the same woman who put people on highwire cycles over the boardwalk. Any time she seemed delighted by an idea, Smokey realized he'd just smiled and followed her lead. He'd changed the farm's name, added the rubber sea monster, and now added this grand pumpkin tower.

Yesterday, Smokey and Hugh assembled the pieces of the tower stored in the barn. It took all day.

Today, the tower was loaded with pumpkins. It was also taking all day.

And where was Dottie Berkeley these days? *Not* with him or this tower.

"I'll be doggone." Hugh considered the arrangement of large pumpkins on the bottom two platforms, stuffing his handkerchief back in his front pocket. He hooked his thumbs through his suspenders. "Looks exactly like she described, don't it? Like an honest-to-goodness tower."

Smokey didn't respond. The grumpier he got, the more cheerful Hugh seemed to be.

Hugh was still looking uncharacteristically happy when he jumped into the back of the wagon for the short trip back to the pumpkin patch. There, the pair would fill the wagon again and repeat the arrangement on the next layer of the tower.

"Better swing by the barn to get the ladder. Gotta reach the upper half of the tower," the other man called up to him on the tractor.

Smokey grunted. Of course he'd been intending to get the ladder. Whose farm was this, anyway?

The late September sky was cloudless, bright blue, which Smokey somehow also found annoying when he bent to retrieve another pumpkin from the field.

Despite his impatience with everything, he took care to leave a perfect stem as he removed each gourd from the vine. They would make better jack-o-lanterns that way. Lids were important. Tomorrow, a bus from Columbus would bring the first group of city folks out to enjoy the novelty of picking their own pumpkins at Holiday Farms.

It would be the official start to the busy harvest season, when Americans in general would fall back in love with their agrarian roots and their small farms.

Smokey knew Holiday Farms more than fit their romantic expectations, snuggled as it was amidst the rolling hills beyond the lake, with its classic red barn and pond, with its patchwork of bright evergreens and its surrounding woods of colorful, changing leaves. Small farm, indeed. Those who traveled here to gather pretty gourds and wreaths for their porches had no way of knowing that Black-Pool Farms went on for miles and miles and earned a tidy fortune in the production of grains and meat. In reality, it was in no way a typical small farm.

Those visitors would be charmed by Smokey in his flannel and his overalls, never suspecting that he had books and books of carefully drawn-up plans and objectives and a business model that was paying off more and more each year.

Even Dottie, he figured, didn't get the full scope of it.

The crowds of families who would come to fill their car trunks with pumpkins would also never suspect the charming farmer was heartsick with love for a woman who thought his farm was pathetic.

She'd said something like that, hadn't she?

It was enough to put a damper on a man's charm.

"Shelby's coming out a little later to help with setup," Hugh informed him after he'd grunted an armful-sized pumpkin onto the wagon. Soon, Hugh would climb in and start scooting them back to make more room. "He stopped by last night to say so."

"Shelby. Great." Smokey headed back for the patch. "Let's go with more medium-sized ones for the middle of the tower now, eh?"

"Thought you liked Shelby all right."

"Sure. Why wouldn't I?"

"Just don't sound as keen as I'd have thought about an extra pair of hands."

After spending the better part of a year trying to get Hugh out of his shell, Smokey considered ways to push him back into it now, so he'd zip it.

"Aren't you just a talker these days."

The fact was, Shelby Berkeley had the same eyebrows as Dottie Berkeley. In one of those genetic quirks — like the one that had turned his own hair gray while he was still in school — the Berkeley eyebrows all flared up into little crests on the outer edges. Smokey would never, ever confess that he couldn't endure those eyebrows just now.

If that weren't bad enough, below those brows, Shelby's eyes were also nearly the same brown as his daughter's. Shelby's were closer in color to whiskey, but making eye contact was still disconcerting.

That reminded Smokey of the fact he needed to check in with the man, anyway, to see how he was doing. One of his "wounded creatures," as Dottie would say, released back into the world. It was just as well he was stopping by, Smokey knew, so he could see for himself the man was still on the wagon, so to speak. The sobriety wagon. After all, Smokey *did* like Shelby.

And it certainly wasn't that man's fault his eyebrows would make Smokey's day unbearable.

Chapter Thirty

The ballroom Grand Opening had delayed a few other post-season routines at the amusement park. Today had proven another long day of catch-up, but Dottie had to admit it was easier working alongside her father lately.

Together, they'd overseen the careful removal of the expensive carousel horses from the merry-go-round. The horses had been wrapped in quilted blankets, loaded onto a flatbed, and transferred to a storage barn on Mill Dam Road.

"I always think we ought to make more of it," Shelby was telling her as the pair of them walked back to the boardwalk under a bright blue sky. "Moving those horses, I mean."

"Make more of it?"

"You know. Put 'em in Heenan's racehorse trailer and have a parade with them. Like the carousel horses are headed to some grand race in … in a make-believe place. The North Pole maybe?" Shelby chuckled. "You know the local kids would eat that up."

As he went on about it, Dottie acknowledged that at times like this, when he wasn't drinking and he was carried away with ways to make childhood even more magical, her father made her think of Smokey Black.

Most things made her think of Smokey, though, these days.

It was getting difficult for Dottie to keep the running tally accurate, but she was fairly certain she had cried, hyperventilated, kissed, actively run from, and now, *yelled* at Smokey Black. Some of those in public spaces. None of them were spaced far enough apart for her to come out looking sane.

So, yes. Sometimes, she worried she might have overreacted on the dance floor that night. She hardly trusted herself to think or speak rationally these days, so there was that to consider. It was true that she didn't sleep much. Certainly, nothing Smokey said that night had been untrue.

The fact was, she *had* been pretending. She *had* spent a good deal of time trying to conceal the darkness beneath her eyes and choosing a dress that didn't make it obvious her ribs had begun to show.

She was not all right. Smokey knew it, all too well.

So, why had she gotten so angry so fast?

She'd gone over it and over it in her mind. Now, walking silently beside her father, she wrestled with it all over again.

Grudgingly, Dottie had to admit she'd wanted Smokey to see her as whole and strong and beautiful for once, rather than as a broken thing. When they'd begun to dance, she had even tricked herself into believing those things were true about herself. The way he'd held her and the warm joy in his eyes had helped her believe it. For a moment, she'd been her old self, and he—Levi Smokey Black, handsome hometown athletic celebrity and war hero—had looked at her with something like desire.

She had believed it.

Then, he'd had the nerve to cut that wonderful moment short by reminding her that he saw her for what she'd become. A poser.

That had been unfair of him.

Still, she had to admit, her anger had been equally unfair.

"We could have a parade on Labor Day weekend, maybe," Shelby was saying now, slowing his steps on the boardwalk to stuff tobacco into his lip. He'd replaced one addiction for another, it seemed, but at least this one didn't end in him running in his skivvies off the end of the pier to nearly drown.

The man was managing. Shelby Berkeley was once more able to participate in the running of his little empire with a "chaw" in his lower lip.

"We could have a marching band play something to do with the races," he went on, catching back up to Dottie and wiping the red-brown flakes of tobacco from his fingertips onto his denim pants.

"Looks like you've got company," he said then.

Dottie's heart stuttered, wanting the company to be a tall farmer. She looked up to see, instead, a little girl sitting on the bench outside the park office.

Not just any little girl, either. Dottie's stomach sank.

It was Delia Stimpson Adams, ward of the late Pastor Skip Reese and recently adopted daughter of Rosie and Gabe.

In her new talent for hiding, Dottie had managed to avoid the child for months, despite Rosie's insistence that she talk with her after the accident. Today, though, Dottie's guard had been down, and there was no avenue for escape.

"Shouldn't you be in school?" she asked, figuring she could at least hurry Delia along somewhere.

"School let out for the day, silly." Delia rose from the bench, clutching a notebook to her chest.

Shelby wandered off the way he often did, and Dottie found herself looking down at the kid's braids, white-collared blouse, and plaid skirt. The blouse was half-untucked, and one of her stockings had fallen around her ankle.

Dottie braced herself. Delia had things she deserved to have the chance to say, and it was time to let her say them. *Past* time to let her say them. Things like: "You killed the man who took me in when I had no one else." Or like: "After watching everyone who loved and cared for me die, you took away the one person I had left in the world."

Dottie thought it was ridiculous to offer the freckled kid a snack, so she just stood there, waiting for it.

"I need your help with an assignment for school," was what Delia said, instead of any of what Dottie had imagined.

"You need *my* help?" Delia lived with Gabe and Rosie Adams, arguably two of the smartest people in Dottie's acquaintance. "What kind of assignment is this?"

"My teacher told us to write a story based on something true that happened in local history."

"Oh."

"I want to write about the amusement park."

Dottie breathed out in relief. This wasn't about Pastor Skip or the accident. "Well, come on in," she said, leading the way into the office. Propping the door open for fresh air, she couldn't help a twinge of disappointment that she wasn't about to get the chance to apologize. Dottie really did need to apologize, but how did a woman word something like that?

Today, she'd accept the reprieve.

"I want to write a story about deaths and injuries here at the park," Delia said as she climbed onto a stool at the counter.

Dottie stopped. "What?"

"Yeah, you know. People who got hurt real bad here when they were 'sposed to be having the best day. Like the lady whose hand got smashed when the boat crushed it against the dock last year. Remember?"

Dottie shuddered. How could she forget? That had been two summers ago, though. She'd forgotten how morbid Rosie's adopted daughter could be.

"What kind of assignment *is* this, anyway?"

"I told you. A story, but it must be based on something true. Charlie's writing about the canal boats, and my friend Margie is writing about Indians and the swamp that was here before the lake was."

"And you're writing about a smashed-up hand."

"No, no. Not that. That's not interesting enough. I want something *like* that, though. Someone coming to the park for a holiday but getting hurt real bad, instead. Dying would be a better story, but I'll take what I can get."

Dottie considered the kid. Did Rosie know she was here or what she was writing about? What was Dottie's responsibility now? Should she call over to Rosie's studio?

I'll take what I can get?!

Dottie sighed. "You want a Coke?"

"Sure!" Delia smiled and arranged her notebook on the counter. A few minutes later, she was slurping soda pop from a straw and gripped a tall, new pencil in her fingers.

"What do you want to know, exactly?"

"I want to know the story of the shooting gallery. The *whole* story."

Dottie blanched. She didn't ask how young Delia knew about what had happened at the shooting gallery. *Everyone* knew about that, so of course she'd heard the story. "Sounds like you already know about that accident. I'm not sure what more I can add."

"A good story is about the details, Miss Berkeley," Delia said. She spoke with a slight lisp because she was missing some important teeth in the front of her mouth, and her grown-up teeth were just emerging through her little pink gums. "Were you here when it happened?"

Again, Dottie debated the wisdom of all this. "Yes. I was about your age."

"Okay, then." Delia's eyes lit, and Dottie's narrowed. "What I know is that a couple of sweethearts were at the shooting gallery, and the fella ended up *shooting* his girl!"

"That's right. You sure you're allowed to write a story like this for school?"

"Teacher didn't say we couldn't."

"Mmm-hmm."

"Did she die? His girl? People say she did die after he shot her."

"Yes, she died." Dottie had tried hard not to think about that incident over the years.

"Why'd he shoot her? Folks say he didn't mean it."

"At the shooting gallery, you got six shots for a quarter," Dottie explained, trying to offer the requested details in the form of ones that wouldn't cause nightmares. Dottie, herself, had lived with those nightmares. "The young man thought he took his six shots, and then he assumed the gun was empty. It was not."

"And he pointed it right at her!"

"Yes. He was playing around. But you never, ever point a gun at someone, even if you think it's empty."

"I know that."

"Well, be sure to include it in your story."

"And he pulled the trigger, and he shot her, and she died."

"That's true."

"What did she *say* to him?" Delia asked, chewing thoughtfully on the end of her pencil. "After he shot her, and they both realized the gun wasn't empty? What did she say before she died?"

"I don't know that. I wasn't there." Instead, Dottie had been wrapping pennies here in the office when Big Fred had run in with the poor young woman's body and put it right on the table where Delia sat now. Nothing in the world would compel Dottie to share that image with the little girl, no matter how the fiendish kid would relish the details. "I don't know what she said, if anything. Maybe you can use your imagination for that part of the story. In Shakespeare plays, the characters always say, 'I die!'"

Delia nodded and looked off into space for a moment. "What do *you* think she said to her fella when she saw he'd shot her?"

Dottie longed for the phone to ring. Any distraction would do. "I really never thought about it before."

"Think about it now."

Dottie sighed. Then she did think about it. She imagined the moment, the realization of what had happened, the way time must have stood still for a heartbeat. The strange sense of betrayal that must have washed through the young woman with that physical pain. "I suppose maybe she asked him why … why he hadn't been more careful," she said, very careful herself with these words.

"Maybe," Delia added, "she made him promise never to marry anyone else."

"Or never to casually point a gun at anyone else."

"I think maybe she told him she forgave him."

Dottie studied the little girl. "You really think so? You think she said she forgave him, right after it happened?"

"Yes." Delia nodded. "Otherwise, she'd worry the fella would spend his life feeling horrible about what he'd done. She wouldn't want that."

"She wouldn't?" Dottie wondered if *she* would. She was afraid her dying wish might be that someone shoot *him* and see how *he* liked it.

"Well, she probably loved him, right?" Delia reasoned. "Weren't they gonna get married?"

"Yes, she was his fiancée. I guess she probably did love him."

"Right," Delia said. "So, if she loved him, she wouldn't want him feeling sad his whole life."

"How can you be so sure?"

"Because it was just an accident. She knew he didn't mean to shoot her. He just thought the bullets were gone. It was a terrible accident."

Dottie nodded.

A terrible accident.

She wished, suddenly, she could clearly remember what all had happened … not on that summer day when a young man had accidentally killed his future bride at an amusement park, but what had happened in that ice storm in March when Dottie's head had been bleeding, and this child's stand-in father had been dying beside her car.

Had Pastor Skip forgiven her in those moments when he'd felt his life slipping away?

Could he have loved her enough for that?

"Do you?" Dottie asked little Delia. "Do you forgive someone right away when they do something awful?"

"Is the something an accident?"

"Yes."

"Then, yes. I do."

Then Delia, who was young enough to still be losing her first teeth, reached her hand out and placed it on top of Dottie's.

Dottie stared down at that little pale hand with ink stains on its fingertips, and something in her throat kept her from speaking right away.

Was this child more like Jesus than Dottie had managed to be in all her own years? Was she more adept at extending grace than most of the adults in the community? It was nearly beyond understanding, and Dottie felt the little soul deserved something more than a Coke.

"Delia," she managed, blinking and clearing her throat. "You're an extraordinary person. Do you know it?"

"Yes," she said earnestly, which made Dottie laugh.

"I need to ask you to forgive *me*."

"No, you don't." Delia knew exactly what she'd been talking about. "It was an accident, that's all."

Dottie walked around the counter and hugged the child tight on her stool.

"Miss Berkeley?" Delia said against Dottie's shoulder.

"Yes?"

"Which part of her body did the fiancé accidentally shoot her in? It's important for my story."

Chapter Thirty-One

Sometimes in the off-season, when she had nothing else to do, Dottie would wander over to help Emily put the paper to bed on Wednesday nights.

It was usually relaxed, involved snacks, and was an opportunity to catch up.

On this particular autumn evening, Emily had deliberately called Dottie in to help because Drew was transporting a prisoner and wouldn't be home until the wee hours of morning.

"I'm not as productive as I once was." The publisher's voice was sullen as she'd waddled from the typewriter to the ad desk. Her stomach was enormous, but at least she was too busy to insist Dottie touch it this time.

"I wasn't doing anything this evening, anyway. I'm happy to help."

Emily handed Dottie new classified ads, which hadn't been typed yet, noting, "A monkey couldn't mess these up." Dottie knew Emily had to deliver this week's copy to Pataskala, to the daily paper there, where they would set the type and print *The Buckeye Lake Beacon* by tomorrow.

"I have to say, I'm surprised you weren't tied up helping out at the farm again," Emily said, groaning as she got up. Dottie thought her friend was being a little extra dramatic this evening, as the clock ticked toward midnight. Still, how was she to know how tiring pregnancy might feel?

"I'm sure Smokey's got the farm all under control."

"What's that tone for?"

"I didn't have a tone."

Emily made another indecipherable sound, and Dottie looked back to see her bite into a dinner roll.

"Is that your dinner?"

"No. Just a snack," Emily mumbled around the chewy dough. She grinned. Dottie had to admit her friend still managed to look pretty, even with a breadcrumb at the corner of her mouth and a colossal mound of baby attached to her.

"There's a crumb on your lip. No. Other side."

"You have a fight with Smoke or something?"

Dottie sighed and turned her attention back to the typewriter and the scribbled note for the classified section. It seemed a four-room cottage was available for rent. She typed the first line before she spoke. "Maybe we had a little disagreement at the ballroom. Not a big deal, though."

"I figured it was something like that. Rosie and I went out to the farm the other day to get pumpkins for Charlie and Delia."

"Did you? How did everything look? Is the pumpkin tower up?"

Emily cut her a sidelong look. "Go see for yourself. He could probably use the help."

"Julia's helping out there."

"And Hugh. And his mother. And *my* mother. But he was slammed."

"Did he seem … like he couldn't handle it? Like he was okay?"

"Please. It's Smokey. He can handle anything."

Emily's easy dismissal bothered Dottie, for some reason. It had to be hard to be Smokey, to have everyone always assume he was fine. Probably as hard as it had always been to be Dottie, who was also always fine. She wondered if *not* being fine was somehow freeing, but Emily interrupted the thought before she'd decided if it was nonsense.

"He seemed sad, though. He asked about you."

Dottie concentrated on typing about the cottage for rent.

"That's why I asked if you two had a fight. It strikes me as odd. All these years, I've never known you and Smokey to fight."

"We didn't have a fight, exactly. Just grumbled at each other, is all."

"Come to think of it, I've never seen you fight with anyone. Nor have I seen *him* fight with anyone. Must've been entertaining."

"Like I said, we just said some things. That's all. It's not like I throat-punched him."

Emily laughed, but her laugh ended in a groan. "Ugh. Is one comfortable chair in this whole office too much to ask? Anyway, I'd like to see you *reach* his throat."

Dottie thought about kissing Smokey's warm throat that day in the barn and felt her face get hot. The subject would need to be changed. Immediately. "Here's an ad for a boat for sale."

"So?"

"So, it says 'no motor, no trailer, no seats.' What does it have, I wonder?"

"Maybe it's a canoe."

Dottie typed. "You said Lil is helping at the farm? I thought your mother was pretty much full-time at the family's marina now. I miss seeing her here, in my office."

"It's off-season for the marina, too. So, she's been working there in the mornings, keeping up with rentals and billing and the like. Then she heads out to Festival Farms."

"Holiday Farms. He changed the name."

"Oh, right. I saw the ad. Clever."

"Mmm."

"Your idea, by any chance?"

"Maybe. But why would you think so?"

"Just a hunch. The man seems to put a lot of stock into your ideas, that's all." Emily's typewriter blasted out a line or two of content. "He gave you credit for the pumpkin tower. When we were there the other day."

"You seem like you're hinting at something, Em, and you might as well come out with it. I'm too tired to play your games."

"And I'm too tired to *have* games." Emily punctuated it with another groan.

Dottie rolled her eyes. "Listen. We argued because he accused me of *pretending* to have everything all together."

Emily's typewriter stopped again. "At the Grand Opening?"

"Yes."

"Well, *weren't* you? Pretending?"

"Yes, but that's not the point. I guess I'm tired of people worrying about me."

"At least the ones who are worrying about you aren't hating you, though."

Dottie laughed. "True." Then she sighed. "I miss him."

"I knew it. You two are sweet on each other. I knew it." Her typewriter dinged like an award bell.

"I don't know what we are."

"You're sweet on him. He's sad and wants to see you. It's simple."

"You know very well there's nothing simple about any of this."

"It's got to be simple for now, though, because I have to finish this school board story. Shhhh."

Dottie settled back in with her ads, smiling a little at Emily's occasional sighs and groans that punctuated the clack of her keys. She knew they weren't done with this topic, but Dottie didn't know what else there was to say about it.

Did she miss Smokey? Yes. Desperately. She'd already stood and stared longingly at his latest half-page ad.

But if he had feelings for her, she felt certain they were all tangled in pity and worry. Smokey was a fixer, a hero. If he'd asked their friends about her, it was because he'd convinced himself she'd been curled in a ball, crying, and probably needed some of that proverbial fresh air.

Still, he'd admitted it took more than fresh air, hadn't he?

Dottie had opened her Bible. She'd gone back to the book of John again, to the verses she'd copied and posted on her desk the winter before. Back then, she'd been worried there wasn't enough fruit in her life, so she'd set about growing some because she didn't want to be "pruned" in some great spiritual way. Below the verses, she'd written ideas for using her gifts for the Lord. Dot's Dash to Business course was there. Providing opportunities for war widows and veterans, whether skills or jobs. She'd had a very good plan for her own spiritual fruitiness.

Then a spring storm made the roads icy.

The problem was, she knew now that she'd set about producing fruit all on her own. It had been easier to make a checklist than it had been to tackle the much more evasive challenge of rooting herself in the ultimate truth of the universe. Of *abiding* in Him, as Jesus had said. If she did that, the fruit would form naturally. That was what John 15 said, now that she read it again and put her list away.

So, she'd been putting the wagon before the tractor, or whatever Smokey's analogy had been. The thought of Smokey on his tractor, of being on that tractor with him, settled something inside of her.

As did the thought of grace.

Smokey's tidy ledgers of debits and credits, and a little girl's easy forgiveness, had made Dottie want to pray again. The Lord had just been waiting there, it seemed, for her to have nothing left to offer Him. For her pride to be shredded. For a complete lack of influence or ability to even tell herself she was producing good fruit.

He'd been there, patiently waiting for her to simply abide with Him, for her to be filled in return.

She wasn't sure the lighter feeling she'd experienced lately was the promised "joy," exactly. Dottie wasn't sure she'd gotten that good at abiding or that she'd use that word. Yet. But something was different.

Something was different, too, it seemed, about the quality of Emily's groans. One of them shook Dottie from her thoughts.

"Do you want to switch chairs?" Dottie turned in her seat. "This one is fairly comfortable."

Emily had stood, but she was leaning forward with her palms braced on the desk. When she raised her head a bit, perspiration was visible on her lip and cheekbones.

Dottie got up from her own chair. "Emily." She crossed the room. "Did you get your school board story finished?"

"Yes," she muttered, her voice tight. "It's right here." She drew in a careful breath. Groaned again.

"What's wrong?" *Don't say it. Don't say it.*

"It's only that the baby wants to be born tonight, I think."

"Well." Now, Dottie let her own breath out. "As long as it's only that."

The two of them looked at one another and smiled, and for a moment Dottie felt excited and happy. Her friend was going to be a mother, and soon! But then Emily moaned again, and her damp face got redder, and Dottie's heart gave one of its flops. She looked at the clock. It was nearly

11:30 at night.

"I'm calling Drew," she said automatically.

"You can't, remember? He's doing the prisoner transfer. He won't be back for hours." She blew out a harsh breath. "Just take me to Pataskala so we can drop off the paper. Then you can drive me to the hospital."

"Drop off the paper! No. I'm calling Rosie."

Emily groaned and moved to pick up her purse. "No time. She's in bed. Let's go."

"Emily!" Dottie called it out with an urgency that broke through whatever painful things were happening to her friend's mid-section. "Emily, I *can't* drive. Remember?"

"Baloney. I've ridden with you a hundred times."

"You know very well that this isn't some whim." Dottie's heart was pounding, and she was sweating just like Emily. Where was Smokey? They needed Smokey. "You know better than anyone a judge *ruled* I can't drive. You published a story about it in this very paper!"

She was losing her battle against sounding hysterical.

"Where's the judge now?" Emily snapped. "You think he's out there waiting at my car to throw you in jail? Let's *go*."

Dottie's reflexes were nearly too slow to catch the car keys Emily chucked across the room at her.

"Are you going to pick up the box of copy to take to press, or are you going to make the very expectant mother carry it? C'mon, Berkeley!"

Dottie was having trouble breathing. She shoved the keys in the pocket of her jacket and crossed the room for the box. She realized she'd forgotten to add the additional classifieds and ran back to the typewriter she'd been using.

"Will you get it together, already?"

"You're pressing your luck, Em." Dottie leaned on the front door with her bum so her friend could push her enormous stomach out through it into the cool night air. "What man agrees to take a criminal to … to … wherever he went when his wife is having a *baby*?"

"I wasn't having a baby when he left," she gritted out, waddling as fast as she could.

"And what maniac finishes putting the paper together when she's in labor? This is all your fault. You *knew* this was happening!" Dottie tried breathing in through her nose, out through her mouth. The last time she'd been behind the wheel … she couldn't think about it. She couldn't do this. "Admit it. You knew the baby was coming, and you sat there typing a stupid story!"

"You can't prove that."

"We could have called someone *else*. Anyone else could've been here by now, if you'd just *said* something." Dottie shoved the copy into the backseat of Emily's Cabriolet and slammed the door hard. "You infuriate me, you know that?"

"Hey. *I'm* supposed to be the one doing the whining and yelling!"

Dottie wrenched open the passenger door then and helped Emily, who had both hands under her stomach, slide in. "I'll never forgive you for this, Emily."

"Just stop talking and start this car."

Dottie tasted blood as she bit the inside of her mouth. Behind the wheel, her hand was shaking so hard she couldn't get the key in the ignition. "Don't worry about me," she mumbled, suddenly deciding she should try to put Emily at ease. The woman was about ready to deliver a human. Dottie could drive them to the hospital.

"In case you haven't noticed, *you're* the only one worrying about you right now."

The words hung there as the car started.

Emily believed Dottie could safely get her to the hospital to have her baby. Her father believed Dottie could still run the park. There might have been a time there when he'd recognized she needed to step away, but he still trusted her. Did Smokey truly doubt Dottie was all right, or did he just doubt her ability to believe in herself again?

She may have been more worried about herself than any of them had been about her.

She put the car in reverse with automatic ease. The streets were empty. The weather was fine.

A full breath inflated Dottie's lungs.

"I'm taking you straight to the hospital," she said with a decisiveness that made her feel bold. She could do this. "*Then* I'll take the copy to Pataskala. You'll have to deal with that because I'm driving."

"That's probably a good idea." Emily groaned and looked down. "Ohhhh no."

"What? What? Did the baby come out?"

"My water broke."

"*What?*" Dottie put the car into drive and she slid the Cabriolet onto Route 79 with ease. "What does that mean?"

"It means my car is soaked."

"Forget it. I don't want to know." Dottie breathed in and out, steadily. It felt good to be behind the wheel again. She could do this. She would allow herself to fall apart later, of course, but she could do this for now.

Emily believed she could.

Father, please help me, she prayed. *Please be with us at this moment and the ones to come. Steady me. Abide in me as I abide in You, and please, please, let Emily's baby abide in her a bit longer!*

"Can't you go any faster?"

"Not a chance."

Chapter Thirty-Two

Dottie was scribbling ideas at the front counter of the office on Friday afternoon when a large bouquet of sunflowers tied in a bright blue ribbon arrived by delivery. The card, from Sergeant Drew Mathison, thanked her again for breaking the law for the sake of his wife and newborn son.

Dottie beamed over it.

She'd wanted so badly to call Smokey yesterday, to tell him she'd been brave, to tell him she hadn't even fallen apart when she'd returned home and had given herself *permission* to fall apart. Instead, she'd simply hit her knees and thanked God for new life and for not forcing her to deliver the baby into the world.

Dottie took a pleasant walk after lunch, boarded-up restaurant windows on one side of her, the sleepy lake on the other. Dry leaves blew in her direction from further up the north shore as trees shed the first of their colorful leaves. The boardwalk always felt like a ghost town by October.

The Beacon was on the stands today, but the office was closed for the coming week. Dottie knew Emily's aunt and uncle, Cookie and Burt, would take over publishing for a while as their niece settled into motherhood, but for now the Graham family had hunkered down together in celebration. Rosie's studio, too, was dark and would be until spring, unless she needed to develop film.

Smiling to herself, Dottie had to admit she was more excited about newborn Jimmy Mathison than she'd been about her own natural nieces and nephews. Just as she'd always been more comfortable in Emily's and Rosie's family than she'd felt in her own. Maybe it was because the women in that Towpath Island bunch were expected to be a bit unusual. Dottie knew she'd always fit better there with them.

She had plenty of people who loved her.

Why, why had she ever let public judgment wreck her so entirely?

The answer to that was also obvious. She'd first wrecked her*self* with judgment.

As she returned to the office, still feeling a bit too restless to go inside, Dottie waved in surprise when she saw Julia Fey and little Penny heading toward her. Penny ran ahead of her mother and straight into Dottie's arms, and Dottie felt grateful for the little souls God had put in her path lately. Delia. Baby Jimmy. Penny, who smelled like laundry soap and cinnamon.

She'd learned so much about love from them.

"Sweet girl, what are you and your mama doing on this lovely fall day?"

Penny wore a little plaid romper with a cotton, buttoned jacket.

"Pumpkins!" the little girl exclaimed.

"Pumpkins?" Dottie grinned as Julia caught up. "Aren't you tired of pumpkins yet, little one?"

"She's been staying with the neighbors while I've been out at the farm for the busy hours," Julia explained. "Today, since Fridays aren't quite as crowded out at the farm, I promised her she could go pick a pumpkin of her own."

Penny bounced with excitement in her arms, making Dottie laugh. There was a lesson in joy here, too.

"Come with us, won't you?" Julia said with her own winning smile.

And suddenly there was nothing in the world that could have kept Dottie from agreeing to go. If she didn't catch sight of Smokey Black soon, she thought she might shrivel up and blow away like one of the leaves on the boardwalk.

~~~~~

It was like she'd never been there before, Dottie decided, as she experienced Holiday Farms with fresh eyes. Julia pulled into the crowded lot beyond the bright white fence that ran along the front of the property. Few parking spaces remained.

The new Holiday Farms sign did, indeed, have fall foliage decorating its edges. *Perfect.* A hand-painted sign below it advertised the hours for the pumpkin patch in orange. Fodder shocks of corn stalks were bundled along the fence posts, and Dottie had begun exclaiming over the pumpkin tower when they were still a quarter of a mile away.

"Look at it!" she cooed with delight. She wasn't sure who was more excited, Penny or herself. "It's all so beautiful!"

Dottie's heart swelled as she watched smiling families toting pumpkins out to their cars. Mothers carried jars of jam and orange-swirled lollipop treats for later.

The farm looked like a beehive, full of activity, and Dottie whirled about to drink it in. In the bundle house, shelves had been arranged with hand-dipped candles, wreaths of dried apples, caramel apple treats, and afghans crocheted in the colors of fall. Mama Pool was in her usual apron, arranging more jars of homemade jellies, jams, and sauces from her yard, and she immediately swallowed Dottie in a firm hug.

"There's my girl."

Dottie blinked back tears. Here was a woman who had loved her without condition, and Dottie was only now understanding what a gift that was.
~~~~~

Mama Pool kept her hands on Dottie's shoulders when she stepped back. "What's kept you away so long?"

"Oh, you know. The Grand Opening. Closing the park for winter." *Being unable to face your younger son after storming off during what should have been a lovely dance.* "Just life."

"Don't I know about that. Sorry I've been so busy out here that I haven't made it in to help with the bookwork."

"You know I can keep up just fine this time of year. Look at this! You've arranged quite the spread here."

"Poke around and take anything you want."

Dottie laughed and did enjoy browsing. She saw a scarf she liked. Maybe she'd learn to knit this winter, when the snow was blowing over the lake. Maybe she'd knit Emily's sweet little Jimmy a blanket, she thought. It felt good to even want to make plans again. For now, she insisted on purchasing the scarf. Then she wrapped it over her shoulders before rushing out to the barn to see her animals.

Er ... *Smokey's* animals.

The edges of the barn doors were framed in stacked straw bales, pumpkin arrangements, and pots of colorful mums. She remembered sitting in lawn chairs there, chatting while it rained in the spring. She remembered, too, kissing Smokey's warm throat there in the heat of summer.

Inside the barn, Dottie had to blink back more happy tears when she saw her sweet Dudley, strutting around with a perfectly straight neck, happy to be petted by little hands. A little boy asked if he could take Dudley home, and his mother denied the request. The other animals were milling about with the children, as well, Hugh looking on to ensure the safety of the animals more than of the kids, Dottie knew. She caught his eye and waved. He blushed and winked, and she laughed.

Hugh looked healthy.

She rather hoped he thought the same of her.

Smokey's farm had been so good for all of them, she thought as Dudley waddled in her direction.

Now, where *was* the man?

"I think the hayride is getting ready to leave, if you want to join us," Julia said, taking Penny by one hand and grabbing Dottie with the other.

"I wouldn't miss a hayride."

Soon, the three of them were settled on a low wagon stacked along the edges with straw bale benches. The wagon was hooked to the old Allis-Chalmers Dottie had come to love, but it was Reggie Black waving from up on the driver's seat.

Wrong brother.

Dottie blew out a breath and settled in, delighted when Penny climbed onto her lap. Others were boarding, and there were more straw bales cut across the center of the wagon for seating. Someone had lit a bonfire by the bundle house, and the wood smoke combined with the scent of fall leaves and the low sun felt like all the good memories of autumn, stirred together in some cauldron of joy.

"This place," she mumbled. "It's exactly what he imagined."

"What's that?" Julia asked.

But Dottie could only think of Smokey submerged in dangerous waters off the coast of France, weapons strapped to his thighs and ankles. This place was what had been in his heart, amidst all that fear and mud and death.

He'd made it all real.

He wouldn't want to hear it said of him, but the man was beautiful inside, and all of this was proof.

And then, there he was, looking just as beautiful on the outside. She heard him before she spotted him because he was calling out a cheerful greeting to his hayride adventurers, asking them if they'd like to explore an enchanted forest.

A chorus of excited affirmations went up all around her.

He bounded into the wagon with one long stride over the straw bales just behind the hitch. Dottie watched him scan his crowd, reveled in the moment he spotted her because his gaze stayed right there on her, and then those pale lines around his eyes crinkled, and the grooves that bordered his lips creased, and he was gifting her one of his full-force smiles.

She thought it would be fine if she never managed to draw another full breath.

Emily had indicated earlier that week that Smokey Black had wanted to see Dottie. The smile he offered her now told her how much. She was glad she'd come.

For a moment, Dottie wondered if he would call the whole hayride off, disappoint all these children, just to come check on her, to make sure she was still surviving, to worry about her.

"And after the enchanted forest," he said, easing her mind on that score, "I'd like to take you to see where the pumpkins grow."

"The pumpkin patch!" Penny yelled, bouncing again on Dottie.

Smokey pointed at her and winked. "You bet, the pumpkin patch!"

"And we can pick a pumpkin of our very own," a boy said with confidence on the other side of the wagon.

"Your very own, to take with you," Smokey affirmed. "So, let's settle in and start our adventure! Stay sitting down for me now, you hear?"

Dottie wrapped her arms tightly around Penny as the wagon lurched gently forward, watching Smokey remain standing, resting his hand casually on the rear of the tractor seat while he leaned up to talk briefly with Reggie.

He wore maple-colored corduroys with a worn leather belt, a flannel that wove in lines of greens and grays, and his scarred work boots. Beneath the flannel was an oat-colored shirt that contrasted with his sun-browned neck. The dark stubble on his jaw was nearly to beard-length, though the shadow of hair on his head remained short, nearly undetectable. He wore no hat, but a pair of butter-yellow work gloves were stuffed into his back pocket.

She could just look at him all night. Pumpkins weren't all that impressive, by comparison.

He met her eyes again when he turned. "I'd like to share a story with you," he said in that deep voice that brought a hush over his little wagon theater. "It's the story of the Three Sisters, an Iroquois legend I think you might enjoy."

Dottie smiled at him as he continued to watch her. She wondered if he was also remembering her first night out here on the farm, when her shirt had been covered in manure, and he'd nestled her against him anyway on that tractor. He'd told her he only wanted daughters so he could name them Maize, Red Bean and Pumpkin after the legend.

He'd been trying so hard that day to put her at ease, she reflected. *Red Bean Black*, his middle daughter. He'd somehow even made her laugh.

Tonight, she relaxed into the sweet warmth of the child on her lap and the deep timbre of Smokey's voice.

"I never knew a story about crops could elevate the temperature of the whole outdoors," the woman in front of Dottie leaned over to tell her friend. "I'm *burning* here."

The friend giggled with delight. "You're telling me. He's delicious, and I think he's looking right at me."

"How are you not an absolute puddle, Norah?"

Julia laughed softly beside Dottie.

"He's looking at *you*," Julia whispered. Something about the happiness with which she said it had Dottie glancing over at her. Julia winked with a kind of satisfaction, and Dottie felt so much like a schoolgirl that she laughed, as well.

Julia was not in love with Smokey Black.

Dottie's plans had not panned out this time.

She looked back at the man who was also *not* looking at Julia. Nor was he looking at the woman in front of her. No, Dottie knew Smokey was finally looking right at her.

~~~~~

She'd come back out to the farm. Finally.

Maybe, Smokey thought, as the wagon rattled back into the forest
~~~~~

and twilight flirted around them, she was done being angry with him. She had little Penny snuggled up on her lap, but he could see Dottie's dress was burgundy, her gloves black, and she'd draped a scarf knitted in gold and green around her neck.

She was bursting with color.

Those little splashes of pink were at the bottom of her cheeks, and they looked healthy. *She* looked healthy. Julia leaned over to say something to her, and she laughed and turned back to him with the laughter still in her eyes.

"Why don't you all jump down and play here for a few minutes?" he called out when they reached the Enchanted Forest. "Before we head to the pumpkin patch."

And the words were barely out of his mouth before he made a beeline for the back of the wagon where Dottie was sitting. He brushed past other parents and children who seemed eager to speak with him, but he couldn't feel guilty for pushing forward. Not just yet.

"Dottie B." He looked up at her where she remained on the straw bale. Penny had already been hoisted over to the Loch Ness Monster by her mother.

Dottie turned at the waist to greet him. "Smokey B." When she smiled, he saw the dimple, as he had when he first spotted her on the wagon, and he had to restrain himself from grabbing her. "Everything looks magnificent," she told him. "I'm not even sure that word goes far enough. It's beyond magnificent."

"Thanks. I mean that. So many of the ideas have been yours."

"The vision is yours, though."

"Well, the pumpkin tower is yours."

"The tree house is yours," she said playfully, glancing over at the children on it, the dimple still firmly in place.

"Nessie is yours."

"Smokey, I've missed you." She said it in a rush and caught him off guard. He'd been so afraid he'd damaged their friendship that night at the ballroom.

"I need to tell you … I need to say I'm sorry for …"

"No. Please." She reached down, a gloved hand on his shoulder. "Smokey, we don't have to talk about that here."

He let out a breath, and he assured himself again there was no visible anger in her eyes now. It killed him, the thought of her getting into Julia's car tonight and leaving after Penny chose her pumpkin. He'd somehow felt he needed to keep her here from the day she'd first come in May. "You know, tomorrow's crowd will be much bigger than this one."

"Will it?"

"Saturdays. Yes."

"Do you … have enough help out here?"

"I won't lie to you and say I couldn't use a hand. But I don't want you to feel obligated or anything. And, of course, I'd pay you."

"We can fight about that later, too. I'll be here tomorrow."

"Breakfast is at eight."

Children were trying to climb him like he was part of the playground. "Mister! Hey, Mister, we wanna see the pumpkins!"

"Your people need you, Farmer Black."

"So, you'll come tomorrow?"

"I said I would."

He nodded once, drank in her face for a moment longer, and then Smokey turned to chase Penny and her new best friends.

Dottie would come back tomorrow. She'd said so.

~~~~~

Outside of the forest, the sun was still just high enough for them to take their time in the pumpkin patch.

Dottie walked the rows, a little apart from the wagon crowd, and remembered mounding those little teardrop seeds. She stooped now and then to touch a vine, to feel the hard, perfect skin of a ripe pumpkin. She marveled at the directions in which they'd all crept off the mounds where they'd started.

Certainly, Dottie was no stranger to seeing a project come to fruition. That had been her life at the park, after all. Yet, this field of mostly decorative fruit satisfied her in some different way. She'd gotten her hands dirty here. Literally. They'd ultimately grown, though, by none of her direct design. It felt like a miracle.

While these pumpkins could be used as food and nourishment, as in the Iroquois legend, there was something delightful in knowing they'd more likely be carved into faces and filled with dancing candlelight. They were part of a culture that brought joy and warmth to the darkness.

They felt playful, these pumpkins, and Dottie thought she was learning the value of playfulness for the first time in her life.

"Which one have you settled on, Penny?" she asked as she rejoined Julia and her daughter.

Penny's dress was now thoroughly dirty, and she was cradling a pumpkin that was the perfect size for her. "Dis one."

"That is just the pumpkin I'd have picked out for you. It's lovely."

"She wants to paint it rather than carve it," Julia said.

"Paint!"

Julia had also selected one for herself. "I've been out here so much, and do you know I haven't taken a single pumpkin home until now?"

"Will you be here tomorrow, working?"

"Yes. Saturdays are very busy. But I'll leave by dinnertime so my girl
~~~~~

and I can paint our pumpkins. Right, Pen?"

"Paint!"

"I'll be working with you tomorrow, then. Smokey told me he could use the help."

"I bet he did."

"What do you mean?"

"Just that I'm happy you're coming out to lend a hand. Would you like to ride out with me in the morning?"

"Thanks. If you don't mind."

Julia extended her arm for a side hug. "I think you'll be easy to train for the job."

Reggie stood on the tractor and called out an "All aboard!" to the wagon. This would be the last hayride of the night, he'd explained earlier, since the farm would close before darkness settled.

Walking beside Julia, Dottie sought out Smokey, as she had since she'd first seen him tonight. They watched him stoop to help a little boy who'd given up carrying his too large pumpkin and was kick-rolling it toward the wagon. Smokey hauled both the boy and the pumpkin up on his shoulder, which earned him delighted squeals.

Julia cleared her throat, and Dottie felt her gaze on her. She looked over. "What?"

"You know there's absolutely nothing going on between Smokey and me, right?"

"It's a good thing." Dottie sighed and smiled. "Because I'm afraid I'm in love with that man."

It felt very, very nice to say it out loud. She'd probably loved him since they were almost still children, and yet, this was the first time she'd ever said the words to a soul. How strange. How cowardly, even.

Julia had her hands clasped against her chest and was sniffling back happy tears. "I knew it. Oh, I *knew* it!"

"Don't get too excited. He certainly deserves better."

"Don't say that, Dottie. No matter what's happened in your life or his, meant to be is … well, meant to be. You are *allowed* to be happy."

Dottie wanted to believe she was. No, she *did* believe she was. She was allowed to be happy.

But at what cost to Smokey? Love was frightening.

"What if I wouldn't make *him* happy, though?"

"I think you need to let him decide who and what makes him happy."

"You're very wise, you know that?"

"Don't forget I've already been married to a man I loved. You keep thinking I need some kind of help from you, Dottie. I mean, I'm grateful for the office skills and that you keep arranging work for me. But now, I think you can learn a thing or two from me."

Dottie hugged her. "More than just a thing or two, please."

Chapter Thirty-Three

Saturday morning breakfasts were the latest tradition at Holiday Farms during the harvest season. Smokey figured he'd just keep those breakfasts coming when it was time to start cutting Christmas trees next month.

The autumn air bordered on chilly, the fallen yellow leaves around his cabin still damp from the night, but the sun had started to burn off what was not yet quite a frost. He whistled as he carried the last tray of pancakes out to the wooden card table beside his front door.

She was *there*. Smokey could hardly believe it.

He leaned against his door frame and watched Dottie work through a pile of syrup-drenched breakfast on her plate in that dainty, classy way that was always so much a part of her. She was seated on the tailgate of his truck, swinging her legs, her plate balanced on her lap. She grinned at something his mother said, then turning, said something to Hugh beside her.

Smokey watched another bite of pancake make its way to her mouth while her laughter played around it.

"She seems happy," Julia observed, snatching two more pancakes from the fresh supply he'd just set down. He supposed it had been easy for anyone to track his gaze, so he left it right where it was.

"She does."

"I told her there's nothing going on between us." Julia managed to cut her pancakes with the side of her fork one-handed while standing. Smokey registered it from the corner of his eye, and he marveled all over again at the talent of mothers. "I told her last night."

Smokey raised his brow. "How'd she take that? She doesn't love it when her schemes fail."

"I *had* to let her know. I mean, you two were practically scorching the air between you with those looks."

"Don't know what that means."

"Oh, yes you do. You're doing it again right now." Julia popped another bite in her mouth, chewing and swallowing quickly. "I don't think she was sorry that we aren't headed toward happily-ever-after, you and me."

"That surprises me."

"She seemed downright relieved, to tell the truth."

Smokey straightened from the door jamb and gave Julia his full attention for the first time. "Relieved? Really?"

Julia's eyebrows wiggled up and down suggestively. "I wouldn't want to say too much or meddle … but yes. She was fine with you and me *not* seeing one another."

Now he looked at Dottie again, in her perfectly pleated work pants and belted wool sweater, her boots still swinging back and forth beneath his truck.

What had their fight on the dance floor really been about?

She glanced over then and met his gaze. The morning sun was bright behind her, golden on the texture of the braid she'd wrapped around her head like a crown. Smokey offered her a smile, and she smiled back, and it felt like they had a secret, the two of them.

He just wished for sure he knew what it was.

"See?" Julia mumbled over her last bite of breakfast. "No woman looks at a man like that if she wants to see him settled with her friend. That's all I'm saying."

Julia wandered off with the others, then, leaving Smokey with his thoughts.

What would it be like to have the right to walk over there just now, pluck Dottie off the tailgate, and plant a maple syrup kiss on those lips of hers? To have the right to do it in front of their friends? To have a woman like her allow it, want it?

Even the thought was dizzying. It was the kind of thought in which he'd never let himself indulge.

An impatient car horn sounded in the distance, from the direction of the parking lot.

"Does no one read the sign with the hours on it?" Mama Pool boomed, rising from her lawn chair with her plate.

Smokey made his way over to the truck to take Dottie's plate from her. She'd eaten every bite, he noticed, and he thought today was already a very good day, based on that alone.

"Let's go make some money," Reggie called cheerfully.

"And some memories," Dottie said, softer, just to Smokey. Her dimple flickered. "Let's go make some memories."

It was not necessary for him to help her off the tailgate, but he took the excuse to touch her. Not for the first time, he was grateful she seemed to understand what Holiday Farms was all about.

~~~~~

The day was simply a perfect one.

Dottie was happy to see her father had come out sometime after breakfast to lend a hand, catching sight of him now and then as he replenished pumpkins on the tower at the entrance. Every now and then,
~~~~~

a visitor decided they must select one from there.

Shelby Berkeley was at home out here, she knew, just as she was. What was this place but another amusement park, after all? There were guests to wow, gimmicks to draw more of those people, and a buzz of excitement in the air.

Since the war, Dottie had been vaguely aware that Smokey's farm was an attraction for both local people and people from the cities of Newark, Lancaster, and Columbus. Still, she'd had no idea on what scale. She was surprised, on this sunny Saturday, by the number of buses that arrived, by the people on those buses to whom a live turkey was a novelty and who had never seen anything at all growing from the ground.

She'd split the morning between the petting zoo, which freed up Hugh to help with other tasks, and helping Mama Pool at the register when the line got long. Dottie loved weighing pumpkins for the children, playing guessing games with them before the scales revealed who was closer. She bought a handful of tiny pumpkins Hugh had carved from pine wood for a nickel each and began awarding them to the children whose weight guesses were closer than her own.

She made sure that was the case for every child.

At noon, Smokey himself had made the rounds with rough-cut ham slices on rolls, which he'd wrapped in napkins. After that, he'd insisted he needed Dottie's help with the hayrides.

So, Dottie got to *play* the rest of the day in the Enchanted Forest, where the trees were gently releasing leaves the colors of rust, sunshine, and almonds to drift slowly to the ground. She went down the slide repeatedly, eventually leaving her sweater in the wagon when she got too warm. She helped small people find the courage to swing down from the treehouse. Then she helped them find the roundest pumpkins. She basked in the friendliness of their parents as she enthusiastically explained the way the vines produced flowers, which became little green balls like grapes, which then grew and grew into the pumpkins.

And, all the while, she felt Smokey's gaze on her.

It energized her.

It made her think of the way the potatoes had sizzled so loudly in that pan before they'd burned. She was *sizzling*. Or he was sizzling. Maybe both?

Dottie was a bit nervous about him suddenly, somehow, though she couldn't for the life of her explain why. At any rate, it was a fear she wanted to move toward rather than away from.

When the last cars had left the parking lot, when the cheerful bonfire had been banked and the money had been locked away, there had been no discussion about whether Dottie would remain at the farm.

She simply did.

Julia had left earlier with Penny, and not a soul offered to drive Dottie back to her lonely apartment at the lake.

"When was the last time you carved a pumpkin?" Smokey asked lazily after they'd eaten the potato soup he'd "whipped up."

Dottie had tried to feel guilty about how he'd cooked the soup for her after he'd worked so hard all day, but it was difficult to feel bad when he seemed so happy doing it. Just as he'd been happy to hand her a sandwich at midday and a stack of pancakes after dawn. Instead of indulging in guilt, then, she'd helped him slice a few potatoes into bite-sized pieces, and she'd watched him add milk and onions and butter to the pan while he spoke warmly and with humor about people he'd met out here lately.

When she ate two bowls of that soup—it had tasted better than anything she'd had for so long—he had beamed with approval, and she'd felt stupidly happy to have made him happy.

What in the world was happening?

Now she'd insisted on washing up the bowls in the heated cistern water, and he was beside her drying them when he suggested carving pumpkins.

"I don't think I've carved a pumpkin since ... hmm. Maybe I did it out on the towpath a few years back? With Charlie, I think."

"I've got a beauty out in the wagon."

"And you're suggesting we slaughter it?"

"For a good cause."

She nodded, and they left the pan from the soup to soak as he went out to retrieve the pumpkin and she eagerly spread last week's copy of *The Beacon* on Smokey's kitchen table.

He built up a fire in the fireplace, Cream Puff rubbing against his ankles on the hearth. Dottie followed his lead and rolled up her sleeves. Under the lamplight, she shamelessly admired the way the muscles in Smokey's forearms flexed as he worked the kitchen knife around the top of the stem of the pumpkin to free the lid.

"Funny or scary?" he asked as he removed the lid. "What kind of jack-o-lantern are we carving?"

"Classic."

"We can display it up by the register."

"But only if it turns out well."

Smokey's lively eyes were half-lidded when he was relaxed like this, and Dottie was enjoying his eyes so much that she was not prepared for him to deposit a slimy blob on the tip of her nose.

She gasped, shaking her head, and onto the newspaper plopped a stringy mess of orange pumpkin guts dotted with seeds.

She narrowed her eyes at him across the table. "You're going to regret that."

"We'll see." He winked. "And I say we display our classic jack-o-lantern even if it's imperfect, Dorothy."

"Don't call me Dorothy, *Levi*." She kept her eyes trained on him as she reached a fist into the open pumpkin. His gaze followed her hand, but he made no move at all as she transferred a chilly mound of goo onto the very top of his head.

He looked directly at her, and she waited. He sat very still, while one mucous-like tendril of pumpkin slid slowly down his temple. She tried but couldn't stop the laugh that burst out.

"Oops."

"Let's get started, then," he said easily, and she laughed even harder as he calmly began transferring the insides of their pumpkin into the crock he'd placed beside them, the mound of pumpkin still balanced precariously atop his head.

"You're just going to leave it there?"

"Leave what where?"

"It suits you, at least."

"Maybe folks can start calling me Gourdy instead of Smokey."

Dottie snorted and took turns with him digging out the seeds and meat of the pumpkin with a large, metal spoon. Soon, she was scraping the flesh of the inside clean. They worked in companionable silence. Sometimes, their hands met, and his sun-browned skin was warm compared with the cool of the pumpkin's insides. She imagined more than simply brushing against that warmth, and she felt her breathing turn odd. Not panicky. Just odd.

What in the world was happening?

Then she looked up from the pumpkin guts and saw the pile of seeds on his head, and she laughed softly all over again.

"Triangle eyes, then?" he asked as he considered their hollowed-out canvas in a business-like way.

"That seems classic to me."

"The only thing I insist on is a round nose."

"Jack-o-lanterns have triangle eyes and a triangle nose."

"Ours will have a round nose," he said, in a tone that managed to be playful and stubborn at the same time. "How about you work on the eyes while I make us a pot of coffee?"

Dottie turned the pumpkin this way and that. Which was the best side for the actual face? She was so focused on it that he managed to catch her off guard when he pulled open the back collar of her blouse and slid the mound of pumpkin guts from his head right down her back.

She shrieked. He laughed like a very large child with a very deep laugh, and then he was clomping around the table fast as she rose, knife in hand. Dottie giggled and squirmed as the blob slid its way down her spine between her shoulder blades.

He was still laughing, holding his hands out in surrender. "Whoa, whoa. What are you doing with that knife, darling?"

Dottie held it in a slasher position, but she blew any level of intimidation she'd managed with another giggle.

"No wonder my mother loves you," he said soberly, backing away. "What is it with the women in my life? Anyway, I'd like to remind you that you started this."

"I absolutely did *not!*"

He laughed.

She made a ridiculous poking motion toward him with the blade.

"Can we call a truce if I let you change into one of my shirts?"

The idea thrilled her. She knew immediately she would wear it home and never, ever give it back.

"You think I'll let you off that easy?"

"As happy as I am to see you playing," Smokey said, "I'd really rather you not do it with a knife. This is becoming an uncomfortable pattern in my life."

"Who says we're playing?" she asked sweetly, but then, blast it all, she giggled again.

Which made him laugh again.

In one swift motion, Dottie dropped the knife on the table, grabbed a handful of rejected pumpkin parts from the crock, and launched herself at him.

Chapter Thirty-Four

Smokey and Dottie didn't clean themselves or the floor or the walls until Mr. Pumpkin was successfully carved and lit with a candle. Smokey had stuck a knotty carrot through the round hole he'd carved for the nose, which earned him another of Dottie's lovely laughs.

She had turned down the wicks of the oil lamps so they could admire the jack-o-lantern lit from within.

"So much for classic," she said now as they contemplated their finished product. "The carrot is the exact color of the rest of him. It's kind of unsettling, that nose. Like a snowman and a pumpkin had a child together."

Smokey pretended to also look, but he turned his head to look at her, instead. She had replaced her sticky blouse with one of his plaid shirts, which was basically a dress on her.

Most distractingly of all, though, she had taken her hair out of its braid-bun.

It hung all around her now, ropes of dark and perfect curls. They were shiny in the firelight, and they reached halfway down her back. She was so beautiful that he had trouble swallowing.

"I think the coffee's ready," he said, needing an excuse to move away from her. He poured into two mismatched cups, and he carried one to Dottie. She'd moved into the rocker by the fireplace, and there was no other chair close to that, which was a good thing. "It's pretty hot," he said stupidly as she closed her hands around the mug and breathed in the scent. Her hair was like a cape around her shoulders. It was amazing how soft it made everything about her look.

"I have something for you." He set his coffee on the beam over the fireplace. She arched an expectant brow.

Smokey retrieved it from the little shelves behind the stove, a smaller pumpkin, still whole. He presented it to her.

"A pumpkin," she said, blinking up at him. "Thank you."

"Not just any pumpkin. Here, look."

He turned it, showing her the back, where slightly raised, cream-colored block letters spelled "Grace." Dottie took it from him and ran her hands over the letters.

"It's called scarring," he said, kneeling at the hearth in front of her. "When the pumpkin was still green on the vine, I took a very fine blade and drew the letters on it. Then, as it grew, the letters hardened into a scar."

"It's pretty." She touched the raised letters, and her eyes twinkled when she looked back up. "Did you make it for another woman named Grace? And then she stood you up?"

Smokey laughed. "Would I do something like that?"

Dottie pretended to consider, pursing her lips. "Well, maybe you wouldn't. I could better imagine a woman named Grace bringing it to you as a reminder of the delicious cornbread she baked you."

"I promise it's for you and not that kind of grace. Promise."

"When did you do it?"

"You have to catch the pumpkin at the perfect time in its maturing for it to work right. And you can't cut too deep if you want to preserve the fruit. But if you do it just right and at the right time, it heals beautifully. Just like people."

"It doesn't hurt the pumpkins, ultimately, then."

"Pumpkins are pretty tough."

"But it does leave a mark."

"Yeah."

"Like your tattoo."

"Yes, kind of like that."

When she looked back up at him this time, her eyes were shiny. "So, you scarred this for me? The word 'grace'?"

"Sometimes it's good to have a reminder of the important stuff, that's all."

"We hadn't even talked about that then. I mean, when we talked about forgiveness and fruit that night on the tractor. Wouldn't you have already done this by then?"

"Right. I had. But I knew all along what you were out here looking for."

"I thought I was out here for the fresh air."

"Fresh air. Grace. Charming farmer."

Dottie sighed and smiled at the same time. "Anyway, thanks for the reminder. I've done a lot of thinking the past few weeks. I've been wanting to tell you that."

"I can tell. There's something different."

"I'm more like my old self?"

"No." Smokey shook his head. "No, not like your old self, entirely. You're … your new self."

Her face lit at that. "You think so?"

"I do."

"More than broken now. You don't just see me as broken?"

"I never saw you as broken."

"You said I was pretending."

"That night? When we were dancing."

"You weren't wrong about it. What you said wasn't wrong. I don't know why I got so mad."

"I know why. I deserved it. It took me some time to figure out why I was saying those things, about you pretending like you were fine when you weren't."

"It was all true, though."

"I was out of line. I think …" He cleared his throat. This was difficult, but she deserved difficult things from him. And more. "I think I was a little scared of you."

He hadn't meant to make her smile just now, but he'd managed it, anyway.

"*Scared* of me."

"Yeah. You were glorious that night. So beyond the reach of a farmer. Beyond my reach as a friend, even. As a dance partner. As … everything." He shook his head, dropped onto his backside on the hearth because he just felt like he should be even lower. "I think maybe I was desperately trying to remind myself that there was a loophole, that I was *allowed* to be next to you because you … well, because I was trying to convince us both you weren't perfect."

Her eyes scrunched with humor. "Not perfect? That's an understatement."

"Except that you *are* perfect, and you know it, and that's why you had every right to get angry with me. I'm sorry."

"Smokey, I wasn't looking for you to see me as perfect. I absolutely know I'm *not*." She forced out a blustery breath. "I really hate that you think that's how I see myself. Nothing could be less true."

"I don't think you see yourself that way, not consciously. I just think you know, in your soul, that God made you perfect. He did. And who in this world am I to have suggested otherwise?"

She was silent, and Smokey stared at his hands hanging off his knees. He heard her rock back and forth in the chair three times before he pressed on.

"You've been going through something awful, sweetheart, and I don't know but that it hasn't made you even more perfect. That's what I should have said that night."

"Like the scarring," she mumbled.

"Yeah. Like that."

He felt her hand on his shoulder, a tentative touch that he still felt right through the flannel.

"I think you're the only person who really knows me."

It made him look up. "I'd be honored if that were true."

"It is true."

Her mahogany eyes reflected the fire behind him.

"I thought you never let your hair down."

She shrugged. "I feel like I can with you."

It was the best compliment of his life.

"Dottie …" He was going to do this. He needed to tell her the truth because she'd told him the truth. He just hoped she'd still feel safe with him, and he couldn't ask to touch those curls of hers until he told her. Until she knew. "I thought about scarring something else entirely on that pumpkin for you."

"Something else? Besides 'grace,' you mean?" She arched one of her lovely eyebrows, and then he lost his courage. When he was silent too long, her second brow joined the other. "Another word?"

The truth was, he'd wanted to carve his initials with hers. Let them grow there together with the fruit in the patch. He'd thought about adding a heart, but the whole thing had seemed too childish and too presumptuous weeks ago. "Never mind."

He loved her. He imagined turning a pumpkin to her right now with the words "I love you," and he wished fervently he'd carved that because he couldn't seem to speak the words.

"Come on. What did you think about scarring on the pumpkin, Smokey?"

"That I …" He cleared his throat. His neck was getting hot, and he hoped she couldn't tell since, after all, she'd left her hand right there on his shoulder. "I thought about, you know, carving a heart on it."

Oh, no. Had his voice just cracked? *Lord, help me*, he prayed. *I'm fifteen years old again, in a grown man's body.*

Dottie scooted closer, leaning down to study him. He found it hard to meet her eyes. "Are you okay?"

"Yes."

"You thought about putting a heart on a pumpkin? That's kind of sweet."

He wished now for death. "Kind of sweet" was no way to win a woman of the caliber of Dottie Berkeley.

"For you, I mean."

"A pumpkin for me with a heart on it?"

He coughed.

"Are you sure you're all right, Smoke?"

"For *love*," he snapped.

Dottie tilted her head, and then her eyes got wide. "Wait a minute. You were thinking about that? Weeks ago? You were going to scar a heart on a pumpkin for me? *For love?*"

All he could do was close his eyes and nod. Wait to see what she'd do.

She actually laughed, then. A small, soft laugh.

When he opened his eyes, Dottie had sat back and, dimple firmly in place, laughed like she was having the time of her life.

On second thought, he did *not* love this woman. He despised her.

"Smokey Black," she said when she'd reigned in the laugh, "are you trying to say that you *love* me?"

He abruptly stood from the hearth before he knew he was going to do it. He needed to feel taller, less foolish. "Well, I'm not saying it right. But *yes*. I was trying to say I love you, Dottie, and you're *laughing*."

Now she jumped up, too, the "grace" pumpkin dropped to roll across the floor, and his arms were suddenly full of her. He felt her fingers against the sides of his face. "No, no, no. I'm not laughing because you love me! Are you kidding me? Never! On the contrary, I think I've waited for this moment most of my life, which should make you realize how pathetic I really am."

Wait. What? Most of her *life*?

"It's just that ... Smokey." And she laughed again. "I think I've finally discovered something you're not very good at!"

He stared down at her, trying to make sense of her words alongside the tenderness of her fingers on his jaw.

"I mean, you're a champion athlete and an excellent dancer, and then you went to war and won commendations, and then you came back and built an actual wonderland out of some fields, and you even cook good meals, and you're an amazing kisser ..."

Well. This was more like it. Something unknotted inside him. "Go on."

"But you're really awful at saying, 'I love you'!"

He looked down at her. She looked up at him. And then they were both laughing. All he could focus on was that she'd liked kissing him that day in the barn, which seemed like a very good starting place. He could work with that.

Smokey bent his head and captured her laugh with his lips, and in no time her caress of his jaw gave way to her arms wrapping hard around his neck. She was pressed so close, and it felt so right. He felt the warmth of her compact body, the sheer thrill of how firmly she clung to him and how determined she was about that kiss.

"You have to admit," he said, pausing to skim more kisses along the soft skin of her cheekbone. "A pumpkin with a heart would have been a real win."

"But you didn't do that." He startled when he felt her kiss his earlobe. "Instead, you stumbled around talking about the symbolism of a theoretical heart instead of just saying ..."

"I love you," he interrupted, and then his lips were back on hers. It occurred to him that Dottie's mouth felt exactly like he'd always known it would feel, like something he'd known his whole life. How many years had he wasted not kissing her?

"You're worse," he said, long minutes later.

"Hmm?" She didn't seem to be able to open her eyes, so he pressed a gentle kiss on each of her eyelids.

"I may be bad at confessing my love because, I might add, I've never done it before ..."

Her eyes flew open at that. "Really?"

"Never."

"I like that."

"Well. Anyway, you're even worse at it."

Dottie made a sound of amused surprise. "Oh. I am! I forgot to say it back, didn't I?"

"Well, you're under no obligation ..."

She was still laughing. "I'm sorry. There's nothing funny about it, but you're right. Smokey, I do love you. I really, really do."

He'd thought so. Not until she'd started kissing him tonight, not for sure, but these last few minutes, with her heart beating hard against his own chest added to that enthusiasm she'd brought to those kisses ... Smokey had suspected Dottie might love him, too.

Chapter Thirty-Five

As it turned out, autumn was a complicated time to figure out a very new kind of relationship with the owner of Holiday Farms.

Because of the amusement park, Dottie understood better than most women the unusual cycle of seasons in certain businesses: the careful, quiet, non-glamorous planning in the quiet season, as well as the frenzy of in-season.

And she'd been there with Smokey for both, now.

Most days, she was able to accomplish her own tasks at the park quickly, and then she'd catch a ride out to the farm as the fall evenings grew shorter. Smokey himself would often just drive into town, grab lunch-supper from the diner with her, and haul her back home with him. There was always something to do there: displays that needed restocking, animals to feed and care for, the general repair from the day or evening before.

There were certainly plenty of families with whom to interact. When Reggie was busy with harvest at the main farm, Smokey had taken to driving the tractor, and Dottie easily slid into narrating the hayrides.

As they worked, Dottie figured they were equally busy trying to navigate this surprising swing from friends to sweethearts.

She'd never been so happy in her life.

There were stolen looks amidst the hayrides, those thrilling moments in a crowd when she knew he was struggling to resist touching her. The way he'd look at her sometimes made her *feel* touched. Now they really did have a secret they shared in those looks, and they both knew it was all about love. Some evenings, he'd have her drive his truck just down to Mama Pool's for supper, and now she could do it without shaking. He'd sit in the middle of the bench seat with his hand on her knee "for encouragement," and she'd swat it away. Other evenings, they'd curl up in the cabin and snack on whatever was there, talking late into the night.

She sometimes wondered how they had so many things to say to one another after growing up in such close proximity.

The single ladies had stopped bringing food out, which Dottie celebrated, and Smokey pretended to lament.

Still, it was his own doing that the bachelor offerings had dried up. One evening—she thought it was a Thursday—determined Lucille had pulled in with a covered basket of something that smelled like culinary heaven. She'd nodded to Dottie, sharing a different kind of look now, after that night in the ballroom.

"I made too much and thought I'd bring you dinner, Smokey," Lucille said sweetly, striking an alluring pose beside her open car door, the basket in the crook of her arm.

Dottie was thinking Lucille had spent a surprising amount of effort on her makeup just to cook dinner when Smokey startled her, clamping an arm around her waist and pulling her to his side.

"We're mighty appreciative of that, aren't we, Honey Pie?" he said, pressing a long kiss to the side of Dottie's head.

Dottie couldn't help it. She'd snort-laughed. "*Honey Pie?!*"

"I'll just leave it for you, then," Lucille said into the long pause that followed.

"Thank you," Smokey said politely.

Dottie couldn't stop cringing. "Lucille, I'll bring your basket back to the park office if you want to come get it. Maybe we … maybe we could have a cup of coffee. If you want."

So far, Lucille hadn't stopped by, but nor had she seemed overtly angry to have lost the game of *Capture Smokey Black*.

Meanwhile, Dottie was very much enjoying the spoils of victory. Smokey made her laugh until she cried, which was something she hadn't realized she'd stopped doing even before the accident. He made her heart beat fast in a wonderful way. He showed her every day what it meant for someone to put her first. Had that ever happened before?

Dottie didn't want to say, not even to herself, that she'd never been loved like this except by God.

But it was true. She hadn't been.

Her father loved her in his way, she supposed. He'd enjoyed sculpting his oldest daughter into what he'd always called "a force to be reckoned with" — something he'd usually said with such pride that Dottie decided it must be a worthy goal in life. Her mother seemed to love her in theory, and Dottie didn't think her sisters wished ill on her, exactly, though mostly they regarded her as odd.

She had good friends in the Graham sisters, of course.

But she'd never been loved the way Smokey seemed to love her.

He read her carefully, at all times, and seemed to anticipate her needs. If her back ached, he seemed to know just where. He seemed to want to hear her thoughts about things, which she had to admit had always been true about Smokey. He knew she was hungry before she realized it herself, and he seemed to delight in feeding her. She made him homemade rolls, in exchange, and was grateful Mama Pool had made her learn to bake bread

"Dottie, hear me out," he said on the last Saturday of October. They'd gone back to the Enchanted Forest with lanterns because a woman insisted she'd lost her diamond earring out there that afternoon.

"Hear you out about what?"

They swung their lanterns near the ground, watching carefully for the light to glint off the diamond. So far, no luck.

"Suppose you went to church with me in the morning."

Dottie's stomach sank. She had not been to the community church since she'd ended their pastor's life almost eight months before. She didn't say anything as dozens of thoughts she hated thinking clattered together in her brain.

Mostly, people had stopped seeking her out with cruelty as the objective. Sure, there were still occasional encounters in which she was ignored by people who would have spoken to her before, and those still hurt, but most days Dottie could pretend the general disapproval away.

Most days, she basked in the magic of Holiday Farms and all the strangers who didn't know her.

"Talk to me, Honey Pie."

"Please, *please* don't call me Honey Pie." He'd taken to using the nauseating endearment ever since that night with Lucille because, despite her best attempts to ignore it, Dottie would react. Now, she focused hard on the mulch under the Nessie tires, watching for the gleam of a jewel. "Look, I know I should go back to church."

"And I know it's not an easy thing. Believe me."

"But you think I should go."

"I think it's time. Not for anyone's sake but yours." He was about eight feet away, scoping the area by the slide. "But of course it's your decision. You're your own boss."

"Even out here?" She grinned in the dark.

"Especially out here."

She heard the smile in his voice, as well.

"No earring over here."

"None here yet, either. Since when is picking out a pumpkin diamond-worthy, anyway?"

Dottie sighed and moved toward the slide she'd donated, the light from both of their lanterns gleaming off the metal waves on its surface. He made a very desirable shadow at its base. In wordless invitation, he set his light down. She placed hers beside it. Smokey sat on the edge of the slide, and Dottie slipped onto his lap.

"If you go with me, I won't leave your side," he vowed, wrapping his arms around her.

"I know you won't. And I know I need to go back." She swallowed and laid her cheek against his collar, absorbing the heat of that wonderful spot where his neck met his shoulder. "I think you're right. It is time."

"Afterward, we're invited to lunch on Towpath Island."

Dottie raised her head. "Wait a minute. Is this some kind of group project between you and the Grahams?"

"Maybe I just wanted to make sure they were going to be there," he said, and paused to press a brief kiss to her lips in the darkness. "And maybe they're planning to absolutely surround you in that pew."

Dottie laughed. "Will Emily and Drew bring the baby?"

"He's being dedicated and prayed over tomorrow morning, yes."

"Then I do need to be there."

"I knew you wouldn't want to miss it. Plus, Hickory is smoking a roast for supper."

"I'm going. I'm going."

She dropped her head back on his shoulder in surrender.

"I don't enjoy both of us wearing coats," he said. "You seem too far away."

"Necessary, though. We'll be lucky if it doesn't snow tonight." Dottie sensed just how cold the end of her nose was, so she pressed it into his neck. He smelled distractingly good. "Plus, we could always go inside."

"Yeah, but there's that poor woman's clip-on earring."

"She describes the diamond as enormous. I don't know that 'poor' is the right word for her."

~~~~~

Dottie, carefully dressed in coat, hat, and gloves, made it into her seat at church with surprising ease the next morning.

"See? Everything is completely fine," Rosie said with determination on Dottie's left, her arm pressed right up into Dottie's. Smokey was on the right side, also smashing her inside the wool of her coat.

"You don't have to sit right on top of me, you know."

"Sorry." Rosie hop-scooted to her left, causing her husband to grunt. "Move over, honey."

"Move over," Gabe repeated to his left, and Dottie grinned as the couple's children, Charlie and Delia, grumbled and slid around further down the pew.

"Did you find that woman's diamond earring?" Rosie asked.

"No. But we had a lovely time hunting for it."

"I'll just bet."

"Can I come hunt for it?" This was Delia, leaning around the grown-ups.

"Me, too!" Charlie's eyes danced.

"It's not my farm, but be my guest."

Smokey leaned from her right. "It *is* my farm, and you can be my guest. But you don't get to keep the earring if you find it."

Delia frowned. "Why not?"
~~~~~

"Delia." Rosie sighed her name.

"I'm mounting an expedition, and I need funds."

"What kind of expedition?"

"I'm going to find a shipwreck."

"In Buckeye Lake?"

"Can we talk about this later?" Gabe put in. "No pirate talk in church. New rule."

"Pirates don't go looking for shipwrecks," Charlie reasoned.

"We wouldn't *hurt* anyone," Delia added.

"Shhhhh."

Sitting there, surrounded, Dottie could not be sure just how she would have been treated by the rest of the congregation. She had not yet had the chance to find out. Instead, she'd moved in a protective layer of guards who consisted of Mama Pool and both her boys, along with Pam and the kids, Hickory Graham and his granddaughters and their husbands, as well as other members of Emily's and Rosie's family. Even Lil was with them, that pale, pinched shame nearly undetectable now.

They'd all moved together like a giant creature determined to keep Dottie tucked safely in its belly.

She was feeling a little ridiculous. Grateful, certainly. But ridiculous.

Emily slid into the pew just in front of them, and Drew followed her, baby Jimmy swaddled like a little football in his right arm. Dottie thought it was lovely to see Emily able to move about like her frenetic self again.

In some strange way, she could relate to that newfound freedom of movement.

Once seated, Emily turned around to grin. To say their friends had been happy for Dottie and Smokey to be dating would be an understatement.

"You two will be seated next to one another at dinner," Emily whispered, wiggling her eyebrows at them.

"You're using place cards now on Towpath Island?" Dottie asked wryly. "When did things get so fancy?"

"Oh, it's so good to hear you being your old, funny self again," Emily said. "You're so *good* for her, Smokey."

"I thought motherhood would make you less annoying."

"That only worked on me," Rosie said, leaning over to whisper.

Then there was the piano, and Dottie glanced up at the wall to see what page of the hymnal to turn to. Smokey had already found it, though, and when they rose to sing, he held his open book so she could see it.

It felt like such a *couple* moment. How often had she watched couples at church sharing a hymnal and wondered what that would be like? To meld praise with someone else's praise so closely?

She considered him with wonder all over again, and he smiled down at her. Smokey Black loved her. She was blessed, indeed.

The new preacher, Daniel, was in his mid-thirties and had a kind smile, soothing presence, and receding hairline. As he eased into a sermon, Dottie's knee started bouncing, and then her foot started tapping. She began picking at the edge of a fingernail until the pain was distracting, but then Smokey's hand slid under her fingers even as he looked straight ahead.

Daniel, having seen her, might decide to preach about Jezebel's idolatry or Delilah's trickery. There was always Eve, too, if he needed to fall back on an easy example of female pride and shame. Everyone would be staring at the back of Dottie's head, thinking about her taking a curve too fast on ice, her history of not paying attention to others in general.

She, herself, was a cautionary tale.

Yet, when she expected her breathing to get difficult, or her hands to shake, or perspiration to slide down her temple … none of those things happened.

Nor did Daniel preach about any of those women. In fact, he'd been talking about Peter for a bit, the rock upon which Jesus built the Church.

Peter had walked with Jesus, eaten with Him daily, slept beside Him, walked to Him on water. Dottie stopped picking at her fingernail and started imagining Peter, imagining what it would be like to munch on a loaf of bread with her Savior. Then she remembered that she would. It was called Communion. She imagined what it would be like to chat casually with Him about the things in her heart, and then she remembered that she could. It was called prayer.

"Abide in me, and I will abide in you."

She'd taped those words to her desk again just Friday morning. It was a lovely promise, yet hadn't Peter denied the One who made that promise? More than once? On purpose? Then, still went on to be the rock for His church.

She was back at church as Dottie Berkeley: fallen, broken, forgiven, and healed, and she liked that Dottie better than any version of herself she'd tricked herself into thinking was strong before.

The rest of her church family might like this Dottie better, too, because when it came time to leave, Tim and Maria Price made a point of coming to tell her they thought the reconstructed pier was beautiful. Neither had ever said anything cruel to her at any point this year, in fact. Glenola Hewett hugged her and simply said it was nice to see her back. The Quicks and Smiths waved and smiled on their way out. The Hupp kids asked if she was coming to their mom's birthday party that Wednesday evening.

Through all of that, as Dottie felt lighter and lighter, Smokey's warmth was right there behind her. She heard him there, felt one of his huge hands on her lower back, even as he talked with friends and neighbors himself.

She knew she owed the preacher an apology for hiding from him so successfully all these weeks. As she turned to find him, though, she discovered Daniel was holding little Penny and laughing at something Julia Fey was telling him. Then Dottie watched Julia touch the man's arm like it was the most natural thing in the world.

Dottie left church marveling that maybe she didn't have to control everything, after all, to have it work out just right.

Chapter Thirty-Six

Smokey had his nice suit cleaned again, as prescribed by his new sweetheart. Twice in one year was a new record, for sure.

Dottie's next instructions for the sleepy Wednesday evening in early November were that he should head back down the pier to the new ballroom in his freshly cleaned suit. Of course, she'd be waiting for him there, might even be watching his approach, so Smokey hooked his thumbs in his pockets and whistled his way along the boards above the silent, gray lake.

Everything was silent, in fact. There were no lines to access the ballroom this time. The door was propped open, a single lantern glowing beside it.

When Smokey stepped inside, his whistling died off.

Dottie Berkeley stood in that same golden, alluring gown from the grand opening, solitary in a pool of candlelight, next to a solitary table. It was the only table not stored away somewhere for the winter months, apparently, its white tablecloth covered in bowls and platters of steaming food.

Music played from a record player situated on the dark, empty stage.

His eyes tracked back to her. She'd left her hair down, which he'd come to understand was an expression of trust and love on Dottie's part that he silently promised he'd never take for granted. She seemed to be waiting for something. Probably for him to say something clever. Possibly funny. Something charming enough to offer a woman who looked like that in a scene as romantic as this one.

He had nothing, though.

No words.

Okay, he had one word.

"Delicious." He meant it. It made her lips twitch with suppressed amusement, and he took a moment to appreciate that he truly was allowed to kiss those same lips.

"I figured I owed you a real dance. After last time."

Smokey closed what remained of the distance between them in just a few strides, but he stopped short of touching her. "All this for me?"

"Who else?"

The miracle went way beyond her lips, of course. Somehow all her creative flare, too, had been directed squarely at him tonight. "Dottie."

He'd always suspected he'd survived the war for some profound reason, and now he suspected the reason stood before him. "*Thank you.*"

The record playing was Louis Jordan, and the scent of beef gravy and Dottie's perfume had Smokey feeling a bit twitchy. She leaned into him, her arms snaking in through his suit jacket to wrap around his shirt along his back. Smokey's own arms naturally kept her there, his jaw dropping to rest sideways on top of her curls. At some point, they'd begun swaying to the music. Not dancing, exactly, just a swaying embrace like tree branches in a late autumn breeze.

"Are you warm enough?"

He smiled against her head. "Yes."

"I have a confession."

"You only love me for the way I look in this suit?"

"Well, obviously."

"I don't mind. I'll take it." He ran his fingers over her shoulder blades, so soft. He hadn't been allowed to touch her like this the last time they'd danced here.

"My confession is, I paid Julia to make this food for us tonight."

"It smells good, but it'll keep. I like holding you."

"You're not disappointed? That I didn't cook it?"

He instinctively squeezed her as he chuckled. "There's something that smells truly appetizing on that table waiting for me, and right now I've got the most beautiful woman I've ever seen in my arms. She's smart enough and rich enough to pay other people to make that food so we have time to dance by candlelight. I'd say 'disappointed' is the furthest thing from what I'm feeling."

She snuggled even closer as she returned his laughter.

"You didn't have to go to all this trouble, Dottie B."

"You're worth it, Smokey B."

The needle skipped to the record's next song with a soft crackle. They continued to sway.

"What I mean is, you don't have to romance me. I was well and truly in love with you before I walked down that pier tonight. There's no falling any deeper, believe me."

Dottie pulled her head back to look up at him, and he dropped a kiss on her nose. "Smoke." She swallowed. "I can't have you start believing I'm … weak."

He stopped swaying. "What?"

"I've been feeling weak, and I don't want you worried that that's who I'll always be in our relationship. That you always have to be the strong one who helps me … you know … pull it together. *I* can be strong for you, too. Okay?"

Smokey shook his head. This woman. "What in the world do I even say to that?"

"You don't have to say anything."

"Dottie." He tucked her back in, started their non-dance again. "First, nothing about this year has had anything to do with a weakness in you."

"All I've done is hide and cry."

"Not true."

"I'm doing better now."

"True." He went back to resting his cheek on the crown of her head, breathed in the scent of her hair, felt a little sorry for anyone who had never gotten to experience the way her hair felt and smelled. "Beyond that, you need to remember I've known you since we were just pups, honey. I don't ever need to be reminded you're strong. I watched you win all those stupid drag races in my brother's car, for crying out loud."

She whipped her head up again, bumping his chin. "You did not watch me racing Reggie's car."

"Did so."

"You ignored me, and you know it."

"I watched you, all right. Which I think I'd know better than you."

"Half the time, you were over here at the park dancing with every summer girl you could find. And the other half, when you did come out to Old Canal Road, you were busy smooching with them."

"I love it when a dignified woman of business gets herself in a tizzy over decade-old jealousy."

"I'm not jealous."

"I won't debate it with you. But hear this." He wound one of her dark waves of hair around his finger, but he kept his gaze on hers. "I remember you always wore those crazy kerchiefs in your hair and those skirts that showed off your legs even though you weren't meaning for them to. You about drove me crazy, Dottie."

She went still. "I did not."

"Did so."

"Did not. You laughed at me."

"I did not laugh at you. I was so far gone over you, I didn't even know what to do with myself."

Her brows scrunched. "I'm not buying it, Smokey Black. You sure knew what to do with all those pretty girls of yours."

"You don't have to believe me. But I'm telling you the truth."

"Why didn't you say something? Or even … I don't know … ask me to come out dancing with you?"

Smokey shrugged. "There was always an invisible shield around you. I was … nervous. I couldn't let you just hand me back my heart, I guess. I didn't want to take the chance of that. Besides, you were *Dottie Berkeley*. Do you even know what that meant to all of us?"

"That I was the late-blooming, strange daughter of a known drunkard?"

He barked a laugh now. "You're something else."

"It's a little tragic."

"You don't even know. No, that's *not* who you were. You were untouchable, sweetheart. Gorgeous. Daring. A step ahead of all of us, all the time. There were precious few of us brave enough to talk to you, let alone ask you to go dancing. Besides, you'd have said 'no.'"

Dottie started swaying again, clearly considering what he'd said. "No, I wouldn't have."

"You said no any time a boy asked you, and don't think the rest of us didn't know it."

"The summer boys, sure. I said no to them. What did I want with any of them?"

"Exactly."

"I'd have gone out dancing with *you*, Smokey."

He considered that. He couldn't help wondering what would have happened if he had invited her, if she'd said yes. The truth was, he'd been pretty stupid back then. His body had grown way faster than his brain, and Dottie Berkeley would still have been Dottie Berkeley. She'd have handed his stupid heart back to him, for sure.

"Maybe we weren't supposed to dance." He slid his left hand up from her back to take hold of her right hand, bracing her a few inches away as he stepped into a simple turn. "Until now."

Chapter Thirty-Seven

Dottie was surprised to be summoned to her mother's kitchen on the day before Thanksgiving to "help with preparations." This was a new page and move in the maternal recipe book.

"Where's Smokey today?" Winnie Berkeley was already wrist-deep in some kind of dough, her gray-streaked hair held away from her face with the mother-of-pearl combs she'd used for as long as Dottie could remember.

"Smokey?" Had *he* been expected to come prepare food, as well?

"Yes, Smokey. What's that man of yours doing today?" A smile Dottie didn't recognize accompanied this chummy question, and she felt confused. *That man of yours?*

Was this how her mother had always talked with her sisters, and Dottie was simply a novice?

"Um. He's driving a Christmas tree to Dayton, actually."

Her second-to-youngest sister strolled into the kitchen, already apron-clad and hauling the lid to the roasting pan usually stored on a cellar shelf. "Hello, Dottie."

"Hi, Joyce."

"What are you doing here?"

"Mom told me to come."

"Oh. Well, good!"

Their mother took the lid and beamed. "It's time she learned how to feed a family."

Dottie's cheeks got hot. She had brought this on herself by falling in love with Smokey Black.

"Mom ..."

"I can show her how to make my special pie crust," Joyce offered, shooting Dottie a tentative smile. "Little Frankie is sleeping in the bedroom, so now's the perfect time."

Their mother folded and thumped the dough. "I was going to start with the rolls."

"Oh, I know how to bake bread!" Dottie put this forth with desperate confidence. "Mama Pool taught me in the summer."

"Did she, now?" Mom plopped the flour-dusted mound into a greased bowl. "I suppose I should be hurt or embarrassed, that another woman had to step in and teach you. But I choose to take her teaching you as a very, very good sign."

Dottie didn't ask.

Joyce did, though. "A sign of what?"

"That Sylvia thinks our Dottie can be trained to be a good wife to her son."

Dottie hugged her own waist and looked around for an excuse to flee. "Where's Dad?" If she was lucky, some disaster was underway at the park. Walter had just brought her from the boardwalk, though, so she didn't hold out much hope.

Still, the silence that fell in the kitchen spoke of some other kind of disaster. One that was all too familiar in this house.

"Mom. Where's Dad?"

The oven was already heating, and the window of the Berkeley family kitchen fogged. Outside, a thin November rain fell on a carpet of brown leaves.

"He crashed the car last night," Joyce finally said when their mother remained silent.

Dottie's scalp prickled. Dad had been in an accident, and they'd been talking about rolls and pie crusts and being a good wife. "Is he *all right*?"

"Calm down. He's not hurt."

"Where is he?"

"He was drinking." Her mom nearly spat the words, and Dottie noticed how tired her mother's eyes looked. Dottie felt tired, suddenly, too, when Mom went on. "He knows he can't stay here in that condition anymore."

"So, where is he?"

"He's probably still passed out in Pete's garage."

Next door, then. Their neighbor, Pete, likely had a supply of whiskey in that garage. Dottie pressed her eyes shut and wished Smokey really were here. He would know what to do to help her father again.

"I'll go talk to him."

"Don't you make one move toward that garage." It was strangely authoritative for her mother. She drew a shaky breath. "I didn't call you here to deal with your father."

That was a first.

"Tomorrow is Thanksgiving. I want you to place a dish on that table for dinner that you made yourself."

Not *I wanted to spend time with you*. It couldn't have been that.

"This way Smokey will see that I can cook." Ah, if her mother only knew just how spectacularly that ship had sunk to the ocean floor.

"Yes," Winnie went on. "He's an active, strapping man who will expect to be fed well, Dorothy. And if you don't do it, some other girl will."

Girl.

As a *girl*, Dottie had been battling middle-aged men with no help from anyone, but now she was a woman with a business degree. Yet wasn't her mother right? It had proven true that others were all too happy to take on the care and feeding of a certain "strapping" farmer.

"Here," Joyce said gently, though she hadn't managed to hide her snicker a moment before. "Let me show you how to make the pie crust before the baby wakes up."

Dottie obediently positioned herself at the counter. "Will Dad be eating with us tomorrow?"

"That will be up to him, won't it?" Her mother was bent in front of the fridge, rearranging something within. Her arms in her plaid house dress looked soft, but they must be strong. The woman worked hard in this house. Yet, when was the last time Dottie had touched or been touched by her mother?

When Winnie rose from the fridge and shut the door, she was wearing that tight smile again. "Now, why is Smokey driving a tree all the way to Dayton today?"

She was as good at changing the subject as she was at making a home.

"One of the men in his unit, one of the ones who didn't make it back … his widow and three kids live over that way. Smokey said he'll always take a tree to them."

"That's nice," Joyce said.

"Long way to drive for that. Aren't there tree lots over there?"

Dottie sighed as she rolled up her sleeves. "I think the family is struggling a little, Mom."

"Well, I meant Smokey could send them money for a tree, of course." She produced a jar of apple slices in syrup. "That way he wouldn't have to drive clear over there."

"He wants to give them one of his trees. Spend time with them, I think." Her mother would never be able to process that, but instead of continuing to protest, Winnie merely shrugged. Smokey Black would be forgiven this quirk of compassion, if only because he had deigned to date her eldest and only unmarried daughter.

"Francine won't be here with Richard and the kids tomorrow," Joyce was saying as she slowly transferred the sack of flour from the table to the counter next to Dottie. Joyce had always done everything at half-speed, and Dottie resisted the urge not to meet her halfway across the kitchen to speed things up. "Annie and Samuel both have high fevers."

"She called a little while ago and said Will has come down with it, as well." Winnie plopped butter beside the flour. "They've been vomiting now, too. Doesn't that beat all?"

"Oh, those poor babies." A line of concern creased Joyce's brow.

Poor Francine, more like. Those kids were too little to clean up after themselves.

"I hope Frankie doesn't come down with it." Joyce shook her head, glancing toward the other room where he slept. "He just got over that ear infection. Three nights. He didn't sleep for *three* straight nights."

Dottie made sympathetic noises but privately felt like the quintessential old maid with her vomit-free apartment up on the boardwalk. Somehow, being an old maid didn't seem so bad.

"We were all together last night playing cards." Joyce barely contained a groan. "Do you think Frankie will catch it?"

"Don't ask me!"

"I was asking Mom."

Dottie followed her sister's dry ingredient instructions, barely listening to her mother's verdict.

She had always been so intent on her dad's advice and the work she enjoyed alongside him that she'd never paid much attention to the fact her mom played that same role in the lives of her sisters. She had known it at some level, she supposed, but now she paid attention for the first time.

While she learned to blend the powdery ingredients with the butter using a little trick with two knives, she thought of her father, relapsed into his drunken and destructive state in the neighbor's garage.

She considered her mother's easy way with cranberry sauce. The woman could manage it while also casually discussing ways to help an infant Frankie's age keep his food down if the flu did attack another branch of the family.

Dottie paused in her mixing. She'd always thought she'd patterned herself after the stronger parent, but now she wasn't so sure.

"Tomorrow you can wear my lace apron, Dottie." Her mother, changing the subject again, had moved way past vomit. "You can put it on when you carry that apple pie out. And, for heaven's sake, do something more alluring with your hair before Smokey comes to dinner tomorrow. Joyce, you can help her tame those curls a bit."

Attracting a man, setting a nice table. They were fine priorities ... if only they'd brought Winnie Berkeley joy. Instead, it was only ever about impressing someone else.

Perhaps Dottie's weaknesses were easy to trace back to both parents, not just her father. And perhaps she'd allowed them to become her own.

She divided the mound of dough, as instructed. There was an eternity between now and tomorrow's dinner.

~~~~~

Late that evening, Smokey found Shelby Berkeley smoking a cigar on the front porch of the Berkeley house in Hebron, a sprawling structure made entirely of stone. Even the porch was stone. In November, there was
~~~~~

no furniture to be found out there, so Shelby was on one of the wet steps.

"This as close as you could get to the house?" Smokey made his way up the front walkway, hands jammed in his jacket pockets. This day felt like it would never end.

"Rumor's already spreading, I see." Shelby sounded mopey, his expression grim in the low light from the house windows.

"If you count your daughter calling me and asking me to stop by a rumor, then yeah." He peered up at the dark sky in an attempt to gauge whether the rain was done for a while. "May I sit?"

Shelby gestured to the step beside him. "Make yourself at home. Where is she, anyway?"

"Dottie?"

"Yeah. She called you, told you to come by? I haven't even seen her." He was clearly sulking. Had the man come to depend upon Dottie's concern for him when he wasn't getting it from the rest of the Berkeley women?

"She was here earlier, from what I understood. Did some baking with the ladies." Smokey struggled to imagine it, struggled even more to imagine Dottie *enjoying* a whole day of baking.

He wanted, more than anything, to leave here and go find her at her apartment. He wanted her to brighten those gray places that had opened up inside of him today as he'd played with Paul's kids, those places that had only grown until he was exhausted on the drizzly ride home from Dayton.

Smokey simply needed to be with her. So, maybe he understood why her father did, too.

"You going to be at dinner tomorrow?" Shelby asked.

"Yes."

The older man nodded. "So? Go ahead."

"Go ahead and … come to dinner?"

"No. Go ahead and tell me how I screwed up bad."

Smokey just pulled his feet up a step and rested his elbows on his thighs. "That's not why I'm here, sir."

Shelby snorted the same way Dottie did when she was incredulous. "You don't have to call me *sir*. I mean, look at me."

"It's dark. Thank heavens."

"D'she tell you I crashed the car?"

"Yes. She's glad you're all right. I am, too."

Shelby dropped his head into his hands, the half-smoked cigar still pinched between two of his fingers. "I thought I could do it." When Smokey didn't say anything to that, Shelby lifted his head a little. "Stay sober. I really thought I could."

"I believe that. I don't know much, but I doubt you'd have given it a go if you *didn't* think you could. Of course you intended to stay sober. You still do, or you wouldn't be easing your way back inside your house."

"I blew it."

"Last night was last night. Doesn't mean you failed."

"This is gonna get folks talkin' again. About Dottie, too. Y'know?" Smokey scowled in confusion, so Shelby went on. "The car crash last night, I mean. They'll all start talking about her again, about her accident, about me. About the whole family."

"Dottie can handle herself." Smokey believed it, without a doubt. Mostly because she was no longer trying to handle *every*thing herself.

The concern brewing under Shelby's words might have been the closest thing to coddling he'd ever seen Dottie get from her family. He was determined to change that part of the woman's story, as quickly and as thoroughly as he could. He would be the one to anticipate her needs. He would be there when there was something to hide from, and he'd have her back when the hiding turned to action.

For now, he tried not to resent sitting on a chilly slab of stone when he could be with her. Maybe the best way to show her love just now was sitting on the slab of stone.

"No one's given up on you, sir. Shelby."

That snorting sound again. "My wife sure has."

"No, she hasn't. She might not want you here drinking, but she and your family are counting on you sitting at the head of that table tomorrow. Carving the turkey. You know how blessed that makes you?"

"That just makes it worse."

"Clearly, you feel lousy about last night."

"Don't you want to know what happened?"

"It's in the past. I guess I'd rather know what you're going to make happen tonight, tomorrow. Feeling lousy is okay, but if you sit down in that feeling, you'll only go looking to wash it away again. You, me, and Hugh … we talked about that this summer."

A sigh. A silent nod Smokey could see out of the corner of his eye.

Smokey sat up straighter and slapped his palms on his knees. "Got too much time on your hands these days?"

"Winter's hard for different reasons." Shelby re-lit the cigar and took a drag on it. The smoke danced right into Smokey's face. "You need help on the farm again?"

"There's plenty to do. You can come out Saturday, if you want. Help tie trees to cars."

"I won't drink."

"I know you won't."

"I'll come out, then." Shelby settled back against the pillar at the edge of the steps. "Dottie'll be there?"

"I think so, yes." He was counting on it. "You both do love that fresh air."

"Reckon you'd rather be with her tonight than me, eh?"

"You're a mind reader."

Shelby cackled and coughed in response. "Maybe you can pray with me before you go, though. And don't forget the part about Winnie not killing me in my sleep tonight."

Chapter Thirty-Eight

Dottie recognized that, for Smokey, Thanksgiving was the calm before the storm. While the rest of America relaxed and stuffed themselves with harvest bounty, he'd been grateful but somewhat distracted.

He'd risen extremely early both Thursday and Friday to deliver truck beds full of his Christmas trees to commercial lots in Lancaster and Columbus. After he'd picked Dottie up on his way back from Friday morning's delivery, she'd spent the better part of the day helping Holiday Farms prepare for Saturday's onslaught of families determined to deck the halls for Christmas.

"It's not the busiest Saturday of the season, but it will still draw plenty of folks," he'd told her. His hands bore fresh calluses now when he took her hand, and she marveled at the appeal of the sensation.

Dottie helped Mama Pool fill the bundle house with homemade ornaments, more candles, quilted tree skirts, and wrapped bricks of farmhouse fruitcake. The evening Thanksgiving supper the night before at Mama Pool's table had been easy and filled with laughter. No tension or careful avoidance.

By that Friday afternoon, the women were building wreaths and grave blankets out of evergreen clippings, wire, and red velvet ribbon. Dottie embedded sprigs of holly and berries into the wreaths, happy to imagine each on someone's front door.

Assembling the fragrant decorations on a worktable beside the bundle house was practical, not just because of the mess but because Dottie was able to luxuriate in the sight of Smokey Black carrying entire trees around on his shoulders. He'd assembled a little pre-cut lot next to the bundle house, with Hugh's help.

Reggie came by with a wood crate filled with hacksaws for farm visitors who would cut their own the next day.

The crew ate only once, acknowledging that they'd been thoroughly stuffed the day before. Turkey slices between slabs of bread had been plenty.

By late afternoon, the sun was already low, but Smokey's farm was ready for its Christmas opening the next morning. The Holiday Farms sign now boasted its own giant wreath and bow.

Smokey and Dottie walked up the lane toward his cabin. Their sap-sticky gloves were in their pockets, their bare fingers entwined. She had him all to herself now, after sharing him so thoroughly the day before with family and friends and then with chores today. The simple cabin ahead had become far more appealing than any fancy resort she could imagine.

He would build a warm fire for the two of them.

Dottie wanted to curl beside him with a mug of hot coffee. She wanted to talk with him about her father, wanted to enjoy the way his aftershave mingled with the scent of pinesap that surrounded him these days. Mostly, she needed this unsettled feeling to be wiped away, whatever it was, by Smokey's steady wisdom and playful charm.

For a few precious hours, he was all hers.

"I want to show you something," he said, squeezing her fingers and tucking her hand against the warmth of his coat. Then he led her up along the subtle sweep of the hillside that took them behind and above the cabin, the rise where wooden stakes dotted the thick blanket of leaves. Their tips, painted bright orange, glowed like torches in the low light of evening.

This was where his "real" house would someday go, even if the stakes just looked to be in a random design now. Smokey was a visionary. What kind of magnificent vision must he have for this place?

"I sure can't fault your choice of a view," she told him, spinning to look out.

"We're standing where the porch would be."

Just below them was the cheerful little cabin, piles of chopped wood behind it. Beyond that, the pines began, and from there hundreds of acres rolled out in various textures and shades of green. The setting sun had tinted the sky purple, only to be reflected in the pond in the distance. Then, there were distant forests marking the end of Smokey's Christmas trees and the beginning of another kind of wonderland, the tree branches surrounding his enchanted forest bare now.

Dottie could follow the deep cut of the old canal in the distance and was able to envision, in her mind, where it joined her lake.

"You ought to have Rosie come up and paint this view. It's incredible."

He tugged her with him through an imaginary door, and then he released her into what he was calling the family room.

"Fireplace here. Don't you think?"

She regarded the stakes and grinned. "Smoke, this right here is an enormous space." She stepped it off. "Does it really go all the way to these stakes? Are you planning an indoor football field?"

"You're standing at the opening to the dining room. It's wider. See? And the room, the family room, needs to be this big. We both have good-sized families."

He went on talking about having a long dining table custom built while Dottie stood still and processed what he'd said. They both had good-sized families.

As in his family *and* hers.

Why would her sisters and their husbands and their ever-expanding band of children be gathered in this imaginary living room?

Was he saying …? Did he mean …?

"The floors should be left bare wood everywhere. Don't you think?"

It occurred to her he was asking for her *opinion* on a different level than she'd expected. Was he actually asking her to decide about area rugs?

Dottie shrugged deeper into her coat collar, following with her gaze where he pointed. She'd been imagining building projects for years at the park, and she was good at it. What he was saying made sense, but … was he indicating it would be *her* moving about in these rooms?

Uneasy, she imagined a sofa covered in afghans, a coffee table with doilies like the coffee table her mother had been polishing for decades. Dottie tried to picture herself moving over those hardwood floors in a house dress like Winnie's, a feather duster in hand.

"Does your back hurt from standing over that worktable today?" Smokey was asking, taking her hand again.

She considered it, shifting gears. "Huh?"

"I thought you kind of … groaned or something." Dottie shook her head. "Anyway, the pantry could go either here or …" Leaves crunched as he walked a few long paces north. "… Here. What do you think?"

Dottie could only stare. His handsome face was ruddy from working outside all day, his evening whiskers shadowing his jaw in the way she found so wildly attractive. It felt strange to her that a man this good looking would be talking about pantries. "See, if the pantry goes here, it would be closer to where the stove and fridge would need to be wired. Now that the co-op is out here, we'll definitely have power throughout the house. But if the pantry was here …" He moved back over the grass, "… then you'd have it near the workspace."

She would have it. A pantry.

Her mother's pantry was organized alphabetically.

Workspace? A workspace must be for rolling out noodles. Her mother rolled out noodles at least once a week. Hands like ice, Dottie stuffed them back into her sticky gloves. She worked to relax her shoulders.

"Nothing needs to be decided until the thaw," Smokey was saying, motioning for her to follow. *Until the thaw. Until the thaw.*

"What will happen when it thaws?" *Things would get decided.*

"I just won't break ground for the cellar and the foundation until then. Whoa! Be careful!" He put out a hand to steady her when Dottie tripped over one of the orange-tipped stakes. "You okay?"

"Sure."

"Know what you just tripped on?"

"Um. A stake?"

His elastic, contagious smile stretched over his face. "The stairway! One set of stairs down to the basement, one set up to the second floor."

"Sure. That makes sense." It really did make sense. She lowered her shoulders again because she discovered they were up by her ears.

Smokey moved behind her, and she welcomed his warmth as thick, flannel sleeves wrapped around her. "Which leaves the question of bedrooms up there. They're easier to mess around with, from a layout standpoint, up on the second floor. I assume we'll want a bigger, downstairs bedroom over there?" She followed his pointing finger with her gaze. "But I'm estimating there should be room for at least four bedrooms upstairs."

"That's nice." What did that mean? *At least four?*

"Not that the number means anything, necessarily. I mean, the kids can share rooms if they have to."

The kids.

Dottie stepped out of his arms and turned around. "The kids?"

"Yeah. I can just see them, running down the stairs there into the family room." He stretched his arm out. "In their pajamas on Christmas morning. Toward the biggest, best Christmas tree on the farm, of course."

This was Smokey's Norman Rockwell-meets-Doris Day voice. And his voice was describing ... what? A *herd* of children. Four bedrooms, shared? What did that even mean? Room for *eight*?

Dottie looked around to assure herself that these walls he spoke of were not even up yet. There was no door to move to if she wanted out. She could just walk, couldn't she? This trapped feeling she was experiencing ... it was all in her head. Or maybe all in *his* head. There was plenty of fresh air out here. Lots and lots of fresh air.

"Let's go down to the cabin," she said desperately. Yes. Cabin Smokey could build a little fire in that space just big enough for the two of them, in the place where they belly laughed together.

"Easy there."

There was something about the way he said, "easy there," something about that steady, deep voice that never got too worked up about anything. It had her changing her mind.

"Actually, would you mind taking me back to the office?" She asked him while she angled down the hill, toward his truck.

"Dottie?" He was right behind her, the hurried crunch of the leaves as chaotic as her mind. "What's wrong?"

She didn't know how to tell him she needed the last half hour to be erased. She was used to panicking about memories of the accident. Now, she was feeling all those same feelings as she imagined dusting some custom-made dinner table or shopping for Christmas presents for all those inevitably enormous children who would *all* get the flu at the exact same time.

"There will be vomit everywhere," she heard herself say out loud.

"What?"

"You paint your happy scenes, Smokey Black, of little angels scampering down to their father's perfect Christmas tree, but do you ever think about them tossing up their dinners when they pass the flu around? Huh? All eight of them, with vomit all over their adorable little pajamas?"

"I'm not sure what you're saying. What does vomit have to do with Christmas? Are you getting sick? Is that why you need to go home?"

She didn't respond as she climbed into his truck, shaking.

Oh, this had all been a terrible mistake. When she'd thought about loving him, she hadn't made the leap, exactly, to all of *that*. All of those things he deserved, the things she'd tried to arrange for him with Julia that neither Smokey nor Julia had wanted. Now he was thrusting them upon *her*?

She'd tried, hadn't she?

He drove without saying anything else, but Dottie kept feeling his gaze on her. Sharp, exploratory glances. The poor man couldn't decide if she had a fever or was insane. Dottie clenched her jaw. When had she last been so scared?

The accident. Everything came back to the accident. Maybe she'd been scared ever since the accident. After a silent ride, they parked, and Smokey walked beside her along the empty boardwalk toward her apartment.

"You know, you never call this home," he said softly, and they hadn't spoken for so long that the words startled her.

"What?"

"You always refer to coming here as going 'back to the office.' Not home."

She considered that as the skeleton of the coaster came into view through the drizzly darkness. The midway slept, and the piers stretched out over black water, the water level lower for winter.

"I don't know why I call it the office."

Did he think it meant she didn't have a real home? That her whole life, which had felt so full, had really just been spent in limbo, waiting for him to build a home for her? The audacity of this man tonight.

"I love you," she said sadly when they reached her door. In white paint, the glass pane read Buckeye Lake Amusement Park Main Office. "But my answer is no."

Smokey looked down at her. He tilted his head. "No?"

"All I can figure is that you've been trying to propose to me. And I'm afraid I need to say no, for now."

"I've been trying to …?" He squinted down at her. He gave a nervous laugh. "I think I'd know if I'd proposed, Dottie."

Her spine straightened. "Oh? Whose eight kids were those, then?"

"Uh …"

"Exactly."

"Okay, okay. I guess I skipped about five conversations we should have had before that one. The most important one being … okay. I understand what you're saying." He laughed a little, apparently, at himself. He shook his head. "I was just spit balling."

"*Spit* balling?!"

"Dottie. Look. Don't just … don't just say *no* like that."

"I won't. Since you didn't ask a question, apparently." Dottie sighed. "Look, you painted a lovely picture. I just wish I could see myself in it, Smokey." Only, she *could* see herself in it. House dress. Duster. The problem was, she didn't *like* herself in it.

"Let's just start this whole thing over."

Panic. "Too tired for that. Good night," she said, instead. And she turned, slipping inside the office that was her home.

Weeks before, she had thought she couldn't despise herself any more than she did. She'd been wrong, she knew now, as she turned the lock in the door and heard the click echo down the boardwalk outside.

Chapter Thirty-Nine

"Not exactly a Christmas card kind of day."

A thin man in an equally thin trench coat said it conversationally to Smokey. The hesitance in his words clued Smokey into the fact his own face must look like an actual storm. He straightened, then, and worked up the kind of smile the man might expect on the day he'd brought his family out to get their Christmas tree.

The afternoon was damp and marked by low, gray clouds over winter-brown grass. Mr. Trench Coat was joined by a woman wearing a lumberjack hat, earflaps and all. She was carrying a little boy in a puffy coat, while the father held a schoolgirl's mittened hand.

"Perfect day to decorate, though, and light up this dreariness." Smokey produced two peppermint sticks from the pocket of his work jacket and offered them to the kids, whose happy exclamations made his smile genuine. "How can I help you all?"

"We want to cut our own tree for the first time," the trench coat man said.

"Tweeee!" Earflaps mom had her arms full of bouncing toddler.

Smokey nodded encouragingly. "Well, let's get you a saw, and we'll figure out the kind of tree you want. Then you can drive right out to it."

Trench Coat hesitated.

"We might need help," Mrs. Earflaps said, casting an apologetic glance at her husband. She had a dimple like Dottie's when she smiled. Smokey saw the man still grinning over his bright red, knitted scarf. His wife said he needed help. He did not seem disabled in any way, but sometimes it was difficult to tell.

"I've never held a saw in my life."

"Ah."

"I'd be willing to pay extra if you'd care to accompany us to a tree."

"Sure." Smokey mentally adjusted his plans for the next half-hour. "I can go out with you, show you how to use the saw." He kept his voice down so no one else would have to hear of this man's helplessness.

Still, who didn't know how a *handsaw* worked? You placed the teeth against wood and moved it back and forth until the cut got deeper and deeper. And what kind of man confessed ignorance of this kind with such cheer? Smokey glanced down at Trench Coat's daughter, who looked at her father as though he could be counted on to somehow see her through childhood.

Bleary-eyed from total lack of sleep, Smokey trudged around the bundle house to retrieve a saw, promising to meet the little family where they'd parked. Around him was the evidence that the bleak day had not kept families away. He figured they'd already moved a quarter of the little pre-cut trees, and a steady stream of cars were leaving with sloppy, self-cut evergreens tied to their tops.

Hugh was overseeing the bundling.

Shelby Berkeley was helping tie the trees to the car tops.

Mama Pool was running the bundle house, where money was exchanged. Smokey had seen Dottie join her there just before noon. He was relieved she'd shown, though he'd keenly noticed her absence at breakfast.

Dottie hadn't come to find him or to wave at him when she'd arrived, either. He'd simply seen her enter to lend a hand, as she'd promised to do.

He put a section of thick twine in his pocket, opposite the peppermint sticks. Then he snagged a saw that had once belonged to his grandfather Pool and started back toward the happy, incompetent family.

Unlike them, he'd had saws at his disposal from the time he was the toddler's age. He couldn't even remember when he'd started cutting and chopping things, first for fun and then for chores.

The family had loaded into their Seacrest green Suburban, all grinning expectantly. The mom in the earflap hat was behind the wheel, the trench coat dad ensconced in the passenger seat.

Smokey leaned toward the open driver's window. "Uh, you can just follow me, ma'am. What kind of tree are you all thinking of?"

"Surprise us," the woman said.

"You know, we have some really nice trees of all varieties over there in the precut lot."

Mr. Trench Coat leaned over toward the open window. "We know that's true, but we want the experience of cutting our own." *Or watching Smokey cut their own.* "We came out this same weekend last year, y'know, and got a very nice pre-cut tree. What kind was it, Honey?"

Unbidden, Smokey thought about Dottie's face whenever he called her *Honey Pie*, and his stomach clenched.

She didn't want to marry him. All that laughter between them, and she was fine just walking away. Locking her door.

"If I remember right ..." the woman said, chewing on her lip. "It was a green tree!"

The little family howled with laughter, and Smokey turned and started walking to the Douglas firs because they were closest, and they were certainly green. He let the saw swing at his side, trying not to envy this strange couple.

They would take one of his trees home soon and drape it in tinsel and colored lights. They seemed the kind who would let the kids help with every step of the process, perhaps even clumping the majority of the tinsel in one thick glob toward the bottom branches.

Smokey wanted a tree decorated appallingly like that. He wanted Dottie, most of all, to chuckle about it with him. He couldn't think that much else mattered, really, except it all seemed so far away now.

Dottie did not want him. Not for the long haul, anyhow.

He could admit now Dottie was all he'd ever wanted, from way back when she'd been a little spitfire racing his brother's jalopy on the Old Canal Road. He'd learned to dance for her, in case he could catch her with a night off at the park. His best swim times were when he knew she was nearby, cheering. He'd memorized Ohio State's academic calendar, so he knew when she'd be back at the lake from college. During the war, he'd taken a chance and written to her once or twice. He needed to know she was still at the park, running things, seeing the place through rations and blackouts.

All the while, it was less this tree farm he'd dreamed of and more what had always seemed the impossible fantasy that she'd be there with him. In a home that overlooked the wonder of the place where they'd grown up.

Impossible might have turned out to be right.

What had *she* been wanting all that time, though? Lately, she'd said it was him, that she'd been watching him even as he'd been watching her, but for what? *What had she wanted from him?*

If he could find out, he would still try to be it.

"Here are the Douglas firs," he announced when the car creaked to a stop behind him on the little stone lane. Ahead of them, three other cars were pulled just off the pathway, and folks milled about arguing or laughing, occasionally visible amidst the trees.

"Look, kids! Let's go find one!" Trench Coat Dad was out the door first, eagerly pulling the little ones from the back.

"Thank you," Mrs. Earflaps said, brown curls peeking out from the hat. She had plump, pretty cheeks and a joy about her that Smokey wished were contagious.

"Take your time choosing."

He leaned against the hood of their car, crossing his arms, still holding the saw. Brooding. He'd never tried brooding before, hadn't seen the point in it, but now he understood a man could find some satisfaction in brooding when he'd tried to do things right and still, somehow, messed everything up.

Admittedly, he should have asked for Dottie's hand in a more traditional and far more romantic way. He hadn't meant to propose, exactly, but he understood her point. He'd jumped way ahead.

But that didn't seem like the kind of thing that would have her closing a door in his face. She wasn't like that. Dottie's heart was big, and she loved him, but she had *closed the door* in his face.

Smokey was a strategist. Standing there in the mud, he decided he would go into the bundle house for hot coffee, and he would thank her for coming out to help today. Maybe she'd simply been in a bad mood the night before, and if he simply sought her out, she'd dimple-smile at him. Then he'd take her to dinner tonight and apologize again as they shared a slice of cake.

Or maybe she'd ignore him completely when he thanked her for her help. Maybe she'd "accidentally" spill the coffee on him so that it chilled him when he headed back outside. In which case, he would ask Mama Pool what in the world to do.

Many plans ended with that as a last resort.

"This one!" the dad called triumphantly, and Smokey straightened from the Suburban. He felt like he was moving so slowly today, like the damp sponge of the ground was trying to suck him in.

"Gueth what we're going to name it!" Both the little girl's front teeth were missing.

"Douglas?"

The whole family giggled. "No, Thilly! Dorothy the Douglath fir, like Dorothy from The Withard of Oth."

"Dorothy." Smokey dropped to the ground, wondering if that was where he'd have to find himself to grovel to another Dorothy. What a fathead he'd been. Holding the saw in one hand, he used the other to motion for Trench Coat to join him.

But the man said he didn't want to get his pants muddy.

"You might be able to manage it squatting." It was unlikely.

"I'll do it." The man's wife climbed right under the branches and listened attentively while Smokey got the blade engaged with the trunk of the tree.

"Ma'am, I can cut it for you," he said in the shadows beneath the fir tree.

"Why?" She reached out and pulled the saw toward her, leaving it engaged in the groove Smokey had started.

Why, indeed. He watched her push, pull, push, pull. She was getting it done.

"Get down here, Marla!" she bellowed. "Give it a try!"

Smokey cleared out to make room for little, lispy Marla, only to find Trench Coat being chased by his waddling son, pretending to holler in fear when he got close to grabbing him. The boy squealed in delight each time.

Smokey couldn't help but smile.

This was not the kind of family he'd ever imagined, but he couldn't deny their joyous appeal as Marla prattled on to her new friend, Dorothy the tree, and the mother also laughed periodically amidst sawing sounds.

Smokey stayed close to the tree with a steadying hand so it wouldn't fall and take out the man of the house, who seemed to have stolen his son's candy stick and was dramatically licking it while Junior giggled and jumped as though he could retrieve it.

In the end, after he'd helped little Marla tie the family's tree to the top of the Suburban and Trench Coat had slipped him a large bill, Smokey was sorry to see them go.

Because now it was time to check in with his own Dorothy.

Chapter Forty

"So, you haven't even talked to him since you shut the door in his face?" Emily was cross-legged on the rug in the Graham's family room, folding white diapers and looking simultaneously outraged and amused.

"I didn't shut it in his face." Dottie rolled her eyes. She'd left early Saturday from the farm, before they'd had a chance to talk. He'd been busy, though. And she didn't know what to say to him. "Look, I didn't come here for you to tell me what an awful person I am."

"Dat's goooood because Auntie Rosie wouldn't let Mommy say such things to Auntie Dottie, would she?" Rosie was beside Dottie on the sofa, baby Jimmy laid out over her colorful, woven skirt, his head by her knees. He was making wide eye contact with Rosie, and she was rewarding him with obnoxious smiles and baby talk.

Emily watched Dottie, ignoring her sister's antics. "What did you come here looking for me to tell you?"

"I don't know."

"Maybe hers just needed to talk," Rosie cooed, eyes never leaving Jimmy's. She'd wandered down from her home beside the inn.

There was a fire glowing near where Emily sat on the floor. The still-new mom had shadows under her eyes and her hair covered in a scarf. "Okay. So, let me get this straight. It's the thing about where the stairway is laid out that gave you cold feet."

Dottie hurled a throw pillow at her, and Emily fell backward, hooting.

"Look, I understand what you're saying." Rosie transferred her nephew to her shoulder, where he curled into her. "It's all a little fast for you, that's all. I mean, you only just started dating."

"But we *have* known one another forever."

"Wait. You're playing devil's advocate now?"

"No. You're right. We haven't meant … we haven't meant *this* to one another for very long at all."

"Exactly. Of course you balked a little. Shame on him."

"Can I play devil's advocate now?" Emily asked, crawling over to the sofa.

"I vote no."

Dottie squinted at her. "Go on."

"Where did you think it was heading, this relationship?"

"I ... I was just figuring out how to be in love. I don't know."

"Smokey's always been a romantic."

Dottie closed her eyes. "I know." She opened them. "I've been enjoying it, believe me." She wouldn't tell them about dancing, just the two of them, that night in the ballroom. She was looking for allies to soothe her heart. But she knew she had to be careful not to stir up resentment in the friends the two of them had always shared.

"I don't just mean he's romantic like woo-woo romantic," Emily said, reaching up to squeeze her son's pajama-clad foot. "I mean he's *a* romantic, in the classical sense. Idealistic, sometimes ridiculously so."

"He's not ridiculous."

"No, you're right. I suppose he somehow makes it work." Emily now propped her chin on Dottie's knee and looked up at her. "He's figured out how to make a living delighting people with pumpkins and sunflowers and Christmas trees. He makes idealism less ridiculous when he puts his mind to it, somehow."

Dottie nodded. She'd never have thought of him exactly that way, even though she'd always wondered at him. "So, this house layout ..."

"Classic Smokey." Emily yawned.

"If Jimmy falls asleep," Rosie whispered, "you need to march right upstairs and take a nap. I'll stay with him. And Dottie."

"I'm not missing the chance to gossip about Smokey Black and Dottie Berkeley, no matter how little sleep I had last night."

"I don't think it's gossip if she's sitting right here giving us the information."

"Do you ever regret it?" Dottie hadn't meant to ask it. It just spilled out, the way things did with longtime friends.

"Regret what?"

"Having a baby. Not sleeping. Folding diapers. Losing your figure."

Emily smoothly reached behind her for the pillow Dottie had tossed a few minutes before, and started walloping on her with it until Dottie was shriek-laughing.

Rosie got up, scolding them both. "Well, he'll never sleep at this rate. Shhhh, little man."

"I added that last part just to get your goat," Dottie said. "Your figure is perfect."

"You bet it is." Emily flung herself onto the sofa where Rosie had been while her sister settled nearby in Hickory's rocker. Rosie was softly humming against Jimmy's fluffy head, and Dottie watched Emily's face soften as she looked at him. "You're seriously asking if I regret *that*?"

"It was a stupid question." Dottie sighed. "I don't mean that you'd regret him. I mean, do you miss things about your life ... before?"

"Hmmm." Emily wrapped her sweater tighter and pulled her legs up beneath her. Dottie knew her friend would eventually go back to working very reduced hours at *The Beacon* whenever she was ready. They'd already discussed that. "I never slept very consistently before, if you want the truth. So that hasn't been as big a change as it might have been." She flashed her teeth in one of her sudden smiles. "Honestly, I haven't thought about it."

She'd never, in these last two months, wished she was threatening town hall or writing a scathing editorial?

"You don't miss work."

"It'll keep."

"Or being with Drew."

"I'm with Drew every day now, Dottie. That's how marriage works."

"You know what I mean."

"If you're looking for us to tell you if Smokey's vision of your future is one that will make you happy, Dottie, I don't think we can really … do that." Rosie spoke softly as she rocked. "That's going to have to be your call."

Dottie sighed. "I know. You're right."

"I wonder how he'll react when you tell him you were just dating him because he's a dreamboat."

Dottie transferred the throw pillow directly over her own face and waited to run out of oxygen.

"Emily." That was Rosie's scolding older-sister tone.

"*Rosie*. Think about it. How else is it going to seem to him? She tells him she's always had a thing for him, she experiences an even bigger thing for him, tells him she loves him … but she doesn't want to marry him."

Dottie let the pillow fall. "I didn't say I don't want to marry him."

"Just that you don't want to have children with him."

"Maybe she doesn't want children at all."

"I didn't even say I don't want to have children." Dottie got up off the sofa and wandered to the window in her stocking feet. Just at the edge of Towpath Island, Buckeye Lake's choppy little waves were gray. She missed Smokey, wished desperately he'd tell her it would all work out just fine. Then she hated that she'd accidentally lost herself so much that she needed the man to tell her how she *felt*. "I think …" *You know yourself, Dorothy Berkeley.* "I think I'm mostly scared."

The rocker creaked soothingly behind her. From it, Rosie said softly, "Now, that's more like it."

"You asked me if I regretted my life with Drew and baby Jimmy. You didn't ask me if it *scared* me. And, Dottie, it does. It has all along, but I don't regret a bit of it."

Rosie made a sound of agreement. "Which still doesn't mean all fear springs from the same source."

Dottie nodded, still facing the window. What was she afraid of? Nothing she could put into words, so it was hard to identify the source. Was it her mother's doilies on the shining coffee table? Her father's life of adventure and intrigue at the park while the coffee table got polished quietly each day? Babies with ear infections and fevers? Husbands who didn't come home? Wives who never left home? Bell jars of beans and tomatoes? Laundry day?

Where would her *ideas* go?

She thought of Lillian Turnbull Graham, mother of these two beautiful women. A dancer who'd loved to dance, one who settled here on this very strip of island with a husband she loved, only to decide she was living as an imposter in her own life. And what had she done? She'd run off, abandoned her daughters, left them filled with longing and resentment they were still battling through all these years later.

Dottie simply needed to figure out from which of these places her own fear sprung.

Or was it that she'd been a different person entirely last Thanksgiving? Dating a shrewd businessman, planning an investment into an extravagant new resort, designing an enhanced pier out over the lake, plotting how to produce more fruit to get herself to heaven.

She was only just getting to know who she was *this* year, after she'd lost herself entirely. She'd already changed so much, but that house on that farm, Smokey's romantic vision … that would be a whole other level of change.

Dottie faced her friends again. "You were right, Rosie." She nodded as she said it, feeling a little settled, still wondering how she'd ever put any of it into words to anyone. Least of all Smokey Black. "When you said it was a little fast for me, you were right."

Somehow, while Dottie had been staring out the window, Emily had risen and reclaimed her son. Now, she stood, slow dancing with him near the warmth of the fireplace.

"Sure," she said, grinning over the baby's head. "Give *Rosie* all the credit."

Chapter Forty-One

On Thursday night. Dottie sat in her armchair by the window in her second-floor apartment, watching crystal flakes fall in slow motion. Snow had finally arrived. There were security lights along the boardwalk and out across the two piers, but it occurred to her she was essentially the only soul on this stretch of the North Shore from September to April.

There was no one else to see the snow fall like feathers in those pools of orange light, dusting the wood of the pier in white.

She had one of her parents' ancient afghans wrapped around her to protect against the chill of the windowpane. She'd brought the blanket from home when she'd moved out here after university "to keep an eye on things." Now, as the clock ticked peacefully past eleven, there was little to keep an eye on.

Until a figure appeared under one of the security lights.

Dottie's throat tightened, and she sat up in the chair, trying to make out what she was seeing. From a distance, it appeared to be a monster of some kind.

As it moved through shadow and into the next closest pool of light, she saw the figure was not a monster but, rather, a large man with an evergreen tree on his shoulder. Speckled with snow, of course.

Now her throat loosened, and she gasped, jumping off the chair. *Smokey!* He'd finally come.

Not that she'd wanted him to come.

All right, yes, she had.

Still, she hadn't expected him to come. Why would he?

And what would she say to him now that he *had*? It was, after all, what had kept her from seeking him out herself. She had no idea what to say. "I'm scared in a whole new way" didn't seem very productive.

But here he was, so Dottie slid into her closest pair of shoes and rushed toward the door beside the kitchenette, where she saw, to her horror, a congealing pan of eggs from dinner.

Quick as a flash, she moved the pan into the fridge, out of sight. He didn't need to see that. Just as she wouldn't reveal that she'd inexplicably cried while eating the eggs alone. She pounded down the stairs like a child, flipping on a light in the downstairs office.

The lock on the door was loud again, as she clicked it open.

"Smokey B.," she called, and she was satisfied to have surprised him by standing there.

"Dottie B." His voice sounded raspy and tired.

The slick boardwalk stretched behind him, and she admitted to herself for the first time that she dreaded this winter in a way she never had before. The blizzard last Christmas, the ice storm after she'd thought winter was done … her heart had only just started to thaw, and here it was, happening all over again.

"Brought you a Christmas tree."

Though not large by any means, the freshly cut tree made an effective distraction for them as they wrestled it through the office, around the tight corner leading up the stairway, and into her apartment. They couldn't talk about anything else while they had this fragrant project between them, and Dottie even surprised herself by laughing a little when she got pinned against the stairwell between branches.

Needles decorated the wooden steps.

Smokey, breathing hard, finally dropped the trunk on the floor of her apartment. The full tree only came to just past the wide leather belt at his waist. Dottie's eyes tracked from there up his waffle-knit shirt under his familiar flannel coat, his knit cap pulled low to his brow.

A dreamboat, indeed.

But then she scanned back to his eyes, and she took a few unconscious steps toward him. "Smoke … are you … what's wrong?" His eyes were glazed in a strange way, and his face had no color under the shadow that always grew on his jaw over the course of the day.

"Never been better."

He grimaced, though, and Dottie moved to take the tree from him. She tried to glare in response to his answer, but worry likely made the glare ineffective. She shoved the tree against the wall near her little table. Wordlessly, she pulled his coat off his shoulders and draped it over one of the chair backs.

"Thank you for bringing me a tree. You didn't have to, but I appreciate it. Please, sit."

Smokey dropped into the same chair as his coat, and then his glassy eyes tracked to the clock on top of her radio. "Oh. Is that the time?" His lids were heavy and pink. "Can't believe you're still up."

"What if I hadn't been?"

"Didn't mean to scare you. I didn't know what time …" He trailed off, swallowing, waving a hand toward the clock. His knuckles were bright red from the cold.

"You didn't scare me. I was watching the snow come down. It's … pretty." Dottie cleared her throat into the silence. He'd never really sat in her apartment before. His big body made it feel cramped but not in a bad way. "With the snow, I suppose you'll have a big day Saturday. For trees,

I mean."

"What?" He slumped a little in the chair.

"Smokey …" Dottie rose from the edge of the armchair. She refused to ask him again if he was all right because she couldn't endure another sarcastic answer. She also had eyes. Instead, she crossed the few feet between them and pushed his hat back off his head.

"Hey."

She ran her palm over his forehead, down the scratchy side of his jaw, and he winced. "My hand feels cold, does it?"

"Yes."

"That's because you're burning up with fever." She'd never felt someone so warm. Standing close to him like this had always felt like cozying up to a heater, but this was something different. "You're sick."

"I just wanted to bring you the tree."

Dottie left her hand on his jaw because she couldn't bring herself to take it away.

"It's a Fraser fir," he told her, staring up with slightly unfocused eyes. "Like you. You're like a Fraser fir."

"Am I?"

"Yeah. They smell good. And the needles look kind of silvery sometimes. Classy."

Dottie couldn't stop the smile.

"And the branches are real strong and can hold the heavy ornaments. Like you."

"Smokey, that's sweet."

"I'm more a Balsam."

"Do you need some water, honey?"

"Balsams have excellent form." He grumbled a laugh at himself and pretended to flex his biceps. "Or maybe that's you. *You* have excellent form, you know."

"For heaven's sake." She leaned over and put her lips on the top of his head. Absolutely on fire. "How long have you been like this?"

Maybe that was why he hadn't come over. Why she hadn't heard from him. And what kind of person was she to feel a rush of relief about him being ill?

"What?"

Alarm thrummed through her. "How long have you been sick, Smoke?" He shouldn't have driven here like this. And he'd been trudging around in the snow with a high fever.

"I just don't feel so great, that's all. Lucille is a blue spruce tree. Stiff branches, sharp needles. I mean, she's a good cook, but a fella ought to wear gloves with a blue spruce. So sharp."

"You look like you're in pain. Do I need to call your mother?"

He managed a thick-throated chuckle at that, but Dottie wasn't joking. Mama Pool would know what to do. Her own mother would, as well. Literally any other woman she knew. Her sisters, for sure. After all, their families all had the …

"Oh nooo." She groaned. "The flu! I'm so sorry. I think my family must have made you sick at Thanksgiving. Have you been feeling bad all week?"

Dottie had been sick before, hadn't she? This had to be the flu, and she'd had the flu. All she had to do was remember what she'd done about it.

Smokey leaned forward, very slowly, until his burning head rested on her stomach in a gesture that felt like surrender. Dottie wrapped her arms around his neck and ran soothing hands along his shoulders while she did some thinking. His truck was parked outside, but he could not drive home. She couldn't drive him home, either, of course. She wasn't even certain she could get him back down the stairway, when it came to it.

"Well, my family might have given you the flu, Smoke, but you'll have the last laugh. My reputation is about to go from bad to worse."

"Why would I want that?" He said it into her blouse, so she felt the vibration of his voice all over. Boy, she must have missed him even more than she'd thought for this barely coherent man to give her goosebumps.

"Come on. Let's get you to bed." She stepped back, half afraid he'd slide right off the chair, but he straightened and looked up at her, heavy-lidded, those gorgeous eyes so unnaturally shiny and red-rimmed. "Come on, Honey Pie."

"Bed?"

"I don't have a sofa, and you don't have it in you to stay upright, apparently." Dottie tugged on one of his arms, and he obediently rose, hissing a little. "Tell me exactly how you feel so I know how to make it better."

"Cold. Hurt."

"Your head?"

"Bed'll be good."

Dottie smiled. "Yes, it's right through here." She leaned down to help him off with his boots, but she didn't even get a chance to peel back the quilt before he dropped back onto her bed with another groan. "Well, all right. I have more blankets in the closet. I'll be right back."

When she returned, she carefully draped the afghan she'd been using earlier over him, followed by two more quilts. She could see him shivering slightly.

"Smokey." His eyelids slid open. "You don't feel sick to your stomach, do you?"

"My stomach?"

"Have you been vomiting?"

"If I did vomit, I'd lose you forever, wouldn't I?"

Dottie couldn't stop the little bark of laughter, and it was herself she laughed at. "I guess I made kind of a … thing of the vomit, didn't I?"

"I never said eight." He said it on a rasp, his eyes closed again. "I never said eight kids, Dottie."

"Shhh. There's plenty of time to talk later."

It was no hardship, she decided, to unbutton the top few buttons of his knit shirt and apply the VapoRub she'd found in her bathroom medicine cabinet. She smeared it along the top of his chest to each collar bone. He mumbled something about a Christmas tree named Dorothy and a trench coat. The poor man was half delusional.

"I'm going to get you some water."

"I love you," he slurred.

She stood for a moment, reminded of her father saying those words in just the same way after he'd been drinking, when he'd been trying to make things right with her mother. The slurred "I love you" should have sparked fear. Dottie waited for it to swamp her, but looking at Smokey there under her flower-pattern blanket, she couldn't picture either one of them playing the same roles her parents had.

Maybe as much as she had trouble imagining Smokey's ideal of their future, she was at least also incapable of imagining her own nightmare version. That was something, wasn't it?

"I love you, too."

"I cut it myself. The tree."

She thought of him scarring the pumpkin for her over the summer, too. He showed love through holiday symbols, apparently, and it made her stomach twist.

"Rest."

~~~~~

When his fever broke in the early morning, Smokey was dismayed to find both his clothes and Dottie's frilly pillow damp. Sitting up, he waited for the room to stop spinning. Pain shot up from his leg into his hip, then all the way to his shoulders.

"There you are."

Dottie was leaning against the doorway, and his mouth went from rather dry to completely dry.

She was wrapped in a white, quilted robe with a red satin collar and sash tied tight at her waist. Over the white of the robe, her dark hair hung in curled ropes that reached nearly down to that red sash. Her skin was flawlessly pale, those two little stains of pink low in her cheeks matching her lips …
~~~~~

He might be on the mend. His thoughts had moved way beyond survival as she crossed toward him on the bed, as her hands bracketed his face, and she made some sound of approval.

"Your fever is gone. Or at least not as high." Her fingers stroked down his jaw, along his neck. It didn't seem strictly necessary, but he closed his stinging eyes and hoped she wouldn't stop.

She did stop. "Do you want some tea? I have some more peppermint. It seemed to help last night."

He'd had peppermint tea last night? Smokey had no memory of that, which alarmed him. Maybe it was his special forces training, but the idea that he had been doing and saying potentially anything the night before filled him with dread.

Still, Dottie was being kind to him. Cautious but kind, which meant he must have behaved.

"Can I bathe?"

She nodded. "I can put your shirt and undershirt over the radiator to dry out and warm up while you scrub. I wish I had something else you could put on."

"Thank you. That'll be fine."

He took in Dottie's space as he moved about in it, realizing they'd spent all their indoor time together in restaurants or in his cabin. Had that been selfish of him? She'd never really invited him here, but should he have suggested it?

The apartment above her office was small, but it bore all the marks of Dottie. Her bedroom had a tidy, bright blue carpet, the exact shade of which was repeated in the quilt he'd been on, the floral patterns in the window curtains, the dozen throw pillows he must have tossed around off the bed the night before. Simple but expensive and tasteful. She moved back and forth through it, filling the tub.

Her bathroom was blindingly clean and white, the copper tub shiny as he squeezed into it with a sigh. A rose-patterned area rug warmed the white tile of the floor, and framed bits of rose embroidery decorated the walls, stitched on white linen and framed in more white.

Smokey imagined Dottie in here herself, reclined in the tub. She would fit much better in it, her curls lathered in shampoo bubbles. She'd probably light the simple, white candles he saw scattered about the little space. There were three kinds of soap in a dish on the stand beside the tub, and when he claimed one to wash away the remains of his fever, his head spun all over again, this time with the scent of Dottie.

Had he been wrong to want those moments still to come with her? All the moments she apparently didn't want to share? He wondered, staring at his big, stupid body in her tub, if he'd ever wanted something he couldn't have. Some*one*. He let his head fall back on the cool copper.

He'd always been very good at getting what he wanted. He told himself it was because he put in the work, but still. It had never proved impossible.

Winning swimming races required discipline in what he ate, in building muscle, in hour after hour of swimming across the lake. He'd wanted to win those races, though, so he had. Fighting in the war was very similar: hard, hard work he'd enjoyed much of the time. And then … victory. The farm had also been about hard work, and then success. He wanted it, he got it.

He'd been pouting like a child, though, since Dottie had rejected a proposal he hadn't made. Hadn't he invested the time? She might have been the most enjoyable "work" of all, but somehow, he hadn't ended up with what he'd wanted.

She was not a trophy to be won or land to cultivate, of course. He had never seen her that way. She was simply … precious. She was all her own. And all he could do now was feel enormously sorry.

When he emerged from her room, she'd made him eggs and toast. Beside his plate, one cup of peppermint tea and one cup of coffee were cooling. Smokey sat at her little table, a dish of oranges in the center of it. He felt weary again.

"Thank you for this," he said, scooping eggs into his mouth.

"Does it taste all right?" She looked eager, mildly anxious somehow. It occurred to him she might not have been happy to see him last night, in the middle of the night, feverish and confused and with so much unresolved between them.

He swallowed. "It tastes good. Thank you, also, for last night. Sorry I just showed up like that. You didn't have to take care of me."

"Yes, I did. Just like you didn't have to bring me a tree, but you did."

"Dottie, I …"

"How about I ply you with warm drinks and you rest while I decorate my tree?"

Smokey stood, hating the weakness that washed through him. He wasn't accustomed to his body not cooperating, any more than he was not used to not getting whatever he wanted in this world, apparently. He shook his head at himself. "We'll have to talk about all of it sooner or later, you know, Honey Pie." He walked to the chair in the window where, it occurred to him, she must have slept.

"I know. We'll talk." Another throw blanket beside the window smelled like that soap of hers, and Smokey sat back and let her tuck it around him. She winked, leaving her face close to his. "You and your five skipped conversations. Or was it six?" She didn't seem angry, even though he was a fathead. "Of course, I'd get the only man in the county eager to talk it all out."

He stared at her pink, perfect lips.

"I'm not going to kiss you," she whispered. "I don't want to get sick, too."

"I hate seeing you have to sacrifice."

She straightened, and her dimple flashed. She'd changed into a cable-knit turtleneck and simple wool skirt. Instead of a bun, she'd tied her curls into a low tail with a scarf.

Soon, her radio was playing the King Cole Trio. Smokey pretended peppermint tea was curing him, and Dottie hung Corning glass bell ornaments on her little tree. She'd arranged the evergreen by herself, right beside him in the window.

"I think a tree should go in the window whenever possible. Something about sharing it with other people, maybe?"

"Hmm. Who will see this one?" Outside, last night's snow was undisturbed on the boardwalk and pier, the lake a half-frozen wasteland.

"Absolutely no one." The little caramel flecks in her brown eyes danced whenever she grinned.

"You're so beautiful. You know? It's not fair to any of us."

She winked over her shoulder at him, but Smokey wondered if she believed him. He resisted twining an arm around her waist. She was that close. He wondered what she'd do if he pulled her into his lap to hold her, but she thought he was sick, so she might elbow him right in the gut.

"Is it strange for you, not being at the farm?" She bent to hang a small, red bulb in the depths of the branches.

"I guess I don't get to sit around in the daylight hours much, doing nothing."

"You have your deliveries to the commercial lots done?"

"Reggie might have to help."

"Good. You've no business hauling trees. And the rest of us will rally out at the farm tomorrow. We'll keep things running. Don't worry about that."

"I survived a whole war without being coddled."

"No one's coddling. I only made you tea, so don't go getting stubborn."

The outside part of the windowsill was big enough for a bright cardinal, catching Smokey's attention. It left tiny tracks in the snow. "It's peaceful here this time of year."

"Yes. The boardwalk is so different with the changing seasons." She smiled out the window. "I love them all."

"Did you ..." He stopped himself. He shouldn't. They were finally comfortable again or at least working toward it. "Did you always figure you'd live on the North Shore here? Or eventually move to a house nearby?"

At first, he thought she might not respond. She took her time hanging another glass bell, eventually turning to blow a bit of glitter off her finger at him. "I don't know." She stepped away. "What I imagined for my life … before … it doesn't sound very good now." She looked squarely at him. "I don't know what does sound good, to tell you the absolute truth."

He nodded through the pain of that. As sometimes happened out of the blue, a wave of love for her washed through him.

"But you know what *doesn't* sound good? I think I've figured that much out." She pulled a claw-foot stool to the base of the tree and sat, wrapping her arms around her knees in her skirt. She was still close enough to touch.

Instead of touching her, he said, "Tell me."

"Last year, I started picturing myself in a grand, three-story home next to the resort I was planning to build there up the shore … you know, sort of across from Cranberry Bog."

"Married to Gabe Adams, right?"

She cracked a grin. "Maybe. Can you imagine?"

"I hope that's in the category of what doesn't sound good anymore. Since he went and married Rosie and all."

"It might not have been a very workable vision from the start."

"I don't know." Smokey had also been able to imagine it when he first heard she was stepping out with FH Resorts' business manager. "Gabe surprised everyone by turning out to be a decent guy." Smokey had been tempted to throw him straight into the blizzard a year ago, though. "Don't tell me you wouldn't have been happy in that big house, in the middle of all the action. Travelling to New York in the off-season, to some other Fairchild Hotel."

"No, I wouldn't be happy. Not now. I can't believe I thought I'd be."

"What else?" He nodded. "What else doesn't sound good now?"

He silently begged her not to say *him*.

Dottie stared at an ornament she'd just picked up. "Staying here in this apartment alone forever. That's sounding less appealing all the time."

"So, you need company."

She gave him a smile, straightened her shoulders. "What I don't want, Smokey, is for my life to … look like my parents' life."

"You mean your dad's drinking?"

"Not just that." She looked like she was trying to come to some decision, so Smokey gave her space and quiet. Instead of hanging the ornament, she set it gently back into the box. "I can't help thinking they must have been in love once, you know? My parents. That they said their vows with hope like everyone does, or at least most people do, and Dad bought Mom that fine house in such a pretty spot. And then … that was all." She swallowed. "You need more tea?"

"No. Go on."

"I can't describe it, Smokey. All I know …. Well. I just don't *want* it."

"Maybe you think your dad's half of their life is a little more appealing than your mom's. Face it. You love this park. Like he does."

"I guess I do."

"You don't want to be the one left at home."

"Definitely not. And more. There's no balance between them. No sense that they're working toward the same things, even. There's so much more to it, and I've never tried to describe it before. I suppose I'd hesitate to betray them by describing it, even if I could."

"I guess every marriage looks different." Smokey thought of his parents, and he experienced the usual stab of grief for the loss of his father. Big Reg and Mama Pool. Their easy completion of one another, the way they'd merged two enormous family farms and somehow got it to work for everyone, for both of them. He wished he could show *that* to Dottie.

When he met her eyes, she shook her head at him.

"None of my sisters' lives either. I don't want their marriages. *None* of it sounds good to me."

"Okay."

"And definitely not whatever life Lillian Graham fled. Not that she was being mistreated at all. I don't know. But it scares me so much, the way she *changed her mind* about what sounded good."

"Seems like there are lots of ways of running away. Sometimes the person leaves. Sometimes they run away even while they stay put, maybe."

"Like my father."

"Like so many people. I met a family the other day …" Smokey had thought about them, Mr. Trench Coat and Mrs. Earflaps, after they'd pulled away with their tree. "They were different."

"How?"

"Hard to say. It's like they'd just agreed not to do things the usual way, and they were having a fine time doing it their own way." He could envision Mrs. Earflaps behind the wheel, cracking jokes about green trees, and Mr. Trench Coat completely unphased by his own incompetence.

"Smokey." Dottie pulled his attention back. A curl had escaped her scarf and was bouncing beside her ear. "Forgive me, but I've been very much under the impression that you expect to do things … the usual way."

Now they were getting down to it. "Which usual way? You mean like all the things you just said you didn't want? That's not …" It panicked him. He couldn't become some kind of villain. "I'm not expecting to play all day with pumpkins and trees or corn on the larger farm while … someone … my wife … what? Washes curtains? I've never even thought like that."

Maybe neither of them understood what the other wanted.

"I think I'm scared." There was open vulnerability in her eyes, though, and he thought he'd take that. At least she was talking. He'd take that. She stood, but she didn't cross that short space between them. Smokey understood she couldn't yet.

"I don't want you scared."

"Aren't *you?*"

"Well, now I am." Another unfamiliar thing to tackle. "I don't want to lose you, Dottie."

"Hmm. The thing is, I love you." She said it simply, an assurance.

"I love you. Please say I'm not yet part of those things that don't sound good to you. That's all I need right now. Don't let me become that."

She sighed. "You're the only thing that *has* sounded good to me for a very long time."

~~~~~

Dottie watched relief wash over him, along with something else.

"I'll take it." His words slurred again. "That sounds good."

She eyed Smokey critically. He looked worse again, and she didn't think it had anything to do with the conversation they'd been having. She narrowed her eyes at him.

"Why do you look like you're in physical pain?"

"Guess I'm still not quite myself, is all."

"Smokey." She walked a couple of steps to him, then, and repeated the hand on his head. Still warm, and he was gray everywhere. It occurred to her she hadn't heard him cough once. "Where do you hurt?"

He looked down at his lap. "I'll be fine. It'll heal. I've had worse."

"Had worse what? *What* will heal?"

"My broken heart?" He flashed his teeth in a smile that ended in a grimace.

Dottie squinted at him. Then she pictured him again, as he'd looked carrying that tree down the boardwalk in the snow. She thought he'd walked strangely because it was slick, but ...

"What'd you do? Twist your ankle? You have a bum knee?" That wouldn't usually cause a fever, though. "Is your leg hurt?"

"Yes."

"*Just tell me.*"

Looking miserable, she watched him shift to raise his right pants leg. Above his sock, a cloth was wrapped around his leg, and the cloth looked spotted with a mix of old and fresh blood.

Dottie gasped and dropped to the floor. "What in heavens ..." He flinched when she worked to untie the linen binding, and then he groaned out loud. His face went from pale to flushed.

"Honey, this is infected." As she unraveled the crusty bandage, she
~~~~~

glared at him. "You didn't catch the flu from my family. *This* is causing your fever." When the wound was exposed, she gasped all over again at the jagged, deep gash running alongside his shin. She would take him over to Doc immediately. "What happened?"

"That's the part I most don't want to talk about."

Dottie angled her head. "Smokey, please. All of us are clumsy sometimes. You're an active farmer. These kinds of injuries are bound to happen."

His jaw was clenched. "It was a stake. A wooden stake, to be precise."

"Good thing you're not a vampire. You fell on a wooden stake?" The poor man. That had to have hurt badly.

"No. I didn't fall. I really didn't need you to know this, Dottie, but … I wasn't thinking clearly." He looked guilty, embarrassed, and infected. "I kicked the stake. Several stakes, really, before one fought back."

"Why in the world would you be kicking wooden …?" Dottie trailed off, her gaze slamming into Smokey's. His expression confirmed it. "Oh, no. You didn't kick down the stakes for your new house."

"No one else needs to know it happened. It's healing."

"Levi Black. Did you have a *temper* tantrum?"

He crossed his arms but left his wounded leg still. "Broken heart. I prefer broken heart."

"Your home site. You had it so carefully measured out." Dottie sat back on her heels, rubbed hands over her eyes, picturing it. "You complete dolt."

She sighed. She was afraid even that came out sounding like "I love you."

Chapter Forty-Two

"We can do this," Dottie told the team gathered beside the bundle house Saturday morning. "Smokey may be under the weather, but we all know what we're doing! Right?"

"Right!" Mama Pool led the cheer, and the others joined in. "I always just allowed him to *think* he was running this show, anyway."

Standing in the couple of inches of snow that had turned Holiday Farms into a Christmas postcard wonderland were also Hugh, Silas, and Dottie's father. Silas had brought two other boys from the high school to earn extra cash, and Reggie had already left with a truckload of precut trees.

"Let me know if you run into any problems, and let's have a holly jolly day!"

Dottie felt cheerful and maybe even playful in her red and black flannel jacket with its fleecy collar that matched her hat and gloves.

"I can't see you helping folks saw down trees." Mama Pool shook her head. "Gettin' sap all over those pretty clothes."

"Only if they need help. Is the hot cocoa heating up okay?" Dottie wasn't trying to take over Smokey's tree farm, but a huge pot of cocoa was sure to set Holiday Farms apart from other tree farms in the tri-county area.

She might have checked to make sure no one else provided hot cocoa.

"Anyway, I'm sure glad you kids worked out whatever was wrong between you." Mama Pool crossed the little building to the pot and peered in. "Yes, it's heating up just fine. You still gonna make a sign about it for out by the road?"

"I've got the red paint right here. Anyway, what makes you think we've worked it all out?" They hadn't. Not really. Dottie's heart was still a mess, which was just one reason she'd jumped on the distraction of working the farm today.

"You've been nursing my poor, weak boy back to health, haven't you?" Mama Pool cackled. "I figured that means you're done being mad."

"I was never mad." She hadn't been. Truly.

"Well, you forgot whatever stupid thing he did, then."

Forgot? That he'd planned their whole lives without her input? That he'd sloppily proposed instead of apologizing? That he'd injured himself by kicking apart his house design in a fit of despair?

"Only a mother would assume it was just *one* stupid thing."

Mama Pool's laugh nearly shook the roof of the bundle house.

~~~~~

Smokey tried to do his sulking when Dottie wasn't around.

She'd taken over his recovery process after peppering Doc with a thousand questions, and then she'd decreed to all that he'd be staying in his bed, in his cabin, that Saturday. She had a schedule to change the dressing on his leg twice a day.

Now, outside, he could hear the distant sounds of his Christmas tree farm. He sulked because he was missing it. Beyond that, being Dottie Berkeley's patient wasn't proving a hardship.

She came stomping in at noon to check on him, her cheeks pink and healthy from the outdoors, her eyes bright. It occurred to him that she looked nothing like she had in April.

"I brought you a Thermos."

He worked up a smile. "Thanks. How's it going?"

"Best day of the season so far." She crossed to him with a second pillow and elevated his foot while she talked. Princess Cream Puff growl-purred at her from Smokey's lap. "Folks are loving the hot cocoa."

"Is that what's in the Thermos?"

"Oh, no. This is soup. You want hot cocoa?"

"I'm fine."

"I'll bring you some later. How's the pain?"

"Gone?"

"Don't believe you."

"Better, then. Don't worry about me." She did worry about him, though, if her expression was an indication. She studied him, so he smiled at her again. Then she bent and pressed a lingering kiss to his forehead even though his fever was gone today.

It would be an easy thing to reach up and pull her down there with him. Her ridiculously fashionable plaid coat had those little frog fasteners, all fancy, and Smokey was imagining fiddling with them when he thought he heard a trumpet.

Dottie backed up, clapping her hands in satisfaction. "They're here!"

"Who's here?"

"The brass quartet! I told you about them, remember? I've gotta go. You need anything, Smoke?"

He heard the first strains of "Santa Claus is Coming to Town," and it sounded good.

"No. Hey. The quartet was a great idea, Honey Pie."

She stuck her tongue out at him, followed that with a blown kiss, and was off.

~~~~~

Reggie's wife, Pam, pulled in at the bundle house just as Dottie finished helping Hugh tie a tree to a family's car.

"New supply of tree skirts ready to sell!" Pam was wearing a hat and scarf knitted from what might have been several sections of leftover yarn.

"Oh, good. We could use more tree skirts. They've been selling well."

"That's what Smokey said, so I was up half the night finishing these." She didn't look it. Her blue eyes were bright as ever. "Reggie's taking the kids shopping to buy my gift today, so maybe I'll get a nap. But regardless, it's worth it. Smokey gives me a hundred percent of the sales."

Of course, he did. Dottie was surprised to find she had no urge to change the man.

Something didn't add up, though. What could Pam Black of Black-Pool Farms need for extra cash? Dottie had been hanging around enough to grasp the enormity of this farming operation. She knew the past few years had been good for crops, and they'd just signed another lucrative contract for beef. Was Reggie keeping his wife on a tight leash?

Dottie added that to the list of things she didn't want in life.

"Hey, there, Pammy!" Mama Pool handed change to a customer, and her daughter-in-law waved.

"Don't tell him, but I'm gonna put this money toward Reggie's Christmas gift." Pam was beaming. "I'm going to surprise him with a trip to Hollywood over the winter. See if we can't spot a few stars."

"Hollywood! That's a lot of tree skirts."

She shrugged. "I love making them. Other things, too. It all adds up, and he doesn't know a thing about the money I've got hidden in the drawer behind my stockings. Makes it feel like the trip's really just from me, y'know? And it'll be just me and Reg. For a whole two weeks."

Okay, maybe the Reggie-Pam marriage had a few things going for it.

Mama Pool strolled over. "I'm keepin' the kids, but if those two lovebirds get to meet Humphrey Bogart while they're out there, well, they're under orders to drug the man and pack him on a train home to me." She smiled at a wide-eyed man at the counter. "You all set, Honey?"

Dottie stepped outside when a car horn sounded over the band's third go-round of "O! Christmas Tree." The horn led to a vehicle that had her grinning.

"Well, if it isn't one of my favorite families!"

She rushed over to the Graham Marina truck, its cab filled with Gabe behind the wheel, Rosie pressed against him, Lillian by the window, and the increasingly lanky Charlie and Delia crushing their laps.

"Hey, Aunt Dottie!"

"Smokey still down for the count?" Gabe leaned toward the open window.

"He's on the mend, but he's not quite ready to be hauling trees."

"Band's a nice touch." Rosie smiled. "Do you have time to come out and show us the Scotch pine you marked for us?"

Dottie nodded. "Need a saw?"

"Got one in the back." Gabe jerked his thumb toward the bed of the truck. "Hop in!"

Delia half-fell out the door. "I'm ridin' in the back with Aunt Dottie!"

"Me, too," Rosie exclaimed, and Gabe laughed behind the wheel as everyone abandoned him for the open tailgate.

"Did you know ..." Delia clambered to the tire well as the truck crawled along the lane. "A hundred years ago, fake trees were made of goose feathers dyed green!"

"I did not know that. How'd they get them into a tree shape, anyway?"

"Wire, of course. I'm thinking of trying it next year."

Dottie looked at Rosie. "You'll put a goose feather tree in your house?"

"I assume Delia will sanitize the feathers." Rosie simply shrugged. More like, she'd have a dozen new plans before then and would forget.

"Of course I will! You can get lung diseases from goose feathers, which would wreck everyone's Christmas."

"Here!" Dottie called up to Gabe, and he eased off the lane. The truck had barely stopped before they piled out.

"Happy first annual Deck the Halls Day," Gabe said, reaching into the bed for the saw.

"We're making a big deal of it." Charlie tugged on Lillian's glove adoringly. "Grandma hasn't ever had a Christmas tree with lights on it. Imagine!"

"I've spent most Christmases in dance halls." Lillian didn't sound sheepish these days when it came to her life before. Delia was swinging the older woman's other hand.

Gabe, meanwhile, leapt out from behind a tree. Rosie was so surprised that she shrieked. The kids laughed and started chasing one another around the pines.

Tonight, after their tree was lit and the halls were decked, Dottie supposed Gabe and Rosie Adams would snuggle up, perhaps with a glass of wine, and talk about how they'd fallen in love making homemade tree ornaments the year before. They would decide what to buy their kids on this, their first official Christmas as a family. Then Rosie would most likely stay up too late painting, and she'd be bleary-eyed but content tomorrow in church. Gabe would, no doubt, let her sleep in and get the kids' breakfast himself, as Dottie heard he often did.

Dottie gestured to a little ribbon she'd tied to one of the tree's midsections weeks before. "Here's the prettiest pine on the property!" She bowed theatrically to their applause. "Can you take it from here, family?"

"You can count on us, Captain!"

As Dottie's boots crunched along the path back to the front of the farm, she thought of what Smokey had said about some couples crafting their marriages to suit them. Not to suit the husband or the wife, but to suit them both.

Rosie, after all, hadn't seemed all that intimidated about a lifetime with Gabe Adams. The two of them hadn't modeled their dynamic after some other couple or some ideal. They'd simply built the life that suited them. As had Emily and Drew.

Dottie waved as Pam Black pulled away, smiling over the thought of her quilting so she could surprise Reggie with a get-away to California. To Hollywood. In pursuit of Humphrey Bogart. Reggie's and Pam's marriage didn't look like Gabe's and Rosie's, or Emily's and Drew's, to say nothing of Dottie's parents' marriage.

Gloved hands in her pockets, Dottie veered off into the warmth of the red barn where her furry and feathered friends were also enjoying a lull in the afternoon crowd. She scattered grain for them and topped off their water.

It was easy to pray here, surrounded by the scent of hay. "I'm having a very good day," she told God with gratitude. She really was, and she knew that He knew it. "I just need some guidance, that's all. I keep saying I don't know what I want, Lord. Mostly, though, I just want what You want for me. That's worked out so much better so far." She thought about all the ways that were true as Pee-Pee nudged her hand. "Maybe You've been giving me that guidance already. Maybe I already know what we both want. But ... God. I need You to stop me if it's not in Your plan, okay?"

Chapter Forty-Three

Because he was taller than average, Smokey had had his Santa suit custom made.

The last Saturday before Christmas Day was always the busiest of all at Holiday Farms. It was the day he traditionally wore the suit. Today, it had snowed more gentle flakes, the brass quartet had returned, and this week Dottie Berkeley—the woman who could draw tens of thousands of visitors to Buckeye Lake's amusement park on a summer Saturday—had introduced the roasting of chestnuts over the fire pit in front of the bundle house.

Why hadn't he considered doing that before?

They had the busiest day in the history of Holiday Farms.

The scent of chestnuts and cocoa still lingered once night had fallen, and Smokey sagged in exhaustion as he shut off the power in the bundle house. He still limped a bit at the end of a long day, though his leg was mostly healed. The others had long since gone home, and he felt a little ridiculous hobbling around, still dressed as Santa, alone in the shadows of a winter evening.

Then, as he turned from locking the door to the rough-hewn little building, he spotted the love of his life sitting next to the still-glowing fire pit.

"Well, Dottie B."

"Smokey B."

He disguised the limp a little. No sense reminding her what a dolt he could be. Not when she'd finally stopped acting wary of him. He dropped into the chair beside her after carelessly tossing a couple more logs on the embers.

"Thought you were Christmas shopping tonight."

"I changed my mind."

He made a humming sound of happiness. Life was better when she was nearby. "Listen. The chestnuts were brilliant, darling."

"Thanks. Next year, hot salted peanuts in little greasy bags. What do you think?"

He stretched out his boots to ease his leg. "I think you can run as wild as you want to."

"You mean that, don't you?"

Smokey rolled his head until he was looking at her, those pretty eyes of hers turning golden in the firelight. "About peanuts? Of course."

"I mean about me running as wild as I want to."

Now he chuckled. "Never figured you'd need my permission for that. Run as wild as you wish."

That was all it took to have her scampering over onto his lap, and his laughter came from surprise now.

"You make a disturbingly alluring Santa Claus, you know."

"I hear that a lot." He shifted her and sighed contentedly when she pressed a brief kiss on his mouth. He bumped the tip of her nose with his own. "What do you want for Christmas?"

"I was waiting for you to remember your line, Santa." She leaned in and made a bigger project of the next kiss. She was so good at it, in fact, that Smokey thought she could ask him for anything in the world, and he'd find a way for her to have it.

"Glad I took the fuzzy white beard off before I came out." That earned him another playful peck, very much in contrast to the kiss she'd just finished.

"So?"

"So?"

"What do you want?"

"Oh. Right. I thought the kiss would say it all, but ..." Dottie pulled back a few inches more so they could bring one another into focus. "I want you."

Smokey let himself smile. "Well, that's easy. Done deal. You've already got me, Dottie."

"No, I mean *you*. I'm saying I know what I *want*, not just what I *don't* want." She seemed to wait for that to sink in, but it didn't completely. "Not just for Christmas," she added.

"Sorry to say, Saint Nicholas is only partly following. Though he likes the sound of it."

She blew out a breath. "What I absolutely want, today and on Christmas and every day forever ... is you."

Smokey studied her, the smile fading. He thought he might just have sat himself down in a much more important moment than he'd realized. "By forever, you mean ..."

Dottie nodded.

"I can't afford to get this wrong again, sweetheart."

Now Dottie smiled and leaned in with her lips like they were magnets. Right against his mouth, she said, "I said no to you before. About marriage."

"Right. When I hadn't even asked. Then you slammed a door in my face."

"I didn't slam it." Now she bit his earlobe beneath the fluff of his

Santa hat. It occurred to him she was in a ridiculously good mood.

"You locked the door."

"Smokey ..." She pulled back again. "I said 'no' to something I'd cooked up in my mind as awful. I think I might need ... time. Regardless, though, it's you. *You're* who I want."

"I thought you said you were afraid."

"I am."

"Well, that's two of us, then."

"Look, all I'm saying is ... I think I've got it sorted out."

"So, if, someday, I asked you to marry me ..."

"I'd say yes to you. But only to you."

Smokey looked around and considered. "This feels like a big moment."

She grinned.

"And I'm dressed as Santa for it. Just my luck."

"More importantly, I've decided ... I think I'd like *being* married to you."

Another brief kiss. "Explain the difference."

"I've been scared about *being* married, not *getting* married."

"Ahh. You don't want to *be* married like some of the marriages you've seen."

"I've started noticing the good ones, too, Smoke. Now I'm paying attention. Not that I want us to look like those marriages, either, but you were right. We can make our marriage *our* marriage. We can make it work for us."

"I do feel like I've heard that somewhere before."

"Well, I'm marrying a very wise man. Someday."

She let him enjoy that for long minutes, during which he rejoiced that it looked like it would be these lips, Dottie's lips, that he'd kiss until the day he died.

"Don't forget you said I can run wild," she murmured.

"The wilder the better."

"What do you think about me running wild at the amusement park?"

"For as long as you want to. Maybe I can come follow you around over there."

"You mean work?"

"Maybe. But I get to run around free and wild too, you know."

Dottie laughed, her dimples making little shadows from the light of the fire. "I'd like to live out here, though, on your farm. You know. *Someday.*"

"You sure?"

"Yes, here at the farm. It's not a bad drive into town, and I'll be allowed to drive again soon. Which means you need to fix the stakes and break ground on the house."

"Now who's in a hurry?"

"I'm not in a hurry for *everything*."

"But you do want everything."

"And more, yes. It's just ... well, I am in a hurry for *some* things."

They were smiling into the next kiss. A little less into the one after that.

"You're in a hurry for happily ever after, I hope."

"Smokey." She tucked her head beneath his jaw. "That kind of thing takes time. A lot of wonderful time."

Chapter Forty-Four

Most guests assumed it was Dottie's idea to get married on a roller coaster, but it was really Smokey's.

It would be his first-ever roller coaster ride.

It would also be the summer of 1948's inaugural ride of The Dips, too, but Dottie had walked the length of the tracks every day for a week with Walter, her head of maintenance. She'd had every bolt memorized for years. The coaster was safe.

This afternoon, though, she had no wrench tucked away into a pocket. Instead, she'd stuffed herself and her mother's lacey wedding gown into Car #2 of the coaster.

"I have to say, I'm a little surprised you went with your mother's dress," Emily had noted earlier. "Don't get me wrong. You're stunning in it. I'm just ... surprised."

"We're doing enough things our own way. I decided to be traditional in this one."

Daniel, the preacher she now considered a friend, was looking alarmed in Car #1. "Dearly beloved, we are gathered here today ..." he shouted.

Emily, matron of honor, was now in Car #3 with Reggie, Smokey's best man. Emily was waving down to the loading platform, where Drew held Jimmy up, maneuvering his chunky little hand into a wave. Emily blew a kiss.

Rosie was with Gabe in Car #4 — Rosie by merit of being a witness and friend, Gabe as a thank you, Smokey said, for "not marrying my wife before I could."

In the cars behind those were Shelby Berkeley, Pam with their oldest, Mama Pool, Hugh, Julia, Charlie and Delia, and Dottie's sisters and their husbands.

"Who gives this woman to be married to this man?" The spring breeze carried the question down the cars ahead of Daniel.

"Her mother and I!" Shelby shouted it, drunk only on life because he loved this entire gimmick, as he called it. He'd wanted to invite the newspapers. Dottie had refused.

Below, next to Drew Mathison on the platform, Winnie nodded her agreement and waved. Others who had opted out of the coaster included one of Dottie's pregnant sisters, Hickory (who was certain any one of those curves would be enough to snap his ancient neck) and a host of other friends and family from around the lake.

Dottie and Smokey sat down after they each said, "I will."

"By the power vested in me by God and the State of Ohio ..." Daniel twisted to grab the handle bar. "... I now pronounce you husband and wife! You may kiss your bride, Smokey!"

Smokey and Dottie kissed one another as the coaster's brakes released and it began rattling its way along the tracks to a great deal of cheering all around. The bride's veil flew off her head on the first hill, but the kiss lasted through every up and down, every heart-stopping plummet and every breathtaking crest.

The End

ACKNOWLEDGEMENTS

Thank you, readers, for taking another journey back in time to the lake with me! Though I've always loved writing, the adventure of the *Together* series has shown me that I love connecting with you even more. Interacting with you all has changed me for the better.

Thanks, Penny, for the earliest reads, and Michelle, for the final ones. I so appreciate feedback from Heidi, Jenn, Cameo, Lori, Leah, and Jenny. I'm grateful to the ladies from Traci's living room, always, and to Carmen for helping me figure out how to get Dottie to say "yes." The fact this book exists at all is partly thanks to my late, dear friend, Shelley Payne. Though she went home before *Patched* came out, she was often the reminder I needed to just *sit down*.

Uncle Bill, thanks for talking me through how back-road racing might have worked in 1935, including what kinds of cars kids would have been "souping up" (and for building me an actual model for a visual).

Thank you to Ed Wasem of Wasem's Tree Farm. I needed to figure out how Christmas tree farming worked, not just now but more than half a century ago, so I got to spend a delightful time with Ed hearing about the adventures of growing trees and being part of the holidays for generations of families. Also, as a bonus, he remembers going to Buckeye Lake Park just after his dad returned from WWII!

Likewise, the harvest celebration at Smokey's farm was partly inspired by Pigeon Roost Farm in Kirkersville, Ohio—not far from Buckeye Lake. We loved taking our family there to get pumpkins. Speaking of farms near the lake, the very spunky and fascinating Betty Hankinson remembers spending her childhood at one, and she was good enough to help me with the details of rural Ohio life in the 1940s. She explained the intricacies of the domestic sphere, and it's important to note here that Betty *did* know how to successfully cook on a coal cookstove. Any mistakes Dottie Berkeley made in this book are entirely her own and nothing Betty would ever have done.

I'm grateful to all the farmers in my life whose spirit of hope is as predictable as the changing of the seasons. Smokey is a tribute to all of you. Speaking of which, I'd be remiss if I didn't note Smokey gets his name from my great uncle Smokey, who was a frogman (precursor to the Navy SEALS). I still think that is *so* cool.

Thanks, as always, to the family living with and near me. Here's hoping we remember that it all starts with love and that we don't get tempted to put the wagon before the tractor, as Smokey would say. Brent, thanks for helping me see that we really could do this thing called life in a way that worked for *us*. It's very true that "every good and perfect gift is from above, coming down from the Father of heavenly lights ..." (Jms 1:17). And thank You, Jesus, for the ultimate happily-ever-after.

Kim Garee

BOOK DISCUSSION QUESTIONS

Here's a lively set of discussion questions for your book club's chat about *Patched Together*!

Themes & Character Dynamics

1. Dottie's moral dilemma: She wonders early in the book if her curiosity about friends' lives is gossip or just "liking the news." Where do *you* draw the line between caring and gossiping?

2. Lillian's sudden return is causing some family tension for the Grahams. How do you think long-lost relatives disrupt family dynamics (in stories or real life)?

3. In what different ways do Mama Pool and Lillian mentor Dottie through her journey in this novel? How do their roles compare to the part her own mother plays?

4. Dottie's resistance to marriage is part of the somewhat unexamined fabric of her life, just as Smokey's traditional romanticism is part of his. Who and what contributes to each of them moving toward a middle ground?

5. Dottie thinks she can balance out her weaknesses by producing "good fruit" in her life, and she's willing to work hard to do it. Have you ever fallen into that trap? What reminders of grace have you needed along the way?

Plot & Speculation

1. Each title in the Together series is a play on words related to the content: *Pressed Together*, *Packed Together*, and, here, *Patched Together*. What is the layered significance of "patched" in this novel?

2. Smokey and Dottie grew up together at the lake. How do you think this kind of life-long acquaintance impacts couples when it comes to romance? How do you think it will impact their marriage and family, moving forward?

3. Lucille has been setting her sights on Smokey and trying to win him with home cooked meals. She's been none-too-nice to Dottie. The reader never learns what Lucille is crying about at the grand opening of the new ballroom. What do you think it

might be? What do you learn about Lucille and Dottie both in that scene?

Reader Reflection & Fun
1. The setting is rich with small-town vibes and lakeside charm. What's a favorite book or movie with a similar cozy-but-gossipy community?
2. If you could join Dottie, Emily, and Rosie for their "gab session," what's *one* question you'd ask them about their lives? Which of them would you choose to have coffee with, if you could?
3. The title *Patched Together* suggests mending or piecing things together. What's something in *your* life that's been "patched" in a beautiful way?
4. Casting call! If this book were adapted, which actors would you pick for any of the Together series characters: Emily, Drew, Rosie, Gabe, Dottie, and Smokey?

Bonus: Share a "patchwork" memory—a moment from your past that's stitched into who you are today.

These questions balance analysis, personal connection, and playful speculation. Happy discussing!

ABOUT THE AUTHOR

Kim Garee is the award-winning author of the *Together* series, including *Pressed Together*, *Packed Together*, and *Patched Together*. Kim has worked as a journalist (yes, at Buckeye Lake) and writing instructor. She loves her current work as a high school librarian and advocate of student-directed learning. She and her husband have three children and live in central Ohio. Kim loves to connect with readers and book clubs! Please feel free to reach out through her website at www.kimgaree.com

THANK YOU!

Thank you for reading this book from Mt. Zion Ridge Press.

If you enjoyed the experience, learned something, gained a new perspective, or made new friends through story, could you do us a favor and write a review on Goodreads or wherever you bought the book?

Thanks! We and our authors appreciate it.

We invite you to visit our website, MtZionRidgePress.com, and explore other titles in fiction and non-fiction. We always have something coming up that's new and off the beaten path.

And please check out our podcast, **Books on the Ridge,** where we chat with our authors and give them a chance to share what was in their hearts while they wrote their book, as well as fun anecdotes and glimpses into their lives and experiences and the writing process. And we always discuss a very important topic: *Tea!*

You can listen to the podcast on our website or find it at most of the usual places where podcasts are available online. Please subscribe so you don't miss a single episode!

Thanks for reading. We hope you come back soon!

www.ingramcontent.com/pod-product-compliance
Lightning Source LLC
Chambersburg PA
CBHW010609310726
48969CB00010B/2623